P9-BXW-289

ANGELS OF NORTH COUNTY

NORTH COUNTY TRILOGY, BOOK 1

ANGELS OF NORTH COUNTY

T. OWEN O'CONNOR

FIVE STAR

A part of Gale, a Cengage Company

Farmington Hills, Mich • San Francisco • New York • Waterville, Maine
Meriden, Conn • Mason, Ohio • Chicago

LIBRARY OF CONGRESS CATALOGING-IN-PUBLICATION DATA

Names: O'Connor, T. Owen, author.
Title: Angels of North County / T. Owen O'Connor.
Description: First edition. | Waterville, Maine : Five Star Publishing, [2018] | Series: North County trilogy ; 1
Identifiers: LCCN 2017029714 (print) | LCCN 2017039052 (ebook) | ISBN 9781432837570 (ebook) | ISBN 1432837575 (ebook) | ISBN 9781432837532 (ebook) | ISBN 1432837532 (ebook) | ISBN 9781432837617 (hardcover) | ISBN 1432837613 (hardcover)
Subjects: LCSH: United States—History—Civil War, 1861–1865—Veterans—Fiction. | Indians of North America—Fiction. | BISAC: FICTION / Historical. | FICTION / War & Military. | GSAFD: Historical fiction. | Western stories.
Classification: LCC PS3615.C5965 (ebook) | LCC PS3615.C5965 A85 2018 (print) | DDC 813/.6—dc23
LC record available at https://lccn.loc.gov/2017029714

First Edition. First Printing: January 2018
Find us on Facebook–https://www.facebook.com/FiveStarCengage
Visit our website–http://www.gale.cengage.com/fivestar/
Contact Five Star™ Publishing at FiveStar@cengage.com

Printed in the United States of America
1 2 3 4 5 6 7 22 21 20 19 18

ANGELS OF NORTH COUNTY

★ ★ ★ ★ ★

PART ONE

★ ★ ★ ★ ★

CHAPTER ONE:
NORTH COUNTY

"You are becoming one hell of a lazy man, John Walker."

"I know, Mother Martin, I know."

Walker was lean, his strength not evident in the bulk of shoulders or back but in the sinewy muscles that snaked out from his midsection like cords of rope gradually growing in size, becoming most pronounced in his forearms, which ended in something more akin to talons than hands.

He had ridden a horse before he could fully walk and had never stopped. It was only now that his legs sometimes failed him, particularly his right knee when he walked too much or stood too long, as he had this long, hot day setting fence posts. The thought of climbing a ladder was too much to consider.

The new stable had been built, the roof was finished, but the lightning rod wasn't in place yet. It lay propped up against the side of the long slats that ran vertically the length of the new sides. He knew it was a lazy fool thing to leave even for a single day. In this season, lightning came in heated blasts that fell from the dark heavens without warning. He knew it was risking all that work, but his legs were telling him it could wait 'til the morning. He was thinking only of supper.

To take his mind off his concerns, Walker looked off in the distance and saw Toby using the fading light of the day to get in some riding. The day's hard work did little to dampen the boy's fire for it. With the sun's dying light spreading out behind him, the long shadows shaped the boy's stature in the saddle and he appeared larger than warranted. Placed in relief of setting sun, he looked like a full-grown man in the saddle.

Toby had grown up on a horse. To those who saw him race in last year's North County fair, Toby appeared to ride with a reckless abandon, but Walker knew he was safe on the back of a horse. Walker had seen him fall once, hard, breaking his arm, when he was five, but in the next ten years since, he had never been thrown. He remembered his wife yelling at the top of her lungs from fear when she looked out the window the day after his fall, riding the same horse that had thrown him, his broken arm fresh in a splint.

Toby had the way with horses too. A horse ain't like a dog. If you mistreat a dog early in its life, a new master, with patience and rewards, can bring that cur out of his shell, take away his hate and fear and bring him close to being a whole dog again. A horse is something different. A horse, if ever mistreated, never forgets and never forgives a man. It carries its fear and hate for life. Toby, though, he could heal a horse. Walker had attained a fortune off horses nobody had faith could be redeemed, but Toby had brought some back and forged them whole again, or as whole as anything broken can be mended.

Walker fell back into the rocker alongside his mother-in-law. He could feel her sidelong glance as he stretched out his legs and fretted she was about to stab him again with another barb from her sharp tongue; she did it simply for the pleasure of it. She sat knitting something for one of his girls, something neither one of them was ever going to be pleased to wear. But his wife, Molly, would insist they wear it to some town event, saying how they'd disrespect Mother Martin if they didn't wear it. Walker swore she knitted the girls horrid things to keep them self-conscious and thereby modest. She had no tolerance for whores and she was intent on using every ruse to keep his two daughters, Maggie and Peg, on the straight and narrow, in what she often referred to as this barbarous land west of nowhere.

As he started to drift into a snooze, Walker heard Molly's call for supper. He rose reluctantly, shaking the thin dust of sleep that had settled in his head, and descended the front porch steps slowly, his legs stiff from sitting. He grabbed his rifle leaning on a porch pillar, hesitating for a moment as he caught sight of Toby in the distance repeating over and over the cavalry drills his neighbor, Gabriel McCallum, had taught him and his best friend, Gabriel's nephew, Seth McCallum.

The two boys would drill for hours. Gabriel never tired of teaching; he schooled them over and over in the horse-killing techniques. Walker watched Toby wielding two pistols, the reins dangling loose on the horse's shoulders, the boy able to master his horse with his knees. He could see Toby's hands gripping the pistols, the glint crossing back and forth in fluid movements, the horse, boy, and pistols rhythmically swaying. The day's dying light glinted and played off the shiny metal parts of his guns and saddle.

Walker raised the Winchester and fired into the spreading blood-red sunset, spending a half-cent to call his son to supper.

CHAPTER TWO:
THE BLACK

Gabriel McCallum took his nephews, Seth and Caleb, and his horse breaker, a mestizo, Joe, on a ride to the North County's upper plateau. Rumors had spread of a wild herd led by a black stallion that was near ten hands high. The word of the black had spread through the county, sending men and boys into the highlands in search of the prize. The first day's ride ended without a sighting, but they had found hoofprints and stools, and from the size of one pie, perhaps the tale was true.

They camped at the edge of a cliff that jutted like a peninsula into the ocean of sky over the valley. The vantage point provided a view across the low country all the way to the wall of mountains to the south. It was all shrouded in a cascading curtain of reddening hues fired by the dying day. After a long day in the saddle, Gabriel could relax; a time of day they all enjoyed because Gabriel's demeanor was at its most easygoing.

Gabriel lay propped on the ground using his saddle as a back rest, his long frame stretched out, his boots appearing impossibly far from the hat that was pulled low over his brow. He was smoking his pipe and using the last of the light to read. The weathered old book by his side, he now gazed out into the vista, burning its image into his memory. Gabriel had chosen the cliff rock because of the sheer drops that guarded its three sides. No sighting of renegades this far north had been reported in three years, but Gabriel, despite some years of relative peace, never lost his wariness.

The boys began telling stories, sharing gossip they'd heard in town, holding their tongues when Gabriel read a passage out loud. Idle chatter displeased Gabriel and his reading was a thinly veiled warning to damper fool's talk. Caleb and Seth took notice and feigned an air of gravity, giving Gabriel time to lose interest in them. Joe was setting the fire as Seth and Caleb skinned the rabbits. Seth had taken both rabbits from the saddle with pistol shots. The heavy spring rains had given the rabbits their plump shapes: They had grown fat and slow indulging on the buds that smothered the plateau's landscape.

They broke camp early the next morning. After a quick parlay, Joe surmised the warm weather was driving the herd to higher elevation, so they wound up climbing switchbacks all day to the high open ridge. The high fields sat atop the high country like green encrusted crowns. As Gabriel crested the last rise, he spotted a wild herd of twenty horses grazing in the meadow. He felt a strong breeze against his face and knew the horses hadn't caught his scent. One by one the four riders crested, all silently taking in the herd. Each fixated on the black stallion in its midst.

The horse was not only tall, but thick, strapped with muscles that ran through his shanks and tapered perfectly. The morning dew glistened on his shoulders and his thick mane waved in the rising light. The other males kept a wary distance from him and the mares moved in his orbit, brushing him with their flanks as they grazed the high field. Caleb's mind became obsessed with stud money, estimating that a horse like that might end up the highest paid stud in North County. Ranchers would pay more for him than Ulysses, and he was John Walker's gold mine.

As the sun burned away the last of the morning, the four exchanged looks, and the unspoken plan began. The plateau was surrounded by thick woods. The woods were choked with short thin trees of scrub oak, pine, and birch. At the base of the trees was wild and gnarled vegetation; it snaked and choked the

13

trees, making it impenetrable terrain to skittish, wild horse running. The horses would avoid that clutter and try to head for open country, and this rise had only one true exit. The meadow ran down to the low country on the opposite end of where they stood. If they spooked the herd, they knew it'd head for the far pass and race down to the flats where they could run hard in any direction. They split into two groups: Gabriel and Joe riding downwind as long as they could without the herd picking up their scent to cut off the exit route to the pass. Caleb and Seth would come from behind and run the herd, single, off the black and rope it.

Gabriel and Joe walked their horses east along the far edge of the meadow, sticking close to the woods to blend with the trees and not spook the herd.

After a spell, Caleb and Seth dismounted and started walking their horses, the tall grasses shading their approach.

As they neared the herd, Seth could see the tops of the horses' heads start to jitter, the nervous energy percolating as the herd sensed an intruder. He could hear the dull thuds of stomping hooves and felt the ripple effect as warnings ran like brush fire through the herd.

The horses got frustrated in their inability to smell what was approaching upwind. Was it a deer? Another stud male challenging? Were wolves moving on them? Their noses searched the morning air, their heads raised, their necks stretched.

Seth and Caleb could sense it too, the rushing of the blood, the herd's eternal instincts sensing predators on the move. The two mounted softly and put their horses into a slow walk, their horses' chests parting the tall, sun-bleached brown and sea-green grass like slow-moving ships on calm, cold, thick waters. Within two hundred yards, they spurred the horses to a gallop. The wild herd shuddered as one, and like a swarm of bees bolted for the far pass.

The herd gained speed and wended its way over the contours of the earth like an elastic band stretching and fattening as the ground dictated, never breaking into lesser groups, always moving as one. Seth was high in the saddle riding atop his horse's shoulders. He came up on the herd and was immediately deafened by the thunder of the hooves. The hooves crushed and turned the earth, the rushing of blood filled his ears. He melted into the rhythm of the wild animals, allowing his horse to instinctively find its place in the herd. He scanned the backs, seeking the black amidst the chaos. He teased his stirrup, goading his horse to seep deeper into the herd's midst.

The wild horses glared at him out of the corner of their eyes, curious at the strange, humpbacked horse staring back at them. Seth searched for the black at the front of the rushing mass. To his surprise it was in the midst of the pack. The black's gait was awkward and the sight confused Seth's instincts, causing him to think. The nervous self-conscious energy confused him, unnerving him. In the midst of the run, fear gripped him: had he done something wrong? Then he sighted Caleb on the opposite side of the black and realized he wasn't doing anything wrong, the black was slow. He pressed into the herd. Like talons of a cloven hoof they squeezed toward the black, the rushing herd's midsection thinning like an hour glass as they pinched its middle, moving to the black. The renewed purpose settled Seth's nerves.

As the two pinched in, they heard the bursts of rifle fire from Gabriel and Joe, who had circled around and were now riding headlong into the path of the charging herd, forcing it to turn. Seth could hear the distinct blast of Gabriel's buffalo rifle even in the din of the run, its distinctive crack bouncing about the ridgeline above. This was the critical moment: If the herd turned left, Seth would do the roping; if to the right, Caleb would have to score the black.

The herd broke left and Seth tugged slightly on his mount's

reins, cutting an angle to the black as the stallion rounded. He was next to it now and had to slow his mount slightly to come abreast of it. As he careened toward it, the deepness, the thickness of its back and haunches, mesmerized him. He had the fleeting notion he could walk across its back. He tossed the lasso high; it billowed out in a near perfect circle appearing to freeze in a halo above the horse's bent ears before it dropped like a stone onto its massive neck. He gathered the rope and quickly cinched the tail end around the pommel of his saddle, immediately feeling the black's power as it tugged and towed the horse underneath him with tremendous force. It had a bull's power.

The rope's drag slowed the black, allowing Caleb to catch the pursuit from the far side. Caleb missed with his first toss, but retrieved his rope and tossed a second that landed around the stallion's neck. The drag of the two ropes slowly drained the black's stamina and it bucked and turned trying to bite the ropes, snatching at the chase mounts. To fend off its defensive stance, Caleb and Seth spread out, pulling in opposite directions, the ropes taut, stretched tight from neck to pommel. The black flailed out with its front hoofs, straining to kick its pursuers; snorting and thrashing, its black eyes wild with rage. Seth's mount thrust its weight deep into its haunches, straining against the strength of the animal. Gabriel and Joe rode up.

The stallion reared back, looking upon the pursuers with a wild defiance, thrashing until it was exhausted and finally conceded to the pull of the two ropes wrenching its neck. It stood there in a menacing stance, leering at Seth, its body spent but its eyes still wild.

Joe said, "Look at its front hoof, cracked bad . . . a good two, maybe three inches up to the flesh . . . don't know how it could run crippled like that."

As if he were guilty of something, Caleb bellowed, "We did it right, ain't our fault it cracked, must've hit a rock or turned it."

Gabriel said, "No, that's not what Joe's saying. The hoof's been cracked three, four weeks. What do you think, Joe?"

"Yeah, yeah, maybe three. I don't see how he run, never seen a horse run with a crack like that. He should be lame; wolves or a big cat should've gotten him. It's cracked more than it looks, it's filled with hard clay, got caught up in there, maybe only thing holding the hoof together is clay, it were gonna be a day or two anyhow."

Seth's face was filled with dirty sweat, he was still breathing hard, and not wanting to believe the horse was lame. "Is there nothing that could be done?"

"Ain't nothing to do but shoot him. You can't try and break him with that hoof. Shoe'n him ain't gonna help. It's cracked to the flesh; no remedy gonna hold that split. Once it's cracked like that it's as good as done," Joe said.

Caleb dismounted, sliding down and drawing his rifle from the saddle holster, drawling "I'll put him down."

"He ain't yours," Gabriel said, "Seth roped him."

Caleb went to speak, but caught himself. Joe could debate with Gabriel, but Caleb'd earn a backhand for his efforts. Seth looked at the black; it was glistening with sweat and its muscles were pumped, the veins spreading out thick and cordlike. It was no longer flailing and kicking but Seth could still feel the steady strain of the rope and hear the hemp cords wrenching tighter around the pommel of his saddle. He studied the flesh of his own mount, which tingled and shimmied, the fear of the black manifesting itself in his horse's hide. He tried to speak but couldn't because he'd lost his spit. Seth sucked on his teeth and squeezed his tongue to the roof of his mouth, freeing it from the dryness, and said, "It ain't for us to put him down, I'm gonna cut him loose."

Caleb scoffed, "Seth, don't go getting sentimental, you heard

Joe, if it ain't us, wolves will take him down eventually. Soon enough, he'll go lame and the pack'll pull him down and chew him up. Them critters catch the scent of someth'n hurt for ten miles; in a day or two he won't be nothing but a meal on three legs."

Seth handed his rope to Joe and dismounted. He moved forward, a few paces back but it felt like he was standing under the stallion. Its nostrils were flaring, its eyes searching him. From the ground, he could fully behold its enormity. It was like the stories Mr. Bibbs taught in class. The ones with knights and armored mounts—he thought of that drawing of a knight and steed, both covered in black armor, the knight holding a gold shield. The black had his own armor in the muscles that pulsed in his chest and in the golden fire in his eyes.

Seth looked at Gabriel, who was also staring at the stallion, he too mesmerized by it. Seth spoke, "Uncle Gabriel, we got no right to kill him, he ain't ours yet, I say cut him loose."

Gabriel cleared his throat, spat, and said, "Interesting statement coming from a man holding a rope around its neck."

"No, I mean it wouldn't be right for us to kill him."

"Not right. What's right got to do with any of this. Rights? I heard talk of rights before, still don't know what they were talking about. I don't know about rights, but what I do know is that if he weren't lame, you would've studded him for a hundred dollars a hump. Yep, and next month at the county fair you would of paraded him in front of forty fools each pay'n two bits to watch him hump. We would've stood as proud owners telling folks this black's McCallum stock. Yep, fool, see what come out the Criss-Cross Ranch, nothing but the finest. And I reckon we both would've soaked up their oohs and aahs, told the story of how you roped him. That'd be some good story telling to see them little girls Caleb likes to see tittering. I reckon that's true too, ain't it Seth?"

Seth took off his hat and held it in both fists, mashing its well-worn fabric with a nervous twisting. He looked up at the black. "Yes, sir. I reckon you're say'n I'm talking out both sides of my mouth."

Gabriel went on, "When a man does a thing, consequences come with it, there's no dodging it. What's done is done—that horse's yours. So, you do with yours what you think is right."

Seth fixed his hat and put it back on his head. He breathed deeply without taking his eyes off the black. He looked at his uncle and asked, "Sir, can I borrow the fifty."

Gabriel handed down the long-barreled rifle and tossed a three-inch round. The round's tip had been hollowed out at the point. The hollowing gave it a menacing flat dull look. The round had been designed to blunt-stop a brown bear; that is, if you were lucky enough to hit it square.

Seth raised the butt of the rifle in his shoulder and strained to steady the weight of the barrel. He sighted in between the animal's eyes; at the close range, he ignored the metal sights and estimated the round's trajectory from his appreciation of the true barrel. He squared the muzzle at the space between the eyes; it was tufted with black mane. He squeezed gently on the trigger; the report shook the entire ridgeline and a flock of sparrows nesting in the trees cascaded into the sky, filling the air with squawks.

The round hit the animal with a sickening thud; it shuddered, and was thrust backward a half-step. It regained itself and rose again to its full height a moment before it collapsed straight down, folding into itself.

The tremendous thud ran through the ground, the waves rippling under Seth's boots, sending rhythms up through his groin and into his ribs. He cradled the rifle lengthwise across his chest, the long barrel resting in the crook of his elbow. The stallion lay like a sphinx, the blood where the round penetrated barely discernible amidst the black tuft of mane. Seth freed the ropes from its neck, straining to lift its massive head.

They headed down from the high ground, dreading the long three-day ride back to the McCallum ranch.

As the pack of two legs departed, she watched without motion in the shade of a low bush. Her silhouette in the shadows framed a pair of pyramid ears marking her as the catamount of the highlands. She gazed with detached menace as the kill lay in the grass without being fed upon. She pounced and sank her teeth deep into the back straps of the horse, her mouth filling with hot blood as she wrenched free a great husk of flesh with a single twist of her neck. She fed for an hour before she heard the pat-pat of their paws. The dozen surfaced from the tall grass with their ears pricked, tongues lolling and tails high. She knew this pack. The gray was wise and he sent two to the west to seek the cradle of her cubs—she snarled, the loose blood and flesh splaying from her mouth, and bounded away.

The two returned and the lupine pack howled and twisted about the carcass, snapping for the next three hours at each other to ascertain their turn in the feed. Bellies extended, they began again their wandering. Two solitary coyotes waited for the perfect dogs to disappear into the tall grass and began ripping at the flesh that held tight to the bones as the sun dipped behind the heights to the west. The dusk raised three red foxes from a nearby den and their dark eyes danced with the snapping coyotes for the flesh, the scavenger ritual dragging in an ever-widening arc the stallion's legacy. In the heat of the next day turkey buzzards in the air tasted the stench on the wind and fell from the skies to tear at the viscera, debating the issue of ownership with a murder of crows. In the cool of night, carrion beetles polished the bones in the darkness and left nothing for the fly to propagate.

Early the next morning, the herd returned, led by a reddish

roan that kicked at the grass where his ancestor had fallen, the only trace of the fallen king the impression in the grass. The sun rose up strong over the east hills on the third day and the bent grass arched and vaulted toward the radiance. By midday the plateau was a wave of tall brown and sea-green grass rolling in the wind.

CHAPTER THREE:
THE WHITE LION

The day Seth killed the black, Gabriel's brothers, Luke and Eli, and Luke's son, Kyle, were finishing the day's work forty miles to the south of the high plateau. The Criss-Cross ranch lay in the middle of a three-sided bowl, with high ground to its north, east, and west. Its southern boundary spread out flat, allowing the Criss and Cross creeks to meander toward, but never reaching, the south mountains. The creeks fed the rich grazing lands that stretched to the south and anointed North County as prime horse country.

On the reverse slope of the north hill overlooking the Mc-Callum's ranch, a renegade warlord sat high in the saddle. He was adorned in garments of white, except for his head, on which sat a black bowler hat. His horse was a grayish-white mare; blood was running harmlessly down its hindquarters.

He eyed the ranch's defenses and counted the number of ranchers and the horses in the pen. He studied the ranch house; its front door faced east and he could see three men, two bent at the shoulders, betraying their age. They were closing the gate to the pen that held two-dozen horses. He could see the stallions stirring in a separate pen, and knew the studs had caught the scent of his mare on the breeze as the aroma of her blood ambled down the valley and mixed with the honeysuckle and rosewood that blanketed the hills. The scent and stirring of the stallions was no matter, he thought, this would all be over soon enough. He wanted the horses, needed them, to push the

22

hundred and fifty head of stolen cattle south past the mountains. Two women, girls, conversed with a young man on the porch. They were sweeping the porch with brooms and occasionally bursting out in laughter. At times, they pretended the brooms were dance partners and they flowed and swayed in long simple frock dresses.

The twenty of his band he had sent moved upon the ranch from the east. They had been crawling toward the ranch for two hours. They approached like snakes through the fields of high grass that was occasionally dotted with dogwoods and a single copse of white pine. The twenty slithered at the speed of the wind, the top of the grass moving as if only to the whim of the breeze and therefore never betrayed their approach. To the onlooker, there was nothing to fear but a soft wind.

The renegade in white surveyed the grass that hid his warriors and he knew it had once been cut down to shear a long flat field before the hacienda, but like everything he had noticed on this raid, North County had some time ago lost its fear of the wastelands and the grass had been allowed to grow wild and long.

The twenty were a motley bunch, some dressed in women's silk underwear, others wearing wigs; some still covered in clown's clothes. Ten years earlier they had fallen upon a wagon train headed west. It had been a traveling circus, a carnival of sorts. The warlord was still wearing the pelt of a white lion he had stripped from a display case after he had disemboweled its former owner. He watched as the twenty descended like a mist; they were clear of the tall grass and making the final approach to the ranch house over the last hundred yards of clear land. Each savage moved with the contours of earth, zigzagging back and forth but never crossing each other's paths. To him, it seemed an elaborate, ritual dance. The twenty stepped with no sounds and their barefooted feet were raised high with each step so as not to stir dust.

The little girl on the porch, the one with tails, was the first to see the face of a warrior streaked with red paint; his hair tasseled with small bones. She let out a piercing scream and the whites reacted better than he would have expected; they did not even pause. The girl's warning sent the whites bolting for the ranch house. He could see an old crow of a woman the moment before one of the old men slammed shut the window. She was already loading carbines and handing them to the men, grabbing more from above a stone fireplace and loading them without pause. She was methodical, without reckless haste. The two young girls dashed about the house slamming closed every window. He could hear the crossbars being lifted and slammed home, and realized his plan had gone from a quick raid to a siege.

He knew he didn't have the time; he had been north too long already and needed to return to the lake to regain his strength. He had left a dozen dead in his pale wake of death through the cattle lands and the news would spread and the whites would mass to destroy him. Stroking the fur of the lion pelt, he considered committing the thirty in reserve. They lay flat against the reverse slope of the rise. Instead, he opted only to send down the two with the cannon.

The twenty opened the pen and drove the horses south. That should have ended it, and they should have immediately started south; that had been his command but he knew the twenty had seen the girls, seen their blond curls, and they were compelled to move on the house.

Rifle fire erupted from the crosses cut into the windows with rhythmic percussions; the three ranchers were staggering their fire, always keeping two loaded as one discharged.

He knew the horses should have been enough; he couldn't afford to lose twenty, but they had seen the girls. Nothing but death would stop them.

The ones in the rut ran head-on, three dropping from the chest-shattering blasts of the ranchers' .50 caliber buffalo rifles. They were thrown backward and down into the crushed stone of the path that led up to the front door. They didn't even reach the shadow of the porch. The rest of the savages lay flat in whatever small pieces of cover they could find, clawing at the earth for cover. The ranchers aimed carefully and sent rock and dirt into the heads and faces of warriors who couldn't claw low enough. One rose screaming, clutching at his face shredded by lead and rock, and as he stood, a second round hit him in the stomach. As he dropped to his knees a third shot sent the back of his skull flaying out in a thousand fragments.

He heard a rancher yell out, "Leave 'em screaming. We'll finish 'em right when they give it up."

The band clung to the ground begging for the dusk to end, darkness to fall, and for the cannon they knew the White Lion would send.

As darkness shrouded the hills, the three ranchers in the house gathered and parlayed in crouches behind the heavily reinforced front door. They spoke in hushed tones and whispers. The parlay was meant to last only a minute, to fix responsibilities for sectors of fire and decide turns for sleeping so each man could keep fresh for the rush they knew was coming. The two older men had helped Gabriel build the ranch, knew its strengths, and they were confident it could hold as it had in the early years.

The women were by the stone fireplace, cleaning and polishing the individual shell casings of dirt and dust, freeing the rounds from anything that might cause it to foul in the breech of the rifle. The cleaned shell casings glimmered in clay bowls on the table. The old woman was setting out bandages, oil for the lamps, and was stoking hot coals in the fireplace, keeping the coals red hot but not burning.

Except for the hushed tones of the men and the soft polishing of the shells, the house was silent.

The cannon shot hit the front door and the force of the explosion shattered it, sending shards of wood into each of the men. Kyle was shredded instantly and Eli decapitated. The oldest, Luke, who was crouching in the middle, dropped to both knees. He was blinded by the flash of light and a large shard of wood stuck out from his chest. It was pumping up and down in sync with the beating of his heart. He lightly caressed it in the fingers of both hands, mesmerized by the rhythmic sensation.

The lead savage came through the hole of the blasted door; he rose up from the smoke and dust wearing a jester's hat and wielded a machete that had been shaped from a plow blade. He slipped with precision to the left side of the kneeling old man and slashed, splitting Luke's Adam's apple in half as the blade flowed smoothly through the old man's neck. He spun to his right and was blinded by the muzzle flash, the old woman fired point-blank into the center of his chest.

She turned and dragged the girls with her to the far corner of the fireplace. She grabbed a second rifle from the table, turned, and fired, hitting a second savage in the left eye, the force of the round sending his eye socket and left ear peeling around the back of his head. She saw the shadows of five more coming through the smoldering ruins of what had been her front door. They were all screaming. She fired an old musket and hit the lead savage in the groin with a mix of rock and salt. He stumbled forward clutching at his crotch, smothered in blood, and the tattered remains of the blue cavalry pants he wore. She turned and grabbed the handle of a long knife; its blade lay in the red coals of the fire. It had been meant to slap onto the flesh of the men to stem the flow of blood in the event they had been wounded so they could keep fighting.

With the knife in one hand, she turned to the girls and in a steady voice said, "No matter what happens stay alive, don't fight, give in. Gabriel will come for you. Take care of one another." She caressed their faces with her free hand, and said softly, "The preacher will save you."

She wielded around blade in her hand, but the savages now feared her. The lead warrior flung a small ax, the blade hit her in the chest and she gasped as she was thrown back against the fireplace. The hem of her dress caught fire and the billows of her linen dress flared out to the sides in wings of flames. A renegade naked from the waist up and wearing women's dress bottoms seized her by the throat and threw her down on the table.

She was still clutching the knife and with her last effort, she jabbed the red-hot blade into the sides of his ribs and heard its sizzle as it scorched flesh.

The savage's scream rang through the house. He fell off her, spinning like a dog chasing its tail as he tried to pull the blade free from between his ribs. A second warrior leapt onto her stomach with his knees and sent the blade of his knife through her chest, pinning her heart to the rough-hewn boards of the table.

The girls shuddered against each other, the young one sobbing in the corner. The savages were turning over tables, grabbing silverware and any shiny item. A huge figure approached the girls. The fires from the spilled oil lamps spread out in thin rivulets along the floor behind the monstrous figure. A savage moved in front of him to reach the girls and the huge figure grabbed him with one hand by his hair and tossed him over a table like he was a man of straw. He moved toward them. The shape of the figure's black bowler hat was stark in relief of the white mane. The long hairs of the mane distilled the fire that burned behind him into vibrating sparkles of light. The older girl could not see his face because it was encased in shadow, but she gazed at the shape: it was perfectly round. The rim of his bowler accentuated the orb making it appear as if he were Saturn rotating in total eclipse.

The White Lion stared down and decided the older one belonged to him. The two who fired the cannon had rights to the other—they had saved him much time. The rest could wait; there would be plenty of time for all during the long ride to the lake. He needed to move while still night. He was already long overdue.

Thunder shook the sky and lightning lit the landscape in brief flashes of brilliance, revealing the small army riding its wild ponies and dragging its ramshackle wagons and stolen cattle over the grazing lands. They headed for the Crossing, the single pass through the walls of the southern mountain. The bolts shattered the horizon; with each blast, the mountain appeared as a black monolith and echoed the crash of thunder. The band chased it like a lost ship after a beacon at sea.

The two girls were tied to the cannon's caisson, which rumbled in the back of an old circus wagon that had been used to carry lion cages. As the wagon rolled and jostled toward the south, the flashes of light revealed two fevered silhouettes upon the young one.

Chapter Four:
The Lightning Strike

As the White Lion made his way south, lightning rolled along the night sky hitting Walker's new stable and sending balls of flame rolling down the roof. The horses in their stalls neighed in harsh and guttural tones. Along with an old nag, goats, and a dog, the best breeders were under that roof—four stallions, each of which had already secured advance stud money for the breeding season. They were all high-strung horses and Walker knew the heat was pouring down onto their backs and the urge to flee the flames was scrambling their brains.

He stumbled down the porch steps cursing his legs and loping stiffly to the front doors of the stable. The fire had already gotten to the hayloft and a burst of flame flew from the roof and descended in a shower of sparks. The flash of brilliant flames illuminated Toby's dash toward the barn. Walker could see him throwing open the tall doors. He wanted to yell for Toby to stop and stay back from the flames but he also didn't want to lose his studs, and he held his tongue as Toby burst through the doors into the midst of the flames.

Walker could hear the wood of the rafters cracking and sensed the roof structure starting to give. The first stallion bolted from the flames and headed off into the night, hay on fire still clinging to the hair of its tail and then another, Ulysses, came out of the doors and ran off into the night. Walker rushed to the doors but a gust of hot, liquid wind sent him stumbling back. He looked through the open doors and saw Toby naked from the waist up draped between two stallions. He was holding the manes in each of his hands, his feet glancing off the ground as he guided the two stallions out of the fire, a ball of flame engulfing the stable behind him. The horses bolted at the door, and Toby let go of the manes and ran to a stop, not even falling. He turned and headed back toward the stable doors when Walker grabbed him.

"But, Pa, the gray mare's still in there."

His father held him, one hand clutching hard a handful of his hair and the other arm thrown across his son's chest, immobilizing him. They both stared in stupefied wonder and listened to the harsh sounds of beams cracking, timber falling, and the groans of the old mare as the agonies emitted from the depths of the fire. Walker glanced heavenward and saw thousands of stars and realized not a single drop of rain had fallen. As he clenched his son, he felt the warm, guilty relief of a man who had gambled recklessly without consequence.

The next morning, Walker stood with slumped shoulders looking at the smoldering ruins of his new stable. His wife, Molly, came to the porch. "John, it can wait until tomorrow; we need to meet the train. He has been gone seven years; that barn isn't going anywhere, it'll still be smoking when we come home tomorrow."

Walker mumbled "Goddamn it to hell," under his breath.

"I don't want the girls to hear that talk," his wife said as she spun and reentered the house.

He thought the woman must have ears like a dog. Of all days, it had to be today that his elder boy, Wesley, was due back from the east. As he turned to the house, he caught sight of the postal carrier sauntering up on his horse.

The postman pushed the bill of his cap high on his head and leaning forward, crossing his wrists on the pommel of his saddle. He let the reins dance in his fingertips as he looked at the stable and let loose with a long soft whistle, saying dryly, "Well, Colonel, I hope there's at least some good news from the post."

"I hope so too, Teddy, but I doubt it . . . Hey, Teddy, can you do me a favor?"

"Of course, Colonel, but I ain't got no new barn in my satchel. There's limits even to the post."

Walker ignored his comment and said, "Tell Raif I need my long saw back, and tell him why I need it, and also tell Jack Straw that it looks like I'll need them planks he was selling."

"Sure, Colonel, anything else I can do?"

"Tell any of them farmhands, I'll pay two dollars a day to work on a new barn."

"All right, Colonel, and congratulations on your boy, a real military academy grad. Cavalry?"

"No, Teddy, he's an engineer, going to Fort Sill in Oklahoma territory. Never could ride worth a shit, anyhow." He heard Molly's sharp response from the inside of his ranch house, "John Walker, stop that talk." Walker frowned, and added, "All right, Teddy, tell them farmhands I'll be back day after tomorrow if they're looking for work."

Teddy reined his horse into a turn and as he rode off said, "Sure will do, Colonel. Congratulations again on your boy. A lieutenant, how about that. I never got promoted past private. Every lieutenant I had lasted about an hour into each fight, brave sort mostly, there was only one fool we had to shoot ourselves."

CHAPTER FIVE:
THE MASTODON ON THE PRAIRIE

As Teddy followed his route through the county delivering the post, the roads began to fill with life. An hour after each delivery the folks started to roll in the opposite direction toward Walker's Nottaway ranch. It was a migration of neighbors: farmers hauling wood in the back of their wagons; ranchers sending their hands in from the prairies with unaccustomed tools; cattlemen donating heifers to feed the folks; grain merchants sending feed for the workhorses; and town merchants riding out with cartloads of nails and shingles. No matter the stripe they all owed Walker, and all knew they would need him again.

Walker had loaned farmers strong horses for plowing when theirs had dropped dead in the harness. He had floated merchantmen interest-free credit when business was slow, that is, before the railroad spread its reach to the town and they became wealthy in their own right. He allowed cattlemen to water their herds in his streams during spring drives to Tin City. On and on they came in wagons filled with raw materials and families all to help the richest man in North County resurrect his stable. By dawn the next day, the pasture surrounding Walker's ranch was a swarming tent city filled with North County folk.

By dusk the next day, the skeletal framing of the new stable rose thirty feet in the air, the roof already framed and ready to be shingled. It stood like the skeleton of a lone mastodon lost on the prairie. As in any gathering, there was also opportunity.

In the shadow of the mastodon, the parson raised up his hands and began his sermon, "People, good people, misfortune has beset the Walker family, but rejoice because you see the power of the Almighty in our gathering—a community of the faithful come together to raise a neighbor struck by calamity . . ."

A few hundred feet away and covered in sawdust and sweat, the three Hanson brothers sat on bales of hay in the back of the crowd. They were part of the gathering, but remained on its fringes.

Jed Hanson curled his lower lip and spat out a stream of tobacco juice before saying to nobody in particular, "Can you believe these preacher boys? They can look in an ass crack and find a silver lining. And it's always bent to their purpose. Parson, help me understand the ways of the Lord because I done sat on my horse for hours plow'n my fields and my reward is an empty field and an ass full of sores. Why has the Lord done this? Parson'll bend you over, look at your crack and say all solemn like: 'Son, I see the miracle of the Lord in that there crack— your hard work pleases the Lord and your sitting displeasure is a reminder of his love' . . . or some other such shit. But, if you say, Parson, I done drank beers and tortillas all night and my crack's as red as a beet from the shits, that same Parson, look'n at that same crack, the same exact ass crack. will say 'Son, that's the devil's work in there, it's a testament to the evil you been do'n.' "

The youngest Hanson, Abner, said, "Jed, what the hell are you go'n on about?"

"I'm say'n they always got it straight because they say whatever they feel like. Imagine we sell a horse and some dirt-splitter asks, 'Is it broke?' And we say, 'depends on what you mean by broke,' that fool look at you like you're crazy. All I'm saying is if my crack's full of sores the Almighty ain't got noth'n to do with it, and I particularly don't need no parson to tell me otherwise. All these fools out here listen'n to this charlatan jabber on. Ain't been a parson worth his salt since Graham passed on."

Raif Hanson listened on with a detached expressionless look. He was lean and powerful and like the chosen few in North County, he was a horse rancher. He stared at the parson. The farmers had built a raised platform of hay bales and wood slats four feet off the ground, raising the parson over the crowd. Atop the hay stage was a raised dais of two more hay bales. The dais was draped with a red-and-gray-striped horse blanket. The blanket's edges were singed and blackened. Raif used every inch of the hay chair formed from the bales, leaning farther into a reclining position and stretching his legs. He glanced around at the dozens of family folk waiting for the parson to finish so the feeding could start. He marveled at the parson's ability to speak to such a throng in a calm measured voice, realizing he could never speak to such a crowd in such tones. He would rather face fifty renegades alone than stand and speak to such a gathering—the difference amused him.

As he gazed at the crowd, he caught a small boy staring at him. He felt self-conscious of the vicious scar that rose above his left eye and cut jagged across his cheek and nose. The forehead had the deepest gash and it was only slightly concealed under the flop of his dirty blond hair. The boy's gaze made him edgy and he was relieved when Jed said in a mockingly threatening tone, "What the hell you look'n at, Blinkton boy? You're a little Blinkton; I can tell by the mule features. Git, 'fore I tan your hide." The boy darted off toward the mastodon.

The Hansons' parents had died ten years earlier, and the brothers had been considered orphans by the rest of the folks in the county. It was a stigma that still clung to them. Their father had been a horse breeder like Walker, and was as good at it. Death joined the brothers alone, and Raif was fifteen when a tax collector from the county office rode out to the ranch and told Raif that they needed to pay the land tax or he would have to foreclose and evict the brothers. Raif had gone to Walker. The walk from his horse to the Walker front door was the longest of his life. John Walker had helped him ten years ago and like everybody at the stable raising today, he was still repaying that debt. Walker had been there when his family needed it, and now Raif was here returning the favor, helping his competitor raise a mammoth stable from the ashes of foolishness.

The parson's voice broke into his daydreaming, and Raif heard the vague snippets of sermon as he continued to eye the crowd. The parson's voice rose in earnest, "By your neighborly acts we have given succor to the downtrodden . . ."

Jed erupted in mock indignation, "What the hell did he say? Did he say downtrodden? Walker's the richest man in this county and he was burned out because he was too lazy or plumb forgot to put up that lightning rod. I seen it over there, the braces still on it, never cut. Downtrodden my ass, shee-it, he could build ten barns 'fore it hurt. Parson knows better than anyone the lining of Walker's ass crack is filled with silver."

Raif looked at his brother out of the corner of his eye.

Jed said, "Oh, all right."

Abner muttered, "It is true, Raif, he ain't downtrodden."

Raif wasn't listening anymore but was gazing on a mother scolding her seven-year-old boy. The finger of her right hand was wagging in front of his nose as she stretched his collar with her left hand. The boy's eyes were cast down in a weak attempt to look penitent for his latest prank.

Jed's voice piped into Raif's thoughts again. "Half-buck she cracks him."

Raif said, "I'll take that."

The mother lowered her face to meet the boy's eyes and released his collar. She took his cheeks in her hands, raised his face, kissed him, and sent him off. He raced away to rejoin the gang of boys climbing on the mastodon's skeleton.

"Ain't fair, Raif, you knew what that squirt done. I didn't see what he did. I only bet because she was wagging that finger in his nose. You must've seen what the squirt did and knew it didn't rate a crack. I'm surprised at you, Raphael, for taking advantage. Ain't like you."

"Half-buck."

Jed blew air and said, "All right, all right, I ain't exactly got it on me. When we get back to the ranch, I'll get it to you and if I forget, you remind me."

The mother wore a bonnet but blond curls billowed beneath it falling in ribbons on her shoulders. She was heavy from child-rearing and her girth gave her a mother's look, but she was beautiful. She glanced at Raif for a brief moment before turning and melting back into the cluster of folks gathered around the parson.

Jed asked, "Was that Edda? I remember her; she was sweet on me. Man, but them kids she squeezed out done did a reckoning on ol' Edda. What she got now, four or five? She was the prettiest girl in Bibbs's class. Wasn't she, Raif? You remember her, don't you? She look like that bigg'n with the curls you always git in Tin City . . ."

Raif drifted off and was lost in his thoughts.

CHAPTER SIX:
RAIF

Ten years before lightning burned Walker's stable to the earth, Mr. Bibbs's class was the highlight of young Raif Hanson's day. The one-room schoolhouse was plain except for an array of books along the far wall. The schoolroom was laid out in columns, four seats across. The youngest sat in the front of the class; the oldest in the back. The boys sat in the right two rows and the girls on the left. The desks were simple, slats of two-by-fours, sanded down so the middle crease didn't cause your grease pencil to puncture the paper. The pencil still cut, especially for Raif, who no matter how hard he tried, always pressed too hard.

Raif sat in the back corner; he preferred it there. He could look out at the entire class and only Mr. Bibbs could look directly at him; anybody else who tried to look at him had to go through the effort to turn around. Mr. Bibbs was young with a pretty wife. They lived in the house adjacent to the school with their two girls. Bibbs had replaced the old Potter woman a year ago. Potter had finally kicked and Raif figured it was way past her due date, anyhow. Raif had hated her. Potter's class had been drudgery: rote spelling, monotonous incantations of prayers, and she used the standard speller same as she used the Testament—no questions asked, lest the ruler across the knuckles. She never strayed from the lessons. He had hated school, detested it with a passion, always longing to return to the horses, so he could sweat out the boredom and idleness of

37

the long school day.

There had been no school for two months after Potter kicked. When Bibbs arrived in town, Raif had begged his father not to send him back, explaining it was a waste of time and that he was needed full-time on the ranch. His father had almost relented when his mother stepped in and said he had two more years of schooling and wasn't finished until he was full sixteen, and that was final.

Raif pondered the notion often in class, how the change of one person could change the way you felt about the same exact thing. It was like that with Bibbs; he had changed it all by simply showing up. Bibbs loved to read classics, and a man he called the forgotten poet, Shakespeare. He loved history and great heroes, as long as they were Christians, and he loved to teach. He had a deft touch with students, finding their weakness and interests, finding what motivated and what bored, and he did it in a classroom of forty kids in varying ages, none of whom were much interested to begin with. Raif drank it in. From complete drudgery, school became a haven to explore new worlds late into the night by candle. Raif would read constantly.

Bibbs saw potential in him and cultivated it. Bibbs spoke to him of far-off places like Tusculum and Bethel, colleges he called them. Raif's father was lukewarm to the idea, but his mother was thrilled, saying "The Walkers always talked about Wesley one day going to the academy; Raif's going to attend a real college, not some Yankee army school." To Raif, it was all heady stuff.

In the late afternoon of one spring day, near summer, the light slanted through the windows of the schoolroom. The dust danced on beams giving the room that hazy quality. In the far corner, Raif looked up from his book and stole glances at Edda's blond locks. He sat there pondering her hair, the way it cascaded down the back of her neck and shoulders. She was toying with a pink ribbon, twisting it in her hands. He fixated on her hands. He stared for what felt like an eternity, until he looked up and realized her hands were on her desk but she had turned her head. She had been staring at him. He had been caught dead to rights, or as his father always liked to say—he had shown his ass. He felt his face flush with the rush of embarrassment until he noticed she was smiling. She simply batted her eyes and delicately looked away. The shame went to a throbbing of his heart.

Raif, Jed, and Abner headed home from school. They hitched a ride on a lumber wagon that let them off at the edge of the Hanson ranch. From the north fence line, for no reason at all, Raif starting running toward the main house, his books slung across his shoulder, dangling from an old belt. He felt as if his legs were those of a colt that got the hang of running and he let loose.

He cut his way across the field, dodging the fresh pies hardening in the sun.

Jed and Abner struggled to keep up. Jed kept holler'n to slow down and the only thing Raif would remember was Jed calling out, "Ah, Raif, you done made me step in a huge pile of shit, and me with my school shoes on."

Raif reached the front porch and bounded up the steps, hardly noticing that Doc Hennon's wagon was in front. Panic jolted him as he recognized it was the doctor's long wagon. His mother had been sick, but they didn't think, they just didn't think . . . He crossed silently over the threshold of the bedroom and none of the adults in the room knew he was among them. The air was thick with a sweet smell of flowers and bile, like that of fruit left to rot under a hot sun. The scent burned into his nostrils and caused his eyes to tear up. He saw his mother, her head lay canted to one side of the pillow; blood from her coughing had speckled down the side of the pillow and its misting spread down the top of the bedsheet. His father sat on a chair near her, holding her hand and whispering to her. She was delirious, talking about the cloth she needed for kitchen curtains. His father's head dropped now and again between his knees. His hands were speckled with his wife's clotted blood. Her eyes were formless, encased in yellowing skin that was stretched thin and run with bright blue veins that cracked in tributaries over her forehead.

Doc Hennon looked on sullenly, offering weakly, "Matthew, you best come away from there or you're liable to be next. C'mon, Matthew, think of the boys."

His father raised his head and saw Raif standing at the door; he muttered a soft "son" before returning his gaze to his dying wife. Matthew rose and led Doc Hennon to the door, not in any forceful manner, but in that way that says the next bit is for family. Hennon kept repeating softly that there was nothing that could be done, that at least the boys should keep clear. The doctor said it with soft earnestness. Raif knew that the Doc was all too familiar with his father's temper, as he had stitched up some men in town who had faced the rage. Raif had seen it a few times and had even seen his father kill a man, but he had always been gentle around their mother. The killing had been done defending Jed from a crazed drunk, but the image of his father's savagery and the swiftness in which he took to the knife haunted his dreams.

As he left the room, Doc Hennon said in subdued tones, "Matthew, keep the boys in for only a moment. I'll need to quarantine you and the boys for at least a month. It shouldn't be too much longer than that. I'm sorry." And with that Doc Hennon waited outside on his long wagon, his two attendants sitting in the shade on the far side of the house, waiting on the word to retrieve the mother's corpse, so they could wrap it in a thick shroud and burn it with whale oil.

Jed and Abner stood on the front porch. Their father saw them; he turned and said, "Come now, boys, say goodbye to your mother."

Abner obeyed, but Jed stood frozen, scared of what was inside, saying in broken words, "I can't, Pa, I done stepped in shit, got it all over my foot, Ma would kill me if I tred inside." At that Jed started sobbing, the tears streaming down his face.

His father walked to Jed and Abner, dropped to his knees between them, and pulled them into an embrace with him. He rose slowly and placed one arm around each and led them inside, murmuring it was all right, it was gonna be all right.

Raif slowly approached his mother's bed. Her lips were blue and the blue was cracked with lines that ran a deeper azure; spittle dripped from her mouth. He croaked a hoarse "Ma" before he felt his father's heavy hand rest on his shoulder.

"Raphael, Jedediah, Abner, say goodbye to your mother."

Tears flowed in torrents down their cheeks and each in his way said goodbye to his mother. She lay there delirious and unresponsive, her eyes opaque shades. The dying light of day diffused in pale cream colors over the retinas of his mother's eyes, creating a cloudy impenetrable mist. The father and boys stood in a half crescent around her, staring at her gaunt figure wrapped in blood and sweat-soaked sheets until their father sent them from the room.

The mother lingered for hours, longer than expected, and his father remained by her side as she coughed out her life. The next day they buried her in the earth, Reverend Graham coming and giving a eulogy despite the fact there was a quarantine in place. The ranch families, Walker and McCallum, were the only folk to breach the quarantine. The three families formed a tight semicircle as the men lowered the mother's ashes in a long hickory box into the earth. They sang gospel hymns, the songs rising into a cloudless blue sky on a perfect spring day.

41

The night of the funeral, Raif lay awake in the loft, his head resting in the crook of his elbow. He allowed his mind to wander, staring unfocused at the ceiling. Occasionally he stared down at his father sitting in his worn leather chair on the floor below as he stared silently into the fireplace. The light from the flames illuminated his father's face. Raif could see the lines of age running from his eyes and down his cheeks. In the firelight, the crow's feet ran a deep black, as if they were rivers that flowed out from the pools of his father's dark eyes.

Raif laid his head back and stared up at the cathedral ceiling of the house. The great beam of wood, dark with pitch, ran the length of the house, giving it its high vaulted center. The light from the fireplace flames flicked in twisting shadows upon the sharp angles of the ceiling. Raif was drifting off when he heard his father cough. The sound came from the depths of his chest. He spit and Raif could hear the sizzle of the sputum as it hit the burning logs.

Over the next two weeks, the brothers watched their father die the same slow, bloody death as their mother. Matthew Hanson passed on the same day Raif turned fifteen.

His father's last will and testament was like the man. As far as Raif could remember, it read something like: Raif, the land is yours and all on it because you're my oldest, but goddamn your soul if you don't take care of your brothers, or something or such like that. The Cuchalainn ranch was at its peak that May, with three studs that ranchers from far off sought. The grazing fields were lush, fed by a natural spring that was welled in half a dozen spots over the ten thousand acres, and the Criss River ran for a good mile and half inside the northern boundary, giving water the year round. Raif, Jed, and Abner were young, but they had been working the Cuchalainn since before they were housebroken and were experienced ranchers. The boys were holding the ranch together until the blight hit.

It was a strange illness. It hit the cattle first and then wove its way into the horses. Reverend Graham called it a plague. It swept North County—the stock dropping in the fields with bloated tongues. The air filled with the rancid smell of death. Even before the stock dropped, the stench of dead flesh started weeks before. It was as if the disease hid in the belly of the beasts and killed slowly from the inside out. Many times, they found steers with beautiful, healthy looking hides being picked on by buzzards.

The rain conspired with the pestilence and failed to fall on the fields that spring. The dry spring led into the driest of summers anyone could remember. The Criss's and Cross's banks caked and cracked under the relentless heat. The Cuchalainn's natural spring ran dry. The stock that managed to survive lived off scrub bush and licks of morning dew. The brothers, caked in dust and sweat, tried to tap a new well on land that showed it could still keep its vegetation. Red, the only prize stud to live through the pestilence, got curious and came over to inspect the dig. He stepped into a rattlesnake den as he trotted over and twenty young serpents emptied their venom into his foreleg. Red broke into a run but crumpled to the earth after a few strides, his eyes lolling over in his head, his magnificent frame convulsing in violent spasms. Raif poured lamp oil into the den and ignited the fuel, sending the snakes slithering out, sizzling as they crawled. The boys watched in a bitter satisfaction as the snakes curled in a kaleidoscope of blackening twists a few feet from their hole.

The fall brought clouds but no rain, and horses and men and every living thing except buzzards languished in North County. By December, the sky doused the land with sleet and snow. The cold winds blew hard and early. And the same as the pestilence had come, it went. The North County prayed for an early spring.

★ ★ ★ ★ ★

In the bitter cold of a December morning, the tax collector, Leviticus Tickers, meandered his way along the fence line. The wind whipped across the fields and cut him bitterly as he went about his business collecting the year-end land taxes. He had been shot at only once and from a great distance at the Brinkley farm. Tickers thought, what did it matter? The Brinkleys were going under. He would wait a few weeks and go out again with a wagon, maybe a hired man or two. He'd seen it before. The Brinkleys would break. Tickers was sure they were already broken. The rifle shot was the last gasp of pride. Brinkley was a fool. There was no steady water on that property. The drought broke them. He would go back in a week or two after Brinkley had loaded up a wagon with whatever he could carry, including his brood. They would head somewhere else and probably starve to death on the way.

Tickers would be the first one to the homestead after the Brinkleys' exodus to see what he could salvage. It amazed him what these homesteaders could accumulate in a few years of farming even on shit land like the Brinkleys'. The Brinkleys were hard-luck people. They had it written on their faces— hard, determined people, yet ones that never got a break, always getting the short end of it. Ah, what did it matter? The place would be empty soon and he'd take whatever was left and sell it in Tin City or at the spring market. The Brinkley girl was scarred by the pox, but maybe a deal could have been worked out—if heh, heh, heh, Tickers laughed to himself, if only Brinkley wasn't so proud. Tickers fretted a little, remembering that the proud ones usually torched the farm as they were pulling out.

Tickers cursed the cold once more and trotted his nag down toward the Hansons' Cuchalainn ranch. He scanned the frozen fields and despondency gripped him. He asked himself how a man of his awesome promise could end up in such a forsaken place. But he knew. That pudgy little bitch, Trini Davis, had sent him from the East to this frozen hell. He remembered how she had batted her eyes at him like all the girls at the theatre when he wore his new green coat cut in the Continental style. They had all flitted about in his orbit, their perky nipples dancing beneath thin silky layers of fine cloth.

Trini had been the most forward with her "Oh, Leviticus, you must come riding with me when the weather permits; father has some new wonderful Arabians." Trini's father was wealthy, but Tickers had questioned the true extent of his real worth at the time, and if he was going to saddle himself to that little porker, he had questioned whether there was enough money. Trini had youth, but it would fade and she'd grow to be like her mother with her hideous bulbous form and its folds upon folds of thick hide. But her flirtations intrigued him, the flash of her eyes as they stole over him. Tickers was titillated, and he had judged that Trini wanted more than to ride a horse.

On the first warm spring day, Tickers and Trini rode through her father's fields, and Tickers's keen eyes evaluated the wealth. The house was splendid, the gardens near the home finely attended, but once past the façade and showpieces, the fields were shabby and ill-kept. The millhouse on the river was a ramshackle affair with no more than a half-dozen hard-looking Irish teagues to keep the wheel turning. Davis had money but not enough to interest Tickers; there was a thinner, richer breed he was hunting. He had asked Trini to join him boating with friends on the Potomac. She had agreed, but insisted he come riding first. As they rode the grounds, Tickers began to imagine Trini's motives for being so insistent they ride together. She knew they would be alone on a ride. On a ride the corsets and layers of cloth were impractical, on a ride, they could . . . Tickers fantasized that she wanted to show him how much she really liked him. Why else the insistence to ride alone?

Tickers suggested they dismount and rest under an elm that had sprouted early buds, giving generous shade. Trini had looked surprised at first, but agreed. Tickers sat down next to her on a fallen tree branch. He moved closer to her. As they sat, Tickers noticed her riding skirt had risen, exposing the flesh above the boot. She smiled her coy smile.

He gripped her shoulders and awkwardly pulled her toward him. She struggled, but Tickers was lost and sensed the squirming to be rapture. He became aroused but a faint, insistent buzzing noise kept annoying him. What was that? Why doesn't it stop? He opened his trousers to expose himself and it was only then he realized the annoying sound was Trini screaming.

Tickers begged her to stop screaming. He let go of her. She bolted to her feet and staggered backward a step or two before tripping on a fallen tree branch. She fell on her bottom, sending a muddy splash up from the wet grass. She rose but slipped again and had to roll over, covering her hands and outfit in an additional layer of muck. Tickers was on his feet. He had forgotten his pants were still undone and he reached out for Trini. He used his hands to wipe the mud from her as his erect penis bounced about. She flailed to distance herself from his exposed member. Tickers looked down and realized his penis was out and looked up to see the millhouse goons making their way across the pasture shouting "Miss Trini! Miss Trini!"

Tickers buttoned his trousers and turned to Trini. "Now, Trini, you must admit, you gave me the wrong impression."

At this she grew furious, and realizing that society had been restored, she became defiant: "I gave you what? How dare you, sir?"

"Now, Trini, it was your idea to go riding, your idea."

"Wrong impression? I am an excellent rider, to think I wanted to impress you, you, you, you monster."

"Trini, you gave me every indication my advances were

welcome, indeed invited."

Trini spun about toward her horse saying, "You are a scoundrel—I am going right to Father."

"Now, Trini . . ." he stammered.

Tickers had grabbed the rein of her horse as the mill men came crashing through the brush, "Miss Trini, miss, we heard a cry—"

"Let go of my horse, Mr. Tickers." Despite the request, Tickers held the reins.

An old workman thick about the shoulders and brandishing a nose flattened by scores of bare-knuckle matches in his youth said, "I think you heard my lady."

"Mr. Conway. Yes, it was me—this brute attempted, ugh, please escort him from the property—and if he gives you any trouble, forcibly remove him." Trini wheeled the horse and galloped toward the main house.

The millhouse gang never said a word; they beat him to a pulp and dragged his body to the property line where they dumped him. By the time he scuttled back to Washington his eyes were still puffy, but the bruising had faded.

His father was waiting for him in the study. It was all so sordid. The usual disbelief followed by "Are you telling me, Leviticus, that Miss Davis concocted the whole story? To what end?" Despite Tickers's protestations, the conversation ended with his father stating: "My God, Leviticus, what were you thinking? A good marriage will be impossible now. Your appointment to the ambassador's staff at King James will be rescinded. You stupid, horny boy, Davis is Grant's man. Oh, this is poor judgment, poor judgment. What this will do to your sister's prospects, I do not know. I'm glad your mother's not alive, this would have killed her."

From there it went to worse: Tickers's peculiar proclivities at boarding school began to surface in polite society. By the end of the season, he was a pariah in Washington and all of Virginia.

Months later in the steaming heat of August, he lay in a boarding room flophouse in Philadelphia. It was near noon when his boyhood friend, Jeeves, knocked and woke him from his stupor. The one-room rental still reeked of the perfume from the whore he had coerced with money and liquor the night before to engage in his deviant wants. Jeeves pulled a dirty footstool over to the bedside and placed his handkerchief over the cushion before sitting on it.

"How are you, Leviticus?"

"Jeeves, please, man, spare me. What brings you to Philadelphia in August: The waters?"

"Ha, ha, Levi. Despite it all you haven't lost it."

"Jeeves, please, do you have any of the hair?"

Jeeves drew a small flask from his jacket pocket and handed it over. "Well, anyway, best to get on with it. Do you remember Braxton?"

"Yes, John or Jake or something. Railroads, isn't it? He was with us at school, a few years younger. Why?"

"Yes, that's him—it's John, but he insists on the pedestrian Jake."

"Well, what about him?"

"Well, Levi, this is no reflection on our friendship, but I come as his second."

"His second? What are you going on about? I don't even know him. What slight? He doesn't have a sister, does he?"

"No, no. Braxton's engaged to Trini Davis. He says there's a point of honor to be settled."

Levi rose and took a pull from the flask and fell back down, his head spinning, "Jeeves, what *are* you going on about?"

"Yes, yes, Levi, that's why I agreed to be his second. Braxton doesn't want to slay you. I told him you of all people are not disposed to violence—that if I spoke with you you'd agree to flee the East for a while. It was Braxton's idea, he is really only interested in getting married to Trini as soon as possible and knows this is an inconvenience."

"Why is he in such a rush to marry that pudgy tart?"

"There's a great fortune there for Braxton; it all fits with his family's railroad business."

"What? The Braxtons have gads more money than Davis."

"Oh, Levi, you really are on the outs; you haven't heard? Davis sunk his entire fortune into a silver mining operation out West. He's hit it. Davis gambled every dime, and they are pulling silver out of his mines by the wagonload. The Davises are moving to an old plantation, Sommers . . . town, ville, something quaint-sounding—twenty thousand acres I hear. The old boy has a hundred men refinishing the old mansion of some driver of slaves moved off by the war, good riddance. It's all so splendid for Jake."

"Oh, please stop. Jeeves, tell Braxton you couldn't find me. Say I'd gone to New York. I need time to think. . . . Would I have any chance against Braxton?"

"You wouldn't have a chance against me. Braxton's a brute. This isn't his first, either. Two wounded, one dead—a Frenchman that insulted his sister, mentioned something about the sharpness of her teeth; Braxton shot him through the middle of the eyebrows at twenty paces. No, no, Braxton can split piano strings at ten paces, can you imagine being able to do that, what a monumental waste of time practicing that."

"Yes, yes, thank you for all of that. I've got to go to Father."

"I went to your father first. He's mixed in with this whiskey ring business—Grant's tossed the lot out. He's going to Italy until it blows over."

"Italy! Why wasn't I told?"

"Your father said he'd send for you after they had established themselves. For now, he's secured you a post in the West."

"What ship? What dock are they sailing from? How much time do I have?"

"Levi, Levi, your father's given me specific instructions—the family wants to give your sister a fresh start on the Continent. The Trini episode, you can imagine the position your father's in. He also said it would be doubly disastrous for the family for you to be killed in a duel over a matter of honor involving a young woman everyone admires."

"Admires! That chubby little tart was nothing until this silver business . . . my God, *how* much silver?"

"A loss in a duel would only compound your family's earlier embarrassment. And if by some chance you killed Braxton your family would be ruined. Your father insists you try to make a go of it in government. He's used his last bit of capital with Grant to secure a position for you in the western land bureau. It's the frontier, Levi—a man can reinvent himself out there."

"Oh, Jeeves, what have I done? I have made such a mess of it all."

"You're going West, Levi. Think of it as an adventure."

Tickers remembered it every day for the past ten long years. As he rode, he looked out at the desolation of this barren trek of North County. For ten years, he rode the circuit of ranchers and homesteaders and had suffered the indignations of countless slurs from these slobs. Slobs that he wouldn't have even noticed back east when they brought him his steak and Madeira. The ranchers were the worst. McCallum had been particularly nasty this trip—not even inviting him to dismount, not even the offer of a cup of coffee. Only a perfunctory "Wait," while he went in the house to fetch his coins. Tickers had sat on his horse in the cutting wind. McCallum had handed him the coins, all silver eagles, and as Tickers went to transfer them to his satchel, his numb fingers dropped them on the ground. McCallum stood over him and glared as Tickers fumbled through the light snow before the rancher simply turned and strode off without a word into the warmth of his ranch house.

But even that was less demeaning than Walker's ranch. There he was bade to wait in a room off the kitchen like a colored boy bringing firewood in from the fields.

To assuage his anger, Tickers ran imaginings of McCallum's niece and Walker's older daughter around in his mind. He toyed with the daydream of hiding out on their property and snatching one of them. He'd dress like a savage, dirty his face with charcoal, and yell gibberish as he dragged one of them into the brush. The thoughts excited him and even in the cold of the saddle, his imagination warmed him. But what if they spotted him on the property dressed as a savage? McCallum would put it together in a minute; old Gabbie would skin him. And Walker, despite all pretenses to being some colonel, he was nothing more than southern trash, as brutal a killer as McCallum. He knew the stories of savages, rustlers, and the odd vagrant or two disappearing on their lands. Tickers knew the risk was too great. They were all killers and could track and snare a coyote that had the impudence to piss on one of their trees.

Tickers grew despondent, but his spirits picked up as he approached the Hansons' ranch. His anticipation grew as he tallied in his mind the telltale signs of decay. The fence posts rotting and slanted, untended for months. The Hansons were replacing fence posts in stretches with wire, using whatever sticks they could find to shore it up. The hay was no longer staged in picturesque bails about the fields but lay in great, soggy, vermin-infested heaps. The horses were thin, ribbed-out, and mangy. Tickers marveled at the rotting corpse of the ranch; even the animals could smell the rot and started to look like death afoot.

Yes, yes, no girls to bargain for, but some currency could be bartered here in horseflesh. Tickers calculated that the Hansons couldn't afford the tax this year. He could make a deal, $500 worth of horseflesh to satisfy the tax bill. The Hansons would do anything to buy themselves a little time—they'd cut off their hands in winter to buy time so they could breed stallions next summer. Tickers's mood improved as he conjured the ways he was going to squeeze blood out of the Hanson stone. His inner voice rattled off his contempt for the ranchers, and it was more vile than the hatred he had for the homesteaders. Who did these people think they were? A bunch of Johnny Rebs who had gotten a good licking and brought all that southern gentleman bullshit out here.

It was the fifteenth of December as Tickers trotted up. He tried to carry himself with a studied, detached air, but he was aware that while his horse was large, it was weak and ungainly, its forelegs bending in awkwardly at the knees. Tickers knew somewhere along the bloodline a crafty plow horse had gotten over the fence and mixed with a prized mare. Tickers adjusted his large green felt coat and tipped his broad-brimmed hat with a matching green felt band so that it slanted down over his eyes. The coat was frayed at the ends and the hat's band was knotted in various places where the fabric had worn through.

As Raif took in the sight of Tickers's approach, he supposed the shabby outfit was probably once expensive. The fact that Tickers didn't dismount, but called him "boy" from the horse irked Raif. The slight cut to the bone. Tickers had always dismounted and greeted his father like they were long-lost friends; removing his hat and saying repeatedly things like, "I know, sir, I know, they must make up the fees at county, they're not horse people like you and me, you know my task is to deliver the news, don't hate the messenger, sir." But now Tickers didn't even dismount; he stared down his long nose at Raif, and spoke in rapid clips of speech as if he was in haste to meet with a more important engagement.

"I assume you are the Hanson son that is now in possession of the Cuchalainn?" Raif nodded, and Tickers offered a few brief words of condolences, calling the deaths regrettable. Without pausing, Tickers continued, "According to the poll records, the Cuchalainn is due for its year-end land tax assessment. This year it is . . . umm." Tickers pretended to search his tax log, a tall leather-bound ledger that he kept in the postman's satchel he'd slung over his shoulder.

Raif was skeptical Tickers needed to look up the assessment for the third largest ranch in North County.

The ledger had a record of $240. "Ah, yes, here it is: $280; payment due by December the 31st. If you like, you can pay me now, it would save me a second trip at the end of the month or you a trip to town. This December is a cold one; one trip out here is enough."

The ranch was down to its last hundred dollars, and Raif needed time to think how to raise another $180. He spat a stream of tobacco and wiped his mouth with the back of his hand. Tickers noticed the pause, and sensing an opportunity interjected, "You know your father would sometimes pay the assessment in horses; sometimes three or four and even five, depending on the quality of horseflesh, of course. I realize cash is tight in these hard times. Perhaps those two—the roan and that young one, the reddish one, and how about that mare, the shaggy one. Those three would take care of it."

The request stunned Raif, and he blurted out, "They're my best three; that's two thousand dollars of horseflesh in Tin City." He silently cursed himself for the loss of composure and compounded the mistake by saying, "I do have a couple dozen more on the north field."

Tickers enjoyed the reaction, a thin smile breaking out on his cracked lips as he sensed an opportunity. "Oh, no, those won't do. I passed those as I rode down from McCallum's. No good, won't do. Anyway, I couldn't sell those nags until the spring, and maybe not even then. Whether the blight has really ended no one knows for sure. No, no, no, I couldn't transport them to Tin City or the fort until the thaw. I would have to feed them through winter, and there's still no guarantee those nags would sell. No, no, I don't think so. No, no, no, they will not do. It's got to be at least those two—Blacky and Bloody, we will call them, that is, unless you have the $280 on hand, then we don't have to keep at this silly talk out here in the cold."

"Mister, I'll give it to you in cash. What's the last date we can pay?"

Tickers perked up. "Well, if you have silver eagles, why have I been wasting my time freezing here talking about a fair trade? Let's settle the account."

Despite the cold, Raif could feel the sweat beading on his forehead. "It's better for the ranch's finances if I pay at the end of the month. What date is the latest?"

Tickers ignored Raif's comment, and said, "I tell you what, give me the two and I'll settle the account for the full year. Listen, I understand everyone in the county is hurting, we all have trouble—farmers, ranchers, the merchants—all have felt the blight, but relief is in sight. Endure this winter, son, and the spring will grant fresh opportunity. If you part with those two, we can even put a little down payment toward next year's assessment, say twenty, twenty-five dollars."

Raif felt as if he was spinning and forced himself to ask, "What's the last date we can pay, mister?"

Tickers's expression grew hard, his eyes squinted, and he hissed, "I have told you twice, boy. It's two weeks." Tickers caught himself and used a softer voice: "I don't see how it does you any good to know the date. I want the two. The two dozen in the back forty are dead on their feet. The only ones desperate enough to buy that trash on hooves is the cavalry, but you and I know the Crossing is snowed in, and its thirty days there and back from the fort if you stick to the flats, and the drifts in the flats are plenty this winter, swallow you whole, son."

Raif spit and said, "It's two weeks over the Crossing, be back December 31st, Tinkers. I'll have your goddamn money."

Tickers was taken aback by the flash of anger but recovered and drew his full frame up in the saddle. "It's Tickers, son, *Mister* Tickers, you will learn that soon enough. Perhaps I am too hasty. I give you fair warning—the price for the red and black is going to be different on December 31st. It'll be different, boy, much different. You heed me now, son, winter's blowing hard this year, and the last bit of your daddy's money will not save that mangy stock from the blow."

The tax assessor reined his horse and trotted off as Raif watched him. The assessor's oversized green velvet coattails flopped against the flanks of his horse as he sauntered away down the road.

Raif, Jed, and Abner sat on the porch. Jed sat with his hands in his pockets, and Raif, with his hat pulled low, was thinking hard.

Jed muttered, "You heard that dandy, Raif. Maybe we shoulda given him what he was squeeze'n us for. Tomorrow's the sixteenth, where we gonna raise a hundred and eighty dollars by the end of the month? And even if we do, how we gonna buy feed without a cent left after that last hundred's gone?"

Raif looked up. "We'll sell the nags, a dozen of 'em. That'll earn us more than enough."

"Raif, ain't nobody gonna buy them nags in North County before winter's end," Jed snapped.

"The fort will buy them or we'll find a buyer in Tin City. They'll pay a winter premium too. The pestilence hit them hard down there. They got cavalrymen walking foot patrols. I hear renegade ponies been riding circles around them. Reverend

Graham said it's bad times down there too. He said Tin City's about to go bust losing one of every three shipments of silver being snatched by renegades. Down there, any North County horse is four or five times its worth at its best price in the spring."

Jed looked at his brother with concern. "Raif, the Crossing, it's closed until the thaw, and we can't hire no party of twenty armed men that'll stick with us to wrangle ponies over that heathen hill anyway. If we try to ride the flats, we're never gonna be back in time even if the snows don't stop us—it's twenty days at best going hard on the flats to the fort in the spring with the weather with you. If we make a thousand dollars, we still lose the ranch to that tax man and we will have to bid at auction to buy back what's ours to start. What the heck has gotten into you? We need to buy time."

"No, we're leav'n first light, you two round up every nag we got. I'm gonna ride to McCallum and Walker. We'll sell some horses for them too and take a cut out of it for the price of transporting their stock over the Crossing. We'll take forty across the pass."

Jed and Abner felt a rush of embarrassment for their brother. Raif looked them both down and said, "I'm not in the habit of saying things twice. Get going."

They moved off.

Raif headed to Walker's first. When he reached the two-story manor house, he dismounted and tied his horse to the hitching post. He cursed himself for not changing and felt self-conscious in his filthy field clothes.

Walker greeted him at the front porch and asked him to come inside.

Raif responded, "No, sir, thank you, no, but I don't have time." Raif offered his deal to take as many horses south through the Crossing as Walker was willing to risk, and they'd split the price fifty-fifty. If he crossed the pass, the probability was, and

Walker knew it, he could triple the price of any nag down in the fort or in Tin City. He factored the winter's feed money that Walker would also save.

Walker stood on his porch in an oversized wool sweater knitted and shipped from the highlands of a forgotten land his family had left centuries ago and rolled the offer around in his head. They walked across his front yard as Raif unfolded the scheme in half-formed sentences. Walker kept factoring the odds of success. He figured it was a no-lose proposition. He'd give him ten nags, the ones that wouldn't live through winter anyhow. Walker was bound to lose at least that many to the cold by winter's end if they stayed in the fields. He looked at Raif and realized he was talking to Matthew's son, and that he was still a boy.

"Raif, it's not likely you'll even reach the pass. The ice is already choking the switchbacks up the cliffs this time of year. Hell, it's near impossible for the hooves to grab. There isn't anything off the end of that footpath at the top, it drops a thousand feet."

Raif said in a steady tone, "Colonel, I figure the drought has fixed us all, the flats is covered but maybe the Crossing's dry. The snow can't be deep this early, and if the ice is thin it'll crack and give a hold. I heard it can be done."

"No one's ever said it can't be done because no one ever thought to try it in December. The dry down here don't mean it's dry up there, that mountain makes its own weather."

Raif grabbed the reins of his horse. "I've heard say that the renegades do it; that's how they used to raid in winter. Luther said he done it one winter."

"Luther used to say a lot of things, Raif."

"Luther had the knowing of many things."

"I don't deny that, Raif. Some say Luther was a papist priest before his wanderings brought him to North County. Some say he was a whaling captain because he could ride at night guided by the stars. But some, including your father, said he was touched."

"Luther had the knowing of a lot of things, and he said the Crossing can be done in winter. He told me how to do it."

"You know, your father and Gabriel and me chased renegades up them switchbacks in winter. We chased them all the way to the base of the Druid Mountains before the wind broke us and turned us back. I could see the outline of the peak before we turned, and we could see them renegades on the skyline and watched them climb away on their ponies. Even if you reach the pass, you'll have them to deal with up there. And that's still their world. Luther told you that too, didn't he? We don't see them much around here anymore, but they're still up there in them cliffs and caves, raiding to the south—Luther told you that too, didn't he?"

"Colonel, the cavalry is paying silver eagles; word is they're running around on foot chasing renegades on their bone-thin ponies that beat the pestilence—sir, I got to be going, it's a fifty-fifty split on each horse we get across and I aim to near triple the price."

"Raif, it's December . . ."

"No hard feelings, Colonel, but I am out of choices. I appreciate what you're saying, and I take no offense, but if you don't want the deal, I got to get going, sir."

Walker responded: "I'll lend you the money. Pay me back in the spring, this county's luck is gonna change. Next year, we'll all be straight again, you'll see, we've seen these years before—I'll stake you and your brothers. I'll stake the Cuchalainn."

"I appreciate that, Colonel, but I got a chance here to sell my own twenty nags for three, four, maybe five times what they'll fetch in summer. I aim to take my chance. Like I said, sir, no hard feelings."

"All right, but I'm only giving you ten. If you're going to make it, you have to keep it to ten a man. I'm in if you give me your word that if the first switchback has an inch of ice, you'll turn 'round. I rode up there with your father. I owe your father ten times whatever Tickers told you your assessment is, don't take it as charity. I rode with your father. We cut this land open."

"I hear you, Colonel; I can't promise you that we'll turn back if there's ice, but I'll give your offer some thinking."

"Oh, hell, Raif, take the ten and good luck."

Raif headed with Walker's ten and took a course that ran long and back through the McCallum lands. Gabriel stood with his two brothers by a freshly dug fence-post hole. His nephew stood off to the side holding a shovel, and the uncles had pickaxes. Even in the December chill the sweat was dripping from all four men as they broke at the frozen earth. Raif gave his pitch and added that Colonel Walker had given him ten. Gabriel listened intently, not interrupting. At the end Gabriel asked, "How many can you handle."

"I reckon we can handle a dozen each, so thirty-six, one man for every dozen horses."

Gabriel responded, "I think eight, maybe ten, but you can choose a dozen from that far pen. They don't look like much, but they're strong."

Gabriel went to a horse nearby and drew a new Colt .45 single action from the saddlebag along with a small leather satchel with rounds in it. He handed it to Raif. "That's a loaner. Bring it back with my cut."

The pistol was so new Raif could still see bits of the packing grease in the grooves of the barrel. The black metal of the weapon was so smooth and polished it reflected even the gray of this day's light.

Raif led the horses back to the Cuchalainn and slept for four hours. In the morning, the three brothers headed out toward the Crossing. The sun was a faint yellow-orange glow on the horizon, giving light but no warmth. The air was crisp, and the horses' breath hung in thick vapors as the men and beasts assumed the natural order and unfolded toward the southern mountain. All around them was the smell of winter fields folding into themselves, shutting down for the dark season. The start of the rise was four days' south.

They rode hard and at the morning of the fourth day, they started their ascent. At a hundred feet the switchbacks appeared out of the mist as sharp angles chiseled into the wall of the southern slope. They tied the horses in a daisy chain and led them up. The horses were eerily docile and took easily to the narrow footing of the ledge. As they climbed, the ice patches deepened. On the fourth day, they rose above the cloud level, and ice covered the path from the edge of the cliff to where it fell off thousands of feet. The lead horse's front hoof slipped on thick ice, and the jolt wakened it to the danger. It began to shimmy and neigh, and Raif eased the pace, giving the nag a chance to regain traction and its confidence. The slower pace forced them to camp that night in the midst of a switchback. They huddled together against the rocks, gripping each other for warmth underneath every blanket they carried. The wind howled and whipped, and the cold seeped through, making sleep possible only in short fits.

In the morning, they continued the climb. The lead horses crunched the ice, and a calming rhythm took them higher. The trail horses had it easier than the leads as the crushed ice improved the footing. Raif pushed the lead harder trying to gain the plateau by nightfall, the dread of another night exposed to the wind on the switchbacks driving him forward. The plateau would offer some open room where the horses could herd for the night and cut the wind. As dusk descended halfway up the last cutback, the lead horse became agitated as fatigue caused the animal to lose its nerve. The second lead remained steady and only seized up when the lead horse bucked. The rope between the two bounced slack and taut as the lead shimmied, creating an electric current of fear that echoed down the ropes.

Raif pulled on the harness, but the lead had had enough and wouldn't budge. The animal's eyes were rounded with fright. Raif took his rifle and cut the tether loose from the second horse and nudged the lead forward with the barrel of his rifle. It moved a few feet forward, then stopped and kicked back with unexpected speed that nearly sent Raif over the side. It flailed again with its back legs, but Raif was positioned now at a safe distance. Raif observed the second horse, and it remained steady, stomping only occasionally in defiance of the cold. He inched forward and put the muzzle of his long rifle a half inch below the horse's left ear and pulled the trigger. The horse dropped like a sack onto the trail. The weight of the animal slowly skewed over, and like a sack filled with water, it rolled off the edge into the ravine, disappearing silently into the cloudy mists below. Raif grabbed the reins of the new lead and moved out again. The line followed the new leader, and they climbed.

They reached the plateau as darkness shrouded the mountain. The horses kicked at the snow to nuzzle at the vegetation, but there was none to be had; the ground was rock. The brothers broke out the bags of feed, reckoning that the going across and down on the far side would be easier and figuring there was no reason to save it. The horses neighed and stamped from cold the whole night through, and the brothers slept in turns with one awake rotating every hour until the morning light broke in the east.

Before dawn on the sixth day, they were passing between the soaring cliffs of the high peak to the right and the first of the Druids on the left. They had reached the Crossing. They reached the far side of the Crossing before nightfall. The path was narrower than expected, but it was shielded between the cliffs and the druids, and the wind slackened to almost nothing as a silence descended upon them. The ice on the trail was patchy, and the horses moved easily. On the seventh day, a crosswind cut their path. The boys marched with one hand gripping a horse's stirrup and their heads lowered into the horse's flank to shield the bone-crushing wind. The slightest movement of their hands in their worn leather gloves telegraphed bolts of pain through the fingers. Their lips chapped and broke into open sores. They blew their noses and rubbed the mucous in their faces to save pieces of it from falling off with frostbite. The wind whipped the powdered snow on the cliffs creating a whiteout, and they feared the snow blindness. They clenched the reins and kept their heads lowered trusting the horses to keep the trail.

At the end of the day, they moved down past the last of the Druids. The three slipped into a crevice between the last two stone monoliths to escape the wind.

Their breaths misted together as Jed said in shivering bursts, "We crossed the top, we crossed it. Lord, I never been this close to heaven. I believed that last crosswind was gonna git us, but we done crossed the top of this heap of shit; strange how there ain't much snow here."

Raif could feel pain as the blood flowed again into the flesh of his fingers once they were out of the wind. "I reckon the wind blows it clean. Anyhow, we ain't beat it yet. Luther said there's snow deep as a man on the short switchbacks down the other side. I reckon we got some digg'n to do before we make it down. The horses are tired. We gotta dig 'em a path down or they'll quit on us. Whatever happens remember to keep digging. We'll do it in relay. We got shovels, it won't last forever, a few hundred feet of deep drift and we'll break to the bottom and run hard to the fort."

They passed the last Druid and crested, beginning the slow descent on the far side. The descent went easy until they hit the drifts. Raif cursed the snow, but felt relieved that Luther must have really done it in winter or else how could he have predicted everything they'd faced. For the first time, Raif had faith they could see his crazy gamble through. They took turns digging lead. The drifts ran four to five feet in places, but the snow was mountain light. They pushed on for the next ten hours, each brother digging until his arms ached and back burned. The going was endless, but they persisted downward. The grade lessened as they descended. The flatter trail meandered along the side of the mountain, which prolonged the digging. They stopped for the night, and on the next day, it started to snow and panic gripped them. They cut the horses' tethers and had them follow in line as the boys all moved to the front, digging faster, believing their luck had run out. By midday, the snow was blinding and the trail pitched down more steeply, making their footing unsteady. The horses became unruly and started to stomp in protest at the pace. The snow became a thick blinding wave making it impossible to see more than a few feet forward. The lead bolted, and Raif's frozen hands could not grab the reins as it raced forward into the snowdrift, nearly killing Jed. The rest of the mounts stampeded after the lead, and the brothers scrambled up the side of the trail barely escaping the hoofs. They watched powerlessly as the line of horses plunged down the switchback into the whiteness. As the last horse bolted past, they dropped to the ledge, gasping from the exertion. The burst of adrenaline that had sent them scurrying out of the path of the fleeing horses drained off, and the exhaustion from the hours of digging washed over them.

Raif was nearly broken, and he crouched on the trail, the sweat freezing on his back as he tried to stifle the wave of shivers racking his body.

Jed rose and moved down the trail following the horses.

Raif looked up, stared into the blinding whiteness, and said, "The colonel was right. I was a plain fool for getting us killed on this mountain. What a fool way to die."

Abner's eyes closed until he heard the crunch of Jed approaching from down the mountain. "Raif, I thought for sure you were gonna get us killed. I would've bet on it, 'cept I wouldn't have been able to collect being dead and all. The horses smelt the river, it ain't frozen fully over and they's water'n. We done it. We're at the bottom."

Jed helped Raif and Abner to their feet, and they walked the last hundred feet down. As they reached the bottom, the winds slackened, and they could see the wide plain. The horses were milling about, kick'n at the snow for sparse grass, and a few were drinking from ice holes in a stream. A single day's hard ride, and they reached the fort with thirty-two horses. They tethered them to a long rail post.

A lieutenant and sergeant emerged from the stockade. The sergeant methodically went down the line of horses, eyeing them in all the right places. He lifted hooves and peered in mouths, snouts, and assholes. He grunted, "Looks like you rode 'em hard, the flats can be tough this time of year."

Raif responded, "We came by way of the Crossing. We are in a bit of a rush, so can we get to it—them all North County from the Cuchalainn, Criss Cross, and Nottoway, out a week or so. Good stock, good breeding lines, all of 'em North County. They'll outride any renegade pony. They need some feed and rest is all."

The lieutenant paused between being impressed and a nagging notion that he was being put on. He said to Raif, "I hear the Crossing is beautiful this time of year."

"Lieutenant, I need to know your offer, I need to sell and get back to North County. If the cavalry don't need 'em I got to head straight for Tin City."

The officer looked to his sergeant and said "McAlary." The sergeant moved to the lieutenant's horse, and the officer lowered his head to hear the sergeant's whispering. Raif could catch out a few words—shoe'n . . . freeze burns . . . foreleg . . . good mounts.

The lieutenant looked up and said, "They've been through a tough ride and cold for extended days. Some horses never recover from that. But the cavalry is interested in a fair price. What're you offering?"

"Three hundred a head."

The lieutenant fired back "Deal," and rode forward and shook Raif's hand before Raif knew what happened. The officer instructed the sergeant to lead the horses and boys inside the fort to finalize the deal. The lieutenant turned to Raif. "The pay is in silver eagles, no gold, but I'm sure the eagles are acceptable. You can stay at the fort until the thaw. Crosby charges a reasonable rent and the board comes with it. I don't recommend Tin City unless you have a taste for that sort of thing, but even though you didn't ask for it, my advice is to avoid Tin City when you're flush with silver eagles. You can run the flats after you rest up."

"Sir, we need to be back to the North County to take care of some business. We're riding back through the Crossing."

The lieutenant stared for moment at Raif, reined his horse, and rode back through the gate shaking his head.

The sergeant eased over to them and put a hand on one of the sold horses. As he brushed its flank, he said, "Fellas, don't take this the wrong way, riding the Crossing at Christmas is plumb crazy, but you boys got it done, and I don't know how. But I been out here five years now and I know them renegades. They may have missed you coming over, that's something short of a miracle itself. But now I'm thinking those crafty devils let you ride past the Druids thinking they'll snare your asses on the way back when you're full of silver eagles. I reckon they got a war party in the flats laying for you and they may even have left a few in the Crossing too, thinking if you were crazy enough to come that way in winter, you might be crazy enough to go back that way, but I reckon they don't expect it. But fellas don't go back up the Crossing, them rocks is powerful magic to them and you've hurt some pride to the extent them sons of bitches have any. Heck, wait a week, we'll rest and feed these hooves, and you can ride with me. I'll be taking a patrol over the flats as soon as theses mounts is fit, if the drifts ain't bad, you'll all be home in no time."

The next morning, fingering his St. Jude medal, McAlary watched from the tower as the brothers galloped toward the mountain. The boys had traded in their ragged clothing for new wool coats, thick hats, and leather boots and gloves lined with rabbit fur. McAlary watched the flapping of their new riding coats as they rode hard for the Crossing. They rode in a flying wedge; snow and clods of earth churned and crushed under their thundering hooves.

The brothers rode their way up over the same path they had cut two days before. The trail had some new snow that had filled in the path but not enough that they had to dig. They rode as high as possible in the daylight and then tethered the three horses. The first night they slept in the nook of a switchback under a bright, three-quarter moon a bit shy of the crest. The night was cold, but no wind allowed the mist to roll off the cliffs to eat the moon's light and shroud the brothers in darkness. On the next day, they stopped two hundred yards shy of the first Druid on the last switchback in the dark light before nightfall. The dying sun's last light was flailing against the sides of the red cliffs. The next day they would pass the Druids and reach the far side of the Crossing. The night was clear, and a full moon blossomed. Abner was pissing downwind and looking up at the cliffs as his waste sizzled into the snow.

Jed reclined, his long frame propped up with one elbow, and twisted a toothpick in his mouth. In a voice dripping with false scorn he murmured, "Three hundred a head . . . three hundred a head . . . I told you to start with three-fifty."

"What, when the hell did you say three-fifty?"

"I said it on the downslope when you was breaking and squealing like a momma sow being fed its baby's balls. I distinctly said the horses done finished it, it's three-fifty, maybe four a head, damned if I didn't."

Raif said, "I don't recall that t'all."

Jeb continued: "Speak'n of what you choose not to recall, you heard that sergeant . . . you don't think they's waiting up there do you? Looking for silver eagles and scalps, and now we got both."

Raif removed the saddle from Buck and said, "It ain't possible anyone can live up there this time a year, that high. We made good time from the fort, and if anyone was chasing us, I can't believe that there's a faster way from the fort to here. They couldn't beat us riding them naggy ponies of theirs. No, we beat 'em. If anything, they'd be chasing us up this rise. I'll tell you what we'll do. Tomorrow before evening we should be across the top and past the Druids. We'll hole up and get us a good vantage point; and, if anyone's following us on the trail, we can ding 'em with the rifles. That's it. We'll stop tomorrow evening when we're at the last Druid. We'll have a good clear look across the pass from some high point, and we'll ding anyone following."

Jeb said, "Yeah, well, what if that crazy old bird Luther was right and they live up here, in caves or something, storing up food, hibernating like bears and waiting for fools with coin and fine hair like mine to come stomp'n along, what do we do then?"

"Luther told tales, and you know Papa said he was touched. No, we just gotta keep moving because they're behind us. They can't out-climb us, not on the good horses we got. We got 'em beat. Get some rest, 'cause we're moving out first light and get ourselves down off this rock and give that son-of-a bitch Tickers his money. I'll take first watch."

Raif waited until Jed and Abner were asleep and then softly holstered the .45 pistol Gabriel had loaned him and slipped Jed's pistol from its holster into his overcoat pocket. He retrieved his father's short cavalry sword from his saddlebag and angled it under his belt buckle. He hooked the clasp to his belt loop and unsheathed it. The skies had cleared as it cooled in the night, and he could see the sharp edge glint in the moonlight. He tested the sharpness of its blade with the leather of his belt and the tough hide melted away as he ran the edge across it. He studied the weapon and thought it was more a long knife than a sword. He returned it to its sheath. He took his long rifle down from his saddle holster and slung it across his back. He wrapped the rifle's sling snug across his left shoulder and down the length of his chest, the muzzle pointed at an angle to the ground.

Raif took a moment to look at his brothers sleeping and thought about Abner being thirteen. He shook his head and started on foot up the pass, moving steadily to the top of the last switchback. The frozen rocks were coated with a thin flowering of snow, and he moved easily up the trail, raising his heels and toeing along in his new boots, using the crust of the mountain for traction. It was as easy as walking on the packed dirt of the sidewalk in town and the hard mantle under the thin sheet of fresh snow rendered his movements nearly silent. He paused beneath the lip of the ridge and peaked out over the side of the crest. The full moon had risen and its cold incandescence lit the landscape like a torch light. He knew that if he stayed on the path, he could be seen for hundreds of yards up the Crossing, so he stole east under the shadows of the first Druids and headed for the abyss.

He paused to catch his breath under the dwarf Druids and took in the immensity of the harvest moon. He climbed up the Druid and looked north up the Crossing. It was now that he evoked in his mind the chess match he had with Luther when he was nine years old. They were on the floor of his ranch house playing chess on the fur rugs that lay before the big fireplace on Christmas Eve. Luther had taken his rook and paused to hold the castle in his powerful hands. He rotated the heavy black piece crafted of some unknown dark stone in a rhythmic rocking and spoke slowly as if he were measuring out every word to stand alone. He stared not at Raif but into the fire as he spoke, as if what he spoke of gave him pain.

"Raphael, the south mountain is like a chessboard, did you know that?"

Back on the mountain, Raif remembered Luther's gaze boring into the heart of the fire. The memory rolled out in his mind in vivid colors; he could see the flames from the logs dancing in Luther's dark eyes. Luther spoke of the lay of the Druids, how each was part of the mountain but how every grouping stood alone and defiant with its own tribal purpose, like chess pieces. Luther spoke of the Crossing as if it were something built, designed by the hand and not of nature. Luther swept away the chess pieces from the board and took up the white pawns, placing them in a neat row down the side of the chessboard running from him to Raif. "The white pawns are the main trail that runs bright in the moon across the top, Raif." He took the black pawns and lined them along the opposite side and described the footpath that snakes along the edge of the abyss. Luther said Raif needed to steer clear of the white side because it ran along the cliffs that held the caves.

He traced his finger along the line of black pawns and said

that it was the footpath along the abyss that must be traveled at night. The renegades would let none pass the white trail near the cliff walls; even with twenty armed men, it would be a bloodletting to pass at night. In the folds of the cliffs, the renegades could see in the dark because they knew the lay of it with their eyes closed. Luther placed the kings and queens between the white and black pawns at the top of the board nearest to where Raif lay on his elbows staring at Luther. He said this is where the great Druids rule, the giant rocks that dotted the pass. He described the Druid kings and queens as mountains unto themselves. He said they were exposed to the bitter north winds and forged of a stone so hard that even the renegades had given up hope of hiding upon them.

He placed the bishops at the bottom of the chessboard and said the southern Druids were low and smooth rocks that held no place to hide but whose shadows hid the path to the black trail. Luther put the rooks in the middle of the chessboard. He said the Druids that dotted the center of the mountain were the bad magic; it was here the renegades built their nests to kill those who violated their sacred ground; the Crossing was holy to them. The only spot where the entire length of the southern approach trail can be seen is from the rooks.

Luther had looked into Raif's eyes, and said, "You need to go alone, Raphael. More than one will never get past the watch in the hide. Let your brothers sleep."

With his back to the Druid, Raif stretched his neck to look out over the mountain's broad chest as it rose to the north. He could see in the moonlight the chessboard Luther had laid out for him that Christmas Eve night before the fire and the image he saw was the same one that Luther had burned into his mind's eye seven years ago. He saw the sheer cliff face to the west soaring for hundreds of feet, and he knew the abyss was waiting to his right. In the moonlight, the Druids looked as if a giant hand had placed them one at a time on the mountainside, choosing grander ones as the pass ascended to the north. The rocks stood defiant and refused to give awe to the staggering cliffs. It was as if the mountain's peak served them. Luther had told him of the fights in the early days over this pass, of men taking a few steps away from the camp at night to pee and disappearing without a sound. The tales he had begged Luther to tell him lying on the bear rug in front of the fireplace now haunted him as he trekked to the black trail of pawns that ran the edge of the abyss.

Luther had told him the main party of savages would stay hidden and lay for them in the folds of the cliffs. He said they feared the abyss, so Raif kept moving toward the edge. He went into a crawl because he sensed the abyss, the emptiness reaching out to him because the light changed along its contours to an almost blue, as if the abyss swallowed even the moonlight. He reached the edge and stretched out his arm, feeling it dip into the chasm. The sense of nothing sent an electric current of primordial fear racing through his balls. He moved north up the thin path that skirted between the Druid's side and the edge. Luther told him that the renegades watching from the hide would eye the main trail running along the cliffs and not the footpath along the abyss.

For the next two hours, he took the gambit on Luther's words and scrambled up the mountain. He reached the gap between the Druids and looked across the breadth of the mountain to the cliffs. He glimpsed the shadows of a fire a few hundred yards across. The renegade camp would be invisible to anyone moving north or south on the trail, but he could see the shadows of the flames dancing on the palisades from where he stood on the edge of the precipice looking directly across. He crossed on his belly across the gap to the shadow of the rooks and waited.

Raif remembered Luther's eyes fixing on him and saying, "They'll switch the watch, it's the switch; that's the time to move." Luther told him, "Don't move until you see them move first; you'll never spot one in his hide nor can a man sneak up on a hide even if he knew where it lay."

Luther told him about the time he had wounded a deer and tracked it deep into a ravine. As he'd followed the blood trail, he'd come across an old oak tree that had been hit by lightning. The bark had been blown off the tree. Luther had looked at the piece of bark on the ground and seen it had a leather strap attached to it. He looked into the hollow of the oak and saw it was lined with furs. He sat inside the hollow of the oak and lifted the bark door, shutting it over the opening. Sitting in the darkness, he'd seen two beads of light; he had leaned his head forward and through the two slits he had a clear view down the trail. The slits had been carved for spying and were invisible from the outside because they ran with the creases of the bark. Luther said you could have walked right past it and never known you were inches from a demon.

Luther had twisted a rook back and forth in front of Raif's eyes and repeated over and over again, "Wait, wait, wait, with the patience of Job, wait, wait, wait, with the patience of Job, wait, wait, wait . . ." Luther's words now churned in Raif's head as he waited in the shadows. The sweat from the climb began to chill on his back, and he did his best to stifle his teeth chattering. His fingers and toes ached from the cold. It inched up his arms and legs and he began to shiver, the shakes rising and ebbing in waves that racked his body. He cursed his teeth for rattling in his mouth, thinking the noise so loud it could be heard a mile away. The more he fought the cold the more he shook. The cold meandered into his mind and clouded his judgment. He took the rifle off his back and hatched a plan to rush the camp. But Luther's warning echoed in his mind—"wait, wait, wait, with the patience of Job . . ." He lay the rifle on the ground and wrapped himself in his arms, believing the cold was swallowing him. The urge to sleep crept over him, and he told himself he could close his eyes but only for a moment. It was then he felt the rush that only shame brings.

As he lay there holding himself shaking, he knew he was on this mountain because of Edda. He needed the ranch, needed it so that Edda would marry him. Without the ranch, she'd never take him for a husband. What a fool. He had risked the life of his brothers who lay sleeping, thinking he was watching over them, for a girl with curls he'd had noth'n with but a half-dozen snatches of conversation. He had to stifle a laugh at his foolishness and decided to turn around and take his brothers back to the fort when he heard the sound of cold leather stretching.

Raif saw a shadow in the moonlight from the top of one of the rooks. He waited and watched as the figure climbed down the far side of a rook. The figure was enormous and draped in skins, but still he climbed nimbly down the rock. He saw the scout's breath misting in the moonlight as he angled across the trail toward the camp. He followed him until he saw him kick a lump of thick furs nestled near the fire. The sleeping hump was reluctant to crawl out from the heap of skins and warmth of the fire.

Raif heard a second dull thud to the ass of the next watch as he raced up the path, feeling the emptiness of the abyss to his right and the side of the rook to his left. He could sense the path thinning under his feet as he ascended. The rook's side was pushing outward and squeezing the path against the emptiness. The trail of the black pawn thinned, and he was forced to put his back and heels to the side of the Druid and move sideways, and realized he'd left the rifle on the ground. It was too late to turn around.

He turned sideways facing the Druid, and moving his feet laterally he inched along the precipice. After another twenty feet, only his toes had purchase on the edge of the trail leaving his heels to hang out over the abyss. He kept moving until the rook's side jutted out to the very edge. He feared it was a dead-end and began searching with his raised hands to find a grip on the rock's face. He found a fingertip's worth of grip on an inch of ledge above him. Taking a deep breath and holding his weight with his fingertips, Raif swung his legs out over the precipice and flailed with his feet for a toehold on the far side. He felt his feet grab on a flat surface. He put his toes on the surface and slid his hands along the ledge above until his hands were even with his feet, and there he clung to the side of the Druid.

The nothingness reached up for him, forcing the blood to course in great pumps through his heart, the beat thudding in his ears. After another five feet of shimmying with fingers and toes along the rock, he could feel the ledge under his feet widening until it was a long, ascending riser of stone steps. He dropped to his hands and began climbing the steps on all fours until he reached the top of the rook and reached his hand over the jagged edge at the top feeling a drop on the other side. He reached across the gap and placed his hands on both sides. He swung his feet over and dropped into a deep path in the rock, landing on his feet.

He moved through the cut and stopped only for a moment to inspect the markings on the side of the cut, which glowed in the moonlight like snakes. He took off his glove and touched the snakes and felt chiseled grooves like those etched by a stonecutter. After thirty more feet, the cut turned sharply to the right and he sensed the path was leading him to the center of the Druid, to the hide.

He knew the hide had to be somewhere that would allow the scout to spy the main trail. Raif started to question whether he'd missed it and had passed it, when the smell of scat struck his nose. He followed the scent to a hole cut in the rock that was full of shit. He figured they couldn't bury the scat in the stone so the scouts dropped it into a cut in the stone and reckoned on the wind carrying the scent into the abyss. He passed the scat and ten steps later felt something snag his shoulder. He could see in the moonlight that it was a crude ladder of stick rungs and leather strips. It ran ten feet up the stone wall and he could see skins at the top of the ladder—it was the hide. He had beaten the changing of the watch.

He scaled the ladder and sidled into the fur-lined crow's nest. A slit cut in the rock formed a window with a vantage point looking straight down to the south. He knew now they had been laying for the brothers. He saw the camp a few hundred yards to the right off the main trail, which glowed in the moonlight, the trail's crushed stone a shade lighter than the dark rocks of the sheer cliffs. He placed his hand on the stone to turn around and felt again the chisel marks and realized the slit window had been hacked out of the stone. He thought of the biblical Egyptians and he wondered how many thousands of years the renegades had been ambushing along the Crossing.

He thought of Jed and Abner and hoped they were still sleeping and hadn't tried to follow him. He questioned himself now about not telling them, but Luther had told him it was the job of one man and Jed would have never let him go alone. He looked out at the renegade's camp again and spotted a short, stout figure draped in skins making its way up the trail toward the rook. Raif watched the scout until the angle of the rock blocked his view, and he guessed rightly that the scout would come along the same chiseled path he had taken but from the opposite side. His pulse quickened, knowing he had a minute to ready himself. He descended to the floor of the path and moved off to hide in the shadows. A moment later he heard the rustle of fur skins as the scout waddled toward him down the path from the far side. The scout was breathing heavily, and Raif thought he might still be sleepy.

Raif waited in the shadows, and despite the cold, the sweat ran into his eyes. He pulled his father's sword from the scabbard and felt its weight and balance. His hands were still a little numb, but he was warm from the climb and felt he could trust his grip. He waited for the renegade to reach the ladder, but it occurred to him that he didn't know how to stab a man to death. He had never stabbed anyone and had no idea how he was supposed to keep the scout from yelling out when he stabbed him. Luther had said nothing about how to kill the watch.

He cursed Luther and believed Luther had tricked him and meant for him to die on this mountain, the crazy old coot. The questions rattled in his brain: would the renegade be wearing thick skins? Would the bayonet pierce the thick skins? The doubts rattled around until he heard the rustle of the fur a few feet away. He felt the heft of the handle in his fingers and placed his thumb lengthwise along the top of the blade.

He sank into a crouch and recalled Bibbs's class and the lines of a play the name of which he couldn't remember but it was about a soldier: "Keep your good blade bare, and put it home quick; don't be afraid because I'm at your elbow."

Only he was alone. He determined to strike like a rattler and drive the blade through the apple of the throat and pin the neck right to the rock. He would use his free forearm to cover the scout's mouth after he sank the blade.

The shadow elongated across his front and shrank as the scout shuffled closer to the ladder. He could smell a mixture of flowers, bile, and rotting meat. He heard the soft clink of metal strike on wood as the scout reached the ladder. He watched the scout lift the front of his furs near the knees to give his feet liberty to step onto the first rung of the ladder. Raif could see a thick fur hat and couldn't help thinking that it must be warm. The step caused a grunt of exertion, and Raif crept out of the shadows. The watch turned in time to see only the flashing glint of steel. Raif misjudged the short stature of the savage and struck high, the blade piercing below the nose. It sank swiftly through the flesh but jammed hard into the bones of the face. The force of the strike snapped the head back, slamming it against the rock with a dull thud. The scout collapsed, and Raif threw himself down on top using his left forearm to muffle the gurgling breaths. He cursed himself for missing his target but realized the scout had been knocked senseless by the blow to the head on the wall. He worked the blade back and forth to free it from the bone below the nose. It had been sloppy, but he was pleased at how easily he had been able to overpower the man.

The moonlight revealed the horribly disfigured face covered in bubbles of air and froth spewing in a torrent out of the nose and mouth. Raif hurried to finish him off and determined that the quickest way was to strike the blade deep into the chest. He ripped back the thick furs until he reached a thin cloth shirt. It was when he placed the point of the knife in the center of the chest that he noticed lumps shrouded in the thin undergarment. He pulled the thin undergarment down from the seam at the neck and engorged breasts spilled out of the cloth. He pulled further, and the moonlight revealed the taut arching skin of a belly stretched in late pregnancy. Raif put his palm on the butt of his blade and as her eyes began to open, he sank it to the hilt in the center of her chest. She sighed softly, a kind of long, breezy hush, and went still. Raif drew forth the blade and crossed the high trail headed straight for the camp.

He crawled within forty yards of the fire and watched. In the fold of the cliff there were six mounds of fur spread out in a semicircle around the fire. He knew the six would be sleeping with their weapons. He crept to within ten feet of the first lump and crouched in the shadows beyond the fire's illumination.

From the darkness, he could see the vapors of breath coursing out of the folds of fur in the firelight. He drew his two pistols. He moved to the first lump of furs with Gabriel's .45 in his right hand. He placed the muzzle inches from the forehead and raised Jed's revolver in his left hand. He planned to fire in rapid succession, firing with his right, then his left, around the arc of furs killing all six before they could rise.

He squeezed the trigger and the report of Gabriel's .45 shattered off the cliff face mixing with the sickening sound of hammer to melon. He moved and discharged Jed's pistol into the next bundle and then Gabriel's into a rising wild-eyed face covered in war paint. The fourth sprang from his furs and ran naked into the darkness. Raif fired but couldn't tell if the shot was true. He swung around to fire the next shot when he saw his planned fifth target rise to his feet and try to raise a long-barreled rifle, but the weapon's front sight post snagged on furs and he couldn't free it to level it. Raif's shot hit him in the stomach and he fell to his knees, dropping the rifle and clutching at his belly. The next shot hit him in the center of his throat.

Raif wheeled, but the sixth savage was up and charging him with a club. As if in a slow dream, Raif could see the details of the club, its perfect round iron ball mounted atop a three-foot shaft of knotted wood. He fired with his left, but the round spoiled in the chamber and spit out nothing but a harmless blue flame. He wheeled Gabriel's pistol, but the club's iron ball hit above his left eye sending a scorching bolt into his skull. The skin on his face was wrenched apart by what felt like the ragged claw of a predator, and an impulse of animal fear raced through him as he was flung violently backward on his back. Gabriel's pistol spun out of his hand into the darkness beyond the firelight.

The warrior rose up over him and swung the round ball club again, but Raif rolled away, the metal ball making a sickening clang against the stone of the mountain. Raif reached for the bayonet in his waistband. He leaped to his knees and reared back with the bayonet to strike when the savage that had earlier run off naked raced back out of the night and at full speed lowered his shoulder into Raif's back. The blow knocked the wind out of him and sent him hurtling forward, his hand and bayonet splashing into the fire. He screamed and pulled his hand from the flames as he struggled to his feet, but he tripped over fur bedding and spilled out on the ground gasping for breath, the blood pouring from the wound blinding his left eye.

He saw the savage who had clubbed him rise up slowly on the far side of the fire still holding the iron club in his left hand. As the warrior moved toward him, Raif saw a twisting black animal horn in his right hand and knew it was the tool that had ripped the flesh from his face. The fire illuminated the warrior's image, and Raif could see the jagged lines of scars from innumerable battles that ran along his features. He had one lazy eye that looked off into the night, but the other was fixed upon Raif. As he tried to rise again, the naked warrior leveled the long buffalo rifle at him, and he stayed kneeling. The one with the horn began chanting, and Raif became absorbed in his music. The chanting calmed him and he regained his breath, feeling the ground moving beneath him and taking away his impulse to run. He grew calm and dreamed it was morning in the ranch house and he was waking up to the smell of his mother's cooking when the head of the naked savage exploded in a fine mist that sizzled into the fire like bacon grease. The naked warrior stood tall for a full second as if he was unaware half his crown was missing before toppling over like a new cut board stood on its end.

The scarred warrior stopped chanting and wheeled at the sound of the rifle fire. Raif could see Jed and Abner standing a short way off as the warrior raced silently at them. Jed fumbled to reload his rifle. Raif was amazed at the speed and distance the savage was covering until Abner simply raised his shotgun and emptied both barrels into the savage's chest, sending him flying backward. He landed on his back, but his momentum carried his ankles and shins underneath him, and he died in an awkward hump.

The pain sliced through Raif's forehead, but the blood went syrupy as it hit the cold night air, crusting his left eye shut.

Jed and Abner approached, and Jed asked, "Raphael, you dead?"

Raif tried to rise, and Abner grabbed hold of his arm before he fell back over.

Raif drawled, "I think he done cracked my skull with that contraption."

Abner sat Raif down on a pile of furs and picked up Gabriel's pistol, reloading it with cartridges taken from Raif's pocket. He walked the line of the dead, kicking each in the head. One kick produced a slight groan and Abner stepped back and fired. He returned to the fire, sat slowly, and said, "Luther told me they play possum."

As they sat by the fire, the first rays of light broke through, and a curtain of light began to draw down the cliffs. Abner stoked the embers of the fire with the shaft of an arrow and said, "I reckon it's Christmas morning." He rose and went to fetch the horses still tethered down the far switchbacks.

Jeb stitched Raif's face, then rustled through the war party's possessions mostly out of curiosity. He rolled over the savage with the long rifle and freed the weapon with a struggle from the half-headed man's grip. The barrel was the longest he'd ever seen, and he whistled softly as he raised the weapon to his shoulder. He expected the barrel to be too heavy to steady, but was impressed with its balance. He held it at arm's length and studied the stock of dark cherry wood that was carved with what he figured was a pack of large-eared dogs chasing a lion.

They were a breed he had never seen nor heard of.

Jed said, "Got to be at least fifty caliber and look how it's sighted, Raif. It's got a tube on top to look through. I bet you could drop a man at a thousand yards. I reckon this is yours."

"No, Jed, you blew his head off. I think that means you practically inherited it. I'll lug it for you. Buck's holster is long enough and my rifle's out there somewhere's on the mountain where I left it last night. We ain't got time to go search'n for it."

Jed whistled again softly as he studied the rifle. Abner returned with the horses and kicked at a clump of skins to clear a path and cursed out as the pain in cold toes rang out from hitting something solid under the skins. Abner revealed a strongbox when he pulled the skins away. The metal latch had been broken off and it was held shut by a crude leather thong. Abner cut the thong and opened the lid, exposing a chest of gold and silver eagles, colored beads, and stones and jewelry of all shapes. Abner looked up and said, "Where do you reckon they got this?"

Jed said, "Probably robb'n Tin City shipments. Will you look at all that? We crossed this hump flat on our asses, and now we're headed back like Solomon. Ain't that the way of it."

"We best be going," Raif said as he struggled to his feet.

The brothers divvied up the treasure in their saddlebags and galloped past the Druids, cresting the north pass the following day and descending toward home. They rode hard in the daylight, and walked their tired horses a good part of the night but they didn't reach the Cuchalainn until late afternoon of December 31st. Raif climbed the front steps to find tacked to the door a decree for failure to pay the property assessment. Attached to the decree was an eviction bill ordered by the magistrate and a notice that all chattel and livestock would be publicly auctioned to satisfy the debt.

Jed sat on the front steps and said, "It ain't right, we're here and it's the thirty-first."

"No, it ain't right," Abner responded.

Jed said, "I guess it don't matter now, we got enough to buy this place and ten more now, at auction or anywhere's else for that matter."

Raif said, "The hell we will. I'll be damned if I'm going to bid with some townie merchant for what Pa built."

He mounted Buck. The horse didn't have much left, but he had some, and Raif followed the path across the back fields to the old bridge. He reckoned Tickers would take the lost trail road out to the old bridge and cut across the opens to pick up the Post Road to Walker's, the homesteads, and on into town. Raif wanted to catch Tickers before he hit the Post Road and spurred Buck hard down the path. It wasn't until the first sharp rise that Buck faltered. Raif dismounted, not wanting to kill his last good horse. He grabbed the dead renegade's long rifle and three rounds and ran the last twenty yards to the top of the rise. He sighted Tickers's green velvet coat flapping as he rode across the field five hundred yards shy of the old bridge. He put a cartridge in the breech and fired into the air.

The report rumbled down the meadow. Tickers wheeled his horse, and Raif waved the rifle and took his hat off with his other hand, hoping his long blond hair would alert the tax assessor that it was a Hanson.

Tickers sat there in the saddle for a long moment with his wrists crossed on the pommel, dangling the reins in his left hand. He pulled his watch from his vest pocket and held it with his right hand, and with a dramatic flourish, he pointed to the watch with his left hand. Tickers returned the watch to its pocket and stretched out both arms with palms turned skyward and pantomimed the universal sign for too late, tough shit. Tickers smiled and wheeled his horse around and started off at a slow trot.

Raif cleared the chamber and loaded a fresh cartridge. He dropped to the ground and laid the barrel on a rock. He put the stock into his shoulder and sighted down the long tube, raising the yardage sight to a distance he figured to be five hundred yards. He'd never hit anything over three hundred in his life. He felt a slight breeze on his right cheek and gauged the wind from the way the tops of the dried grass fluttered above the snow dusting. The rifle's windage bolt was strange to him, so he decided not to fiddle with it and factored Kentucky. The sight filled with nothing but the green coat of that fool, and he positioned the sight to the right side of Tickers's back. He took a full, slow breath and exhaled slowly, squeezing the trigger, which had a much lighter pull than his rifle. In a half instant, Tickers was thrown over the neck of his horse. The round hit him dead center high in the back between the angel bones. Tickers's foot caught the stirrup, and his horse dragged him twenty yards before it tired of the effort and stopped.

Raif raced over to the dry creek bed that ran the length of the meadow. He tried as best he could to jump from rock to rock, trying not to leave tracks. He was amazed by the clarity of his mind and lack of concern at having killed Tickers. His eye was still hurting but he was fired up and determined to fix it so that it looked like renegades did the killing. He removed his boots within a hundred yards and ran in the snow-dusted grass to the tax collector's body. Tickers lay on his back with little indication of where the round entered, but when Raif flipped him over there was a gaping hole in his upper chest. Tickers's face was ashen with open eyes fixed in eternal amazement.

Raif riffled through Tickers's satchel and pulled out the tax log. He fingered the pages to the day's date and right below the entry for McCallum he found the entry for the Cuchalainn. It was still blank. He found a grease pencil in the bottom of the saddlebag. He studied the entry for McCallum's ranch—Gabriel McCallum, proprietor of the Criss Cross, paid $200 silver eagles, and one colt sired by Charlemagne (value agreed of $95), total: $295. He studied the stroke of the tax collector's writing. He saw the Cuchalainn was $240, and he knew Tickers had tried to cheat him. In the entry for the Hanson ranch, Raif wrote, "Spoke with Hanson boy, claimed to be proprietor, paid $240 in silver eagles." Raif reached into his pocket and pulled out $240 in silver eagles and put it in the dead man's purse. He fretted for a moment over being able to copy Tickers's signature. It had a scripted "T" written in an elaborate flourish and he decided to not even try.

Raif returned the logbook to the satchel the way he found it. He stood to run but thought better of it and opened the satchel again. He took out all the money. There were silver and gold eagles, pennies, foreign coins, and many small coppers, all in all he guessed about a thousand dollars' worth. He also found a wedding ring, silver spoons, brooches, and a bronze medal from the war, and, to him, the thought that folks had to part with these because of this fool sent a warm feeling over Raif. He relished killing the son of a bitch.

A crow's caw startled him. The caw-caw came again, and he saw the bird circling. He scanned the horizon and knew he was taking too much time. He walked back to the river gully holding the satchel but stopped again and looked back at Tickers's ashen face, his eyes appearing to follow Raif. He studied Tickers a moment and reflected that no renegade would leave a dead man like that. He went back and rolled Tickers over, grabbed him by his hair, placed his chin and mouth into the grass, and drew his long blade. Raif scalped him from his eyebrows to his neck and wrenched the pelt free.

Tickers's horse grew skittish at the smell of fresh blood, but before it could bolt, Raif grabbed it by the reins and plunged two feet of his bayonet into the big vein of the neck. Blood vomited and the horse bucked, but Raif held hard to the reins until the animal collapsed. He took the scalp and put it in the money satchel and slung it over his shoulder. He grabbed Tickers's hat and waterskin, grabbed his boots, and headed back to Buck. He emptied the waterskin into Tickers's hat and Buck drank feverishly from it. He feared for Buck because he was still sweating but he figured the horse'd cooled enough in the winter air. The water finished, he buried the hat in the soft sand of the riverbed. He scanned the horizon and saw nothing but the circling crow. He put his boots on and led Buck by a tether, trekking on foot toward the ranch.

He reached the fence line of the Cuchalainn and cut the wire. He took the saddle off and slapped Buck's ass, sending the horse into its home range, knowing that Buck would go for the stable. He hid the saddle and long renegade rifle as best he could under a hay pile a hundred yards inside the wire. He twisted the wire back and started walking east across the open fields.

He covered five miles on foot until he reached the old Kaiser homestead. Raif knew the Kaisers had been slaughtered and the homestead burned down years ago by renegades. The chimney and one wall with a window cut in the bricks was all that was left standing. Raif remembered the older kids at school teasing the girls that the Kaiser place was haunted. He went to the fireplace and found a loose stone with a hollow space behind it. He pushed the satchel into the hole, but it snagged on something. He reached into the cavity and retrieved an old-style buck knife, the handle charred but still solid, and put it in his belt. He put the satchel in the space and replaced the stone. He turned west and headed for home. As he walked, snow began to fall, and he trusted his luck that his footprints would be covered.

★ ★ ★ ★ ★

Two months later, a cavalry detachment rode up to the Cuchalainn with the new tax collector. Raif put a pistol under the flap of his jacket and walked down the front steps to the gate. Jed and Abner waited behind the curtains. Jed held the long rifle and Abner the shotgun. The cavalry officer asked if this was the Hanson ranch and introduced a Mr. Thompson as the new tax assessor. Thompson was a scrawny man with a fidgety disposition. Raif thought tax collectors must all be molded in the same government workshop. Thompson started talking about how they'd uncovered a second set of books in Tickers's office. According to Thompson, the county board had learned Tickers had a series of oversights and handed Raif a coupon for $180. He could redeem it in town or its value could be put to next year's assessment. If he redeemed it in town for cash there would be a $10 processing fee.

"A hundred-eighty dollars don't seem like an oversight," Raif told him.

"Well, the review of Mr. Tickers's recordkeeping is still ongoing, son."

Raif said, "You can put it to next year's assessment. I ain't got no pressing need for the money. And you'll refer to me as Mr. Hanson. I'll be damned if I'm going to pay my hard-earned money to some stranger crawled into North County yesterday who calls me 'son.' "

Ten years later, Raif lay stretched on the bales of hay at Walker's barn raising. He tracked Edda as she moved among the farm families, watching her exchange smiles with womenfolk. He knew he would never know family. He knew the women whispered about him and any decent woman had a father that wanted no part of a Hanson, especially him. When Tickers was killed all those years ago, no one gave it much thought other

than a party of rogue renegades did it. The thought never occurred to anyone that a polite and handsome boy shot him in
the back and then carved off his scalp from his eyes to the back
of his neck. But the years passed and Raif's reputation as a
wanderer in the wastelands and a killer of renegades, rustlers,
outlaws, trespassers, and the half-lunatic shaman Lobo trickled
into the town gossip. The gossip turned to folks conjecturing
that maybe there was more to the mystery surrounding Tickers's
killing, folks knowing the last ranch Tickers visited was Raif
Hanson's.

Edda caught him staring at her and instead of a smile, she
took the look of a frightened animal that had fallen under the
blank gaze of a predator. She had married a good man, Tom
Burke, and had four children. Raif dreamed for a moment of
the children she would have borne him. He had vowed after the
Crossing to go to her, but as soon as he had healed, Gabriel
had come to him, saying a gang of rustlers led by Lobo, the
crazed half-breed, had targeted the Criss Cross. The colonel,
Gabriel, Raif, and their men had tracked the rustlers for weeks
before the butchering, followed by Raif's lone odyssey tracking
Lobo into the wastelands. Every time he thought to go to Edda
there would be another reason to ride, and he had the ranch to
run.

A decade of killing and building the Cuchalainn took his
youth. By the time he got around to marrying, Edda had given
Burke two sons.

It didn't matter, he was unfit. Every night since the Crossing,
it was the same dream. It started with him feeling warm and
wrapped in blankets, then he would hear the warrior's chant. It
would start slow, and the cadence would build. As he was drawn
deeper into its familiar rhythm, he would feel the cold seep into
the folds of his blankets. The cold would crawl toward him, and
he knew that he was the child in the mother's belly clawing at

the womb because its fire was dying. He could see the vision of himself kneeling over her as he had that night in the chiseled path of the Druid, the moon's light flowing over her skin like poured milk, revealing the shapes raised by the quickening. The chant would grow louder and he knew the only way to stop the cold before it consumed him was to stab her in the heart. He never used the bayonet. In his left hand he held the scarred warrior's long black horn and he twisted it down into her womb where he knew his soul was crying out against the cold.

He gazed at Edda holding the small hand of her son and whispered to himself, "Ain't that the way of it?"

CHAPTER SEVEN:
GABRIEL

Reaching the Criss Cross ranch house after the hunt for the black, Gabriel and Caleb entered with pistols drawn. They moved swiftly through the house. The house was empty except for the dead. Seth entered and let out a gasp and backed out onto the front porch stifling an urge to vomit. He held his head in his hands, and his body swayed with sobbing.

Gabriel and Caleb rushed on to the porch when they heard Joe approach on horseback and say: "Maybe forty warriors, pulling something heavy. Cannon maybe, looking at the door; hundred or so head cattle, plenty horse—they've got a full day, maybe two on us."

"The girls are gone. Take Caleb, don't engage. Track 'em—meet me at the old mission tomorrow next—get close enough to know if it's the flats or the Crossing they're tak'n."

Caleb and Joe swung onto their horses and sped south.

Gabriel watched them ride out, then grabbed Seth by his collar. He slapped his hat off and told him to shut up. He dragged him by his hair into the ranch house and threw him down onto the bloody floorboards inside the door. Gabriel lifted him up again and dragged him to his dead grandmother still pinned to the table. He forced Seth's head up and shook him until his eyes opened and said, "Look at your nanna, boy, she's the only mama you ever knew. Your pa's over there with his head cut off and he'll be lay'n next to your ma in the dirt out back soon enough. Everything you and Caleb ever loved is dead except

your sisters and they is all that matter now, so stop your sobbing. You're going to ride to Raif, tell him straight what you
seen here. Tell him not to head south; tell him there's too
many—tell him we'll meet at Walker's." Gabriel dragged Seth to
the door and down the front steps. "Ride to the brothers, tell
them we'll need everything they can bring. Now ride and if Raif
ain't at the main house, find him."

Gabriel reentered the house and moved to the fireplace past
his brothers' dried pool of blood. His mother still lay pinned to
the table. He flattened her shirt and pulled the knife from her
chest. He lifted her up and brought her to the porch; she was as
light as a straw doll. He retrieved his brothers' bodies and his
dead brother's son. He laid them out on the front lawn of the
ranch house, placing the severed, scalped head of his one
brother with his body. He covered them with blankets and then
fetched wood and kindling. He poured the oil from lamps on
his dead kin and set them on fire. He stood near his horse making sure the fire got burning well enough to keep the animals
uninterested. He would bury his family when he returned.

Gabriel stood there looking at the flames consuming his family and remembered his dead father, The Most Right Reverend
Jeremiah McCallum, thundering from the pulpit so many years
ago before the war: "The bondage of one man born in Christ's
image by another is an abomination in the eyes of the Lord. Let
the word go forth that John Brown is the righteous messenger
of the Lord's wrath. One cannot thunder about rights whilst in
his fields he chains a child to its mother; we, all of us, will pay
the price for the pride and greed of the few. This land will be
set aflame by the armies from the North, but make no mistake,
it is the torch of the Lord's justice that the invader will carry to
set this land aflame. And cast not a believing eye on the slave
master's newspapers which pronounce his lies—the only rights
offended are the sins of slave masters."

Gabriel looked up at his father railing from the pulpit, his arms extended, holding the Bible in one hand and a fist in the other. Reverend Jeremiah McCallum was once the most successful preacher in the slave county of his youth. Gabriel could remember the pews full with the finest slave-owning families, poor whites at standing room only and the slave hands crammed into the balcony, all to hear his fiery sermons. Back then the good folk used to take the reverend's medicine every Sunday. But back in that day, he only railed about the venal sins, taking the Lord's name in vain, coveting the neighbor's prize bull. These days, for weeks on end, it was nothing but the sin and abomination of slavery—every sermon, every Sunday. Gabriel looked at the dark cherry wood pews set against the stark white of the walls as they sat empty except for a scattered few sharecroppers. The only ones left were the aged and one odd family of northern abolitionists that had moved south for reasons known only to them. Each Sunday these odd ducks would be the only ones at service. And each Sunday they heard the same lacerating screed against the sin of slavery.

These sermons had started unexpectedly. On a wet fall day, Gabriel and his reverend father had ridden to the McHales' plantation for supper. The reverend often enjoyed the McHales' hospitality and their commitment to the church. In turn, the McHales needed the reverend's approval to overcome the loss of the family's good name in society. Rumors had circulated for years that their oldest son, Tucker, was going to the McHales' slave shacks on many a night in a drunken stupor to rape the women and threaten the children. The problem was not the act of fornicating with his father's property but the indiscretion of being drunk and the tales of his wild violent temper on the young. It was said he would wander into the shacks and threaten to rape children, boy or girl, unless an older black woman took him into her shack and satisfied him. Afterward, he would stumble from the shack with his pants undone, the pent-up hostility drained from his inebriated body, and stumble back to the manor house in the darkness. On many an early morning, the McHales' houseman, Old Charles, would find him in the fields with his pants around his ankles and a spent liquor bottle in his hand.

Tucker's antics became a problem because on some drunken nights he would forget where he was. It was one thing to violate your own property, it was quite another to violate another's. In this case, it was the New Year's Eve Ball at the Monroe plantation. Once a year, every notable slave-owning family in the county would be invited to the Monroes for the grandest ball of the year. One year, Tucker drank himself incontinent and wandered into the Monroes' kitchen. He shoved the kitchen women around until he spotted a twelve-year-old slave girl adding frosting to desserts. He coaxed her into the root cellar claiming he needed her to find him a bottle of brandy. Once down the cellar steps he flung himself at her. She was able to elude him and ran out the root cellar door, but not before he tore her dress, exposing her breast. The sight of the child exposed fired up Tucker until he was wild. He chased her into the courtyard below the back porch. He grabbed her by her hair and bludgeoned her unconscious with his fist by rows of Old Man Monroe's cherished peach trees. He started to rip her dress bottom off when Old Charles, who had driven the coach to the ball, arrived with two field hands to restrain him. Tucker filled the orchard with vile oaths at the hands as they dragged him away, his pants around his ankles.

In the midst of the tumult, the girl regained consciousness and scrambled away down the orchard path, the sounds of her sobs echoing among the trees. Unfortunately for the McHales, the incident was witnessed by every male guest standing on a second-story balcony enjoying after-dinner brandy and cigars.

To a man, each guest had taken his own liberties with his slaves, but they found the lack of discretion and violent nature of Tucker's attempted rape ungentlemanly.

More troubling for the McHales, the girl was rumored to be Old Man Monroe's daughter. It was said he had a special fondness for the mother and doted on his daughter, treating her with special consideration, even going so far as to teach her to read and write. Old Man Monroe's quest was to see the McHales shunned and Tucker dead.

Tucker was shipped off to Europe to dry out, and the family set about repairing their reputation in genteel society. The McHales knew the only way to soften Monroe would be through the reverend's intervention, and so the reverend became a regular guest at dinner. On this night, after a large supper and conversation in the living room, Reverend McCallum asked about Old Charles's absence. McHale told him that Charles had taken ill and now lay dying out in an old shotgun shack with the field hands. Old Charles had lived in the main house for fifty years, but the McHales said the house was filling with the tangy smell of death, so they put Charles out to die in the far reaches of the plantation.

The McHales' daughter, Vanessa, insisted that they would be honored if the reverend would say a few words over Charles. She claimed it was propitious that he had asked about Charles, because the very next day Doctor Roberts was visiting to relieve Charles's suffering. She reminisced that Charles always loved to attend the sermons on Sunday and that he cherished his time in the balcony. Thus, it was agreed, after dinner, the reverend would ride with Gabriel out to the shotgun shack and say the unction over Charles.

The reverend had known Charles for more than forty years and remembered him fondly at meals and seeing him in the front row of the balcony on Sundays. Charles had a shock of white hair and beard that always stood out in relief of the dark faces in the balcony.

The night air was cool, and Gabriel could see his breath as he and the reverend rode out to the field shacks. The reverend and Gabriel entered the shotgun shack, and both had to duck under the doorframe. Once through the door, the room opened to the left. The interior was smaller than Gabriel expected, the wooden cot taking up more than half of the one room's space. As the reverend approached, he laid the Testament atop the wooden crate near Charles's bedside. A crude candle burned on the crate—it had a thick rope for a wick that gave off a dull, flickering light and left a sinewy trail of black smoke to travel up the wall and mushroom in a cloud at the ceiling. Next to the candle shimmering in the candlelight lay a crude cross bent to its shape out of the metal of some long forgotten farm tool. The candlelight threw shadows about the room, but Charles's face glowed.

Reverend McCallum bent so close that his face was illuminated by Charles's glow, and he looked directly into the dying man's eyes. He reached for Charles's hand, holding it firmly, and began the Lord's Prayer. He admonished Charles not to be fearful; that the Lord would shower on his soul righteous justice. The reverend asked if Charles wanted to clear his conscience of sins, if he wanted to make his peace with the Lord.

Charles responded, "Yes, sir, I do, but I need to tell what the sin is so I can confess it true." Even on the door of death, Charles's voice was clear.

The reverend said, "Say to me what's been riding your conscience, Charles."

Charles said: "Reverend, I never saw the baptism of my own. I know I had me at least three; to this day I don't know if they was baptized."

The reverend said, "Every child of this plantation is given the chance to be baptized when they are old enough to decide for themselves."

"Yes, Reverend, I know that, sir, but I'm tell'n about my own. They took all three of 'em when they was babes, you know how they do before they attach to da mother. I always wanted to speak up about baptiz'n when they was taken, but it wasn't my place. And, you know, Reverend, there's them that don't think the hands should be baptized. So, I always feared that maybe my young'n never got the water."

"That was out of your hands. God cannot punish you for what you cannot control. He will reward you for your obedience. He will not punish you if others fail to carry out His works," the reverend consoled him.

"I understand, sir, that's what I mean to tell you. My last one was still suckling with his mother and wasn't sold yet, but I knew he was paid for and Mister Powell com'n for him. I stole out the main house one night and went to his mother in the shacks after his feeding and I took him down to the creek out yonder. I had heard the preachers do it with grown hands, so I kicked through the ice and I dipped that child's head in that water and I said the words over him, the words I heard a hundred times. I knew he was too little to understand, but I thought he might never be baptized if'n I didn't. Ever since that night I always feared I done wrong. I ain't no preacher, and I didn't have no right. I feared since that the Lord be angry with me, and maybe with that young'n for him being falsely blessed. But I was worried he'd never get the sin washed off him; you know how some folks don't baptize theirs, that's the reason I did it. Reverend, the only reason I feared for that child to get to heaven without the water."

For the first time in the twenty years of his life, Gabriel saw his father at a loss for words. The reverend's countenance was grave, and he was staring at the floor unable to look at Charles's face.

Charles said, "I know I done wrong, Reverend, help me make it right 'fore I go. I don't want no trouble with the Master above when I go."

His voice quavering, the reverend asked, "Charles, did you baptize that, your child, your son, in the name of the Father?"

Charles nodded and said, "Yessir."

The reverend said, "What was the child's name?"

Charles said, "I called him Jonah, that's the name I used, but I reckon that weren't up to me."

The reverend said, "Did you let the water pass across Jonah's forehead?"

"Yes, Reverend, jest for a minute, he being so small and it being so cold that night."

"And did you say 'Jonah'?"

"Yes, sir, and the child smiled, I swear to you, Reverend."

"You did it better than I ever could have, Charles. You did it right and well. Your reward will be heaven, and there you will be the master, and men like me will toil in your fields."

Gabriel backed out slowly and retreated to the horses tied to a fence railing in front of the old shack. He was unsure of his father's reaction to Charles's story. In a few moments, the reverend filled the doorway of the shack. His tall frame silhouetted by the candlelight flickering behind him. He took a step down from the shack's landing. He was holding the Testament in his left hand and pulling at his collar with his right hand as if trying to keep the night air from choking him. The reverend walked a few steps and dropped to his knees; his shoulders slumped forward as if he had a great weight upon his neck. He keeled forward placing his face in his hands, the only thing between the dirt and his nose was the Testament. He began pounding the earth with his right hand and crying out:

"Lord, more than Saul, I was blind. Hypocrite. Man of God, hah, whore for the prince of lies."

Gabriel saw the hands emerge from their shacks and appear like wraiths in the darkness to look into the yelling. They stared with blank eyes at the preacher as he wailed and beat the earth with his fists. From his knees the reverend reached up with both hands in great clawing motions as if he was trying to tear the fabric of the heavens. He was bathed in shadows, and the flickering candlelight bounced and danced in the doorframe behind him. The flames cast the shadows of his father's movements to be elongated, grotesque. As Gabriel went to his father, he snapped threats at the hands to return to their shacks or there would be a reckoning. Gabriel looked down upon his father and his prostrate form and swore to himself that he would never again kneel.

Gabriel bent and said, "Father, we need to leave."

The reverend rose but seemed to collapse in his arms. He stared at his son who was now dragging him toward the horses. As he reached his mount, the reverend grabbed the pommel and pushed Gabriel's hands from him and said, "Is it your pride, son? I was once proud—yet an old man dying in bondage in a shack of old boards showed me the truth."

Gabriel gripped him, and the preacher allowed himself to be lifted into the saddle of his horse. Gabriel grabbed his father's reins and led both horses slowly down the road. The reverend's eyes were a mix of sorrow and madness, and the look unnerved Gabriel. He would grow accustomed to the look. It would appear thence forward every Sunday as his father railed against the sin of slavery from the pulpit. As they cleared the McHales' plantation and climbed up the main road's embankment, Gabriel mounted his horse. He looked at his father slouched in his saddle.

His father looked at him for a long time, then said: "Do you know what Charles told me, son, do you know what the dying man told me after you crept from his shack? He told me he feared you—the prophet in chains said you had the mark of Cain upon you."

The attendance stayed the same at church for a short time. The first break came when the folks stopped allowing their slaves to attend, believing their attendance might be what was prompting the reverend's sermons. It did not make a difference. The sermons grew shriller as he castigated the slave-holding families sitting in the pews before him with righteous invective. They quit the church. The merchants and craftsmen stopped attending when the reverend turned his wrath on them as witnesses of injustice who remained silent because they profited from the sins of their slave master neighbors. The McHales were one of the last to leave, but after a few weeks of the attacks directed at the source of their wealth, they too departed.

The flock moved to a new church in town. The young preacher there was handsome with a pretty wife, and his sermons were about the white man's burden. He preached that teaching industriousness to the hands would free them from their natural idleness. The message sat better with the gentry. Yet, the reverend pounded on, preaching to the few poor hardscrabble farmers that remained about greed, vanity, and the monstrous evil of slavery, though they owned no one and worked from first light to the end of the day's dying sun to feed themselves. Rather than confrontation, the town simply ignored the church, and when secession fever and war rallies rolled through the county, the church faded into the background of the coming storm.

Fort Sumter splayed across the newspapers, and Gabriel could hear the whooping and pistol fire in the streets. As his family sat down to dinner, the reverend said grace and finished with, "It has come. The Lord will not turn a blind eye to it any longer. He will send his legions to smash the Egyptian slave masters. You boys are of age now. I think we'll travel west to St. Louis. It will end as all wars do, and we'll return."

There was an awkward silence, and the reverend looked around at the table. He asked, "What is it?" Gabriel had worked out his speech prior to that night. He had even practiced it late at night in the church, alone. He would speak about the fight for home and rights. But, as he looked at his father, he knew the man would hate him more if he tried to explain, so he simply said, "Reverend, Luke and me and Eli have enlisted in the cavalry. We leave tomorrow for Fort Donelson to join the fight."

Gabriel knew he could not lie. His father knew him, knew more than anything that Gabriel wanted to ride and that he did not care if it was Indians, Yankees, Missourians, Mexicans— he'd ride against anything or anyone. Gabriel had listened for years to the old men in the country store sitting about the stove smoking their cigars and pipes. He would hide among the shelves and listen to the tales of battle. On special nights, one old soldier would be at the store. He came only in winter and only on those rare nights when you could smell snow on its way. He kept the look of the first Americans—the woolen cape worn over a threadbare colonial uniform, his hair knotted in a short ponytail, leather riding boots that were hobnailed before the birth of the nation. Everything upon him spoke to the old days, the first days, when men were giants. The men in the store who took the stock of every customer that entered with a single glance always gave him special consideration, shuffling chairs around the stove upon his appearance, allowing the old warrior to take the first place, the one closest to the fire. His name was Uriah but the old-timers passing time before death around the stove's iron belly had named him Captain.

When he was a boy, Gabriel would climb out his window on those biting winter nights, run across the roof of the front porch, and descend the tree limbs, making his way to the far side of town. He'd climb through an old wood chute at the county store and hide amid the shelves in the back of the store. He'd wait, knowing the others would take their turns to talk of elections, the latest gossip from the chancellery court, but he knew that if the captain came in from the snows to call upon them, the old boys would save his tale for the last. The captain had fought with Marion when barely more than a boy and by twenty he had commanded a flying cavalry squadron under General Jackson. He had fought the Creek and Cherokee nations, the Chickasaw and Shawnee, and the British in the Rebellion and at the time of New Orleans. The captain's tales were woven with the sinews hardened through a life of battle. The legends fed Gabriel's spirit. Listening in his hide secreted amongst the shelves, Gabriel vowed to himself that he would one day sit as a warlord.

Now, atop his horse outside the ruins of his ranch house, Gabriel watched the flames engulf his mother and her sons; yet his memories went back to the night his spirit became the captain's. He recalled the skin of the captain's face, so aged it looked as if old parchment had been dried taut over his prominent features. The only signs of life were the simmering blue embers that burned in the sunken hollows of their sockets. His face was pocked with the scars of the same disease that had taken all five of his siblings as babes, he the only one to live. The face was without hair. It looked as if each individual hair had been plucked out as the vanquished tribes had adorned themselves long ago. He drew on a tobacco pipe carved from a single piece of stone, the secret of its shape and hollowing lost in the currents of the past. Absorbing the heat from the flames, the old men would sip whiskey from tin cups and prod the captain for tales of Jackson and Marion. Stroking the stem of his pipe across his chin, the captain would peer into the wood burner. Other than his soft voice, the only noise was the sound of the fire popping and roaring, as if his breath fed the flames.

As Gabriel hid, the captain began a tale of how a band of enemy irregulars, British officers dressed up as Indians and their allied tribesmen, violated every woman in a small town. The captain cleared his throat and began: "I won't tell you the name of the town, for every woman in it from eight to eighty was dishonored, and the womenfolk there still bear in their hearts marks of shame though it be our failure and not theirs. The bucks humped two at a time and left some of the young'ns bleeding to death from the wounds. I won't be the one to mention the name of them honorable folk, all their brave sons away staging for New Orleans. It were late in the winter of '14, the war had become bitter, and each side lost its sense, but none yet had become so as these, they had gone back to man's first nature. It was madness if you had to give it a name.

"I led a squadron of horse in them days, seasoned hard. There weren't a man had not proved himself. Only a fool could fail leading such men; not a single one needed tell'n in a fight. All of 'em gone now; I'm the last."

The captain paused and reached over to unlock the stove's gate. He would look to the stack of wood and peer at each cut with deliberation. He would select a single piece of wood and place it alone into the belly of the stove; he did it with the forethought that each had been carved to its shape and meant to serve the nature of the fire at this, its moment. After he placed the cuts into the flames he would study his work and doctor minute adjustments to the flue, and then with a flick of his pipe's stem he'd sling closed the hinged gate and cage the racing blue flames back into the gaol of the stove's belly.

He sipped whiskey slowly and claimed it was only to clear his throat to speak, and he started again, "We chased 'em deep into Creek country. Lasted a fortnight, ran three hundred leagues. I could not let them go. General Andy had brought me into his headquarters in an old Tory manor house and sat me down in its great room. It had a fireplace, the kind you don't see too often nowadays, you could stand in it. I remember the long white birch logs burning. I can feel the warmth even now and the smell. We were alone except for an old Indian fighter that never left his side; one I never knew to utter a sound. The general told me the price for what was done to them womenfolk, and he was sending me to gather it. I said something about the march on Orleans, and he said this was more important. The general took me by the shoulders, and to this day I can still feel the power of his hands upon me. He raised me up to meet the steel of his gaze, his eyes ablaze as if the great birch fire reflected his light, and he said, 'Do not desist from this undertaking, Uriah, until the account is settled, Hell will have its bounty.' "

The captain placed his cup between his feet and took out his pipe. He pinched tobacco from a crude leather pouch that hung under his shirt from a hemp cord fastened about his neck. He unhinged the flange gate again with a flick of his pipe's stem and took a long stick out of the metal bucket near the stove; the sound of the running flames echoed from the belly of the stove in a low hushing rumble. He placed the end of the stick in the heart of the fire and pulled it out, the end aglow with a soft yellow ball of light. He put the flame to his pipe and drew on it until the tobacco accepted the heat, and he dragged slowly upon the pipe, drawing out the flavor. As he exhaled, the smoke billowed about his face and Gabriel would swear he disappeared behind the haze.

The captain continued, "They run us deeper and deeper into the Creek lands, all the way to the Red Sticks. This were after Horseshoe Bend so there were no Creek left, but there were something odd about Red Stick mound country, something mighty odd. In parts of that bog the roof was so thick and deep you lost sight of the sun in day and stars at night, but the ground was soft and the trail stayed fresh, as if the earth in there wanted to give up its secrets and direct us to 'em. We found horses dead along the trail, hacks of meat cut out of them, so we knew they were riding their mounts 'til they dropped dead under them.

"We found no fire, so they were cutting raw strips from the tenderloin to keep running, always kept moving—like scared animals, rabbits that know the hounds is chase'n without looking back, they could smell us upon them. Every so often, we'd catch prints making off left or right, buying into the fool's philosophy to split from the pack hope'n we would beg off tracking the stragglers and stick to the main party.

"But I had me two brothers from the Carolinas had got their liv'n chasin' runaway slaves 'fore the war; I also had me a Spaniard that spoke Seminole from his days being raised in the swamps of Spanish Florida, his family been killing Creek for more'n a hundred year. It would take them three no more'n hour or so to track some poor Harry trying to slog his way in that bog. They'd catch back to us and present me with a right ear.

"I don't know if the main pack of Harries were dumb enough to trust the Shawnee they had with 'em or if they fixed a compass point and stuck to it. My hunch is the Harries know their acts of dishonor meant death and they reckoned to go as deep in them bog mounds as needed to lose what'd been elected to give penance. Lord knows I never in my day saw another purpose to go into that country again."

The captain eyed Gabriel among the shelves, and gave Gabriel that pipe-smoker smile—half grin, half leer—the prevailing emotion secreted by the pipe's stem. Gabriel froze in the captain's gaze, but the old warrior winked and relief coursed through Gabriel's body; he wondered how the captain could see into the dark recesses of the shelves where he hid. The captain had pardoned him from the old boys cuffing his ear and tossing him to the cobblestones of the road, the harshness of the slaps coming from their jealousy of youth and its invasion of what the aged men defended fiercely as their province.

As the captain's eyes turned again to the stove, the lamp ran out of oil and the room dropped into total darkness. Clem, the storekeeper, got up, saying it'd take a moment to fill with whale oil but the old hands feared the interruption would stay the captain's telling and hissed for him to be still. The only light now stole out from the slats of the stove's grate, bathing the captain's face in the caged flames' amber aura; the old hands about him receded into the flickering shadows waiting for their eyes to accustom to darkness. The shadows heightened the radiance of the pipe's stone bowl when the captain drew his breath upon it, burning a deep crimson.

The captain sipped the brown liquor and cleared his throat— "We chased 'em 'til the path led into stone outcroppings allowing the sky to open again. The Harries were all but on foot now; two horse left if memory serves. The sun had set and twilight gave us enough to find the foot falls vanishing into a cavern, its maw high and wide, bigger cave I never seen, a man mounted could gallop into its opening. We thought better to rush such a hard position, so we set about the cave for two days, waiting for 'em to come charg'n or creep'n out in the night, as we saw little option for 'em, figur'n hunger and thirst would drive 'em out.

"Second night late two tried to run for it, but we shot them in the legs, one was regular English that had adorned hisself as a Creek, t'other was Shawnee. I heard a year later the Shawnee were Tenskwatawa's kin, a nephew if I recall, a rumor anyways was that he was related to The Prophet. Who really can distinguish, though, how they consider kin, everything running from the mothers.

"We tried to get him to tell, but he died without a sound, most impressive. The Harry cried out for his mother as he lay dying from the cutting but would not tell about the cave, the strength or disposition of the unit, or their aim.

"Funny though, the Harry's eyes never changed from a blank, odd stare, 'til the very end when he called for his mother and his eyes flashed over, but he was on the doorsill of the next world by then and spoke no more.

"On the mornin' of the third day, my patience wore thin and I called a war council, said it were my thought to rush and conclude it. We weighed us the options, and I let some back and forth, but no man in that troop ever was keen on waiting for a fight. We figured if Andy were here he'd've wanted it done sooner than later. We rushed in preparing to blaze away, but the cavern were empty, there were enough light to show its only occupants were two mounts lolling by a pool of dark water at the furthest point yonder the entrance. Otherwise noth'n to speak of, not even bats, only some old bones strewn along aged fire pits. The pits used rings of smooth stone, the builders I reckon were there before the Creek nation were even born—I never knew tribes to use river stones.

"We brought in torches and lit every inch and found no way to learn the sense of the vanishing. It was then Davey said he recalled the Harry and Shawnee were soak'n wet when he tied 'em, he recalled he had to pull the hemp cords tighter because the wet let 'em stretch. It was then we went to the pool of water sitting in the back of the cave; first thought it to be a stagnant pool from the drips of the cave wall but when you bring the wet to your nose you smelled it were fresh. We knew they had found a way out through that pool.

"Most of my troop had been boys along the Duck and Cumberland 'fore they took to the horse, so they could fin like otters. We sent Davey with a catch of breath under, and he were gone so long we thought for sure he were taken by the pool or by a Harry, but no sooner did he poke his head back out gulp'n for air. He told of a ledge near ten feet across he negotiated to the rival side, and he could see from under the depth there were lights burning above on the far shore. We knew there were more caves on the far side of the rock ledge, the riddle for us was how to keep our powder dry and fin under to finish 'em. After a bit we knew there were no means, at least none any could think of, we had no oil or wax paper, no good bolts of cloth."

The captain coughed and apologized, laying blame on never having the habit to talk so long. He picked up his pewter tin and sought to drain it, but it was empty. The act prompted the old boys to spit blasphemies at Clem for letting the captain's cup go without a fresh charge of whiskey. Clem fiddled in the darkness begging the captain's pardon, and the jug emerged in the glow tilted hard to bring the color of rich amber to the pewter's rim, the fire's light shimmering off the circle of liquid. The captain politely nodded and took a sip allowing the burn to meander, savoring its slow passage, allowing it to harbor for a good spell in the catch of his throat before he let it sink to warm his innards.

The captain went on, "We had little option other than it to be blade-to-blade when we come forth from the water on the far side, so we begun whet'n the edges. We knew they'd be waiting, and if one thing could be said of them Harries, odd sissy ducks to parlay with but no stranger to the fight. The Shawnee was with 'em, so any advantage we had of the blade was lost. I was seasoned by that time, scores of fights and quite a few charges against Harry cannon, the devil's breath, but in all my days there was none more than that day standing on the shore of that black pool that I did judge it inscribed in the heavens that there'd be no back to this shore for me. We left none on the close side but Tom Jordan, he being the youngest with a wife little more than sixteen carry'n his first when we left. Gave Tom his orders, if'n it's a Harry or Shawnee come up from the pool, he were not to miss the first to emerge with a musket shot, but then he were to quit the cave, ride to General Andy, and let it be known the debt was still outstanding.

"I led and crept into the pool, trying so as to not disturb the waters and give 'em warning on the far side. I readied to stifle the chill, but the pool were warm and thick and easy to float in, as if'n it were meant to hold you. I drifted out, and eleven more crawled in after, and we put out to the rock, some had knives in their mouths, it looked foolish but any man go'n on that crossing were free to go as he liked. With a common nod, we took breath and went under the ledge and forded our way across to the far shore. The water was thick and hardly splashed when I came up, I were gasping for breath.

"We stormed the far shore but there were no one there. The cave went back, and torches were still lit. Where they got the torches or means to light, I don't reckon, but it were like a full moon bright in there. We looked about and at each other wonder'n if they had found a ways out, and then they came pour'n out of the shadows. No sound, no yelling, not a single utter, Shawnee and Harries storming at us holding ancient weapons, spears, stone clubs, axes, as black wild-eyed madmen silent as the dawn. You had to stab them three or four times before they quit, and even then they didn't utter word one, nor cry out when cut.

"A Shawnee clubbed me across the right shoulder separate'n it not for the first time, but the blow did drop me to my knee—he were huge and he drove that stone-and-iron club down again, and I parried it with my sword, but it be my left hand and the blow overpowered me and sent the sword flying and me onto my back. The Shawnee stood over me and chanted some song fore he was fixing to finish me when his chest split

107

and a torrent of steel and blood spit forth. The club dropped to my feet and the Shawnee stood looking at the shaft of blade that run through his heart. He dropped to his knees and then I seen it was Tom Jordan behind, sopping wet holding the hilt of that blade. Tom drew it back from the Shawnee and sent his head rolling with another cut.

"We gathered up and finished the last of them, cutting each down, the last was wielding nothing but a stick with a stone ball atop it. After we finished 'em, we found their muskets and a good bit of powder dried up over them two days on some of the altars, no explanation we could ever figure why they come at us with clubs. We collected up our wounded and dipped ourselves back into the pool, any of our number that passed back through them waters no matter how deep the cuts, lived to tell about that fight, though I suspect many told no one. We had collected the debt."

Clem said, "Captain, what brung about Tom Jordan's choos'n to cross over?"

The captain stared out from the glow of the fire and looked at Gabriel and said, "There are only two things that bind a man to another. The first is blood—we all seen it, a tradesman can run a commerce and for all the years he labors, he can have by his side a trusted hand, a hand that can be counted on to never pinch and cut the rows with him 'til both are sore of back and bone. The tradesman without such a trusted hand might never see the fruit of his endeavor—and through the years the trades-man will pound his breast and spout oaths that the hand is dearer to him then his own profligate son—the hand is the son of promises. He will grow to love the tradesman and have faith that his sacrifices will be rewarded and that the tradesman is not a liar, but the son of promises' faith is fool's gold. Time and ag'n the tale be the same. As he age, the son of promises learns the tradesman cannot hold the promise, he must break away and build his own commerce, he knows the tradesman will give his legacy to his son of blood. If the son of blood be shiftless, if in the tradesman's heart he knows the son of blood will destroy what his life's toil built, the son of blood still takes. Though he can't give voice to his knowledge or reason, the son of blood takes what is his father's, as the sow's cub knows the mother's milk is his.

"The son of promises must move on; the son of blood once in possession means the end for him, the time he remains may vary but no matter, long or short, the son of promises' time is done—the jealousy of a son for his father's favor is a vicious obsession and brooks no competition. The son of promises will learn that his master's oaths were no more than the ripples of a pebble tossed in a swift river. It is the way of it. The father knows that as the gravedigger's first blade of dirt spills over his pine box, his profligate son of blood will curse him saying the commerce is failing because the tradesman had not built it strong enough, or had kept the secrets of its running from him. The son of blood will spew vile oaths on his father's name for not preparing him for a life of toil, resentment will be his only lasting birthright.

"Hard work is learned over time, the muscles and sinews cannot be born overnight, and those who do not work in youth find like the colt that never walks that it can never run. Years by, the tides of this world will bring the word of the tradesman's death to the son of promises who has built his own commerce in exile. Upon hearing of the loss of his father of promises he will look upon his own son of blood, whether in the crib or crawling about and there he will understand that his father of promises was bound by blood. Just as he be. The son of promises will carry himself to a quiet place, and there he will not curse the father of promises, but on that spot he will pray for his soul and forgive him.

"A man's only loyalty is to his blood—all other bonds between men be like the fire in this stove's belly, it may burn for a time, but come morning the embers be cold, that is, lest the bond be forged in war. Tom Jordan come across because he were bound to us in war. Other than blood, war is the only forge that binds men's souls one t'other—the crucible of battle brings out in man his first nature—when without reason or proper religion, he ran wild in the forests bound to his tribe, to those who first crawled the earth in packs the tribe is all. Jordy come across because he could not do other—he were bound to his company, he had fought with us and so, like a twin in the womb, his fate was burned to ours—if'n he had fled he would've walked the rest of his days in his own exile, like the outcast, the old drunk you see muttering to himself begging for scraps about the town streets, the one you wonder about, as to the cause of his madness. Yes, two things bind men's souls, blood and war, the rest be ashes."

Gabriel crawled through the woodbin out into the cold of the winter's night. He waited down the road and watched as the captain mounted and walked his horse over the crushed stone of the roadway, the hooves clopping in the steadiest four-beat rhythm he'd ever heard. The captain came upon him and halted, the two stared at each other, and after a long moment the captain spoke.

"You're the reverend's boy."

"Yes, sir."

"Why do you hide about the shelves?"

"I come to listen."

"About what?"

"War."

"Strange vocation for a reverend's son."

"My father says each man to his own path."

"I don't reckon the path I trod is the one he'd see fit for his kin."

"I heard in town you bought the old Fletcher's place. Fletcher never had much luck bringing anything out of the ground on that rocky patch."

"I live on my pension, it's enough. Anyhow, I reckon if I had any knack for farming I'd have set a different course than the one you hear me tell. What do you want, son?"

"I can bring you food. We always get plates from the womenfolk. My mama don't know what to do with it half the time. There's bottles too from menfolk that the reverend don't never touch. It stays stacked in the cellar; there's crates of it down there dusting up."

"Why would you do that for me?"

"I can't ride or shoot worth a shit, sir. If I bring you food and bottles, will you promise to teach me? I got two shooters my uncle left me 'fore he run off. I got them hid, and he left me with thirty ball and some powder, said I was not to tell the reverend. I'll barter with you for the knowledge."

"You come tomorrow and we'll start. Oh, Gabriel, that's your name, ain't it? Leave the ball and powder at home for the time being, as I ain't fixing yet to leave this world, but bring a bottle, the dustier the better."

"If I keep my end of it, you'll teach me to ride and shoot?"

"If you keep your end of it, you got my word."

Six years later, Gabriel stood below the pyre. Gabriel had sworn a blood oath to him that the morning he found the aged man dead he was to take his body deep into the bog country and there he was to build a raised platform of dried wood. He was to wrap Uriah in a shroud, and Uriah gave him two ancient gold coins to place over his eyes and upon the pyre he was to burn Uriah until God could take nothing but the ashes.

Gabriel never lost his lust for war from the fall of Vicksburg to the end. His specialty was raids behind the lines. The taking of prisoners was not practical, so killing became the only way. He rose in rank until he commanded a flying squadron. A certain type of horseman was attracted to him, and his ranks swelled with the remorseless. They rode deep and surprised many. Gabriel had gunned down more men with their hands in the air than he cared to remember. To him, if a man wore blue, he had bartered his own deal; he asked for no quarter and gave none. The worst of it was dealt to any black found helping the North. He ordered them cut down with the sword. He would drive his horse into their ranks and hack at them in a furious rage, the exertion causing froth to spittle from his mouth.

The Union papers discovered he was a reverend's son and tried to belittle him, referring to him as the preacher's boy. But on a clear day in late July 1863, the squadron rode to New Bethlehem to attack the railhead deep behind Yankee lines and storm the garrison. It was defended by green and unskilled quartermaster troops. The entire unit bolted into the nearby woods at the sight of charging cavalry. The flying squadron looted the rail cars and then set them aflame. They piled the goods on any flatbed wagon they could find and pushed back south when they came upon a hundred blacks fleeing with their women and children. The blacks ran to the sanctuary of a church. A black soldier fired at the cavalry as it rode toward them, dropping a southern horseman in the road. The Confederates caught him and dragged him to the church and ordered every male inside to come out. The minister came out and pleaded with Gabriel to spare them and was shot through the head for his effort. Gabriel had the church doors and windows nailed shut and he bade his men to burn it to the ground. The cavalry surrounded the church as the flames licked up the sides and waited until the roof collapsed in a great wrenching moan. Those not killed by the roof broke windowpanes and began

jumping to escape the flames only to be shot down by the horsemen. The terror did not end until the church was a smoldering
ruin and there was no sign of life.

After New Bethlehem, the northern papers knew he could
not be stopped and the insults about him being a preacher's
boy grew hollow. The enemy papers began to refer to him as
simply the "preacher," and to his unit as the devil's horsemen.
With each month of southern defeat that brought the end
nearer, he grew stronger. The defeat meant nothing to him
except that it meant the end of war. It was not until two years
after Appomattox that he returned home. Late one spring night
he rode through the mists of the old town's deserted streets. It
had been looted, and many buildings had been burned by the
invader. The only building left untouched by the war was his
father's house. The Union knew he had been an abolitionist.
The reverend had died that winter.

Gabriel entered the house, and its small size unnerved him.
He recalled memories of his father's large presence filling the
main room. He sat slowly down in his father's chair and stared
into the embers still alight in the fireplace. The act of sitting in
the chair was the first time his father's death was a reality to
him though he had known for months. He could smell the scent
of his father's pipe in the weave of the blanket that lay draped
over the arm of the chair, and it brought no emotion, merely
the recollection of things past.

His mother came in from the back door, carrying wood to
the fireplace. Neither spoke. She placed thin kindling on the hot
embers and stoked the embers until the kindling caught and
then placed larger sticks of wood until a good flame started.
She placed two well-seasoned logs on the fire that caught, and
the small hearth was soon engulfed in flames. Gabriel knew she
had fallen asleep in the chair and had let the fire go out.

She rose and walked over to him and put a hand on his

shoulder and said, "I didn't reckon to see you in this life. Appomattox was two years ago, where have you been, son?"

"West, Missouri mostly."

She said softly, questioningly, "Luke and Eli?"

He could feel the tremble in her hand and responded, "They're in the hills west of here, three days' ride, waiting for us." He could feel the tension leave her as if a great load had been lifted from her shoulders.

She looked down at his face and saw that it was furrowed with dark lines and thick crow's feet. The last time she had seen him he had had the complexion of a boy. She said, "Every week, he read the notices in the newspaper and looked for your names. He would pray and thank the Lord each time it were thought you still lived. He would say 'the war will end before it is too late.' But then the papers started talking about you. The Atlanta papers said you were a hero. I think that is when he started praying for your death."

Gabriel stared into the fire, and she moved her hand to his face, saying, "A Yankee colonel came to the house about a year back. He brought with him Yankee newspapers. They told a different story. The Yankee said you were a butcher that killed anything that had the misfortune to cross your path. He said you were responsible for the massacre at New Bethlehem. He told Father that if you showed, that the reverend should send a message to him. He said the end of the war meant nothing when it came to what's coming to you. The North had already found you guilty and condemned you to death by a jury 'in absentia' he called it, I think he called it that. He was a congenial Yankee, said in all honesty, his men weren't exactly in any hurry to catch up with you, anyhow."

Gabriel said, "It weren't right for him to bring that talk here."

"Oh, I think it was his way of getting at you. He didn't want to run into you so he found another way to punish you. After his visit, father started to fade. Most nights he would sit in this chair and stare at that fire like you're doing. One night sitting here I heard him cry out as if in a dream that you would taste the vinegar."

Gabriel rose from the chair and stoked the fire. He returned to the chair and sat down again and watched the fire grow in the hearth. It was here before this fire his father had read him the Old Testament. Before the flames, the reverend would practice his sermons, invoking hellfire and thunder, teaching the Book the only way he knew how: through the scars of its warriors, of Goliath and the Philistines, of Aaron and Jericho, Joshua and Gideon. He would stride with book in hand, fulminating at the king of the ten tribes, his whore, and the prophecies of Elijah—dogs licking the blood of warriors false to God. Before this hearth the shape of his soul had been forged and now he learned that the craftsman had cursed his creation.

His mother moved close to him and moved her hand under his thick black hair; she felt the path of the knotty scar that ran across the top of his skull.

Gabriel said, "There's nothing left for us here. There is a place far west where we can go."

"Your father asked you to leave once, and you told him this was your home and you were willing to fight and die for it."

"That doesn't matter now. I rode with a Colonel Walker in Missouri. He tells of good land for horses that lay out past the edge of this world. Open, and none of it claimed. The war is chasing him too."

"Son, you know land is never free. Who's on that land?"

Gabriel shrugged. "There were Shawnee here when Granddaddy come through. He cut his first row through graves he filled first with their sons. We'll build again, we done it before— there's nothing left here for any McCallum."

She stroked his hair and then held a fistful of it in her powerful hand and whispered, "You done seen to that, son, you done seen to that."

CHAPTER EIGHT:
LIEUTENANT'S HOMECOMING

The train took a last turn before its long straight run to the station. Colonel Walker stood rigid, almost at attention in a fine suit. He wore his long frock coat and thick slacks despite the heat. Molly had on her best dress and wore a hat the brim of which stretched out to the edges of her shoulders, the sisters in bonnets. The Walkers looked like respectability frozen in time, townfolk milling about to admire the landed gentry that was gracing them with their presence.

A handful of townies and their ladies had turned out for Wesley's return, the first from the county to graduate the Academy. Wesley hadn't been home in seven years. Two years before his appointment to West Point, Mother insisted he be sent east to spend time in Chattanooga with her kin to learn manners and perfect his studies before entering into the rigorous curriculum at West Point. In those two years, Wesley had summered in Europe. He had traveled from Sweden to Egypt since graduation. He had spent time in Rome and took extended vacations with distant English cousins in a country house outside London, or at least that's what his letters home said he was doing.

Toby sat there fidgeting in his collar, scraping and pulling at it and rocking from one leg to the other as the wait for the train to complete the last stretch seemed to last an eternity. The last time he had seen his brother he was eight, and he didn't recall feeling sad when Wesley left. He also didn't remember his being all that sad each time Wesley's planned returns home fell through as some new and exciting opportunity would present itself—a chance to travel to New York or Boston. Each time it happened, when Wesley wired for more money, he could sense the sting for his father. His son was being raised by people he didn't know and with whom he had no blood ties. Each planned return home, Molly's relatives would find something new and more wonderful for him to do. I guess that was the way of it, though, to any child, it was the mother's family that got their hooks in.

Walker never protested, each time he wired the money for travel and appropriate new clothes. Wesley's letters with each year contained less and less information and became nothing more than cries to mother to increase his allowance. Wesley would play to her sympathies, warning her that her cousins from Chattanooga were going to Philadelphia, and every male was going to the tailors for formal wear. She always saw to it that the expenses were wired.

Now, here he was, graduating at the top of his class, the new lieutenant of artillery. Before reporting to Oklahoma, he was given leave to return home. The train was crawling now, its mammoth engine breathing in and out in great gasps of power. The train's brakes whined under its weight. Toby could hear the engine's pipes rumbling, like a giant beast perpetually out of breath, the great steel sides appearing to expand and contract with each breath of smoke from the stack. Young townie boys ran the last hundred yards waving at the conductors and trying to keep up, the conductors rewarding their efforts with pulls on the shrieking whistle that drowned out Maggie and Peg's chatter.

The engineer hung over the side watching the small crowd as it entered the station. Toby never understood why he watched because he couldn't stop that thing short if he wanted to. Like all engineers, he had that look of pride. The train coming this far southwest was new and the entire train crew preened like martinet missionaries bringing the word to heathens. In a year or two the train would be old hat, and the next new station down the line would suffer the condescension.

Wesley didn't waste any time, he stood out from the rail car on the short ladder. His uniform was still a shiny blue, and each button and epaulet glinted from the sun. He held the guardrail with one hand and waved his cap with great sweeps in the other. Toby swore there was a look of disappointment on his face when he realized the townie boys were there for the train and didn't give a hoot about him.

Mother was beaming and his sisters were enthralled. The girls had hoped he'd brought friends, other new officers to visit, or cousins from back east, but he was alone.

Toby thought he had dandy hair because it was parted not exactly on the side but more toward the center. The same way the dandies wore it in the Roebuck catalogue. Wesley's expression was one of bored amusement, using it to press his perfect white teeth out from his lips. The train rolled to a squealing stop and the half-dozen boys stared out of breath at the lieutenant. Wesley leapt to the platform like a stage actor. He approached the colonel and gave him a salute with a mock flourish, then they shook hands with his father saying, "Welcome home."

He embraced Mother and Maggie and Peg, remarking in vague terms about their growth and how promising and healthy they looked compared to the dowdies back east. The two gushed with pride. It was undeniable that he was a good-looking dandy and he acted the part of an army officer. He reminded Toby of that painting that took up nearly a whole wall in the courthouse. It was of some long-ago battle in the Old World. Wesley looked just like the dandy officer in that painting standing amid the smoke and chaos holding a sword, the same sharp features and piercing blue eyes.

Toby dreaded his brother's approach: "Well, well, look at this fine young cavalryman. When I left, you stood maybe two hands; now look at you, but still in knickers. I bet you can ride like the dickens, can't you?" Before Toby could respond, Wesley spun on his heel, and said, "I'm famished."

The family strolled to the hotel. The family would eat dinner and stay for the night. Two liverymen struggled with Wesley's trunks and heaved them onto a flatbed wagon. Their groans telegraphed the weight.

As the family walked, Toby caught snatches of Wesley speaking with his father. Wesley said: "Father, as a lieutenant, I require a minimum of three mounts. Some of the Yankees are going with six . . . I understand that, Colonel, but the salary is at best subsistence, I'll need dress uniforms and winter fittings . . ."

It went on with his mother's occasional—"Of course, and if you take a wife, they'll be expectations . . ."

Colonel Walker kept nodding his head, and Toby knew his father was preoccupied in his thoughts about the burned barn and wasn't listening. Toby feared that Wesley would take Ulysses.

They ate at the hotel and Wesley demonstrated for the ladies the proper etiquette presently being observed in the East and he prattled off the nuanced differences between the use of spoons in Paris and London. He would drop French occasionally. The girls jittered at his stories.

Toby knew the day he rode off on Ulysses, he wouldn't even say thank you. At that moment, Toby felt his father's gaze and it felt like his father was reading his thoughts. Toby looked down at his plate.

As Wesley sipped his coffee, he said: "Colonel, to the extent the horses aren't all available at the ranch, perhaps we could trade with McCallum or that Raif, if he's still alive, for a suitable horse."

The colonel raised his pipe and began packing it in that

methodical way pipe-smokers use. He tapped the pipe seven times and as he finished lighting the tobacco he said: "I've already got the six in mind for you. We've got a dozen older ones roaming and twenty that are newly broke. Toby knows the good ones. We'll select the right ones for you, won't we, Toby?"

Wesley said, "Colonel, no slight to the workhorses and no slight to little brother's judgment, but I've learned a little about what an officer requires with respect to his mounts. I'll need at least one to stud."

"Well, I see your point," the colonel said.

Maggie blurted out, "If you take any stallion, you should take Ulysses. He's the most beautiful."

Toby was overcome by an urge to put his fork into her ear, when his mother said, "Ulysses is Toby's. He raised him from a colt." She was like that, keen on keeping up appearances and all the refinements, but there was a sense to her, a hard sense that could never be shaken.

Wesley said: "Mother, let's not be hasty, if Toby is fine with it, I don't see the harm."

"Ulysses is a one-man horse. He's too temperamental when others ride him. No good for pulling cannon, anyway," the colonel said.

The following morning the family clambered aboard the wagon and headed out to the ranch. It was a long ride from town and took the better part of the day. Wesley sat on the leader board with Father and along the route pointed out various landmarks that he had remembered despite his long time away.

Late that afternoon, the Walkers crested the rise before the ranch house and Wesley said, "I thought it burned two days ago. You had it framed out already."

The colonel said, "No, it's the neighbors. They must have caught wind of it somehow."

Wesley viewed a commotion in front of the house and said: "It looks like the good folks building the barn are about to lynch that boy on horseback in front of the house."

CHAPTER NINE:
TOBY RIDES

Seth had ridden hard and now screamed out from behind the mastodon for the farmers to clear his path. The farmers were around Seth astride his stallion, and Raif could hear angry voices from the throng swearing oaths at the boy, "Watch your mouth, boy"; "there's no call for that talk"; "I'll take you off that horse if you don't curb that tongue . . ."

Seth kept at it. "You all got no fight in you, chickenshits, clear out."

Tom Burke came out of the fold and said, "Now, that's about enough out of your trap I can stand," and reached up with his powerful hands and grabbed the reins of Seth's horse.

Seth pulled back but Burke's strength was too much for him.

Raif watched the tug-of-war and reached for the buck knife that lay sheathed on a bale of hay.

Jed said, "Ain't seen no reason yet to be skinn'n some splitter."

"I don't plan on it. But I'm not rolling around in the dirt with some ham-handed pig-pusher. This'll keep 'em from getting any hero notions. I'll wear it prominently so if it comes to that afterward I can tell his kin his demise came a surprise to me too," Raif said.

Raif wound his way toward Seth, traveling along the seams in the throng of folks that were watching the altercation. Seth was wheeling his horse back and forth, but the farmers continued to close in, and Burke wouldn't let go of the reins. Raif pushed the knife down in his belt, concealing it as much as he could so that little of the hilt showed. He knew Burke's strength, so he was going to rely on speed and slash Burke across the throat. Raif closed toward Burke with no quick motions. As he flowed toward Burke, he caught glimpses of him on the far side of Seth's stallion and channeled his path so that his movement was shadowed by the steed's neck. He wanted to be blind to Burke. It would look like it was all Tom's fault. He would come up from behind Burke and grab the reins out of his hand hoping Burke would flail before he knew it was him. Once Burke put his fist to him, Raif was going to carve his apple from his neck. As he approached, his thoughts all seemed so logical to him.

Jed turned to Abner, "Grab the shotgun and the pistol we brung, Raif's found himself an excuse to kill Tom Burke. I don't think they got the nerve, but we may have to blast a few if they go for Raif."

Abner said, "How do you know it's trouble?"

"Brother's got that crazy eye thing going. Git ready."

The farmers sensed a predator and like a freshly lit candle that splits the darkness, a path opened for Raif. Burke sensed the odd movement of a cluster of so many and looked over to see the blank lifeless eyes fixed upon him, Raif's hand caressing the hilt of the knife in his belt. Burke's flee instinct triggered, and he melted back into the folds of the farmers on the opposite side, disappearing like an ebbing wave back into the sea. Raif sensed the loss of the prey as it fled back into the fold and the fire of the hunt melted in his chest. He shambled to Seth in a partial daze. With the moment gone his sense of his surroundings slowly surfaced and he understood once again the depth of his madness.

Seth saw him and exclaimed, "Raif, there you are. I rode past the ranch and looked for you. Gabriel said to find you, Raif—

they're all dead."

Raif grabbed the horse's reins and squeezed Seth's knee hard and said, "Easy does it, brother, don't show these fools nothing, Seth, steady up."

Raif led the horse and rider over to the porch; a few farmers followed a short distance until Raif stared back but they still tried to cluster within earshot.

"Who's dead?" Raif asked.

Seth started sobbing and the words came out in fits, "Mama, Uncle Eli, Tyler, Luke—Clara and May are gone. There's fifty of 'em with a cannon."

A collective gasp went up from the farmers. Raif turned to them and said, "You all need to wait for the colonel. He'll be back shortly to give orders."

The men dispersed, hurrying toward the mastodon, and gathered in a large group to discuss the situation.

Raif turned to Seth, "Jed and Abner and me are gonna gear up. Where's Gabriel?"

"He said to meet here at Walker's. He told me to tell you to bring all you got, Raif."

"That's right, Seth, we're gonna ride. What about Caleb?"

"He's with Joe, and they're tracking 'em. We're to meet at the Old Mission."

"We'll be back in four hours, Seth. We'll kill every last one of them. We'll get your kin. Stay steady." Raif headed back to Jed and Abner.

Jed asked, "What's all the fuss about?"

"The McCallums been butchered by a war party of fifty—a cannon took out the front door, killed the ma and uncles; war party took the nieces—Gabriel and Joe was hunting the black with Seth and Caleb. We ride."

Jed spat and said, "Fifty and a cannon, shee-it! I will tell you what, though, since we're in such a hurry, I'll get that half buck to you when we get back."

Colonel Walker and his family rode up in the wagon as the Hansons were mounting their horses. Raif rode over to the colonel and told him the news, and added, "You best see to Seth, Colonel, before he opens fire on them farmers. We'll be back 'fore sundown."

"Who's the advance guard?" the colonel asked.

Raif knew the colonel was taking command. "Caleb and Joe're at the Old Mission, trying to see if they're running the Flats or going for the Crossing."

"How many days they have on us?"

"Joe thinks two, more or less. Ma'am, Seth's taking it hard. I put him on the porch."

Molly jumped down from the wagon and climbed the short steps to the porch.

"Colonel, maybe you can get more out of Seth. Be back in a few hours."

"Seth can stay at the house until we get back."

Raif reined up, and said, "Seth says he rides."

"He's a boy."

"He's fifteen, nearly sixteen, Colonel, but I'll leave it to you and Gabriel."

"That boy's in no condition to ride," the colonel said more to himself than Raif.

"It's his kin been butchered, but like I said I'll leave it to you and Gabriel."

Raif reined his horse, and the Hansons galloped off to fetch fresh mounts and their killing kits.

As they rode Jed said, "He's balk'n 'cause he don't want Toby to ride."

"No, he don't, but if Seth rides, Toby's rides. The colonel ain't one to give up command," Raif responded.

★ ★ ★ ★ ★

Molly was on the porch with her arm across Seth's shoulders. Wesley and Toby gathered around. Molly had listened to Raif and her husband talk, and she watched Walker closely as he climbed the porch steps. The colonel placed his hand on the back of the boy's neck and bent down and said, "Seth, son, I'm sorry, but I need to know if Gabriel said for you to tell me anything more."

Seth responded, "No, sir, he said I was to tell Raif to bring all he had and to tell you fifty with a cannon killed our kin and that my sisters is nowhere to be found."

The colonel stood and looked off to the south scanning the horizon and said, "Fifty and a cannon." He said it without fully comprehending it. Even in the early years he couldn't recall a raiding party of more than fifteen. In the last five years, it had been nothing but the one or two that crept down at night from the mountain to steal horses from the flats. Fifty with a cannon, fifty with a cannon, he rolled the fact in his head but couldn't fathom it.

"Seth, I don't want you to worry, we'll find your sisters," the colonel said.

"That's right, Seth, we'll bring them back," Wesley added.

The colonel looked at his elder son. It was the first time he realized his son was a soldier, and an officer.

Seth looked back at them from one to the other and said, "I ride, Colonel."

"Seth, son, I'll talk to Gabriel; we'll work it out." The colonel tried not to sound harsh.

He turned to Toby and said, "Saddle Bull and pick a horse for the lieutenant."

Toby said, "Yes, sir," and ran to the horse shed out back that was being used as the temporary barn.

The colonel turned to Wesley and said, "There're Colts and

Winchesters in my study. The key for the gun case is under the quill holder by the letter stand. My irons are on the right side; you can take your pick of the rest, but make it a .45 pistol and a .30 rifle. We need to keep the cartridges as simple as possible. If we need to resupply those two will be the easiest to find down there. Bring a good amount of ammo, but don't weigh the horse down. Time is against us."

Seth looked at the colonel. "Sir, they took near everything, I didn't have no ammo from the house. Can I borrow cartridges?"

Wesley said, "Seth, fella, we need you to stay here with Toby to guard the women; not everyone should ride."

The colonel liked the tack and said, "The lieutenant's right, Seth, I need you here."

"It ain't my call, Colonel, Gabriel told me straight I ride," Seth said.

The colonel looked at the boy and saw that his face was as smooth as a marble statue's. He remembered Toby when the fever almost took him and how his face had splotched. When the fever broke, he recalled Toby's face smoothing out again and regaining its luster and as he looked at Seth's face, he thought of his son. He looked over at his wife, and Molly's eyes were fixed upon him.

She hugged Seth closer to her bosom as she stared at Walker.

The colonel said, "I'll be right back. I need to organize the folks and farmers."

Wesley went to the case and selected the two newest pistols and grabbed a Winchester rifle. He pushed his way out the back-door shutter and strode to the old shed looking for a saddlebag to stow ammunition. He entered the shed, and his eyes adjusted to the darkness so that he could see that it was Toby and three saddled horses. Wesley looked at the black and knew it was Bull, because it looked like one. The second was a roan, well-proportioned and tall. He caught sight of Ulysses and was floored by the horse's amber coloring and the power that radiated out of the animal. He moved toward Ulysses.

Toby had his back to the door and didn't hear Wesley's approach.

Wesley reached for Ulysses's reins, and the horse shimmied and reared back to strike.

Toby wheeled and drew his Colt pistol in one smooth reflex action thinking a snake had crawled in the barn. He holstered it with the same dexterity when he saw it was only Wesley. He grabbed Ulysses's reins and put a hand to the horse's muzzle and said, "Easy, boy, easy." The horse calmed. Toby turned to Wesley and said, "He don't take to being handled by someone he don't know. I reckon he only been rid by me and maybe Jed a couple times."

"He's magnificent. Do you mind if I try to work with him when I get back?"

"Let's see if he takes to you on the ride. For now, you can take Vengeance, he takes to anyone."

"Toby, why is Ulysses saddled?"

"If Seth rides, I have to," Toby responded.

"Seth's not riding, Toby. Father . . . I mean the colonel won't allow it. He'll talk to Gabriel."

"We'll see," Toby said.

"Toby, Mother will never let it happen."

"We'll see. Vengeance pulls to the left if you try and start him at a gallop; you need to ease him into running."

Toby handed Wesley the reins to the roan, and Wesley led him out to the front of the ranch house. He tied him to the hitching post. The women had taken Seth inside, and he could hear them giving the boy supper. He looked at the house and wondered what if it had been his family. It could as easily have been here as the McCallum's, maybe easier because the Nottoway was farther south. McCallum's was more remote from town but it was better prepared for a raid than this ranch house. The colonel's original had been a fort, but the new one offered no special protection; it was nothing but a stately home, a miniature of the one the colonel had quit back east.

Wesley had visited Sommersville on a military summer assignment two years back and knew this was a poor attempt to capture the grandeur the family once knew. McCallum's was still the original bunkhouse, a fortress upon the land. Wesley wondered how he would feel if he had gotten off that train and everything he knew had been destroyed, his sisters being dragged to the wastelands. Would he chase or would he board that train and head back? He went in to eat without answering the question.

Three hours later, Gabriel and the Hansons converged on the road and entered Walker's property. The colonel strode out onto the porch. He went to speak but heard the door unlatch behind him and saw Seth running to mount his horse. Seth leaped up and reined the steed around until he sat tall in the saddle next to Abner. The colonel looked at Gabriel and before he could speak Toby came running up leading Bull and Ulysses. The colonel took Bull's reins and mounted.

Toby stayed on the ground, but he was dressed to ride. He was adorned with three pistols, the butt loops tied by strings to his riding coat so he could empty them and drop them while riding hard without needing to reholster; a fourth pistol was holstererd with a cord to a belt loop and a Winchester rifle sat in the saddle holster—adorned in the killing trade as he'd been schooled by Gabriel.

Wesley ambled down the porch, looked about slyly, and mounted Vengeance.

The colonel looked down at Toby and said, "What are you waiting for? Mount up! Daylight's burning."

Wesley was struck and blurted, "Father, you can't be serious?"

The colonel wheeled around on Bull. "I'll not have my orders questioned, Lieutenant. If I want your counsel on this mission, I'll ask for it."

Wesley responded, "Understood . . . sir."

Molly was out on the porch, and she was shaking. She raced to Walker with three quick steps and grabbed the reins of his mount and motioned him to come closer. He leaned down to her and she whispered, "When I was inside feeding that boy, I looked at Maggie and Peg and knew if it had been them taken that Gabriel, bastard that he is, would be sitting here like he is now and Seth with him. And I knew in my heart that I wouldn't have tried to stop Seth from going if it was Maggie and Peg, so, John, I can't stop you from taking Toby."

The colonel responded, "Molly, if it were Maggie and Peg, Toby would ride."

"I know, John, that's why I won't stop it. But you gave me a promise once, do you remember, John, do you remember?"

The colonel stared at her green eyes, and he remembered looking down from his horse at her an age ago.

"I remember."

"You promised me you wouldn't let go of the rope. You're going to promise me something right now, John Michael, or Toby goes over my dead body."

CHAPTER TEN:
JOHN MICHAEL WALKER

Walker's grandfather still wore the uniform of a cavalry lieutenant when he went riding—the simple blue coat, tan breeches,
and leather boots that folded over below the knee. Sommersville
had one knoll of any real height and it held the stone markers
of three generations of Walkers. John followed on his mare
behind his grandfather's lead to the top of the knoll and
dismounted. Despite his age and rheumatism, his grandfather
still dismounted in a single thrust down from the fifteen hands
of his dapple gray, landing on two feet.

The two looked out over the growing fields of the plantation.
The porch and large pillars had been built a generation ago, but
the main house's entire rear wall had been removed and John
could see the scores of carpenters milling about and hear the
knock-knocking of their hammers driving home pegs and
flatheads to join the wood. The main house would double in
size in a month's time.

The field hands were crossing the rows harvesting the cotton,
and John could see the overseers high in the saddle on their
black stallions trotting back and forth along the red earth of the
paths that ran among the fields.

"Johnny, do you see this one here, the simple stone marker?"
his grandfather asked.

"Yes, sir," John responded.

"It's my father's daddy. We called him Pappy. He was the first

Walker to come to this land, but you know that already, don't you?"

"I do, sir."

"No one knows where he really came from. My grandmother used to spin yarns he was the last of five sons born to a duke. There were land for only four in the old country. The fifth in line had to find his own way in the world and he yearned to be free in a new world. Grandma'd tell he come to this land with nothing but a handful of guineas and a bushel of grit. I guess it does not matter where a man comes from but what they say about him when he leaves. John, I care for your father very much. He doesn't seem to like to do much good other than attending balls and dancing; but he does have a head for commerce, I'll give him that; credit to his mother—she was smart as a whip. I think I'm near'n eighty now, give or take, my time should've been finished long ago. Your daddy criticized me t'other day saying my days riding and shooting with you was interfering with your tutoring; that you had schooling to accomplish."

"I don't mind, sir."

Grandfather let out a loud guffaw. "You don't mind—what boy wouldn't mind riding and hunting the day long? You're smart as a whip like your grandmother, school'n come natural to you in time. I don't have time, though, to wait for the schoolmarms to finish with you before I teach you what's important to our kind. War's coming, Johnny; I seen a spell of it. It gets so you can smell it in the air like the scent of a good leaf fire gusting your way; there's no mistaking it. It's drifting this way from up yonder." The old man pointed north as he said it.

"I hear the talk, sir."

"I was gone five years fighting that tyrant king and his red butchers. Folks forget, Johnny; folks got a way of forgetting.

Silly cartoon of nabobs standing about some parchment with flowery words; all of 'em all patting themselves on the back for doing nothing more than scratch'n their names on it. It'd be kindling I ever got my hands on it.

"I had a cobbler for my first captain, a wife and eight sons when he left home for the fight. The redcoats had dug themselves a fort on a hill and we were taking an awful licking from their cannon, an awful licking trying to take it. Captain got both his legs taken off below the knee. We dragged him back beyond some trees and laid him on some grass. He lay there with the bright red running thick out over the dark green of the grass, we couldn't stem it, the legs so tore up, life runn'n out of him. I was a boy, no more than seventeen or so, looking down at him with a handful of other fools waiting for something to happen, as if there were anything to be done, and that cobbler raised himself on his elbows and cried out, 'Boys, no nation was freed by gawking, to your guns, lads, to your guns, finish them red sons-of-bitches.' That cobbler's name was John Michaels, and you bear his name.

"Anytime a tyrant tells a free man how he ought to live—the matter is settled by blood. Tyrants come in many guises; my sense tell'n me another is bound to rise out of the ashes of the old one, and again the call will come to the Walkers. I gave your father that name so he'd give it to you; so when your nation calls you, you'd never forget what it means to be a Walker—honor bound to ride to the sound of the guns; the days com'n, Johnny, when you'll need to draw your sword and throw away the scabbard."

"Yes, sir."

John Walker was in town when the news of Fort Sumter came. He watched as the streets exploded with yells, church bells ringing and the music hall band striking up Dixie on the steps of city hall. He returned to his family's Sommersville plantation that afternoon and told his father and mother that he had received a commission with the cavalry. They were delighted. His mother suggested Crimshaw's shop for a winter and summer cut uniform. His father voiced displeasure with his decision to join the cavalry, saying a man of John's station should be with the infantry. Yet, despite the minor disappointment, his father understood that his son was a horseman like his father had been; so he relented, but insisted that he would speak to the governor to see that he was billeted under a capable commander and not some pony-riding brigand.

Molly came to Sommersville when she heard the news. They had been engaged for three months and she was thrilled that the family was celebrating John's going away with a soiree. She counted fifty hands landscaping the gatehouse road, planting five thousand tulips along the borders. The newly minted captain of horse would ride out the following day through a portal of dazzling white. It was planned with exquisite detail. Molly and John sat on the porch swing. They sat talking, oblivious to the hands swarming about the house grounds when his mother came out onto the porch.

She was prim and austere, and said, "John, so you know, we are fixing up your bedroom. I think it is high time those items you've collected over the years running about in the woods are put aside."

"Mother, springing this on me on the day before I leave to serve our country," John replied with mock indignation.

"Oh, don't worry. Missy Jay is doing the work. I know she'll put your knickknacks in a safe place." She wheeled in her perfectly tailored dress and disappeared through a large door divided by a dozen glass panes; the door was opened by an old white-bearded slave whose father had had the same task for John's grandmother for the fifty years before him, his only task—to follow her around and open doors for her all day.

Molly asked, "What do you have in this boy's room of yours?"

John answered, "Let's go see."

They climbed the steps taking two at a time to the third floor and detoured to a remote staircase, only used by the servants, that entered into the rear of John's bedroom. As they climbed the stairs, Molly could hear the sound of shuffling feet and bickering. John put his finger to his mouth and signaled Molly to be quiet. They crept up the stairs.

"No, no, don't go throw'n everything in one basket, we need to split it out," came a woman's sing-song voice.

"Why? When he come back, he ain't never going to look at this stuff again, this is boy's things," a raspy man's voice responded.

"You heed me, Jess, and put the stuff that's bones and rocks in that basket, like 'em arrowheads and flints; the feather stuff go in a cotton bag so it keep and the copper stuff need to go in a wood box. Git and go find me a hardwood box, there's empty wine crates in the pantry."

John eased the door open and crept into the room. He tried to sneak up on Missy Jay, but before he could startle her she said, "John Michael, you got feet of stone. I heard you coming up them steps, didn't I, Jessup?"

"I reckon she did, Master John, she winked at me as you coming."

"I done told you a hundred times you can't sneak up like no Injun," Missy Jay said.

Missy Jay was a large woman, and she dwarfed the diminutive Jessup. She was of a light complexion giving her the look at certain angles of a white woman of mixed blood. Jessup was dark and always wore a friendly smile. Molly looked over the room. Native American artifacts filled every shelf of the room. On one shelf, there were glass-top-looking boxes filled with arrowheads of multiple shapes; under each arrowhead there was written in neat printing a description such as: "flint; Chickasaw"; "shale; Cherokee"; "bone; unknown." In other cases, there were exotic beads, another with pipes carved from bones, and antlers carved with animals in minute and intricate beauty. Nine handheld axes were mounted across one wall, the blades arranged in the same direction. The first three were crafted of stone, others bone, crude iron, and one of copper.

Looking about the room, Molly remembered her brother finding a single arrowhead once and the jealousy and excitement of the other boys at his find. She had never seen anything like this, it looked like a museum. A round table in the far corner of the room was laden with maps, drawings of foliage, sketches of animals, and a dozen dog-eared journals of the British Geographical Society. There was also a daguerreotype of four young boys all about thirteen years of age in what looked like costumes. She recognized a young John wearing a bush hat and a vest adorned with shotgun shells.

She looked at John. "How is it possible you recovered all this? You must have looked every day as a boy."

"We did quite a bit of searching I must admit."

"Who are these boys in the picture?" Molly asked.

Missy Jay snatched a glance at Molly and Jessup grabbed a basket and headed out the door and down the stairs.

John hesitated for a moment and said, "When I was eleven I was a founding member of the Intrepid Explorer's Guild. We read too many British Geographical Society journals for our own good."

"This one boy looks so young. What's his name?" Molly asked.

John took the daguerreotype in his hands. "That's Addie Sparrow. She was the only girl ever let into the guild, but she proved her mettle always. She's gone now, caught in the river during a summer storm."

Missy Jay said, "He was wild when he was young, Miss Molly. Yes, ma'am, he were wild for 'em woods. I told him not to go messing in those places but he never heed me, uh-uh."

Molly's curiosity was piqued. "John, what is Missy talking about?"

"We had great adventures tracking in the old Indian lands; we'd head deep into the bayou looking to search the ancient mounds. Boys' dreams of finding a lost city."

"Are those the Indian mounds you can see from the riverboat?" Molly asked.

"Yes, that's the start of the mound country. The mounds are ancient; built a thousand years before the Nation got there. The Geographical Society has stories of mounds of similar size and shape in Africa. It was Courtney's idea to explore the mounds for a lost city."

"The Collinses' boy?" Molly asked.

"Yes, Courtney was the first to buy a subscription to the British Geographical Society's journal. We read every one we could get our hands on. He's gone too. He went with a British expedition to explore the mound country in the great desert of Africa, lost at sea is what I heard."

Molly could see in John's eyes he was far off, a thousand miles from where they stood. "Was the bayou dangerous?"

"We rode out on horses and brought our guns. I tried once to wrangle some hands to carry our packs like I had seen in a journal drawing about an expedition to Africa; Father gave me the switch. Was it dangerous? I suppose—we crossed rivers, climbed cliffs, tested our mettle, as Grandfather used to say." John took a copper ax down from the wall; he paused for a moment and added, "We discovered an old abandoned village, possibly Chickasaw, deep in Miller's bog. The village was old, maybe a hundred years or so; it looked like the entire village up and walked away one day leaving everything behind right where they left it. We explored the village, that's where most of the collection comes from."

Missy Jay interrupted, "Master John, it don't do to go talking about that explor'n that years ago."

John smiled and said to Molly, "Don't worry about Missy Jay, she's a superstitious one. She remembers the old slaves telling tales of that bayou."

"Oh, no, Master John, I ain't meant you to share that," Missy Jay said. Missy turned to another box of relicts and shook her head.

"What tales John?" Molly persisted.

"It was Pierce Briggins's passion. He supplied us with machetes that came from Old Man Briggins's sugar plantations in Hispaniola. An old hand on his estate told Pierce there was an ancient burial ground, a lost city in Miller's bog. Many years before, the hand had gone with Old Man Briggins on one of his hunting trips into the bog. The guild set out to cut our way in and find it."

Missy's interrupting became more urgent, "Now, Master John, don't go telling Miss Molly about such stuff. It ain't for a lady."

"Missy, I have teased you enough." John said.

"I am impressed that you were such an adventurer. Did you ever find the burial grounds?" Molly asked.

Missy Jay looked down at the row of arrowheads she was packing and grimaced.

"I don't know if it was a lost city; we found a cave, a cavern really; tales were told that Old Man Briggins used to venture into that cave. Missy remembers, don't you?"

"Now, Master John, you can tell your tale but don't bring Missy in it," she said.

"You see, Missy knew all these stories as a little girl on the

Brigginses' plantation. Isn't that right, Missy?"

"Oh, Master John, there's no cause to go on about them Briggins. They all gone now."

Molly was intrigued. "Why was Pierce Briggins so obsessed with it all?"

"The town gossip about Old Man Briggins infuriated Pierce. The old man had attained his fortune sailing slavers from the west coast of Africa to Hispaniola. The gossip was he paid his sea captains a bounty to barter with the tribal chiefs for women who had the mark."

Molly asked, "The mark?"

"In Africa if the shamans think a girl is a witch they brand her with fire; sometimes on the forehead, or cheeks. Old Man Briggins wanted witches. Isn't that right, Missy Jay?"

"Master John, that all a bunch of hooey and it don't do nobody no good raising dust about them Briggins, they gone. Tell'n such stories to a young lady, shame on you."

Missy shook her head and opened the top drawer of an old dresser and started removing clothes. From time to time during the conversation Missy Jay would steal glances at Molly.

Molly picked up on Missy Jay's pained expressions and changed the subject. "Missy Jay, was he always such a mysterious rogue?"

Missy Jay smiled. "He never had a cross word for me, Miss Molly. Always a gentleman, so daring though he needed the switch every so often. Used to scare Missy Jay so. I remember once he with those intrepid boys and they were build'n a rope swing down by the river. It was springtime rains and that river was angry, crashing against itself. I came up to his room to see to things. I found two leggings cut off a pair of brand-new long pants. I gist knew he'd cut short pants for swimm'n, so I ran 'cause I remember them boys pulling rope out the back stable and talk'n about the river. I never gave it no thought 'til I seen the leggings. I broke hard for the creek and I come out the brush and see them swing'n out over that water and back ag'n to the ground. And I seen it was Master Johnny's turn. I so out of breath I couldn't holla. He took that rope and ran and leap out. I gist knew he was gonna let go o' that rope; had it in him since he was a babe, as soon as he start crawl'n turn your back a second and be headed to trouble."

Molly turned to John who was looking at Missy Jay. The smile on his face was radiant and loving.

Molly asked, "John, why did you let go of the rope?"

He turned to Molly. "The challenge was to build a rope bridge and you had to get one rope across the river to start. I went last. Nobody before me had let go of the rope. For the sake of the honor of the guild, I had to do it."

John burst out laughing.

Jessup came into the room with another basket. "Master John, I'm gonna place all this stuff in shed in t'west field. It stay driest, and the critters seem to leave stuff be in there."

"That's fine, Jess."

Missy Jay let out a sniffle.

Jessup said, "Now, now, don't be go'n on again. She go on when she thinks about you leav'n for this here war, sir. This pack'n up done brought the memory to her."

John walked to Missy Jay standing by his old dresser. "Missy Jay, don't worry."

"I worry about you doing your stuff. I won't worry though, Master John, if'n you promise Missy Jay."

"Anything, Missy Jay, I could never say no to you."

"Promise me this time you won't let go of that rope, and I won't worry so much."

John smiled. "Missy Jay, I learnt my lesson. Remember how you tanned my backside when they pulled me out of that river downstream? If the water didn't kill me, you almost did."

141

"Go on now and promise Missy Jay you won't let go of the rope in this here war com'n."

Missy Jay was searching his eyes for an answer. John turned his gaze to Molly and Missy knew he wouldn't promise.

Missy Jay looked down into the top dresser drawer and pulled out a baby's swaddling cloth. She held it close to her face, breathing it in. "I remember the first time I swaddled your backside. You come into this world and Doc Fields put you face down on them sheets. I reached for these; they was so soft, softest I ever knew; and you being so new, you still slimy. I turned to bring out the swaddling and Doc Fields says, 'Missy Jay look at that, Missy Jay look, look' and I see over and there you was on your hands and knees lift'n your head look'n at the world. Said to Doc Fields, 'we got a strong one, like Sampson'; and Ol' Doc Fields jest shook his head repeat'n—'I'll be damned, I'll be damned.' "

John placed his hand over Missy's hand for a moment before he spun around and grabbed Molly's hand. Missy stared at the swaddling as the two departed down the back stairs.

As they descended the stairs Molly could hear Jessup saying, "Now don't go on again, Missy. It be all right. This war over 'fore Christmas. You know folks don't stand to be out in the cold. Johnny back and you be tended to his little 'uns. Come on now; we got a boat of folks com'n t'night."

Dinner lasted well into the evening. Speeches were heard around the table with the same themes—the southern cause, states' rights, the Philistine armies of the North will fall to the sword. The speeches went on until brandy and tea was served. The young officers and their ladies stole out on to the sprawling back porch, gathering about the porch railings and swings to enjoy the cool night air. The ladies floated around in billowing dresses; the young men preened in new uniforms.

The next day there were over a hundred guests as John

mounted his horse. He bid his farewells. His mother and father stood on the porch. He was in his new uniform and was leading four horses. The family, the guests, and all the plantation hands waved as he mounted, and a great hurrah went up from the crowd.

Molly descended the porch and walked up to John. "So handsome."

He responded, "I'll be back before you know it. We'll give them Yanks a licking; it'll all be over before Christmas."

"Promise me," Molly said.

"Molly, I wouldn't ask you to wait if my intentions weren't true."

"Hah, you were mine the first time I batted my eyes at you. I'll wait for you only if you promise me something special," Molly whispered.

"Anything."

"Promise me that you won't let go of the rope," Molly said looking in his eyes.

"Molly."

"You can fly above the waves, John, but there's no letting go this time, promise me."

"Molly, I can't."

"I won't wait five minutes after you leave that gate if you don't. Without this promise I won't waste one second of my life waiting to hear about how you died." Molly almost hissed it.

"All right, I promise, I won't let go," he said.

"I'll be waiting, John Michael."

John reined Pegasus and headed for the gate and another hurrah went up from the throng that echoed along the columns of the porch.

Augie Powell pulled the bridle bit from the horse's muzzle and raised its head and looked up its nose. He pulled on its lips to

143

lay bare the gums and teeth and nodded a silent acknowledgment to himself that the prospects of the horse enduring the journey north were middling at best. Billie was loading feed in the bed of the wagon as his wife, Bea, stood on the porch of the Powell cabin, their little Willie squatting next to her, fixating on a frog in his hands.

Angus limped sideways down the stairs under the pair of two oversized horseshoes that adorned an old awning in front of the house. He climbed down the steps sideways, favoring the leg that had grown arthritic to the point he could hardly walk. For forty years, he had been the overseer on the Sommersville plantation, but the pain of standing had retired him. He lived out his days on a rocking chair on the front porch of his shack reading his books, a lot in life that suited his temperament. Angus saw Willie within earshot and snapped, "Put water on the back that toad, tortur'n it for no good cause." Willie darted off the porch and ran to the brook that trickled down rocks out back of the shack. As Angus approached the wagon, Billie climbed the porch steps to Bea and they gently nodded their foreheads to one another and spoke in soft whispers.

Angus limped to the horse and studied Augie over the withers and said, "I knew you'd do it, and go'n and dragg'n Billie into it. You two been runn'n to trouble in them woods since you was knee-high—it's my fault for lett'n you run wild, I shouldn't've spared the rod."

"Huh, I don't recall you spare'n it all that much."

"This war ain't gonna be like all that Caesar crap in 'em books I was a damn fool to fill your head with. Them Yankees is rich as Solomon and their side got their own pack of prideful nabobs. Son, they no different than the fools you two is follow'n up there. Neither one gives a hoot how many got to die so long as they keep their coin. Who is this Walker kid, anyhow, think'n he know someth'n about soldier'n?"

Augie synched the billet strap and stared back at Angus. "Pa, that's it, you done beat your drum enough. Anyhow, Walkers done fitt'd out a hundred Sommersville boys with horse and kit. They put their money up, John Michael go'n; so he ain't like the rest of all 'em all pay'n some other boy to take their place."

"Walker got five hundred hands in them fields; he could fit out a thousand and wouldn't feel no pinch; and lo' and behold that sapling is now some captain of cavalry. Walker's daddy let'm go 'cause he thinks it's good for business. I swear every fool in this county caught the fever of this here nonsense. Walker's daddy gonna earn coin off this war, you mark my words and heed that. And it be Bea over there with her two pennies, she be the widow giv'n more than any of 'em money lenders."

"Pa, we leav'n. I'll bet you two bits to a penny we back by Christmas morn."

"In a pine box if you is back by Christmas. Son, you got to use them blessed smarts of yours. You watch out for you and Billie, and don't go follow'n some biggity fool down a rabbit hole you two can't crawl back out."

Through his field glasses Walker surveyed the hill in the distance swarming thick with Napoleons and 24-pound howitzers. The great gamble of the infantry flank attack had shocked the Yankees and they had fled in disarray down the roads and across the open fields. He stood on a high knoll south of the Yankee hill next to Corporal Powell. He took a moment to scout the land about him and bore witness to the fiery chaos stretching in every direction. To his east, he could see plumes of black smoke and hear the deafening thud of mortars as the missiles crunched and pulverized the earth into submission. Lone Confederates mounted on fast steeds darted to and fro across the scarred and broken tree lines, carrying hastily penciled orders from high command that reached maneuver units at the very moment changed circumstances dictated different strategies. To the west, he witnessed a column of five hundred rebels marching down a farm field road at double time in his direction only to halt and about-face and head with equal urgency in the opposite direction.

Walker had waited in the shadow of this knoll for two hours for orders. The Yankee artillery unit was digging in and barricading its flanks with caisson. He knew enemy support infantry would eventually reach the position and render it impregnable to cavalry. The thick smoke carried on a spring breeze drifted across his vision, and he waited until an alley of sight swayed open. He spied a mounted officer through his field glasses. The Yankee sported a trim mustache and a little spot of hair beneath the lower lip. He had adorned himself with polished brown leather boots that reached nearly to his crotch and the cuffs of his white leather gloves flared to his elbows. Walker could tell he was highborn New England, probably Massachusetts; it would not have surprised him to learn the officer's kin had shuffled down the plank of the Mayflower. Walker watched him upon his magnificent black steed. He handled the stallion with deftness and rode back and forth across the cannon line encouraging his troops. Walker saw the artillery men rallying to the patriot in their midst; the lone man trying to seize the day and alter the fortunes of a nation.

Walker handed the field glasses to Corporal Powell, who stood beside him.

After a moment, Walker said, "It's now or never."

Augie responded, "I reckon, that pilgrim work'n them boys up into a tizzy."

Walker knew the moment was now but his orders were to hold. He was not to assault until he heard from Colonel Smith.

He had two company of horse under his command ready to charge and every minute of delay ticked an eternity in his mind. The captain of the second company was dead. Handsome Jack Carlton had been shot in the mouth and died choking to death on lead and blood behind a muddy parapet. Colonel Smith had joined Carlton's company to his boys some two hours ago and that was the last he had heard from his commander. He looked down the reverse slope of the knoll at the two hundred horsemen. They sat their horses in ranks of fifty as quiet as church mice. The only movement was the reflexive hunch of their shoulders when mortars landed in the distance and the air cracked with lighting strikes of sound. Walker knew the farm boys were uncomprehending of such noise, and the idleness, the lack of action, amidst the madness, was eating away at their resolve.

"I expect orders shortly," Walker muttered.

"Snow get here too, eventually, sir," Augie drawled in response.

Walker grimaced at the remark and took back the field glasses. He looked but the enemy position lay fully shrouded in the waves of black smoke that drifted from an artillery duel somewhere off to the west. They mounted their horses and rode back down the knoll. Walker reined up in front of the ranks and sat his horse, feeling foolish. He looked at the familiar faces of his Sommersville boys and it fortified him. They had fought in a half-dozen skirmishes and he knew they had gumption, but his doubts mounted again when he realized he had never asked them to charge a fixed position of cannon. He sat there brooding and his doubts multiplied, including the notion that Handsome Jack's men didn't know a goddamn thing about him. He cursed again his indecision and muttered to himself, "Ah, the hell with it, luck favors the crazy."

He would gamble. He figured he could fire up his boys and

flirted with the vague confidence that Handsome Jack's boys would catch the fever and follow because anything was better than standing still in this madness. He stood tall in the stirrups in front of the ranks, the butterflies churning in his stomach and his heart thumping so hard he worried the boys could see it pulsing beneath the thick wool of his tunic.

"Men, our brothers in the infantry have kicked some Yankee tail today."

And a muted hurrah went up from the ranks.

"But our enemy is not broken; the invader holds positions on this side of the river. On that hill a half mile to our front he is building a citadel of cannon. We cannot let him finish that task. I cannot tell you what the next hour of this day will bring, but, here, now, at Chancellorsville, the Almighty has chosen this moment for we few to show them damn fool Yankees how stupid it is to cross our border, invade our homes, and pick a fight with southern boys." He raised his sword. "For our nation's freedom let us ride, my brothers, and drive them blue-bellied sons-of-bitches into the river." Walker angled his sword toward the hill and spurred Pegasus, and a great fear mounted in his breast that nobody was following him. Then he sensed the surge after him, as if he had grabbed a fistful of blanket and dragged it behind him off a newly made bed. He never looked back because he could feel that he was the head of some great pulsing venomous snake. As he galloped northeast around the knoll and gained speed, they were with him. He could feel them in the slightest change of direction of his mount; the vibrations of the earth crackled in waves beneath him, like a swarm of yellow jackets, the two hundred mimicked their leader's actions—they were many and one.

He hit north and then reined hard west and headed straight for the side of the hill trying to flank the guns before the Yankees could turn and mass their cannon fire. He could see the

guns being wrenched from their forward positions and the Yankees dragging them so the barrels faced the charge of horse,
and he knew it would be a close-run thing. He spurred Pegasus
and the steed surged beneath him. The shuddering of the two
hundred shook the earth and a throaty hurrah roared in the air.
Two Yankee cannons belched fire. The blast of smoke and heat
washed over him but he emerged unscathed and spurred again.
He gained the foot of the hill and looked up to see an artillery-
man drop a long cannon plunger and flee. The Yankee officer
atop the black steed swung the flat of his sword across the
soldier's back and sowed the air with curses upon his soul but
the man ran unheeding.

Pegasus climbed the hill in great bounds and the rebels about
him screamed bloody oaths. Walker vaulted over a caisson and
the mounted Yankee drew his long revolver and fired; the round
spit the top of Pegasus's ear but the animal did not break stride
and Walker closed and slashed the man from jowl to shoulder.
The blood spurted out from his neck in two faucet spouts and
his steed rounded about like a little boy's wooden toy horse and
trotted down the row of cannon. The dead rider bobbled about
in the saddle and anointed the ranks of his men with the
droplets of his blood. The macabre visage sent a primordial
compulsion through the Yankees, as if a dead man riding a dark
horse were the incarnation of some ancient superstition, and
they fled in streams down the back side of the hill trying to
escape the divination.

Those with courage tried to hold, but were slaughtered with
sword and pistol. Walker watched in awe as his boys dismounted,
turned and loaded the cannons, and unleashed volley after volley, the Yankees scattering for the woods like roaches fleeing a lit
candle placed on the floor of a dark kitchen. Walker became
wild-eyed with the killing, the blood beating in his ears and the
hairs of his body tingling. He dismounted and ran the line of

cannons and bade his men to fire and fire again. He vowed that they would charge the woods and butcher every last one of them and not stay the slaughter until the river flowed red with blood. His passion frothing, he mounted again and reined Pegasus but his eyes looked upon the western sky and he saw the deep and wide expanse of crimson being devoured by the land. He raised his fist and railed at the day's end, wishing he were Joshua and could summon the Almighty to arrest the day so the battle could rage on eternally. Walker stared at the sky and a flood of fatigue washed over him.

Later, as the shadows blanketed the woods to the north, he was ordering the boys to fix the cannon and brace for a counterattack when Colonel Smith and adjutant, Major Barnes, crested the rise on their horses. Walker formally greeted the colonel, who dismounted and strode toward the vantage point on the north side of the hill with a martinet's prance. He held out his hand and Major Barnes filled it with field glasses.

The scores of dead and dying in the field below looked like the scattering of toppled scarecrows. The soft wind carried the moaning, and the twilight revealed the shapes of bloody hands raised from awkward piles of limbs begging for water or beseeching for a mother's comfort. The silhouette of a lone Yankee could be seen with his right leg torn from his body; he kept trying to walk on the phantom limb, only to fall again and again, like some broken stick-figure puppet manipulated by a sadist.

The colonel scanned the north woods, which lay dark and silent without a trace of the enemy, and paid little heed to the vestiges of life in the field. He lowered his glasses and nodded slowly, as if the torments had been righteously called forth into this world by an act of his will. He twisted his upper body to engage Walker, "Captain, I can tell you that this day has not gone unremarked, the general sends his regards. He has been briefed that you were trusted with the point of the regiment's lance this day. Regrettably, my duties prevented me from leading the charge. I envy you Providence's favor to grant you such a station on such a glorious day for our nation."

Walker nodded.

"Yes, a fine victory, very fine. The tax, of course, for victory is paid with the blood of patriots. Carlton died gloriously, as did Powers, and Major Hughes lays in a cot from which I fear he shall never rise. The birth of a free nation, like a new soul, cannot be brought forth without blood, don't you agree, Captain?"

"Yes, sir."

Colonel Smith bade Walker to sit with him on the parapet overlooking the field and like a father congratulating a child he placed his hand on Walker's shoulder.

"John, I understand your people came from old Virginia, built their fortune cultivating tobacco."

"Yes, sir. The story goes a hundred years ago my people sold the tobacco fields and headed south to raise cotton because the old Virginia families would not forget they were newcomers."

"Hah, hah, hah, we are a stuffy bunch. I understand too that you and I come from highborn blood in the old country. A duke? Hah, I had the order of a knight on my mother's side. As fathers to slaves, you and I understand better than most how time does little to diminish what runs in the blood. I wager noble warriors in our clans joined ranks in centuries past on hills such as this one. John, I am entrusting you with Carlton's and Powers's companies. You have a battalion to command now, *Major* Walker."

"Yes, sir."

Augie stood holding the reins of Pegasus, dabbing liniment on the horse's mangled ear, using the handkerchief he took from the pocket of the dead Yankee officer. He listened to the two talk amidst the anguished cries in the field below and he fought the dread that rose in his chest. He was convinced now the colonel was a plumb fool. Walker was no fool but he didn't know if Walker believed a word of what this colonel was spouting or if he was just pretending, playing the part of the junior officer. The colonel's chattering raked the coals of his memory and the embers of Angus's forebodings rose from the ashes and burned in his mind. He tied the reins of the dead Yankee's stallion and Pegasus to a caisson and sat down heavy on the muddy traverse, holding the reins of his cagey old mount, which took to nuzzling him about his shoulder. A work crew in the deepening darkness lit a lantern and he gazed at Billie hefting a cannon wagon so the two soldiers could reattach a wheel to the axle. He cursed himself for dragging that big boy into his adventure.

Nearly two years to the day after they took the hill at Chancellorsville, Walker sat his horse and watched the half-crazed stares of Rebel infantry spill out from the killing tangle of the Wilderness. When the field was taken at Chancellorsville, the Yankees had scrambled away leaving wagons and horses standing in their traces, whole regiments collapsing in a great dash north. Walker rode forward on reconnaissance and from a wooded ridge he spied the Union army, which had lost the field at Spotsylvania the day before. He saw a sea of blue stretching in serpentine lines to the horizon, marching on despite the rebels having filled the woods full of their dead. A few days later at Yellow Tavern, the Sommersville boys were thrashed for the first time by Union cavalry, losing a score in a single cavalry clash lasting a moment, and the fabric of their courage frayed.

In the camps at night the boys took the only solace they could, sipping Colonel Smith's pilfered whiskey and telling tales about home. They took turns conjuring up ghost stories from the past. Three nights after Yellow Tavern, the Sommersville boys lay about a fire pit in a half circle of strewn blankets, using their saddles as headrests. The night was without a moon and the fire crackled with wooden fence posts. The boys had torn the posts from the ground where they had stood unmolested for a decade. Savage acts to the locals but to the boys it was their right to gain a moment's respite from the war–a soldier's means to carve out a chunk of time from the eternal clock before it tolled again in the morning, summoning battle and another day of dying.

Three dozen had defied the odds these four long years, and they sat close, resting and leaning on each other, the fire's light illuminating the sharp angles of the salt lines that scarred the tattered blankets they shared. Moment to moment the jug of stolen whiskey would surface and navigate about the half circle filling canteen cups until it sank again into a hole secreted under a worn saddle. Most nights they would sense Walker's approach and one of their number would ring out with a "Fine evening, sir, think we'll have rain" to alert the others to an officer's presence. The storytelling would ebb to silence. Walker would exchange a greeting and before the awkwardness seeped into his bones he would retreat to the officers' tent to engage in their formal exercises of banter. As he would depart, the familiar cadence of their storytelling would flow and the easy laughter of their world would once again punch the night air.

This night he had emerged later than usual from the colonel's tent and the rowdiness told him his men were deep into their cups. The fence posts burned bright and reduced the world outside their circle to sheets of black that no eye could pierce. Blinded by drink and flames, Walker hung outside the ring of light and took a seat on the root of a towering maple, draping a gray blanket across his shoulders to keep off the dew. He eavesdropped, trying to comprehend the men who followed him without pause into the devil's breath of cannon, and yet, would begrudge him a seat close to the fire's warmth or a sip of whiskey. He knew the task to understand the mysteries of the troop was a fool's errand. The bond they shared could not be fathomed. He had seen other officers try to seep into the fold, try to shed their skins and be baptized into the ranks, but they always spiraled from leader to object of ridicule. The men are an eternal mystery to those with rank, and maybe that is for the best.

From his solitary in the darkness, he studied them as they drew on pipes and spit chaw. He observed the leathery faces, the crows' feet furrowing back from blank eyes that eternally searched the horizon. The fire's glow at times masked the truth with tricks of light and he imagined he saw flashes of the boys they had been, the illusions evoking in him dim memories of the heady days after Chancellorsville. The talk then was only of going north. Buck privates would crow of how they were going to ride down Pennsylvania Avenue and smack Abe and tell him to hold the reins of their horses while they took a piss off his White House steps. All faded now, the boasting drowned in the ceaseless torrent of their brothers' blood. All they ever talked of now was fleeing south, of going home. They chatted of simple things, of sleeping for a week under the roofs of their shacks; eating roasted rabbit and chicken 'til they burst; drinking whiskey by the jugful; and always hunting and fishing the day long. They studied the letters from home like monks searching ancient texts for the hints of revelation until the paper feathered and tore and melted in their hands, and then complained that their women did nothing but squawk about the harvest, the chores needing tending. Walker knew the war was lost from the melancholy of his men.

But on nights when the war ceased its churning, they returned to their ritual, voting a different storyteller to conjure up the past. The elected would don a captured Union general's field jacket with its gaudy epaulets of gold braid and wear atop his head the great black stovepipe hat of a fallen Pennsylvanian. Billie was the elect this night and he leaned against the stack of fence posts that was stacked to provide a stage of sorts. He looked like some great Tecumseh adorned in a jester's costume. Big Billie was that affable breed, a giant of a man but an eternal boy that harbored no grudge against man or the Almighty for being born. He rambled on in that easygoing yapping way that the amiable share with the world, spinning his yarn of home.

"Nah, nah, we called him Stinky, but his given name were Wyatt, if I recall. Stinky didn't have all that's supposed to be given in a man's head; crazy as a shithouse rat but he were cagey as a calico cat too. All his kin took the long way home in the cholera o' '32. The only kin he had left was his mama's sister in Chattanooga. She sent a letter to Sheriff Dunning and told for him to pack that orphan up and ship him to her. Yep, but Sheriff Dunce-cap, of course we all know that crooked goat couldn't find his ass with both hands at noon on Sunday, he told that boy what he was aiming to do. He claimed later he told Stinky so as to give him time to say his thank-yous and goodbyes to the folks who'd give that orphan charity aft' his kin took the dirt nap.

"Well, Stinky, he hated that god-awful great aunt, and you can't give a rat an out 'cause sure as shit he'll take it. He'd already spent one August in Chattanooga with that shrew stuck in short pants and he forever claimed that's what caused his alergees to church'n. So Stinky weren't about to have none of that crud for the rest of his days. He said 'thank you, dumbshit sheriff, I am off to say my goodbyes' and he up and tailed it to the one place ain't nobody gonna find a boy if'n that boy is try'n to get lost, Miller's bog. That crazy squirrel spent the next twenty year in that godforsaken swamp. And it were in Miller's bog that Stinky learned to catch the biggest catfish you ever seen, but to accomplish his feat of fish'n he had to fish as naked as the day he fell out into this world."

"Aww, go on, Billie, how you know Stinky fished naked and all this?"

"Miles, it's my darn night for the tell'n. We voted wit' all democracy and I could get to tell'n it, boys, if'n Miles'd shut his piehole."

"Ah, get on with it."

"All righty, then. I apologize for the heckler in the theatre tonight, folks, tickets were sold to the public and jackasses can pay for tickets same as any t'other. Anyways, me and Augie was boys work'n a bow and arrow out back of Angus's when Stinky come out the woods with a sack o' catfish. It were so fresh it like it'd jumped out the swamp and ran to us. Angus gave him his coppers and let Stinky take on some work cutt'n some dovetails. It give Stinky an 'cuse to stay for supper. Angus knew Stinky wouldn't take no more charity.

"That night after supper Augie and me swiped a jug of Angus's whiskey and got Stinky, well, stinky drunk. We told him that we'd rob him another jug if he told us about how he caught them catfish."

"If Stinky were drunk when he told it, how'd you know it were true?"

"Holy grits and shits. Once again, if a certain fool shut his piehole he'd realize that's what I fix'n to tell. My story's called the secrets of Stinky. I'll tell you what. I'll do it t'other night when I'm not stymied by a heckler from the back pew. And I darn certify that everything I'm tell'n can be vouchsafed by Sergeant Augie."

"C'mon Miles, you need to shut up or you're sleep'n with the horses," one of the circle yelled. Miles sensed the threats could go from jovial to a smacking party in a fly's life and he shrank into his blanket.

"The secrets of Stinky shall commence ag'n since the agitator has been relegated to his rightful place in shutupsville. Stinky fished naked, and I'm telling ya'll how it come about, but you gotta swear me an oath. What I say ain't to go to no one outside this here circle when we get home or I warn ya'll there won't be no catfish left in no time. Swear?"

Hurrahs went up from the circle signaling their consent.

"All right. Stinky were no more than thirteen runn'n in that bog. He said he was hav'n little luck catch'n fish and were about to starve hisself to death when one day he slipped on a mossy rock and dropped his fish'n pole in the water. And, wouldn't you know it? Right then a big old catfish come swimm'n along and snatch that nightcrawler sitt'n on his last good hook. The fish took t'bait and the whole dang pole down a hole in them rocks. Stinky said he was fit to be tied he was so hungry.

"He sat on the rocks and about forsake his life of freedom when out in the middle of that bog river, he spied two inch of his pole poke straight up out t'water and set there like a tombstone. He took off his pants and jumped in and swam out to the middle and tried pull'n on it but float'n there he couldn't get enough to budge that ol' fish. Said that catfish had buried itself in a hole at the bottom and set itself like a pig in a pen gnawing away on that nightcrawler. He was float'n there like a log when he looked to the heavens and told hisself, 'Ah, the hell with it.' He dove in and followed that line to the bottom; said his ears were about to blow when he reach'd in that hole and tried pull'n his good hook out that fish's mouth. I shit you not Stinky put his hand in that mouth up to his elbow. He said it were the meanest catfish he'd ever wrastled with. He said he were matched against Goliath hisself at the bottom of that there bog river and do you know what that whiskered devil-fish did next?"

A voice from the circle cried out, "No."

Billie cried out in response, "Of course not, fool, cause I ain't told you yet," and the circle erupted in guffaws of laughter until boys shushed each other.

"That fish clamped down its jaws on Stinky's arm. Stinky said to hisself, 'this is it, fool, the Almighty punish'n you for not go'n to Sunday school in Chattanooga.' But you know Stinky, he never one to shirk from a fight so he pounded that fish with his free hand but it weren't lett'n go. His breath about done he says he started thinking that he's about probably feel'n like a catfish hisself that done grabbed a hook. He said that's what give him the idea. He think'n he done lost him a hundred cat-fish after they'd grabbed the hook, so why not him gett'n away? Hell be damned if Stinky didn't start fight'n like a catfish. He starts pull'n for the top with his good hand and kick'n for all he's worth to git to the light. Lo and behold that catfish starts rising wit' him; its big ol' sucker still stuck to his arm. He broke the top gasp'n for air and damn if he didn't see that catfish ain't still suck'n on his elbow. He drags it to the blessed shore and once it bellies up on them dry rocks Stinky said it flop twice and its mouth open; and out his arm pop like a cork out a whiskey bottle, a bit red and sorely scraped but none the worse for it.

"Stinky's sitt'n there suck'n for wind and he look and god-damn if it ain't the biggest catfish bottom monster he'd ever seen sitt'n thar next to him. Got the fire started and couldn't eat but half of it. After supper, he's sitt'n there stuffed like a pilgrim at Bethsaida and starts to think'n the Almighty must have spared him for some purpose of biblical prophecy. He figured his ordeal were heaven's means to teach Stinky to lead his fella fallen man to a greater good. So he sat there by the waters and waited, and waited, but not a goddamn thing hap-pen in the follow'n three days, so Stinky went back to pole fish-ing. But ya'll know that one way to certify you ain't gonna catch noth'n but a cold is to mix fish'n with an empty belly. Stinky said the second time he stick his arm in a catfish at the bottom of that there bog he was more scared than a girl on her wedding night, 'cept of course for your sweetheart, Taylor."

"Ah, go on, fool, and leave me out of it."

"Anyways, Stinky pulls that second one up and he said he were like Christian Columbus discover'n the new world, a world wit' the easiest fish'n cause you the one that done git caught by the fish. And that's how Stinky learned to fish naked."

"I don't believe word one of that catfish horseshit!"

"That's 'cause noth'n but horseshit ever pumps out of your piehole, Miles."

Hutch asked, "Billie, what happened to Ole Stinky? I hear he took himself deep into Miller's bog and didn't never come out ag'n."

"That's right, he most certainly never did come out."

"You think he hook'd him some catfish that didn't let go?" Hutch asked.

"I reckon not. Augie, should we tell 'em?"

Augie looked about the circle of fire. "I reckon it okay."

"All right, then, ya'll know the tales of Miller's bog. Well nobody knew that bog better than Stinky 'cept a course that top-hatted devil hisself, Old Man Briggins. When me and Augie got him right drunk that night Stinky told us he had found him a cave that was chock-full of Briggins's treasure and he was aiming to rob it. Stinky weren't taking on no partners neither, no matter how much me and Augie begged him. When we asked him how he discovered the treasure Stinky told us one of Briggins's witches told him. He liv'n in that shack by the ford and still catfish'n his secret way, when one evening with the sun about to drop he pull him up a catfish for supper. He were stand'n there naked as a jaybird on some rocks when an old slave from the Briggins's plantation came down a doe path.

Stinky said she jest about floated out them trees. He feared first it was a haint come to chew on his soul. Stinky said she had on a white . . . Augie?"

"Toga."

"Yeah, a toga, like a bedsheet dress. Stinky says she tall like a reed and swayed like one do in a soft breeze. It were the oldest woman he'd ever seen; her faced stitched up with a quilt of scars on the cheeks—the devil's drawings. Stinky said she raised one long bony finger at Stinky and hooked it to signal him to follo' her back in them woods; said she had nails a bayonet blade long on t'left hand. Stinky said he nearly wet hisself. He stood there froze; didn't move 'til that witch smiled and pointed at that catfish and curled that finger again at Stinky. That plumb nut forgot he weren't wear'n pants and threw that fish o'er his shoulder and follo'd Saul's hag into them trees. Stinky says that old witch had a hut you had to climb halfway up the biggest Cyprus tree he ever seen to get to it; and she went and fired up the best catfish stew he'd ever taste. She mixed about anything in them woods a man can eat in her cauldron. Stinky says it delicious; he sat there a good part of the night squatt'n naked on her treehouse floor stuff'n himself wit' her stew. He says that ol' witch told her name were Clarabelle. I knows you all ain't heard that name for the first time t'night. Every one of our mamas kept us from sneak'n out after bedtime with ghost stories of that sorceress lurk'n in the bog snatch'n naughty boys. Anyhow, Stinky woke in the morn' and she were gone, so he took back to catfish'n but she had warned him the night 'fore not to run no deeper in that bog; she foretold they were runn'n his scent."

"Who Billie?"

"Whatever runs in them caves, you all know the stories of Old Man Briggins. He used to take his slave witches into them caverns and have'n 'em dance to the sun of the morning's fiddl'n. Stinky for years after give Clarabelle a fair share of his catfish until one day he asked for her to tell him the cave Briggins's treasure were hid. Clarabelle wouldn't tell him, told him straight the price of find'n that coin be his soul. Stinky told us he threatened Clarabelle that she weren't feast'n on no more of his catfish 'til she tell. Me and Augie told Stinky he were crazy to wrastle with that witch; the son of the morn whispers in her ear; he were ask'n for it. Stinky said he were tired of being poor his whole life and he aimed to have that treasure. He gone the morn after we got him drunk. Stinky was aim'n to fetch that treasure and he ain't never been heard from ag'n in the county."

Walker sat there alone in the darkness ruing the upending of his entire world. Molly was alone at Sommersville with no family but Missy Jay and a young hand named Sally. Jessup had died and the rest of the hands were moved on by the war. Three years earlier on a winter leave he had married Molly and had returned to the front without respite. After the folly of the invasion at Antietam, his father predicted with a bookkeeper's accuracy the outcome of the war, even the year it would end. He took his mother and what fortune was not nailed down to the plantation and sailed for England. Molly refused to leave.

In London, his father had invested in a shipping company and had tripled the family fortune, running munitions to Havana and to Boston to feed the insatiable Union war machine. He could feel the last letter from his father folded over in the breast pocket of his tunic, his father's perfect script forecasting the destruction of the Confederacy in the bland language of commerce: trade, manufacturing deficiencies, manpower shortages, and the brilliance of Anaconda. He even examined the concentration of power in Washington, predicting that there would be no negotiated peace, remarking that Lincoln had become a dictator more bloodthirsty than pharaoh, and that the man simply had no business sense. The letter laid out detailed instructions for John to sneak his way to the Union lines and upon his surrender to immediately request to be rendered to the custody of a Major General Bradbury of Massachusetts. The general was the brother of one of his father's Boston shipping partners and the two dined together on Thursdays in London. The contract had been agreed upon over dinner for a thousand British pound sterling. Bradbury would commute his sentence and secure him a berth on the next cutter out of Boston bound for Liverpool. If he would not do it for himself, his father pleaded for him to do it for Molly, who, out of misplaced loyalty, stayed in the path of the barbarian.

He gazed at the men settling into their blankets for the night and looked at the fire pit. It blazed bluish gold, feasting on a score of fresh fence posts. The fire's golden hue reminded him of the first time he was taken by Molly's beauty. It was on Christmas Eve when she had come of age and was attending her first ball at Sommersville. He remembered her standing alone by the fireplace; she stood mesmerized by the massive heads of the pair of lions forged into the iron of the fire dogs. Her amber face glowing in answer to the lions' magnificent fangs. He dreamed that if he could go back in time to that night and hear its music and laughter, if he could flirt again with Molly before the lions, this world of blood and loss would fade away. The universe would spin once more in his orbit and the approaching war would still be the stuff of a boy's dreams and not this waking nightmare.

Yet, despite the blood of the fallen and the cracking of his gentrified world, he knew if he had the power to shape time, he would change nothing. He would resurrect that moment in the magnificent past and sacrifice love, life, and fortune to be born again, to have another chance to lead the gallant boys in those lost days when they were heroic. His mind flooded with the vivid images of the early battles, the visions of poor boys striding about the parapets with the gait of princes, lording on steeds over the dead of their enemy that had fallen to the charge of horse.

He was lost in reverie, back on the hill at Chancellorsville, when aged sap buried in an old fence post popped and sent a brilliant burst of sparks into night. The shower of light pulled him from his dreams and reverted his vision to the reality of the broken souls before him crawling drunk into their filthy blankets about a smoldering pit of rotted fence posts. He lowered his gaze and drew the blanket around his shoulders to stifle the chill of hate coursing through him. He spat and cursed them as cowards, his mind lashing out with vile condemnations that they were nothing but shades of the warriors he had shown them they could be; foul scum, weak of nature, and filled with nothing save the base instinct to scuttle home and hide in their horrid shacks.

Walker rose from the maple exhausted, the damp blanket hanging like a yoke about his neck. He laid down in his tent and fell into a fitful sleep. As he thrashed, his nightmares filled with phantasmagorias of the boys who had been slaughtered in the war. They appeared in his visions as he remembered them in the glory days, as gallant young men. They assembled this night to magistrate upon the curses he had laid against their brothers. The apparitions bore witness and cried out from the grave that he was unrighteous and judged the slave masters as the damned; it was they who had lifted the veil of the apocalypse. The gallant boys molted into the shapes of grotesque fiends without eyes and they lurched and pitched about holding their fevered snouts low to the earth. He ran and the ravening caught his scent and hunted him down the labyrinth of the bog's wooded paths, and he was the boy again, running upon awkward legs of lead, straining to reach sanctuary, to plunge into the warm waters of the great cave and swim under the ledge to the far shore in the faith that the dead could not cross beyond the pool of dark waters.

Walker and Augie entered the colonel's command post located in a red schoolhouse twelve miles south of Appomattox Court House. As they entered Augie shuddered when he eyed the colonel squatting in his chair. His tunic lay open and the once white undershirt with its mother o' pearl buttons flowed yellowed and frayed over the soft fat of his belly. The corpulence pushed the fabric in streams around his suspenders and cascaded it over the top of his trousers. Augie thought he looked like a tallow candle that'd been rolled ag'n for its second burn'n. It were only a little past noon but the colonel's fine whiskey was already flowing into his gullet without being tasted. He was trying to add fuel to the lamp, but it was too late, Augie could see the flame in his eyes was out. Major Barnes was in no better shape. He never drank and his tunic still lay starched and regulation straight on his ramrod frame, but it was a funeral sheath about him. Augie saw his nails were bitten to the nub and a quick search of his eyes showed they flittered like a critter's does in the corner of a barn watching the pitchfork rise up. He weighed these fools had no more than a slippery handle on reality and he fretted what new madness this parlay would call forth into the world.

"Major Walker, I need to speak with you and Major Barnes about some important matters, a strategy of top secret boldness, ask your sergeant to give us a minute."

In four years, the colonel had never asked Augie to leave Walker's side and the stench of men plotting stung his nostrils like the trailing of a scat burn. He hung close to an open window and tried to listen as best he could. "John, I have counseled hard with the general and, well, he agrees, you see, it's my leg, Doc McKenna thinks it's gangrene. I keep the boot on to keep it from swelling, but, well, I spoke with the general and he says that I cannot in good conscience lead this fine regiment in this dire condition. The general spoke of you personally with affection. With much regret but with the knowledge that the regiment will be led by a well-bred and steady officer, well, with a touch of sadness and joy, I say congratulations, John, or I should say congratulations, *Colonel* Walker."

Walker emerged from the schoolhouse and he and Augie walked to their mounts. Augie said, "Congrats, Colonel."

"Augie, don't be harsh. It's that leg of his."

"Did he mention the general's wife's his sister?"

"We have orders. We are to find a way behind the east flank of them blue bellies. The high command strategy is a bold double stroke, a Cannae, to turn the Union flanks on both ends. We need a great victory to gain leverage in peace negotiations."

"Colonel, that's fine think'n. I'm for bold strokes and all. They's good stuff. You and I been riding these past months and both know there ain't no flank. Heck, the line run on so we'll need boats in the Chesapeake to circle 'round."

"Pick twenty, we ride tonight. We have got to find a way or the war is lost."

"Major, I mean Colonel, there ain't no flank."

"Twenty men, Sergeant, the best we have."

"Tak'n elephants?"

"Augie, please."

As the day melted into evening a score of riders saddled up for the night run. Walker trotted to the front, and he felt the eyes of the men upon him, a silent insubordination as if after four long years he was betraying his unspoken oath not to send them to their deaths on a fool's errand. He motioned silently with his hand and like condemned men they cantered into the woods trailing behind Walker as he led them north.

By midnight, the full moon lay low in the sky. The two sent ahead to scout had found an old logging road heading northeast that was wide enough to carry caissons. In excited whispers, they talked of it running in thick woods near high grounds and about ten miles up it forked with one lane hitting west and the other straight north. They moved up the road and when they reached the fork Walker half-believed they had found a secret blue vein running to the heart of the enemy. He had a waking dream of a second Chancellorsville; of the early days, the great sport it had been to ramble behind the Yankee lines and surprise rear units. He caught himself knowing too well the Yankees had learned hard lessons in the war and that each blue was now as hard as his own boys. He also knew there was more Union cavalry running in the Virginia woods this night than there had been at Manassas. They were legion.

They reached the crossroads and Walker signaled the men to take the lane heading north for a mile or two to see if it was clear of Yankees. He would leave the crucial road heading west for later canvassing in the night. He changed the scouts and sent Billie and Augie ahead. A mile later they returned and reported wagons advancing. Walker's heart sank knowing that if supply wagons were using the road, the Yankees knew of it and in a day, maybe hours, it would be swarming with mounted patrols and studded with sentry posts. He grimaced at the foolishness of his daydreaming. It was a fool's errand. There was no road, no trail, not even a hunter's path within a hundred miles that didn't lay thick with blues like the frogs that had plagued Egypt. Walker looked at Augie and the silent covenant rang out in the night.

Walker ordered them into the trees and Augie nodded, telling the men to stay quiet and muzzle the horses. The wagons approached and the sound of axles turning slowly wandered

toward them from up the road. The moon had risen to the tops
of the trees and the square shape of the lead wagon emerged
with shadowy clarity, the orbs of the drivers' heads silhouetted
in the moonlight, jostling back and forth as the furrows of the
road dictated. The first wagon drew so close Walker could hear
the harsh whispers of the drivers.

"Hell you say. We lost and need to hold up or we run into
horse rebs. We dead reckoning south; that the Big Dipper."

"Dipper my ass. You Ohio, what you know about navigate by
stars? That local boy said there's a west road up ahead goes
straight to the courthouse."

"We musta passed it."

"These wagons need to be at that courthouse by morning or
Captain have my ass; west road up ahead I knows it."

"Ain't seen the escort in a hour; god knows where they run
off."

"They close; any shoot'n start they be here in shake of a
baby's rattle."

Walker was tempted to assault and take the wagons south but
the Yankees had talked of an escort. He weighed his options and
had decided not to risk a running battle this far north when
Miles burst from the trees and emptied his pistol at the lead
wagon. The follow-on wagons scrambled to turn and Walker
called for an assault, the rebels pouring out of the trees with
wild yells and pistol fire. The Yankees on the two lead wagons
popped from the seats like hedge birds and dashed into the
woods. The two rear wagons were far enough back to round-
about and Walker could hear their axles spinning as they jostled
upon the ruts back north. A single Yankee lay dead in the road
and the three others could be heard breaking brush and yelling
absurdities as they ran east through the thick woods.

Walker hissed at Miles, "Damned fool."

Miles scoffed and said, "It a raid'n party we on, ain't it?"

Augie dropped from his horse and mounted the first wagon and told Billie to mount the second. They tied their horses to the rear of each and began to drive the wagon teams south. Augie ran his wagon hard until he reached the crossroads and reined up. The horses were well trained and the team stopped on a drumbeat in the middle of the fork. They stood like statues sweating in their traces. Augie stood on the toe board with the tugs dangling in his left hand and stared with a fixed gaze down the west road.

Walker reached him and asked Augie what the problem was.

Augie held up the palm of his right hand to signal quiet as he continued to stare west. The moon was conjuring up dark shapes floating in the distance. The shapes swayed back and forth and Augie stared mesmerized by the phantasms until the sound reached him. It vibrated in the crushed stone beneath him and it strummed along the thin trees lining the road. The branches in the road's canopy echoed the awful rumble like a thousand tuning forks. He processed the sounds and his mind pulsed with the vision of the hundred horsemen charging down the road.

He sat and lashed at the team and Walker yelled, "Augie, we will hold them for a spell, head for the river crossing." Augie and Billie slashed the reins again and the wagons jolted and bounced down the road.

Walker tried to yell for the troop to form up but the air was shattered by fifty deafening rounds of awesome velocity. Hutch's head expanded with a sickening thump and he lay back and still on the rump of his steed with his boots still in the stirrups, the contents of his skull running off the dock of his mount. Walker knew the Yankees had the new Spencer carbines. He saw his men start to rein left and he commanded "hold" but Miles burst out with, "the hell with that, boys, I'm gitt'n out o' here." Miles spurred his horse and galloped down the road. The fever ran the line and in an instant Walker sat his saddle alone at the crossroads. He felt a wind from the west on his cheeks as if the hundred were squeezing the very atmosphere toward him. For the first time in the war a gasp caught in his throat. He reined his horse and sped south, the carbine bolts shearing the sheets of night sky about him.

Walker cursed bloody oaths, vowing before his death to cut Miles down with his sword the moment he laid eyes upon him. His wrath rose and he spurred to gain speed but the horse's right foreleg buckled and the steed's legs splayed. The momentum carried the horse skidding along on its belly over the crushed stone of the road until rider and stallion dropped four feet off the side of the road into a stone culvert. Walker lay in a half foot of stagnant water with his right leg trapped beneath the horse. He expected the horse to buck and fight to gain its hooves but it lay still with a strange calm. He ran his hand along the crest and it steamed hot and slick from ear to withers. He figured the animal must have been hit at the crossroads; shot through the big pumper in its neck and its lifeblood had run out at the gallop. He lay like a condemned man on the blocks of stone in the culvert and listened to the Yankees rumble around the turn in the crossroads. He whispered to himself, "So be it."

He gazed up the road and saw the moon behind the rows of trees that had not yet gained their leaves. He steeled himself to his fate and drew his pistol, shaking the water from it. The hundred hammered south down the road, the horsemen fracturing in and out of the moon's leaden light as it flowed out from between the trees. The shadows and hooves clattered above him without recognition, and like some passenger train hurtling through the dilapidated depot of an abandoned town, the horsemen vanished down the road as they had appeared, as swaying phantasms pouring away through a funnel of darkness.

Walker pushed the horse with his arms and slid his leg from beneath the dead beast. The leg emerged, and he gritted his teeth and nearly screamed, the pain in his knee aching out once it was freed from the weight of the horse. He sat there in the water and placed his hands on the animal and thought to say a word, but the horse had no name. It was the ninth shot out from under him since Pegasus and he had stopped naming them two years ago. He sat in the woods the entire next day listening from the trees to the incessant rumbling of wagons and caissons ferrying the Union war machine south. He dared not move until the pain in his leg waned. By the next morning the agony subsided, and he was able to splinter the leg with tree branches and synch the brace tight with leather strips cut from his saddle. He chopped a fallen tree branch smooth with his sword and used it for a walking stick. He found a wooded trail and began his tramping back to camp.

Down the road on the night of the fool's errand, Miles raced past Augie and Billie and yelled out that Walker was dead. He told them to drop the wagons and mount up and run for it because there were so many coming he'd be damned if Little Phil himself weren't leading them. Augie and Billie dismounted and ran to their horses tied to the rear of the wagons. They could hear the killing herd coming down the road and Augie mounted and started to rein when he saw Billie fiddling about in the back of the wagon. He yelled, "Billie, jump out that wagon. They loaded for bear. C'mon."

Billie hoisted a strongbox on to his pommel and climbed into the saddle. He sat his horse and was trying to balance it with his knees when the metal and wood of the wagon near him rang and splintered in a dozen places sending sparks and shards of wood peeling aflame into the night. They spurred their horses and about a mile down the road Augie knew the Yankees were gaining and that it were all but done. He saw a lighter patch of earth up ahead in the moonlight and he guessed it might be a trail running into the wooded heights to the west. He gambled and yelled to Billie to follow and they bolted off the side of the road at a full gallop. When he hit that lighter patch, Augie didn't know if it was going to be some terrible mistake or deliverance until his mount's hooves churned on the patch of light and he thanked Providence it were a trail. They bolted into the woods and the trees about them splintered and popped with the sizzle of carbine rounds.

The trail led to smaller trails that split in a half-dozen directions up the hills and they chose one without reason and climbed hard. They could hear the sounds of gathering horsemen in the roadway below and the Yankees' peppering of the woods with random shots. Augie knew it would have to be one crazy sumbitch Yankee to ride up a blind trail in the dark following rebels and he thought he heard, "All right, you first." He heard grunted orders and the Yankees began again their rumble down the road, chasing Miles and the rest of the fleeing rebels. He whistled softly and believed for the first time they had shook them.

They climbed for half an hour on a path that crested to the top and dropped from their horses into an old hunter's clearing. Augie squatted by the trunk of a tree aside the trail and listened for the sounds of horsemen. The only sounds were the muffled reports of rifles a good distance off in the lowlands.

Augie turned and swore at Billie, "Boy, that were about the dumbest thing you ever done, there were a hundred of 'em."

But he got no answer. "Billie, where you at?"

"By the big rock."

Augie could see Billie had his back propped against a boulder that was adorned with a great arched top. The feldspar in the granite gave the rock a copper sheen in the moonlight. It had been dragged to its resting place by a glacier a hundred millennia ago and had slowly risen with the heights as the innards of the world warred against itself.

"What is it?"

"My back."

Augie said, "Let's see what you got go'n." He rolled Billie on his side and struck a lucifer against the flat of the rock. It flared bright revealing the tunic was soaked with dark blood. He trussed up Billie's tunic to try and plug the hole with his handkerchief when he felt a second hole bleeding an inch away, both shots had cut through his liver. Billie sensed the tremor in Augie's hand.

"Done fish'n?"

"What you do'n grabb'n that box?"

"I hear Walker dead. I'm think'n this here war dead. I figur'd it were a payroll; raise them horses like you always say'n. What color is it?"

"Stripe of a swamp moccasin."

"Figured, felt more thick than slick. Go'n open it."

"Billie, I don't give a goddamn about that box."

"Go on, boy, the curiosity kill'n me."

Augie dragged the strongbox over and wedged his bayonet behind the clasp. He put the heel of his boot to the box and pulled hard at the latch and it sprang with a loud clang.

"Didn't say ring no church bell."

Augie flipped the lid open and struck another lucifer. He cupped it in his hand to shield the breeze and the gold coins shimmered like a drawing in a little boy's book of pirate tales.

Billie cried out, "Holy grits and shits! It a dang regiment payroll. Briggins's treasure, Augie, always said we'd find it."

Augie lay there holding Billie. He tried to staunch the wounds but the blood soaked through the handkerchief and the vile warmth of his best friend streamed in rivulets over his forearm.

After a few minutes Billie said, "Gett'n cold, ain't long now. Same spot as Coop, he bled out no time t'all."

"Billie, why'd you . . ."

"Ah, stop nagg'n. Just get my share of the treasure to Bea and teach Willie the secret horse stuff."

"All right."

"I want you to promise me someth'n."

"I promise."

"How can you promise I ain't told it yet?"

"Treasure for Bea, teach Willie."

"Nah, that ain't the promise, you do that anyhow. This war done and it too damn late to be dying. Take my bayonet and put it thro' your leg. You know how it's done. Twist the blade and make it look like a ball shot. Promise me."

"Billie . . ."

"Swear to it."

"I swear."

The next morning Augie began stoking a fire and for the next ten hours he seeded it with dry pinecones and cedar. The cedar was from the fallings of a tree he figured was born two hundred years before the Revolution. As the sun spread out in the west he squatted by the fire and took out Billie's bayonet. He rolled its long thin rapier over in the palm of his hand before carefully placing the tip between two rocks and sliding the full length of its blade into the blue flames. After three hours, he wrapped his shirt around his hand and used it as a furnace mitt to grab the handle of the bayonet. He drew the blade forth from the shimmering rocks and saw the fire had sewed its nature into the fabric of the iron. He reached for the round rock by his side and began to beat the blade with heavy blows, using a long flat slab of granite as his anvil, not giving one damn if the Yankees heard him. The ancient sound of the blacksmith shop rang in the woods as the steel gave grudgingly to the altering of its first

173

shape. The heavy strikes of the bluestone orb blunted the blade's edges and mooned its tip. He put the blade back into the stones, and the flames licked out again to embrace without prejudice the fabric of its twisted form.

He looked across the flames at his best friend and he bartered with his conscience. After a few hours, he wrapped his shirt around his hand again and picked the knife up by the handle, staring at the fierce crimson running the blade's warped length. He placed the bayonet back in the fire. The day was ending. The shadows of the pines surrounding him grew deep and sanctioned the fire's glow to echo off his bare skin. He rocked back and forth on his bottom, holding his knees to his chest and wept for his friend. He stopped rocking and saw that the crimson had swallowed the blade to the very crossbar of the hilt.

He took off his pants and muttered to himself, "It gotta be deep or ain't no one gonna believe in your tale." He put a stick in his mouth and tied his belt around his upper thigh and waited until the numbness in his toes became unbearable. He grabbed the handle of the bayonet and raised the long blade up with both hands like the sacrifice on Moriah. He held the hot steel but his instincts revolted and he relented to his nature, tossing the blade away into the night. It skittered along the rocky soil until it came to rest, the crimson pulsing like some crucifix beacon on a dark sea warning mariners of dangerous shoals.

He stared at the cross and cursed his foolishness for not heeding the auguries that Angus had prophesized to him as a child before the blacksmith's forge. On winter nights as a boy, he would sleep on old blankets in front of the forge, so he could nestle in among Angus's three runaway slave-tracking blood-hounds. The shack of his home had once been a blacksmith shop and a giant stoker that opened on two sides separated the kitchen from the sleeping spaces. It still burned hot and its thick red bricks arched over the fire gave the dwelling its structure. Angus would come home deep in his cups and on many a night he would fetch a jug and pull a stool from the kitchen up close to the fire where Augie slept and shake the sleep from him.

Angus would sit there sipping his rotgut and Augie would listen to his father's coarse voice spewing out sermons of resentment amidst the snapping of the soft pine in the hearth. His tongue loosened by drink, Angus would rattle off the names of the slave masters and tell of the crimes that had given birth to their fortunes: "Sumbitch Briggins, his granddaddy pack'd his ships three times their hold, stack'n 'em like chopp'n wood one upon t'other know'n he'd lose half his cargo. The captains'd toss 'em overboard without so much as an amen, ships making a wake of bloated dead and sharks all the way to Hispaniola where those without the fortune to be thrown to the sea died of hunger cutt'n his cane.

"And Walker, what a piece a shit his granddaddy be. Pappy noth'n but an indentured servant born of a whore come crawl'n out Whitechapel. He was in Ol' Virginia when he got his freedom and started cutt'n his first rows of tobacco. I turned down Old Man Briggins to oversee Walker's fields. When I told Briggins he sat me down and told me I'd regret it. Them Walkers was hard cheats, and their granddaddy, Pappy, he were the worst of 'em all. Pappy Walker had him a partner in Old Virginia, a Scotsman that first come over in a coffin ship, named McCrary. The two planted fifty acres of fine tobacco they'd killed and cheated the savages for, but they had a fall'n out, so McCrary bought Walker out with his last cent and took the fields. Walker went the next county over and tried again but couldn't do it alone. McCrary's fields grew a bounty and his profits done took off, but Walker's fields was fallow, giving up noth'n but a tangy tasting weed. Walker couldn't beat him square so he harvested horn

worms and sowed McCrary's fields with 'em 'til there was nothing left for the merchants to trade for 'cept Walker's filthy leaf.
McCrary never found out; put a hog musket to his mouth
think'n it were Providence that done took a crap on him for his
sins."

Angus would take his last drink and stretch his back and
shoulders as if he were trying to free himself from a yoke of
weighted stones and Augie knew the sermon would turn to
salvation. Angus would stare with penitent eyes at the forge's
flames dancing off the copper pots that hung about the kitchen
and tell of the evil of his work, the torments he inflicted on the
hands. He would whisper, "My daddy told me to get close to
'em; work hard for them that's got coin and you'll not go
hungry; carry the whip for 'em, there's money to be earned
from 'em. My daddy was a fool, and his daddy a bigger fool.
You end up tell'n yourself you do it for family, you need coin to
feed your own, nobody gonna feed yours but you, but what
good that gonna be in the next world? I'll be kneeling in the
snow 'fore the gates on Judgment Day, and when I do my
beseeching the Lord know every goddamn deed I done in
Walker's fields. I'll plead it were my job but all the Almighty
will hear will be the hollers for mercy of 'em souls I tied to the
hitching post. Who be more damned, son? The fool that sins for
coin or the bastard that pay a fool to sin. You got to take your
blessed gifts, son, and free yourself, the only thing to strive for
in this world is to earn enough coin so you be behold'n to no
man, and then your soul be your own to tend."

Augie looked up from the forge of his memories and stared
at his best friend wrapped in the shroud of an old army blanket
and said, "I can't do it, Billy. I got to tend to gett'n the rest of
them boys home."

Augie spent the following day burying Billie in the earth, using his hands and knife to scrape away a shallow grave. He placed the strongbox under Billie's arm and covered him in the heaviest stones he could carry so animals wouldn't dig him up. Before he laid the soil over him, he did his best to mimic the words of the militia chaplains he'd heard a thousand times on a hundred different days, but all he could recall were remnants and his prayers rang hollow on the mountain. It wasn't until he whispered, "You keep that safe for me, you old pirate," that he was able to bury his friend.

In the morning, he tethered Billie's horse to his own and rode to the southern tip of the highlands. He crawled out on a ledge overhanging the valley and took out his spyglass. He spotted a lone man about a half mile off shuffling across a furrowed farm field with a walking stick under his arm. He thought at first it was a farmer and marveled that a soul could sow amidst these killing fields, but he twisted the glass and saw that it was Walker. He saw the cavalry hat and the sword, the lion's head at the end of the hilt scattering the morning's sun in a dazzling prism.

As Walker crossed the farm field, Augie saw thirty horsemen rise up in his path from the trees to the west. The horsemen emerged as if they had been waiting in those shadows their entire lives to carry out Walker's execution. The horsemen approached in a shallow arc of mounts that soon blocked Walker's path. Walker did not waiver. He dropped his walking stick and drew his sword from his scabbard. He tossed the scabbard to the side and drew his pistol. Augie's impulse was to race to his horse, a habit these four long years, but then he said to himself, "What good would it do?" He surveyed the spectacle as it unfolded through his looking glass and muttered, "That man's no bullshit." He anticipated a volley of shots but the sergeant of the horsemen took off his hat and slowly walked his horse to Walker. After a brief parlay Walker holstered his pistol and awkwardly tried to return his sword to the scabbard until he remembered he had tossed the scabbard away into the field. He paused and slowly turned the sword and grabbed it by the blade. He handed it to the Yankee and the horseman took it by the hilt. Walker picked up his walking stick and limped away, vanishing into the tree line.

Augie saw the sergeant wave his trophy about his head and heard a cacophony of hoots from the horsemen rise in the air. Augie was trying to fathom what had happened but could not and judged it best to wait for night to navigate his way back through the Yankee lines.

The following day near evening, Augie straggled into camp, emerging from the woods covered in burrs and scratches from dodging Yankee patrols throughout the night and day. The old-timer that worked the kitchen wagon said, "God Almighty, we thought you were a goner, where Billie at?"

Augie shook his head.

The old-timer said, "Ain't that the sorriest luck."

Augie looked quizzically, and the old-timer said, "We quit day 'fore yesterday. Rider come this morning wit' a sheet of paper from Richmond with a scratch'n on it the war done. We showed our belly at Appomattox."

Before Augie could comprehend the war's end, he sighted three corpses hanging from the low branch of the maple. He approached and gazed at Miles, Caldwell, and Taylor dangling from gallows' ropes. Their faces were swollen and glazed with a sickly orange pallor. They looked like jack-o'-lanterns that had been carved by a madman, their eyes bulging and their tongues swollen and lolling out the sides of their mouths. Augie didn't believe his eyes until he smelled the scat and he realized all three had shit their pants after the drop.

The old-timer said, "Caught 'em three head'n to Sommers-ville. Yesterday morn they dragg'd 'em here in shackles. The high command said they was shirkers and condemned 'em. We thought Walker dead, so it were left to Major Barnes, but you know he ain't much on decid'n. They sat there. None of us eager to git it done. Walker, though, he come limp'n in to camp at sundown yesterday like Lazarus. Colonel didn't waste no time order'n them three strung up. I reckon one more day and them three home come summer."

"Where's that sumbitch at?"

"Sergeant?"

"It's Augie, goddammit, where's Walker?"

"His tent."

Augie strode to the tent and threw back the flap without an-nouncing himself. Walker was sitting at his field desk, his leg in a splint, writing a letter. Augie came to the desk and pointed at Walker and spat out, "You murdered them boys."

Walker looked up and stared at Augie, trying to size him. He slowly placed the quill on the table aside the parchment. He spoke slowly, measuring his words, "The order came down from high command, condemned. I had nothing to do with the judg-ment."

"There ain't no command no more; none of ya'll had the right to string them boys up."

"I was in command of this regiment when the execution order was rendered. What's the difference? That son-of-a-bitch needed killing, and the two who followed him got what he got, cowards, the lot of them."

"Cowards? They the same three follo'd your glory hunting ass up the hill at Chancellorsville."

"That's right, Augie. On that day, I showed them a soldier's honor but in the end they had no honor. They left me to die on that road. They ran like dogs from the Yankees."

"You sitt'n here. Why ain't your dead ass sitt'n in that crossroad?"

"I gave my word, a promise that I wouldn't throw my life away."

"Billie dead. What about the promise I give to his Bea? Tell me how you tried to stop them Yankees at the crossroads, Horatio? You ran too. I know 'cause them sumbitches caught us up and shot Billie down."

"Is that it? Is that what is causing this? My condolences for Billie. I considered him a friend."

"A what? Billie and I know you since we was knee-high and we never shared so much as a fish'n hook wit' you; always riding off in that bog with them snotnoses. Call'n Billie a friend, your kind ain't got no friends. We the same county but different as coons and coondogs. You sumbitches got loyalty to noth'n but coin."

Walker grabbed his crutch and with effort rose from his chair. He'd had enough. "My kind? What would your people be without us? A life of dropping hooks for catfish, coon hunting. We gave your lives meaning and purpose beyond your shacks. I saw you at Chancellorsville, you strode the earth like a king. I gave you that Sergeant Powell. We showed your kind how to fight for your rights, for freedom."

"Aww, stuff all that freedom shit. This war was noth'n other than to save ya'll's fancy-ass living. And ya ain't got noth'n to be high and mighty about. My kind? Yeah, it were my daddy that strung 'em to the whipp'n post, only so ya'll could hide behind your lace curtains play'n piana and pretend'n not to hear 'em screams for mercy. You think you better than us 'cause you held title? You may o' owned 'em, but you paid coin to my daddy to take the skin off them backs. Sure as shit, Walker, ya'll's hand was on that whip too."

Augie gathered himself and looked Walker slowly up and

down. "I know your kind better than you do. You indentured in Virginia, ya'll people come from noth'n but white slaves jest like all 'em hands in your fields. Duke kin, horse-shee-it, the way I hear it too Pappy's mama a rung or three lower on the highborn ladder, her nobility been a bit exaggerated."

Walker straightened himself the best he could and knew now this would end in blood. He glared at Augie and went to offer his challenge but thought of Billie and relented. "Augie, that is the last insult I will tolerate without raising this to a point of honor. We are going home. I will forget this because I believe Billie's death is bleeding this out of you. We will go and build our county, our homes again. Together. Stronger this time."

Augie sneered at him and said, "Point o' honor? You think I'm getting my ass shot at twenty paces after dodging Yankee lead all this time? There ain't no go'n home for you. Angus writ me, your daddy done hightailed it. I swear Angus had ya'll pegged from day one. I jest didn't want to believe it."

"I'm not my father."

"You ain't listen'n. That my county now. It chock-full of boys wit' torn limbs that were as stupid as me to go and fight for ya'll. The scarred gonna be looking for some fool to take it out on. I get back I'm tell'n Angus what you done. He'll see to it them three's kin know it and then they're gonna see to it your indentured ass swinging from a maple tree for murder."

"I was in command."

"The hell you say. I seen you in that field. Where your sword at, Colonel?"

Walker looked about but caught himself and eyed Augie.

"Them boys told you it were all done. Now, you clear out my county. For what we been through in this stupid ass war of yours I'm giving you three days to git, but you heed me, come sundown on the third day we com'n for you at Sommersville, to burn you out."

The Sommersville mansion had a chapel built on the ground floor. Missy Jay stood in front of the altar in the middle of the night. She listened for any sound of Molly but heard nothing stirring. Sally entered from the servant's entrance carrying a basket. Missy Jay went to the doors of the chapel and peered out through the door making sure Molly was not about in the great room. She closed the large chapel doors and bolted them shut from the inside.

Missy said. "You got the eye?"

The girl nodded.

"What do you see?" Missy pressed.

"I sees things that sometimes ain't happened yet, and then they do," the girl responded.

"Has Augie come to you too?"

"Yes, he say'n I should tell him if Master John been heard from," the girl answered.

"Why didn't you tell me he talk'n to you?" Missy snapped.

The girl got scared, and Missy Jay reached out and held her by the shoulders. "I didn't mean to snap at you, Sally. Gist tell me what Augie say he want."

The girl's face was filled with fright, but she answered, "Augie say this all done for Master John; I'm to tell him if'n he show up."

"Go over now and listen for anyone climbing them steps. You watch me and heed what I do. It'll be your turn one day to protect dis family when Missy gone. You still got learn'n, so watch now."

"Augie say this is all end'n and you can stay jest do his bidding."

"Shush, child, the first thing you got to learn is to listen and the second is not to believe a thing Angus's kin tell you, Powell mix truth wit' lie. You listen to me good now. Augie gonna come ag'n to you, if'n he ain't already; he gonna offer you someth'n to turn Master John. Now you listen to Missy Jay. I knew your granny Clarabelle and she was most powerful, but you got Briggins's blood in you too, and that's fool's blood. Your granny taught me the secrets when I was your age, that's why I'm will'n to teach you, but I'm tell'n you no matter what Augie offer you, don't try to turn Master John Michael, if'n you do, I be the one sew'n you mouth shut, you heed me?"

The girl nodded and her eyes searched Missy's to see if she was going to die.

Missy took the cloth back from the top of the basket and removed a white chicken. She retrieved a knife from her sleeve and held the bird so its throat lay exposed to the blade. She looked down into a basket on the altar. It contained arrowheads, a copper ax, hemp from the rope swing, and the daguerreotype of the Intrepid Explorer's Guild. Sally lit a cigar and blew the smoke over the basket's contents and she began to speak in a strange tongue.

Missy Jay turned and asked the girl, "Before beginn'n, did you see Miss Molly about?"

The girl shook her head yes.

"Yeah, what you mean yeah?"

"That's what I been trying to tell you. I don't need to try and see noth'n. I read the letter that come by that rider. She don't know I can read; she left it lay'n open on the nightstand by her bed. It from Master John, the letter say for Miss Molly to take them four good ponies and meet him at the four corners bridge tonight."

Missy Jay stared at the girl's eyes in amazement as the sounds of horses clopping down the gatehouse lane echoed in the chapel. She continued to listen in stunned silence as the sounds disappeared into the night.

"Master John wouldn't leave me, this our home. Where a man go to 'cept home? There ain't no other place out beyond these fences. He wouldn't, he wouldn't leave me."

Sally said, "They gone Missy Jay, gone for good, he told for her to come alone."

Missy Jay trod the paths in Miller's bog for the next two days until she reached the cave. Though the night was cool, she was panting and she knew her heart was quitting. She entered the cave and walked past the fire pits where she had danced for Briggins all those years ago in the black masses. She half fell into the water and pulled to cross under the ledge but her life ran out and she bobbed to the surface on the near shore before sinking into the pool.

A year and a month after Appomattox, Augie journeyed north and passed a few lost souls still tramping south upon the sides of the road. The last of the hobbling gray wraiths retracing their steps to the shotgun shacks they'd quit in '61. The wagon was headed north to Virginia with a load of peaches and Augie delivered them to the grocer in Fredericksburg. He had contracted for a fair price and the merchant did not try to cheat him. He took his profit and purchased supplies from a funeral home and a dressmaker in the city. As he took the main road out the sound of hammers and the hawking of goods filled his ears; the city had traded the exigencies of war for the rapid life of commerce. The wagon was loaded with a fine bolt of velvet cloth, sturdy needles and a good pair of scissors, strong thread, and a jug of embalming fluid. The leather satchel by his side contained the tools of the undertaker's trade. The wagon ranged out of the city and up tree-lined lanes headed east to Billie's mountain.

Augie hid the wagon off the trail and covered it in cuts of

pine branch. He took his shovel and unhitched the sorrel horse. He loaded its saddlebags and led it by tether up the trail to the old hunter's clearing. Toward afternoon he started digging and by nightfall he had rolled the rocks away to free his friend from his tomb. He held his lantern and waved it over his friend. Termites and other critters scampered around his body and his eyes were eaten away, the sockets now hollow orbs of pure white bone. He built a fire and by its light he took out his undertaker tools and split Billie's belly and chest open with a straight cut from the loins to the neck. He washed out the dried and parchment-like innards of the stomach and chest and scrubbed the bones of the rib cage with a wire brush that he dipped in the bucket of embalming fluid. Augie worked with a bandana tied around his nose and mouth, the sound of a gospel tune humming beneath the cloth. He spent the late evening by the fire sewing each gold coin from the strongbox into a little pocket of fine velvet cloth he had cut and sewed into squares. He placed each piece in Billie's innards, hoping the cloth would keep them from jingling in the wagon. In the morning he sewed Billie up and carefully wrapped him in the white undertaker's strips of cloth like the ancient pharaohs of legend. He lifted Billie from the ground loaded with treasure and straddled him across the back of the sorrel, tying his arms to his legs under the girth, and led the horse down the mountain.

The wagon rolled south for fifty miles until, on the horizon, a bridge with a toll rose out of the wavering heat. A hundred yards out he heard a rough brogue and saw the stripes of a huge red-bearded Union sergeant emerge from the tollhouse. Ten riders on fabulous stallions came abreast of the tollhouse and he knew they were the chase crew, the hunters whose prey were the smugglers who saw the tollhouse too late and tried to turn and run for it. Augie knew the tollhouse was there and he knew it was manned by Irish. He kept his pace and whispered to

Billie, "This is it, brother, I hope you made some friends up there."

The sergeant held up a mammoth hand and lilted the air with his brogue.

"All right lad, let's see what's in the wagon; you have your bills of lading."

Augie handed over the bill of lading for the peaches.

Two riders dismounted and circled round behind the sergeant to the back of the wagon.

"That's fine lad, but this is for the other direction. What're you bring'n back to the boys in Sommersville, whiskey, guns?"

"My best friend, Billie Dunphey."

The two who had approached the bed snapped the tarp down when they saw the shrouded figure in the wagon. Their eyes were wide like they'd seen a banshee in a graveyard on a moonless night and they looked to the sergeant for guidance.

Angus had told Augie that the crazy Irish would fight any living thing at the drop of a hat but their superstitions put them in a dreaded fear of the dead.

"How's that, lad?"

"He died the night 'fore Appomattox. Had me promise 'fore he bled out that I lay him to rest on a knoll overlook'n his field."

The sergeant looked off into the distance and back at Augie and asked, "Is it green, his knoll?"

"Lays like a blanket, grass so thick."

"Raise that gate. Can't you see this lad needs to be on his way? Danny, a tune, your caps lads, don't be daft, Billie Dunphey go'n baile."

The ten horsemen doffed caps as the wagon passed; the sergeant warned, "Keep to the east lad 'til the gap. It's my boys the way down, tell 'em Sergeant Riley seen to you. Don't go west, roads full o' English. Danny, pipe up now, lad."

As Augie crossed over the bridge he could hear a harmonica and a ballad gliding in the air behind him following him and Billie home, *"Come all ye that hold communion . . ."*

The next spring Augie took his team of sorrels down the great road that ran like a thread through Sommersville County. Its high center and smooth crushed stone eased the way for the two Belgian sorrels pulling the wagon. It was the boulevard of the fancy folks that his father had damned, and, as he passed the ornate gates of the plantations every mile or so, saw each one still had its hinge bolts knocked loose from the stone pillars. The foreigner had let it be known the conquered had no privileges; that there was no sanctuary from his will no matter the rank you thought you had bought before Gettysburg.

He reached the Sommersville plantation and rolled over the shadow of its black wrought-iron gate in the roadway. The top hinge was wrenched free of the stone pillar, and the weight had leveraged the gate over, twisting the bottom hinge into the shape of a gnarled horseshoe. The iron lettering "SOMMERSVILLE" lay upside down upon the cobblestones. He looked down the lane and saw the windows of the top floor shattered, and the shutters showed the blackings of a fire that had gutted the garret and licked to the roof.

The ruins of a lost civilization. He spat and nickered his mounts to move on. Augie drove the team at a trot to the farms near the river and did not let up until the wagon reached a newly built farmhouse. It was on good land, fed by a fresh spring, and a creek ran out back of the house. Augie jumped down and knocked on the door, and Billie's widow, Bea, answered, saying with a warm smile, "Hey you." He whispered a greeting and she said, "It okay to talk, it so warm tonight I put Willie and Hick in the loft, they swimm'n all day so they tuckered out."

Bea had the wiry look of a hardscrabble daughter, but she had beautiful eyes, the impossible green that is found only among the folk that'd come down out of Appalachia a hundred years ago.

Augie said he had forgotten something and went to the wagon and pulled a haversack out from a cavity underneath the seat and returned to the kitchen. Bea had lit a small candle, and the light throbbed upon the simple surroundings of her dwelling. Augie emptied the contents on the rough-hewn pine slats of a table cleaved from a single stump. The sack spilled its bounty of candles, cans of lamp oil, apples, peaches, bread loaves, a smoked ham, tobacco, cuts of bacon, coffee, mixing flour and yeast, and a sewing kit upon the knots of the wood.

Bea gushed at the sight of it. "Augie, you do'n us right."

"I didn't look when I come up, but did Tay finish that fencing like I told 'em?" Augie asked.

She gushed, "Tay come out with six hands and they split and fenced it for three days solid and Tay said you got them do'n even more next week. It don't make for no sense, we got pigs but ain't got no horse and don't need so much fencing."

"I'm getten studs. I'm gonna put 'em here and work 'em with Willie. And if cousin Hick stay'n on, they'll both need to start learn'n; I'll bring some colts."

Augie looked at her now across the candlelight, and she came across to him and sat in his lap. He put his arm around her waist and she twisted to face him, brushing the hair from his forehead with her fingertips.

"I think of Big Billie often times, Bea. I think if it weren't for you tak'n to him first, it would have been us that got hitched," Augie said and smiled at her.

"It was 'cause Billie was so nice and you were so ornery when you was young. I didn't know you real good then."

"Don't ever apologize to me again, Bea, for lov'n Billie, you need to see to that, it's a stand'n order from now on, woman."

She looked at him and nodded.

"Hey, I hear tell Casey had t'others go'n in Sloane's the other night tell'n the boys the crazy money you spend'n on horses in Orleans. He says you been bringing 'em up and that you got folks all over hold'n 'em for you." Bea said it with questioning eyes.

"I aim to raise a thousand of 'em right here, and they all for you and Willie."

"Where you gett'n all this money?"

"Billie give it to me."

"What? Go on now, you funn'n me, Billie didn't have no two coppers to rub together."

"Is that right? Best then you heard it from me. Billie were hold'n out on you."

"I swear you're a man of mystery. What we gonna do now with a thousand horses? The Yankees here already; they'll take 'em."

"Take 'em? Hell, they too damn lazy to steal, steal'n hard work. I swear them fools got more coin than a hundred men in a hundred years could count, and they got some hanker'n for good steeds. They gonna buy 'em by the score from us. They ain't even gonna blink an eye when I tell 'em the price. We sell five hundred of 'em for a profit, we won't know what to do with all the coin that's com'n our way."

"A thousand you said? What we gonna do with the other five hundred?"

"We're gonna sell to our boys at cost. They gonna need 'em in a few years when they chase them fools back up the same roads they're burned crawl'n down here. You'll see. Those fools gonna be gone soon enough; it gonna be our county ag'n. And this time, no more yes, sir'n a bunch of prideful fools like 'fore the war. It'll be our kind runn'n things."

"You got it all planned, huh?"

"All of it. I already told the reverend we'll be down Sunday morn."

"Gosh Almighty, is that your way of ask'n, no kneel'n?"

"Am I stay'n here tonight?"

"You're putt'n the cart before the horse, ain't you, Mr. Powell?"

"I ain't never bought a pony yet I didn't see could run first."

"Is that right? You should reckon on gett'n throw a few times."

"That right? I ain't met a pony yet I couldn't break."

"You ain't tried to break a wild pony with green eyes as far as I know."

"Truth be told, I usually don't even name 'em until they broke."

"You ain't got to worry about that, Mister Powell."

"How's that?"

"This one gonna be named Missus Powell 'fore your ass get in any saddle."

"Hot damnation, woman."

Toby was staring at his mother and father and he knew they were discussing whether he would ride. He couldn't hear, but he could see the intensity in the taut frame of his mother and the iron grip she had on the reins of his father's horse as she pulled herself up to meet his face. Molly said, "Promise me, John, that no matter what happens you don't leave Toby down there."

"Molly, I would never . . ."

"No, John, he comes back, we put him in the earth here. Promise me you won't leave him behind. You won't leave him down there. Promise me!"

"I promise, Molly, Toby comes back."

Molly let go of the reins and John wheeled Bull toward the

group. "All right, daylight's burning, let's get to the Old Mission and catch up with Caleb and Joe."

The company spurred their horses and in a tumult raced south toward the southern mountain.

Molly went to the porch and watched Toby flying along with the war party. Without turning to her mother she said, "Toby didn't even say goodbye."

Mother Martin rested her knitting in her lap, and with a quiet wave of her hand said, "Boys is boys; he thinks it's an adventure. That shouldn't be what concerns you. It's Gabriel that will bring the brimstone. Gabriel's ridden his whole life searching for a reason to justify his need to kill, and now it came, like a gift and knocked in his front door. The killer angel hunts them heathens now and justice be his wings. Toby left a sweet boy, I fear what Gabriel will bring us back from down there."

★ ★ ★ ★ ★

PART TWO:
THE DESCENT

★ ★ ★ ★ ★

Caleb and Joe rode hard for two days but never caught sight of the raiding party. The trail was fresh, though, and the prints of the fifty tracked to the Old Mission of Saint Peter of Alcántara. The mission was built at a crossroads. It was one of those places that for reasons lost in time rose as the foci of travelers and wanderers that would last millennia. Whether it be the folds in the land or the alignment of the stars, the pagan nomads of the old world and the missionaries in the new deemed it the place where the last leg of journeys began. These places are sacred until such time when for reasons unknown the world moves on and the land swallows the sacred again, and all that remains are the ghosts of unanswered prayers.

It was at this point that migrants to Tin City had to decide if they were taking the flats around the mountain or over the Crossing.

The mission stood as nothing more than four broken-down walls. To stave off the cold, the wood had been burned by pioneers making their way across this empty track of land over the last hundred odd years, causing the stone walls to crumble without its bracing. The ruins had a bell tower, and somewhere in the mists of time, the tower's base broke free from the top of the adobe walls and slid off its mounts. It toppled vertically so that it landed upright. Twenty feet of it stood unbroken along the outside wall looking as if the mission beneath it had been swallowed by the sands, and only the tower with its crowning stone cross pierced out of the fabric of the earth like a sewing needle.

Joe spotted the tower's cross in the wavering light of the horizon and told Caleb to look for the scouts of a rear guard. Caleb and Joe split by fifty yards and moved toward the mission, the horses moving in a steady walk as if they too sensed a predator.

Three hundred yards in the distance, Caleb saw what he thought was a foot behind a flowering bush.

He signaled to Joe who said softly across the expanse, "Don't kill him."

Caleb drew a bead on the leg from three hundred yards with his long rifle. He estimated where the knee would be from where the foot lay and aimed his rifle, waiting for man and horse to balance; waiting for that quiet moment the horseman feels his and his mount's breath are the same, and he squeezed gently. The report was swallowed by the expanse of sand, and only a faint echo off the tower rumbled back to him from across the plain. The warrior spun up and ran for three steps before collapsing on his shattered knee. He began crawling for the wall of the old mission.

Joe yelled, "Great shot," and galloped after the lookout. He rode hard and caught the crawling warrior ten yards from the wall and clunked him over the head with his rifle butt. Joe leapt from his horse and jumped on the man's back, tying his hands with a cord.

Caleb remained on horseback and scanned back and forth across the landscape thinking there might have been more than one warrior left behind to delay pursuers. Seeing nothing moving, Caleb raced for the old mission. He let the reins drop and grabbed two pistols and bolted into the four walls of the mission ready to fire in any direction, but the mission was silent and empty. Caleb ran back to Joe.

They took one arm each and with the scout's face pointed at the ground they dragged him to the mission, his toes cutting rows in the sand. They tied the warrior's hands around one of the last remaining adobe columns. Caleb took another rope and bound his feet. The knee wound was horrific, and Caleb could see the top of the kneecap peeled around, but the scout remained stoic, not so much as a grimace when Caleb flipped the patella back into place. He took a bandana from his pocket and put a tourniquet above the scout's knee and cinched it tight to keep him from bleeding to death.

The warrior had on a red vest that looked like it had once been bright but was now faded and worn, as were his dungarees. He was barefoot and wore nothing on his head and his hair lay long, wild, and tangled, the strands running in no navigable course.

Caleb said to Joe, "Is he bleed'n out?"

Joe answered, "No, good shot—all bone through the knee, he was easy to ride down."

The warrior held his head face down, the twisted locks of hair concealing his face. For a brief moment, his head rose slowly, and Caleb and Joe saw that his pupils were like the hot red embers you find still burning in the hearth the morning after a night's hot fire. The burning melted in a callow yellow. He looked from Caleb to Joe, slowly turning his head from one to the other as if he were measuring them. He appeared to have no fear or apprehension about the flames he knew were coming and slowly lowered his head again without making a sound.

Joe said, "He's dying, see his eyes. His insides have quit on him, that's why he got left behind, he's rotting from the inside out."

"Should we find out what he knows?" Caleb asked.

"Nah, he's a tough one, and he knows he's dying, so he'll be tough to break. We need Gabriel; Raif; they'll have a trick or two. We wait, you did a good shot. He's got plenty of life. I'm gonna put a flame on the wall so they know it's safe."

Six hours later, the party rode up hard, and the sound of their hooves thundered into the mission reverberating off the walls. They dismounted. The bound warrior didn't look up.

"How bad is he?" the colonel asked.

Joe responded, "Caleb hit him in the knee, all bone; he's been tied off since. He's sick from something else. He's dying slowly."

Gabriel looked over the warrior and grabbed him by the hair, lifting his head to look into his eyes, and said, "Jaundice, poisoned blood, but he still has a lot of strength. Bring me some of that fire from the wall, Joe, and keep it hot about ten feet there or so. Seth, there's a black satchel with metals in it in my saddlebag; bring it to me."

Raif said, "I got the ear thing; it need to stoke in the fire a good bit."

Gabriel rose to his full height and looked down at the warrior. The warrior raised his head as if he knew Gabriel would be staring and returned the same stone gaze. Without taking his eyes off of the warrior, Gabriel said, "I reckon I'm gonna need that. This one thinks he's up for it."

Wesley said, "What's going on here, Colonel?"

"We need to know how they're moving, what path into the wastelands, and this savage knows it and he's going to tell us," the colonel said.

Wesley watched as Gabriel rolled out the black leather satchel revealing what looked like a doctor's instruments. The colonel ordered Seth and Toby to mount up and ride south for three miles and scout for any stragglers. He told them not to kill them but to wound them like Caleb had dropped the warrior. The colonel was sure this would be the only scout.

Wesley turned to the colonel. "Colonel, torture under your command?"

"What choice do we have? We need to know the route his war chief is using to get past the fort to the wastelands. If they get too far ahead we can't follow, sixty miles south of the fort, there's nothing but a thousand like this hard son-of-a-bitch— you'd need a brigade. We can't delay; we have to catch him before he reaches the lakes."

The warrior groaned as Gabriel applied fire to his feet. Wesley turned and saw the blackening of flesh and spun toward his father. "Colonel, torture wasn't on the curriculum at the academy."

"Not everybody's got the stomach for it, Lieutenant. I suggest you ride south and assist Seth and Toby."

"To the contrary, Colonel, I see no other option. My expectation was that you wouldn't choose such a . . . practical approach," Wesley said.

"Wesley, if those were your sisters we were chasing, I would be the one pulling that heathen apart a piece at a time."

The colonel spun and walked toward the interrogation. As the colonel neared, he could hear Gabriel say, "This is going to take some of Luther's ways."

The colonel turned and walked out of the mission. He saddled his horse and ordered Wesley to follow him on patrol.

"If it's all the same, Colonel, I'd rather watch. You never know when certain military tactics will come in handy again."

Less than an hour later the party emerged from the mission. Gabriel and the colonel discussed the information.

Gabriel said, "They're cross'n the Ash Run River twenty miles east of the fort, taking the big valley of the five hands to the lake country. He said they hailed from the western lake, and before he died he said his chief is the White Lion."

The colonel pulled his glove tighter on his hand, "They're

running the flats to save from losing too many head. This warlord is one brazen son of a bitch. He ain't worried about the cavalry or us catching him."

"Well, if he's trying to save heads, he can't go south from the east ford. It's all a desert stretch south from there," Gabriel said.

"That heathen gave it to us straight, he's got to cut west again if he wants to feed and water that herd; he'll need one of the five canyons lead'n to the great lake," the colonel said. He eyed the southern mountains. "We need to ride to Tin City and see if we can buy a safe passage through the Stone tribe. From there we fortify a position in front of 'em in the canyons and lay for him. He'll slow too once he gets across the Ash Run, think he's in the lake country already, he'll let 'em water and feed on down and we'll be lay'n for him in the canyon."

Gabriel responded, "I reckon that's the way to carve that son of a bitch up."

"Did he say anything more?" the colonel asked.

"That he hopes we catch up with the White Lion so that his daughters can wear our skins this winter."

CHAPTER TWELVE:
TIN CITY

They rode hard for the southern mountain and crossed up the ridgebacks as darkness fell, making the last stretch in total darkness, trusting the horses to keep from paying the price for recklessness. By midmorning next, the company reached the druids and picked a defensive position to rest the horses.

Raif took Toby and Seth and walked east across the pass to a squat-looking druid. They searched the side until they found a climbing path of jagged stone with good handholds, and they ascended the rock. The boys followed Raif atop the druid as he swung out over and dropped into a chiseled channel that cut through the stone. As Raif landed he drew his pistol and moved slowly; the boys mimicked his actions. Raif didn't think there'd be renegades about, but the years had taught him to be wary of hides, even old ones. He reached the crow's nest, but there was no sign of the woman, her body having disappeared years ago, taken by the band of warriors without a name that still wandered these cliffs. The only thing that stood where the scout had been silenced were two stone cairns, one of them three feet high; the other a foot. The ladder had since worn out, and a few pieces of hemp and old dried wood lay strewn about the stone floor. Luther had said a nest once found is never used again. It was their law. Raif boosted Seth and Toby up the rock wall, and the two boys climbed into the crow's nest and looked down the path of the Crossing to the top of the south ridgebacks.

Raif told them the story of his night on the Crossing. The

boys looked down at him in silent rapture. They had heard only the rumors, and now they sat motionless as Raif told them how he was born anew that cold night. He told Seth and Toby of the black pawn trail along the abyss, and the camps in the cuts of the cliffs. He schooled them on hides, how they'd never find one by searching for it, you needed for them to move, the need for patience. As they dropped from the window, Raif showed them how to kill a scout from the front and back with the knife so he dies swiftly, silently. Raif drew the black antler from its hide scabbard and told of the warrior of scars that had bested him and how it was Jed and Abner that had come for him as he was set to be scalped. As Raif stood there looking at the two boys, he saw they were near his age when he crossed that first time. He never told anyone the scout was a woman and kept the secret buried within him.

Toby looked at Raif and envied his scars, the way he carried himself, and his knowledge of the killing arts.

As if reading his mind, Raif said, "You two will learn our ways on this trip. I can see it in you. Don't worry, you'll know what to do when the time comes. And don't do the mistake I did back then; Jed and Abner done proved how wrong my ways were that night. We ride and war together. Ya'll took Bibbs; the ancients had their notions of war—the first of their kind were warriors like Achilles, the hero nonsense, but as Greeks started fighting savages, courage came to be the fighter in the ranks, the one who could keep his feelings in check and stand with his brothers in battle. You'll see when we catch these sons-of-bitches, they fight each to his own, there'll be lots of 'em all scream'n gibberish but watch 'em, they're fighting one at a time—each trying to earn his place in whatever belief in a next world they cling to. You'll know what to do when we catch 'em and don't be feared by the first time you hear the crush of it.

"Ya'll shot a lot, but when someone's shoot'n at you it's different. The sound of slugs is like the ripping of a bedsheet, tearing the very sky—it sets the air alive. The ripp'n of that sheet in the air gonna cause near every hair on your body to stand like a cat's whisker, each one pumping fire to your blood. You think at first there ain't no stand'n it; and someth'n inside will be tell'n you not to fire. You'll think don't fire and they won't see me, won't come at me, you'll be think'n like you can hide right in the middle of it all. It's fool's stuff you're thinking, they get to you soon enough. You got to pull that first trigger, that's the bitch—after the first pull, the rest ain't nothing but a thing, and ain't that the way of most things."

Raif paused and looked at them hard. "There's something more important than even the fight—you heed me now—any man that asks from another what he could do for himself on this ride is gonna give rise to a provocation. You got to dig down and hold your own—you're not sons or nephews no more, you're part of the company. The grit you need to face them devils when the time comes is one thing; another grit is to deal with what's go'n on inside you on the long ride. The ancients called it the ironness of heart: to carry on when you think you ain't got noth'n left. The first time you think you can't go a foot more, I'm telling you now you got a thousand miles left in you—remember your mind quits before your heart. These good men you've known your entire life will take on death masks— dark shadows of the eye from lack of sleep, and fear—you'll be wear'n that same mask so each got to keep his own iron heart. All right now, let's get back before the colonel thinks we're in trouble."

As they stood to move out, Seth asked, "Raif, why you suppose they put two piles like that, when it were but one watch?"

Raif responded, "They didn't put 'em up, I did. Let's get back 'fore dark or we gonna get the colonel agitated."

Raif led them to the wall and watched as they descended the

rook to the trail. He told the two to hold, said he was going back to check the lookout one more time and look down the Crossing to see if he could spot any warriors lay'n for them. He plodded his way down the cut until he reached the cairns; muttering "ironness of heart, bunch of shit," he kicked the cairns and sent the rocks scuttling like billiard balls across the channel's stone floor. He gazed down at the scattered rocks and muttered, "Bibbs is a goddamn schoolmaster, wannabe poet. What the hell did he know of anything about war? He's back there giv'n the ruler to saplings 'cause fools like me out here do his kill'n."

His mind went to the two boys about to have the world forever shaped by the killing to come, and he slumped down, putting his back to the wall with his knees slightly crooked due to the narrowness of the channel. He thought, *them two boys either be dead and scalped or com'n back like me and the colonel put'n on me to feed 'em nonsense.* He recalled the scarred warrior stripped to the waist chanting in the hard cold of that night long ago. He stood and looked over the scattered rocks. It must have been the third time he'd kicked the cairns down and he vowed it would be the last time he'd knock 'em down. He'd let it stand; *hell,* he thought, *it's the only statue ever gonna be built for me, anyhow.* It'd stand until the tribe of this mountain was dust and all they ever built perished in the wind, as do all the trophies men leave for the dead. He reckoned that Toby and Seth, if they lived, were bound to become like him and he knew it was a sin, the same wickedness he had visited upon Jed and Abner. Preacher and Colonel sinning by bringing these boys, and them two knew it too.

He stood in the channel and put his hand to the wall and ran his fingers along the chisel marks in the stone and whispered, "If the renegades had let me pass that night, I'd be tending littl'uns and watch'n 'em crawl by the fire on cold winter nights.

I'd of been tender to Edda and raised sons proper, even have
'em kneeling in the pews obedient to the silent invisible power.
I keep pining for it, heck I even prayed once for it. Shit, I been
trying to live some other life, be a man that ain't ever coming. I
reckon I got more in common with that stitched-up sumbitch I
ran into on top of this heap of shit ten years ago than any of
them in that world below. So be it; they coulda let me pass but
they didn't; they tried for my scalp and missed. White Lion
wants a piece of my soul—here I come again, you son-of a-bitch;
Raphael, the angel come to kill your mothers with the twisted
horn of a beast and eat the sons that I rip from their wombs."

Three days later as twilight settled, Toby witnessed Tin City
glistening on the horizon, a glowing flame upon the field, the
backdrop of the southern mountains magnifying its radiance.
The company reined up outside a large hotel that doubled as
the whorehouse. The horses were spent and Seth and Toby went
with Joe to acquire feed and shelter for the animals. The Hansons and Wesley and Caleb entered the whorehouse for a drink.
The horses would need at least four hours of rest, maybe more.
The colonel and Gabriel went to parlay with the administrator
for a passage over the Ash Run River and through the Stone
tribe to the five canyons where the White Lion was descending
on his southern passage.

Seth and Toby held the horses at the front of the hotel while
Joe went looking to find room at a barn.

Joe returned, and said, "Take 'em around back. There's a
livery; tend to the horses, I'll be there in a few with grub."

The boys led the horses past the back of the whorehouse and
across their passage was a cone of golden gaslight that flowed
from a missing knot in a sideboard of the hotel's wall. The light
danced upon the dust mites in the thickening darkness.

Seth went to the hole and looked into the light and beheld

Wesley with a young whore; he was behind her and had his hand over the back of her head forcing her face sideways into a pillow. He wore upon his face a countenance of awful pain.

Seth motioned Toby and as he looked through the fissure, Toby beheld his brother in an aura of gaslight in an oval room the shape of an egg, the golden glow vibrating about his shunting.

The boys took the horses on. In the cool of the stable, the flesh of the animals steamed great wisps, the vapors rising in elongated signs of infinity. To the rest of the company, the horses were nothing more than a steer to a butcher; an animal to ride to its death and then eat if chance called for it. Toby looked at Ulysses and wished he had left him in the stable and that he too rode a nameless beast. He feared he would have to shoot him at some point or ride him until he dropped, his heart bursting in the dust. Ulysses would ride until his heart gave out, Toby knew it. He looked at the thinning of the steed already, the leanness sharpening the once inflated muscles, giving their former magnificence a hard sinewy look.

He stroked Ulysses's muzzle. "I know, boy, it's gonna be a few more days, we'll catch 'em and you can rest, just a few more days," but he feared how it would end.

Joe returned with bread, hard cheese, and venison jerky. They ate in the stable using a hay bale as a makeshift table. After tending the mounts and eating, Joe sent the boys to the hayloft to sleep and stood the first watch. There was a hatch to the roof in the loft and the boys ascended into the night, sitting in the darkness on the slanted roof to cool some before sleep. The roof canted toward the whorehouse and they could gaze into the hotel's second floor, which housed the bar. The bar was raised to the second floor so the patrons could use the enormous raised porch that wrapped itself around the four sides of the hotel. The porch's circumnavigation was checked in one area near the back where an earthquake had cracked a piling, causing a jagged angle in the floorboards. The whores and men ignored the cracked spine of the flooring and sailed over it looping the porch, mixing and mingling, laughing. Their high-pitched laughter pierced the night air, ringing out as more drink and guarantees of fornication floated over the stream of revelers.

Toby could see Wesley tied up in talk with a fat whore until his eyes steered from her and traced the passage of a skinny whore with a busting cleavage. The skinny slut flowed past with rhythmic thrusts of her hips as she sauntered. The fat one kept prodding until Wesley hailed the bartender and yelled for him to "heel this fat bitch." The bartender spoke in a voice without inflection, but its sound cut through the fog and din of the bar to the stable's roof. The boys saw the terrified eyes on the fat whore as she sank into the darkness of the cigar smoke, signaling a single sneer in her wake at the skinny whore before dematerializing into the smoky bar. Wesley and the slight one nuzzled their lips to each other's necks below the ear and began whispering as schemers do in a stage play. They broke out in a shrill laugh that pierced the night, both looking after the path the fat whore had taken. She was in the middle of another whisper, her nose edged to Wesley's ear, her breath tainted with cinnamon and whiskey, when Raif reached across and tendered him a double whiskey. Wesley shoved the skinny whore off in the same direction as the fat one with the flat of his hand to her ass and took the whiskey, raising it to acknowledge gratitude to Raif.

The bartender stood behind the barrier of the bar's rich mahogany. He stood upon a slat floor purposely raised a foot higher than the patrons' floor, so he could command a view over the multitude. He held court like a sultan, the rows of multicolored bottles making a prism of the light that bounced off the great mirror. He intertwined his fingers and folded his hands knuckle down, a prayer position he kept to protect his loins from a sudden assault. He was moored directly beneath the bull, the great bust mounted high on the wall ruling over the liquor bottles. The bull was carved out of a single piece of dark wood; the deepness of its black cherry gave the silent beast its voice. Scores of mirrors about the bar angled to capture its image, and it reflected out again a hundred-fold upon the panes of the windows. The points of the horns twisted to the ceiling, and its black eyes floated above the bartender's in such synchronicity that they appeared to survey the inhabitants of the public house together as one. The bartender's red vest and buttons reflected in the lantern lights, and Toby could see through the flickering, smoky illumination that he was smiling, his grin ebbing and flowing with the tide of revelry that reeled about the bull's compass.

Seth said without haste, "I can't ever think of a reason to give that smiling man my money. Couldn't imagine spend'n a single night in that dungeon, let alone every night of my life."

"It sure didn't look like I thought it would," Toby responded.

"It surely don't, it looked like it hurt'n Wesley so, you got to wonder why a man would pay coin for such pain." Seth said it without looking at Toby and then he went on, "Gabriel says a man's got to keep that stuff in check otherwise he'll lose himself. The old ranch that's burnt out, you know the one that sits south of where the Criss bends toward the Hansons'? The one we were afraid to explore on account of Smiley say'n it was haunted?"

"The old Kaiser homestead, I know it," Toby responded.

"Gabriel told me the story of that family, and he says stay away from that place because it is haunted."

"What? Go on, tell me."

"All right, but don't tell no one, lessen I'll pay for it from Gabriel."

"Course, go on now."

"Your father knows the story too, he never told you?"

"The colonel never talks to me about such things, I get some stuff here and there from Abner, but you know he ain't much on talking."

"All right, I'll tell you but you got to swear, Toby, it stays with us."

"You got my word, Seth."

"Kaiser had a wife and three little ones, the oldest a boy about eight. They was do'n jest fine, Kaiser had a business rais'n feed for horses. Gabriel says he was a man of vision. Knew it was gonna be good horse country and he started a feed business when there was still much doubt the ranches would hold. He was a god-fear'n man too—but they was Lutheran. They built that homestead and had a good well. The wife had the touch and raised plenty stuff. Well, the husband's brother done come out from the east on a scrawny pony, how he wandered west through them lands without los'n his hair is a mystery itself. He was a drifter and good-for-noth'n, but being that it was Kaiser's young'n brother he took him on. The brother took to working the homestead, plow'n, fixing up. The feeding business took Kaiser to travel, though. He had to deliver the feed and he had to man the storefront he built in town. You know it, it's Drier's now, but it was Kaiser's 'fore that. Well, one night the husband came home and found his brother reaming his wife."

"Go on now, how did Gabriel find that out?"

"I'll git to that, don't question the truth of something until you heard it all," Seth scolded.

"I reckon. Go on, though."

"All right, well Kaiser catch his brother lay'n wit' his wife. The old man ran to get his shotgun, but he had a bad limp from the war, so he weren't able to reach the rack over the fireplace 'fore his brother ran after him and sunk a buck knife into his back. Funny how every good-for-noth'n extra hand we had the misfortune of taking on during the brand'n season always slept with a knife close. Probably from all those years of have'n to sleep with one eye open on account of how many they've done wrong. The shiftless always think their reckoning's gonna come at night. Anyhow, he stabbed his brother in the back, and Kaiser fell into the fireplace, buck knife stuck out his back. He lay there bleeding, cook'n in the fire, and there was his good-for-noth'n brother stand'n over him stark nude," Seth continued.

"Go on now, Seth, you're pulling my leg, how you know he was naked?"

"I told you I was gett'n to that, hold on. Anyway, the wife come run out naked too. I guess to stop it but she was too late; so there's the two of 'em standing in the raw with Kaiser in the fire; and the three kids up with all the commotion come climb'n down from the loft. The kids see the brother and mother stand'n naked and the good-for-noth'n with the blood sprayed all over 'em and the father in the flames with the buck knife sunk in his back. So they all start scream'n. The mother drops to her knees sobbing, and the son is trying like mad to pull his father out of the fire, but Kaiser was no small man. The good-for-noth'n brother realizes he's gonna swing for this, so what's he do? What's he do? He kills them all."

"Nah, go on, how do you know it this good?"

"I ain't funning. Gabriel told me the year I got hair down there. He took me aside and told me, said I was forewarned about the trouble that come with lay'n with any woman, even your wife, whoever she was to be, he said straight lay'n with a woman can bring ruin on a man at any time, it always come with a price."

"You swear it was Gabriel told you straight?"

"I swear, and ain't nobody ever seen Gabriel lie."

"Well, go on, what happened next?"

"The good-for-noth'n kills 'em all, even the little'uns. He reaches into that fire and pulls that buck knife out his brother's back and slashes 'em all. Then he dresses it up like renegades done it. Like it was a raid'n party or something. He took that buck knife and he stabbed that little boy and he stabbed that whore mother. He scalped 'em all and carved 'em up with that buck knife. Yep, they were no more than five or six, them girls. He loaded up his brother's wagon with everything in that house that shined, anything he figured he could get a penny for in Tin City; set that house to fire and headed south. Gabriel said he was headed for Tin City to barter what he could git and try to hide his sorry ass out in the wastelands. Only too bad for him it rained that night, so the ranch was still stand'n except the roof, which caught pretty good, but most stuff only got charred not burnt through.

"The post come through the next day and found the ranch all busted up, the slaughter and blood. He rounded up the colonel and Gabriel and Raif's pa, Matthew, and they searched that ranch and started putt'n the pieces together. They started shift'n through the house, and Gabriel said it was like putting a puzzle together. First they found no tracks, no signs of renegades, and they had Joe with 'em, so you know if there were tracks Joe would've found 'em. Gabriel says the key to figure'n it out was when they searched the barn they found the bedding for the good-for-noth'n, but couldn't find no body to match that sleep'n roll. They rode hard for eight full days 'til they spotted the tracks of wagon wheels oddly break'n east off the flat's road and on into them east woods.

"They found the good-for-noth'n wrapped in noth'n but an old blanket, still naked, and mak'n camp in a patch of trees eat'n fruit from a jar the wife had pickled. Gabriel said his hair was still matted with the blood of them kids. They followed the buzzing of flies and found the scalps under the wagon seat, he planned on sell'n them too. Gabriel says the good-for-noth'n was half-crazed, his eyes round and lifeless. He tried deny'n it at first, said he was out riding and returned when he found what the renegades had done and he were out chas'n 'em himself. But they weren't having none of it. Raif's pa was fit to be tied, weren't gonna tolerate something like that done to a family. They put the good-for-noth'n to the wagon wheel and broke the truth out of him. Gabriel said it didn't take long at all to break him; said they did nothing special; Gabriel says most men want to confess their sins.

"The good-for-noth'n told how he and the wife were spend'n more and more time together alone because Kaiser was always off sell'n his feed and building the commerce. The good-for-noth'n told how he dug a new well closer to the house and when he pulled that first bucket of water up, it was pure. He hit right on a spring; said it was the first bit of luck he'd ever had in his miserable life. He said the wife hugged him when he pulled that first bucket up, it being pure spring and all; he said he knew it were no ordinary hug. She come to him the night they hit the spring. She came to his bed in the loft. He said he was half asleep and she crawled naked into his blankets; said it took him by surprise; said he gave in to her 'fore he knew what he was do'n. After the first time, they would come to each other in the night when old man Kaiser was away, and on some nights she would feed Kaiser liquor, so he'd sleep and they could hump, they were crazy for it.

"The good-for-noth'n said the wife started whisper'n to him in the night about how she hated the sight of Kaiser every time he came home. She hated that she had to lay with him. She started tell'n the good-for-noth'n that Kaiser was rough with her, especially when he were drinking. The good-for-noth'n said he knew now she had all of it plann'd out to make him jealous, and she started talk'n of how good it'd be for 'em if Kaiser were gone. The good-for-noth'n said he was tired of drift'n and that it were not just the wife to blame but Kaiser's fault too for what he done. The good-for-noth'n started begg'n them to understand, say'n his brother didn't appreciate all the work he was do'n and with him gone all the time, the work of the place were falling more and more to him. The good-for-noth'n confessed that he figured if he got rid of the brother he could lay with the wife; that he could step in like it were all noth'n but a new boot, jest take Kaiser's place.

"He told how he was surprised as all get-out when the wife started screaming after he stabbed Kaiser in the back. He think'n it's what she wanted. You won't believe this, the good-for-noth'n told that he'd killed them all to ease their suffer'n. The wife was scream'n and she was beating him on the chest, say'n it was all his fault. The little ones were screaming. The boy was try'n to pull his father out of the flames. The good-for-noth'n said he wanted to end their suffering, he wanted to stop the cry'n. He went naked out on to the porch and the screaming and holler'n was com'n from inside. He said it were the most horrible wailing he'd ever heard, said he'd looked through the door and he could see the mother and children all try'n to pull the father from the flames. How they were all reach'n into the fire, howling in pain, but they couldn't budge him. The good-for-noth'n went back in and stabbed 'em all so the scream'n would stop.

"Gabriel says the Kaisers were good folk until that jackal showed up. Gabriel says if you put your thing in a hole that ain't yours, it never comes to no good. He says nothing good ever come of whore'n and that you got to guard your flock against the wolves, because they come in sheep's clothing. Gabriel says the wolves are always close, always closer than you think."

"What happened to the brother?"

"They condemned him to hell on the spot. They parlayed and agreed such an evil needed to be washed from North County. They had a mind to bring him to town, but Raif's pa weren't have'n none of it, someth'n like kill'n a family needed gett'n done right then. They scourged him and nailed him to an old dogwood tree, took a big cut to his belly, and left him there, I guess 'til his insides rotted or critters got him. They burned the wagon and took the scalps back to the ranch and did the best they could to bury them with the right heads. They gave the Kaisers a proper burial 'cept for the wife. They told Reverend Graham, and he wouldn't see her buried in no holy ground; wouldn't let no words be spoken over her, neither. He said 'she be bound in hell with that jackal they left nailed to the dogwood.' They told the folks, though, that it was renegades done slaughtered the Kaisers. The colonel told the townsfolk a story about how they tracked two renegades and caught up to 'em in the flats. I guess the Kaisers all but been forgotten about now. You know folks try t'forget every chance they get."

Seth and Toby sat on the barn roof in darkness staring at the porch. Toby turned to Seth and said, "I guess a man that prays as much as Gabriel knows it's wrong in the eyes of God to be in that cathouse."

"Pray? I ain't never seen Gabriel pray."

"But he's never without his Bible. It's dog-eared as all get-out. Every time we stop he pulls it out."

Seth looked down and spit off the end of the roof. "Yeah, I reckon he reads it, but I never seen that man kneel. He never been near a church as long as I known him."

"Why do you suppose he's read'n it then?"

"You'd have to ask him why, though I'd hate to think of the

214

backhand one'd get to ask Gabriel such a question."

"Seems odd, don't it, reading the book but not pray'n?" Toby asked, not letting the matter drop.

"If'n I say what I think, you swear it stay between me and you?"

"You got my word."

"Gabriel reads that book because he thinks he can figure out its meaning."

"Well, ain't every preacher trying to do the same thing as that?"

"No, not like that. Gabriel isn't trying to interpret the words or find what the writing's meaning is like a preacher. He thinks that book contains something hidden in it, secret meanings. I seen him one night. There's a room off the main house that I only ever seen Gabriel go into. Even Nanna didn't have the nerve to cross that threshold. It had a writing desk and loads of pencils and papers and an old sea chest Gabriel always kept locked; he built a trapdoor in the floor to hide it," Seth said.

Toby could see the wariness in Seth's eyes telling the story.

"Toby, you done give me your word on this, I need you to swear it again on your sisters' eyes and on your mother's soul."

Toby said, "You have my word—eyes and soul, I swear it, I'll never tell another soul."

"All right, that room sits right 'neath the loft and I would always hear Gabriel in that room at night. He would pull that door in the floor open and lug that chest out. When I was a real young'n I would hear him down there most every night, scribbl'n away with his pencils. Lately, not so often, but enough to wonder what he's up to. The only other soul ever in that room when that chest was open was Luther and I barely remember that; I was near seven I reckon, it were before the time Luther done vanished. On some nights, I could hear them talking down there, whispers usual but sometimes you could

215

hear them snapp'n at each other. The whispers turn'n to hisses, arguing for hours; the whole time, Luther's drink'n whiskey. Gabriel never tolerates no drink around him, but he would buy whiskey for Luther. I could hear him lay'n in the loft hissing at Luther that he knew something, say'n things like: 'I know you were permitted; tell me what that number means?' and I would hear Luther say, 'it's each to his own, the mystery is each man's. It means different things to each man.' Or some such shit you know he were always talking in riddles. Gabriel would hiss, 'I know you don't believe that, tell me, if you say it's truth, why do you fear it? If there's power in the know'n what good the know'n ever do you?' "

"What were they talking about?"

"I got no idea. It's close to my first memory of anything. I don't even know if I remember it right. I got it in my head, though, and it got so I needed to see what was in that chest. Something came over me, and it was an urge I couldn't get a hold of, like a stud after the teaser mare in front of him. I tried the door one day with Gabriel out in the back forty, and it was bolted clean. I knew even after I loosed that bolt there'd be another puzzle to get that floor open. Still I couldn't stop, I needed to know."

Seth looked over at Toby with a pained expression, and seeing as Toby was riveted to his tale, he continued. "I heard him down there one night scratch'n away with his pencil, it was real late. He had been riding all day and come in late. He still went to that room and was up until the middle of the night. I heard him hit the cot in there with a thud and I knew he were dead to this world.

"I climbed my way down from that loft, I coulda snuck up on a cat the way I was moving. It were hot and the door were a little open and I could see Gabriel asleep. I pushed that door and I feared that tiny squeak would shake the world. I crept in there and Gabriel had three Bibles on that desk and some other old books—they looked a thousand years old by the bindings. There were drawings all over his writing desk with all kinds of shapes: mazes, circles, numbers, all sorts, like different cattle brands. Atop each of the shapes there were Bible scripts, passages written out in print, and above each of the letters there he written numbers . . . the numbers were written on a separate sheet of paper and circles that spun around and around—it were all, well, it were crazy."

"Crazy? I never seen Gabriel ever do something to be ashamed of."

"Like I said I don't know what he was doing, but I seen into the trunk. It were facing the other way and I crept up to it and pull it back; there were more books and more writings. Some of it was in letters I couldn't sense no head nor tail of it. There were a skull in there with gold about it and coins and these stone tablets, look like small headstones with writing going down 'em in lines going this way and that, not like normal writing. But there were also a Spanish cross in there. It were forged of some gold metal, but Jesus was twisted such that he was hanging upside down on it. I reached in there and tried to lift it, to get a feel for its weight, but it were heavy as all get-out. I stared at it, there's no way you could deform that thing by hand or by dropping it. It were crafted twisted. I crawled back out of that room. Ever since I been want'n to ask Gabriel, but he ain't ever brought it up. I remember him in there and Luther saying the last night I seen him, 'No soul needs to reach for that, Gabriel,' and him just grunting."

"What do you reckon, Seth?"

"I guess he been dodg'n bullets with his name on it so long, I think he wants to believe he got one last dodge left in him. I figure he knows his soul's in peril with all the kill'n he's done. He were gett'n squirrely, talk'n about things he never talk before, but then this happened and you could see it in his eyes, he were bent again; told me flat out we were going kill'n and we ain't stopp'n until it be fifty for every one of ours—his eyes on fire."

As the darkness thickened, the lights from the hotel lanterns spilled out through the doorways and windows bathing the porch. As the whores and their flesh crawlers sailed about the porch, the light spilled over the revelers, creating a kaleidoscope effect. The angles of light traced the shadows of their figures into elongated grotesque outlines, the shades of each indistinguishable from the other.

On and on they danced in a minuet around the porch, moving to each, ebbing, flowing, spinning, their shadows clattering in waves upon the tides of light. The night chill caught the boys as the wind changed, bringing the Crossing's air down upon the city, and chased the boys to the warmth of the stable, but the revelers did not heed it and danced on. They crawled to the hayloft and slipped under their blankets with their heads resting on their saddle rolls.

They could hear the Hansons and Caleb and Wesley enter the barn and Jed say, "Let 'em sleep, Joe. I got this one. Abner's next. It won't be long and we'll be moving."

Seth and Toby pretended to sleep as the others grabbed space in the loft for their bedrolls. They would sleep for six hours before they were on the move again.

CHAPTER THIRTEEN:
THE ADMINISTRATOR

As the company bedded down, the colonel and Gabriel walked the slat bridges that floated above the muck of Tin City's streets and reached the new government house still under construction. Three Cordoba mastiffs were chained near the entrance, their necks straining at the links and emitting low guttural growls at every living thing that passed. Gabriel kicked dirt at one close to the walk. The animal pulled not in pulses of effort but in one steady course, wrenching the leather of its tether. The dogs had no prominent canine teeth but jaws of endless, razor-sharp pyramids. The row of teeth neither shortened nor lengthened but like a shark's measured back the same size to form snapping mouths the entire length of the snout.

Gabriel recalled twenty years ago watching a great brown bear take down a mule deer, breaking its spine with a single great swipe on the banks of a swift river in the northlands. The great bear dragged the massive bulk of the mule deer like a rag doll across a meadow toward its lair in the mountains when seven wolves came out of the tree line. The pack tramped along with their tails high and tongues dangling out the sides of their mouths. Gabriel had looked through his telescope and could see their yellow eyes laughing as they spun about the bear. The bear snapped and dashed at the wolves in great bursts of powerful speed, but the wolves danced around him in a merry-go-round of yapping. The alpha snapped at the snout and then spun away from the great bear's swipes as the second of the

219

pack snapped the ass. The bear emitted groans and slashed at the air with its mighty paw only to get nipped in the ear for its trouble from a third wolf. The players baited the bear for ten minutes as he hurled at them with mad abandon. The wolves rotated about with tails high and tongues dangling out the sides of their mouths. The soft pink of their tongues accentuated the white of the great canine tooth, which sat a king in their snouts. The bear tired of the game and lumbered off disappearing among the birch trees, the feast of mule deer left in the grass. The wild dogs howled and nuzzled each other as they smelled the blood of the kill and anticipated its warm taste.

Gabriel looked to the three mastiffs, who snapped viciously at each other when the chains kept them from reaching Gabriel and the colonel. Gabriel knew that these beasts would have hurled themselves at the bear. The satisfaction gained not from the feast of the mule deer but the simple impulse of sinking their razor teeth into the bear's hide. With a swipe of the paw the bear would have snapped each of their spines in turn. He could see in his mind's eye the three beasts dragging their useless rear legs after the bear, hoping to snap one last time as the bear paraded off with his kill, leaving them to die from hunger and thirst in the meadow; such was the peculiar nature of these black-faced beasts propagated by Spaniards to hunt down runaway slaves.

The new courthouse was being built by laborers from the east, and in the lamplight you could see their shadows moving huge blocks of stone to the base of immense scaffolds. The Asians were dressed in dark costumes and in the lamplight you could see them gauging Gabriel's and Walker's actions as they passed. The laborers draped the large trellis ropes across the stones and prepared them for the morning lifts that would raise the blocks skyward to the vast unfinished dome. Gabriel and Walker climbed the steps and entered the rotunda.

An officious-looking man approached and said curtly, "The match is out back, gentlemen."

The colonel ignored his comment. "I'm Colonel Walker and this is Gabriel McCallum from North County. We need to see the administrator."

The clerk sized them up and said, "If you could, wait here while I check to see if the administrator is available." He spun and climbed steps only to return in a few moments, saying "Colonel, please follow me."

The clerk led them to a great marble room containing little furniture. At the far end beneath a large stained-glass window etched with Moses holding the tablets sat a dimly lit face with a great shock of white hair, his mustache and short pointed beard adorned with the same whiteness. He was seated at a small desk scratching at paper with an old-style quill. As the colonel and Gabriel entered, the officious man said, "Mr. Lutus, the colonel, sir," and departed with brisk steps between two of the marble pillars that held the roof on the east side of the room where he vanished, the door of his exit invisible in the shadows that swallowed him. Out the great window, they could see the lights of torches in the rear courtyard and the heated sounds of a sporting event beyond.

Gabriel and the colonel strode the length of the great marble room and reached the desk.

The colonel said, "I was on good terms with Jake Braxton—" He froze mid-sentence when he recognized Pierce Briggins's features in the administrator's bearded face. The colonel swallowed to regain his composure. "I apologize, Mr. Lutus, but you look like someone I knew a long time ago."

"The ancients believed that each of us had a twin in this world," Lutus said. "What brings the ranchers that supply us with such good horse stock to the city?"

The colonel was still mesmerized and stunned by the

resemblance, so Gabriel broke in, "We need a passage through the Stone Tribe lands; we're willing to pay what's necessary."

"The Stone Tribe land, why on earth would anyone go there, or beyond it?" Lutus asked.

"A renegade chief, calls himself the White Lion, raided North County. He's running the head he stole through the valleys and we need safe passage to stop his war party before he reaches the lakes; we'll pay whatever it costs," Gabriel hastened to add.

"Tin City has thousands of renegades to the south that steal a third of business every year. The Stone Tribes are the only thing between me and them. The renegades fear the Stone Tribes or they used to. It's mostly a spiritual fear now, the tribe is nearly gone. Tin City's had an arrangement with the Stone Tribe that's held for ten years. I don't allow trespassers to cross the Ash, and they have license to kill anyone who ventures there without a commission from the city," Lutus said.

Gabriel looked straight at Lutus and said, "I got kin taken by that raiding party. That chief put a cannon shot to my front door and killed everyone except two of my nieces. I need to get to that raiding party before he gets to the lake country, or I'll never see those nieces again."

"A cannon? The White Lion has a cannon? The contract was that the Germans would not give them field pieces."

"Germans?" the colonel responded.

"To the south, there is a cadre of Germans that fought with the San Patricio, now outcasts from both lands. They are master craftsmen of weapons, including field pieces. I had an agreement with them that I would leave their gun-running alone as long as they didn't forge field pieces for the tribes. It looks as if they've broken that agreement. How many men do you expect the Stone Tribe will allow to ride through? They won't allow an army no matter what I ask of them." Lutus said it calmly, analytically.

The colonel said, "We're ten; the footprint will be small."

The administrator rose from his desk and moved to a table that rolled on wheels to his right and held his cordials. He poured himself a whiskey and put down two glasses in front of Walker and Gabriel and poured freely. Gabriel didn't refuse but continued to stare at the administrator.

"Ten men? I understand your kin being taken, Mr. McCallum. I have also lost kin to the heathen, but so few men. The White Lion has risen from the ashes it seems. There were rumors he was dead, but I guess he was only waiting patiently, plotting this raid. He is the most powerful warlord to come out of the lake country, very cunning. I met him once under a parlay arranged by the missionary priest. The Lion speaks Latin, I think. He and the priest talked in a language I had never heard spoken. If he went north, then he must have ridden with a small army. How do you plan to stop him with ten men?"

Gabriel's frustration flowed, and he spit out, "Mr. Lutus, we ain't got time to build an army, and if ten can't do it, then so be it. We're burning hours, and we need your help. Are you going to give it?"

The administrator smiled. "Gabriel McCallum, your reputation is well known in the city; the rustlers in the saloons often complain about the challenges they face doing business in North County. I have no reason to place you on my enemies list, but I don't want a grudge with the White Lion, either. But ten men against his killing horde, he can't begrudge me that. I'll secure your crossing in the morning; go to the papist mission, you can't miss it, it's ten miles south of the ferry landing. I'll send a guide with you. I'll give you a letter with the seal of the city you can give to the priest. If any man can obtain a safe passage through the Stone Tribe, it's that crackpot."

"Crackpot?" Gabriel asked.

"Excuse me. The priest holds himself out as some sort of

mystic. There are rumors of dark arts, the occult, ritual sacrifices, that sort of thing is bandied about, perhaps nonsense."

As the administrator scratched away with his quill, he said, "This is going to be the courtroom when it's finished. It is time for this land to receive justice. The judge will sit here—where I sit. Take your drinks gentlemen; let's watch the end of the match."

The administrator rolled the paper into a scroll and dripped hot wax from a candle onto the roll. He sank his ring into the wax and, pressing it on the fold, sealed it. He handed the scroll to Gabriel, took up his whiskey, and asked the colonel and Gabriel to follow. They emerged into the torch-lit rear stone terrace that lay opposite the great room's window adorned with Moses.

They walked the stone colonnade until they reached a vantage point that looked directly down on the large gathering around the empty pool of a half-finished fountain. The walls of stone were in place, but the floor was not yet finished, and it was awash with a black, soupy mud. Rows of rowdy men stood around its edges, some in the work clothes of laborers; some garbed as bounty hunters; most in the garish vested suits of the merchant class. All circled the pool looking down upon the two combatants thrashing in the mud. Barks of wager were flung among the crowd, the bookmakers crying out the combinations of odds on the first to die.

The two men were stripped to the waist and barefoot. The two covered in the dark mud circled each other like wary animals. The smaller man was bleeding from both nostrils. The mucous and blood mixed and ran down to his chin and dripped onto his chest. The smaller man's torso was smeared with handprints, similar to those found adorning the walls and ceilings of the caves of lost peoples. The two men lunged at each other grappling like Greco-Roman wrestlers uttering no words but allowing grunts to communicate their intentions.

The administrator said, "The two are, eh, friends. A pair of outlaws, petty thieves really. They broke into the manor house of a merchant; contrary to most of his kind, he was well-liked. The merchant had a pistol, but the two wrestled it from him, and it fired, spreading the merchant's heart out a hole in his back. The winner gets to join the Chinese chain gang and slave until the stone for this courthouse is finished, if he lives that long. The loser dies tonight in that mud. The railroad is coming. We have been an outpost out past civilization long enough. Justice is coming, gentlemen; this courthouse is the future. The rule of law is coming; you really can't do business without it, but until the world reaches out with rail, this works. Take the ferry across at first light. I will tell the ferryman, he will guide you to the priest."

In the pit, the large thief clutched his friend about the waist and raised him as if a child and the two toppled over in a great spatter that sprayed the black mud upon the crowd to the hoots and hollers of all surrounded, as if sharing the filth had bonded them to the blood contest in the arena. The crowd's anticipation rose up in one great laughing cheer as the large man gained the advantage and drove his little friend's face deep into the mud. His meaty hands clenched the small man's neck until the color of his fingertips purpled with the blood of effort. The little man's arms and legs flayed out in four directions, like a newborn babe when it's placed on its stomach for the first time.

The large man cried out, "I'm sorry, Petey, oh, Petey, I'm so sorry," which raised a ruckus of elation by the mud-splattered mob ringing the fountain.

The administrator said, "The priest may not help you. He is converting the southern tribes with some success and is partial to them. He detests the city, he detests me, but he still needs me. He's building the Garden of Eden down there or the Tower of Babel, take your pick, but for now he still needs money, tools, and livestock, which I provide him and he keeps his renegade converts from disrupting commerce. Don't trust him; he's a liar. I want forty horses if you ever lay eyes on North County again, and I want the Germans to stop selling guns to the renegades. Do we have a deal?"

"Yes," Gabriel said.

The colonel said, "Goodnight."

The administrator said softly, "Goodbye, Johnny."

Gabriel and the colonel crossed the mud flat bridges back to the stable.

CHAPTER FOURTEEN:
ACROSS THE ASH RUN RIVER

As the sun simmered above the rim of the horizon, the North County riders filed out of the stable and began shedding their stiffness as they moved to the river. It was the first time Seth and Toby beheld a city rising to the day. The city was a warren of the wood-framed housing that lined crooked and twisted streets. The morning drove the laborers out from the maze laid by necessity and not design. The wood could not contain the multitudes of miners and they came forth from canvas lean-to tents that stretched from the walls of the shacks over the mud alleyways.

Toby watched as the canvas covering a single cart in the street was yanked clear to lay bare a dozen men asleep like kinked spoons in a drawer. Strange tongues meshed in a guttural dissonance. The harshest were the thick brogues that excoriated toilers to "Get a move on!" from the saloon's front porch. The house breakfast special was two boiled eggs and a stein of beer. It slaked the dust that still lay in the catch of their throats earned the day before in the mines. The steel carafes topped with foam were emptying and the piss trench in the street filling.

The whores lined the second-floor porch still clad in their evening costumes of gaudy dress, mascara hiding the eyes of the bone-tired laborers of the night. The madam prodded them to wave, smile, and yell the names of regulars trying to sow the seed of lust in the minds of what she considered a herd of imbecile cattle. The seed would germinate in the darkness of the mine all day and bloom as a flower when the wretched passed from the depths into the night to waste the wages earned through hours of toil with the pick on a moment's time with flesh. The workers coagulated onto the broad avenue that stretched below the skeleton of the rising town hall's new dome. The miasma flowed toward the holes in the mountains that brought forth the silver that fed the city.

Peddlers bobbed on the shores of the street hawking steaming meat pies and great shakers of coffee. The hawkers brayed the fabulousness of their ingredients and tried to captivate the mob by donning garish outfits.

Jed's mouthful grunt roused Toby from his gawking and he saw in Jed's extended hand two great doughy rolls smothered in greasy fat; a second grunt conveyed the need to pass one to Seth. Jed passed back again thick strips of meat from a horned cow slain less than an hour ago. The flesh was hot and tough, bubbling warm with the same grease that had flavored the rolls.

The laborers choked the roadway but the broad chest of the colonel's horse separated the workers like a scythe. To any man that looked afoul upon the rudeness, the sight of the ten adorned with pistols and sundry killing tools stifled the old-world urge to raise vile oaths and generated only insolent stares instead. Hitched to Raif's pommel, hung a score of scalps woven into a cord that showcased the life of each prior owner, not all the hair dark; remnants of a decade of slaughter. The laborers were violent men but acknowledged the fragility of life when it came into conflict with such a company.

Toby knew Gabriel would drop any who slowed the passage with a shot to the forehead, his horse not even breaking stride. He could feel the new intention as soon as they woke in the stable that morning. He saw it in the hard looks of the men he had known his life whole. Men who had bounced him on knees and taught him to shoot were leading him to the wastelands for a reckoning. Toby watched the great migration of laborers as they climbed up the cutbacks to the dark circles that marked the entrances to the burrows carved by man into the side of the mountain to pull out the soft white metal that shined like no other. The line, like a colony of zigzagging ants returning to the nest in service to the queen, dissipated into the darkness.

Seth asked Jed, "How long they stay in them holes?"

"They get six dollars for every twelve hours, more depending on if they're the one to find a good sleeve of silver in the rock," Jed said.

"You couldn't get me in there for no amount," Seth said.

"You talk to 'em in the saloon and most send the money back east for family or stor'n it up to buy a good cut a land back in the old world of Ohio, or Pennsylvania; they don't reckon to do it forever, enough to get 'em started on something else," Jed said.

"It's plumb crazy, Jed, a man spend'n his days in a hole," Seth said.

"Yeah, well they're looking at us say'n, look at them fools head'n to the wastelands to get their balls and hair sliced off while they're still breath'n, and no pay to boot," Jed reasoned.

They met the administrator's man, Philippe, at the ferry crossing. He was the only one permitted to ferry men across the Ash. The first mate was an old sot with a gnarled nose that was cracked like a broken mirror, sprouting a hundred crooked lines of red. He blew an endless stream of phlegm, spraying it into the river as they crossed. He had small pupils encased in small eyes permanently fixed in a squint, the deep furrows of his brow the tell that he had voyaged through a lifetime plying sun-beaten waters.

The horsemen fed onto the long flat deck of the ferry and the great pull to the far shore began. The river had a slow current, but it flowed in such a leaden way that the secret of its fathoms depth was betrayed.

As the ferry neared the far shore, Philippe's eyes darted about the sandstone cliffs and the old sot rocked from foot to foot as if he was testing the lightness of his step, judging his spryness to see if he could steal back across to the far shore, running atop the water.

Phillipe turned to the old sot. "You can let it drift with the current out fifty yards but not a yard more, I can swim that if I need to."

The old sailor looked up at the cliffs, an uncontrollable tick beating in the temple of his left eye. He grunted, "If they wanna get to it, you ain't making it to no damn river."

"You keep it fifty yards out and not an inch more. I better not find you drinking. I'll be back in less than two hours. And, if my ass is runn'n for it, you ding the closest ones to me. I need to clear it to the water, they ain't much for swimming," Phillipe enjoined him.

"I don't like it. We bringing white riders—they done been clear enough about that, they're watch'n us now, I believe it." The old man shook his head and pushed the ancient pistol with its awkward three-foot barrel around under the buckle of his thick leather belt. He hacked up a great ball and sent it into the river where it disappeared without so much as a ripple, twisting once before it disappeared into the black water. He looked at Seth and Toby, weighed their age, looked straight ahead at the sandstone cliffs, and said, "You boys is crazy."

Philippe mounted a beautiful brown pony, its hindquarters dappled with white spots. He led the line up a dry arroyo that had not seen flowing water in a thousand years, but the lines running lengthwise in the stone walls betrayed the strength of the tributary that once fed the great inland sea. The forgotten bed of the river was hard-packed sand, and it made for an easy climb despite the steep pitch from the river. Philippe's horse still had wild in him, and it grew more skittish with the new smells it encountered on the far side of the river. Philippe handled him deftly, but both rider and horse were jittery as if they both knew it were a fool's errand.

It took an hour to climb to the top of the arroyo; once atop, Philippe turned to the colonel. "The administrator told me to take you 'til I could see the church steeple, so that's what I'm going to do. If Farinata is not there cause he's out doing whatever he claims to be do'n, I ain't stay'n; but show his people the seal and tell'm you're allowed to wait for him at the Mission of St. Pedro."

"You are supposed to introduce us. How's this priest going to know we have permission from the administrator?" the colonel asked.

"I spoke to the administrator three days ago, and he told me that riders were coming and needed a ferry to the wastelands. I already told Farinata's people to prepare for you. You have the letter with the seal, take it to the priest," Philippe answered.

"I don't understand. How'd you know we were coming?" the colonel asked.

"If you don't understand, Colonel, how do you expect me to understand? I am just the ferry man; maybe you're not the riders I was told to expect. I don't know. The administrator tells me what he thinks I need and nothing more. Take the seal to the church; it's all you'll need. The administrator's seal will carry weight with the priest."

They rode for another hour along the top of the arroyo until it crested another hundred feet. The vista looked down upon St. Pedro's Mission. It sat like a crown in the midst of a varicolored checkerboard of farm fields. The patchwork quilt of the earth stretched in its pattern across the valley floor as far south as the eye could behold. Philippe's manner eased upon the sighting of the mission, but his eyes now darted about the hills as if he felt some force closing in upon him.

St. Pedro's Mission was enormous, and for half the length of the main building it had a second-level adobe floor that overlooked a great courtyard, surrounded by stone walls, with a large well in its midst. To the back were stables with three fenced paddocks, the split-wood railing circling to form a great clover. The mission crackled with a colony of life; farmers, women, and hordes of children milled about in white cotton frocks all synched at the waist with sashes of fine, colored cloth.

The new church was under construction. The sacristy wall of adobe brick and the soaring steeple topped with an angel blowing a horn were finished. Dozens of artisans and apprentices worked upon the scaffolding, eight tiling the giant mural of St. Peter kneeling before Christ as he grasped a fishing net on the shore of Gethsemane. The mural would sit one day fully encased in the north transept on the Gospel side. Toby looked out over it and could not figure so beautiful a hacienda with the image of the wastelands that had been forged in his mind by the rumors and fantastic tales he'd learned as a boy.

Philippe turned to the colonel. "There's the mission, you can ride on from here. You don't need me." He reined his pony and added over his shoulder as he rode back to the river, "Don't trust that son of a bitch, Colonel." He moved off at a clip, and the ten watched him disappear down the arroyo galloping hard until he reached the banks of the Ash.

The old sot pulled hard to reach him; Phillipe rode onto the flats of the ferry's boards, and he and the old sot began pulling for the far side, the old sot yelling, "Who said thar's no such things as miracles, you lucky son of a bitch."

When the company met Father Farinata, he had his back to them supervising the craftsmen working on the mural of the south transept depicting Christ's temptation in the wilderness.

The artisans eyed the priest warily and hastened to complete his direction even if he communicated it, as he often did, with no more than a nod of the head. Lucifer was depicted as a spirit wrapped in a modest reddish-brown cloak. The Savior lay prostrate, with a lean and hungry look—the forty days in the wilderness captured in his prostration. The mountaintop looked upon the glowing cities of the plain.

The riders entered the half-erected church and saw the priest was tall, powerfully built, with a strong jaw and an angular profile most pronounced in his Roman nose.

The colonel said, "Good morning, Father."

The priest turned, and the left side of his face was horribly disfigured with burns etched into his eye decades ago.

"Good morning, Colonel, the administrator informed me you would be coming."

Farinata looked into the eyes of the ten gunmen standing in his church with his left eye, the horrific scarring encasing the right orb in a ring of pure white.

"Father, we've been told that you could secure us passage through the Stone Tribe country," the colonel said.

"There's been peace here by the river for ten years. Why do you come so adorned with weapons? May I ask why you want to head into the wooded canyons and challenge the peace I have with the tribes there?"

The colonel said, "We're hunting a warlord savage by the name the White Lion."

The priest eyed them all in the room again. "Why would eight men and two boys ride in and challenge the army of the White Lion? You'll never climb out of his world."

"Father, why don't you let us worry about that. Can you get us the passage? We need to track that savage before his trail goes cold," the colonel said.

"What impresses you to believe he's a savage?" the priest asked.

"Father, he killed a family, blew the front door off with a cannon and slaughtered them all. He's dragging that cattle back to the wastelands, and we aim to stop him," the colonel said.

"He's no savage, Colonel. He was educated by Spanish missionaries in your lands more than forty years ago. He lived in a village that sat between two rivers in the North County. He reads Greek, Latin, can speak Aramaic. Have you ever spoken with him, Colonel? Would it surprise you to learn his entire family was hacked to death by whites and his tribe forced out of their lands? His people were chased into the Stone Tribe country, and there they were attacked again and forced to migrate farther south. They call their journey to the lakes, the Path of Blood. And now you want me to help you pass into lake country to butcher those people again?" The priest appeared to study them closely, but through the cloudy aura of his opaque eye that was encased in the scars of melted flesh.

"The administrator told us you would help," the colonel said.

To reach an accommodation, the priest softened his countenance. "I can help, Colonel, but not the way you propose. I will send a message to the White Lion. I will tell him he has taken the kin of powerful warlords to the north. I will offer a deal for the hostages in exchange for horses. He can return the hostages to me. We can avoid any further bloodshed this way. I suggest you remain in Tin City. I will send word to you. It won't be long; you would be surprised how fast information travels now between the peoples here."

The colonel parlayed with Gabriel, and Gabriel walked up to the priest. "I don't recall us telling you that he had taken hostages, so maybe you're right, maybe word does travel fast down here in this shithole, or maybe you knew what this White Lion was up to go'n north. Either way, I'm tell'n you now you best stay out of it. If he's got an army, you're right, what can ten do against that, so get us a safe passage through and you can keep clear of it."

The artisans could sense the tenor in the room and put down their tools and moved for the door, but Raif, Jed, and Abner drew pistols and told them to stay put.

"Raphael, why do you draw your weapon in this place? Have I ever denied you anything in my mission? You and I have always been friends, when you searched for Lobo, did I not help? Have we not always understood one another?" Farinata asked.

"I reckon, Padre, but this is North County business, and I always told you that's where it ends," Raif retorted.

Gabriel asked, "How is it, Priest, you can operate this mission? How come a foot south of your fields, if it walks, crawls, or slithers it has to hide to live, yet this is no fort, and I don't see a single man on this hacienda carrying a weapon."

"I share creation with the White Lion as I share it with you too, Mister McCallum. The mission is here to heal the bond between God and his creation, to care for the children of this land. Salvation underlies everything you see here. I know you, Mr. McCallum. Luther journeyed here many times and we talked of the souls in North County. Have you forgotten all the reverend taught you: 'in his own image, and each to his own way'? The White Lion has his way, and I'm not ordained to judge God's creation, Gabriel."

"You've bartered with them devils, and I don't know what you've given them, but you gave something so that you could build this, whatever it is. You been out of the world too long, in such a place as this; I reckon one day you wake up and it all appears normal."

"When I came to America, Gabriel, I heard wondrous tales about the Mississippi, tales of riverboats and cities along its path, how the river gave life to the delta. The first time I saw it was on a hot August day on my journey west. I trekked to the top of a rise and asked a farmer how far to the river. He paused from his toil and led me on a path through his fields to a wood atop a short hill. He said the knoll would give the grand view of his river, a river he loved and feared since he'd first swam in it as a boy. As we reached the hill, he told me to keep straight and I would see the ruins of an old stone house built by an unknown people that had arrived and disappeared even before his people had reached the fertile land along the river.

"I cannot tell you how great my anticipation when I climbed to the ruins and placed my hands on the stones and looked out to the Mississippi, the sight that had lived to that day only in my imagination, the wild and fabulous tales that had shaped my mind's vision of it. What did I see as I placed my hands upon that wall and looked out? I saw nothing but a brown muddy slop. Oh, there was power, it moved things and people and fed the land, but it did it with no beauty. It was there upon that old stone wall for the first time, after years of trying, that I understood the world. Each man has a muddy river that runs through him, it is his first nature, it is the spring that feeds him—all of us, you, me, the White Lion, the same muddy river flows through us, and like the Mississippi, no banks can hold it. At times it will flood and kill the very things on its shores that worship it."

"I'm not a missionary, Padre, and I don't much reckon to discover the White Lion's nature, don't care if it's evil, good or not, whatever it be I'm going to find him and kill him," Gabriel said.

The priest seemed to relax into his cloak as he sat at a table, "The mixing of good and evil in the heart is the fabric of life—evil, Gabriel, evil is invincible. Accepting it is the only way to move forward until that day comes when we learn to stop killing each other, and until that day, some have no choice but to taste of the vinegar."

"Padre, you can worry about my and that heathen's soul all you want; it's his ass I need to shoot 'cause he took my two nieces, and whatever you're doing here, you're right about the river flooding, it's gonna flood here and wash all this bullshit of yours away, ain't nothing can be built in this land," Gabriel said.

"The North County exists with its Gabriels, and the wastelands exist with its White Lions. Mr. McCallum, there is no repentance for the angels after their fall, and there is no repentance for men after death. If you venture down there, you all will die bloody, and your nieces will be enslaved. The Lion will return the nieces to me, show patience. These men know it is your decision, Gabriel. Think of these two young boys, to die before being given the chance to fully live, to be men. I promise you there is no reason to venture down, the Lion can be reasoned with," the priest said.

"Padre, I hear them levies creaking; I'd hate to see the river start flood'n this day," Gabriel said.

The priest eyed Gabriel and knew the soil must cry out with blood. "Ah, each to his own way—you will have your pass through the Stone Tribe. The poor box is in the sacristy near the baptismal fount, it is one of the first things I had built after the roof—fill it with gold eagles and I'll send word to the ancients to let you pass without violence," the priest said.

"We'll fill it, Priest, but a man with one eye shouldn't try to keep watch of two camps. Don't send word to that heathen or we'll come back through here after we're finished crucifying him," Gabriel said.

"Gabriel, like you, I was blind before the shamans of the Great Desert scorched me; now I see more with more clarity than I ever did. One more thing: Luther borrowed a golden crucifix, it's unique, please return it to me if you ever see North County again."

They rode in single file through the Stone Tribe lands upon a trail that had once ringed an ancient sea. They saw a single tribesman standing sentinel. Toby and Seth looked upon him on a stone ledge above the path standing in front of a cave carved out of the sandstone. He was more aged than any man they had ever seen, nothing but a sheath of dry skin shrouded over bone and sinew. His hair hung in a monkish halo stringing down to his shoulders in great wisps; it was bleached by the sun a radiant white and glowed in relief of his scorched skin. He held a spear by his side; one leg tucked up behind, standing like some rare amber pelican. He watched without passion. He had been born betwixt the ages. As a child, he ran wild in the woods without fear, his people ruling without challenge from the Ash to the southern lake. He gazed now through the cloudy aura of an aged man's eyes upon intruders beneath his home that in his boyhood would have been torn to pieces by the warriors of his tribe. He had never weighed time, to him there had never been a past or future, only the day. Yet, he dreamed the handful of newborn males suckling in his valley would never reach manhood, their deaths written in the arrows already honed by the tribe rising to the south, and the women would be taken as slaves, to propagate a new race.

The sentinel's flaked spearhead had been honed to its razor's edge with millennia of learned skill but it stood useless against the tide of the future crashing upon his tribe.

CHAPTER FIFTEEN:
FORGERS OF WEAPONS

The trail led to five canyons etched from the world by four rivers running south to the great lake. Three of the canyons were impassable to cattle, the rivers having cut narrow, deep gorges furrowed with a tangle of vine and scrub along sandstone cliffs. The fourth canyon was the path the White Lion would take. The Germans had raised their village in exile in this swallow of the third canyon.

The colonel rode next to Raif despite the tightness of the red clay path. "Why didn't you tell me you knew that priest?" the colonel asked.

"Colonel, it were you give me the commission to hunt down Lobo, where'd you suppose I was gonna find that liver-eater?"

"I reckon, but I didn't reckon on you making friends along the way."

"North County hospitality, I guess."

"We got a new commission from the administrator. He's done his part of the deal and got us through the Stone Tribe, so now we got to find the Germans."

"They built a settlement in the passing canyon, where the Stick run, the one with the high peak to the west that looks like an Injun on horseback."

"I know it," the colonel said, and squinted ahead as if he were trying to see beyond the wall of ridges to the very spot.

"Last I was there, they had tamed that land like their people do, farms and a forge built right into rock, crafty sons-a-bitches."

"How many?"

"I reckon twenty, I suspect by this time there's women and kids, they tend to breed."

"Children?"

"There were none a few year ago, but once they got it go'n, they were bent on send'n for wives," Raif said.

"What's the move here?"

"I reckon we need to look like we're chasing something, I expect if they think it's the White Lion we're chasing, they might get ornery with us. Every day they siesta around noon, eat and drink some, play that awful polka, oompah—the play is to tell 'em we're hunting cattle thieves that raided North County. They'll act like they're surprised and won't tell us it's the Lion—we spend a shitload of gold, that always gets them a happy drunk on, and after we tilt a few cups with 'em we turn and commence blast'n—I reckon they won't suspect its com'n, they being friends of mine and all."

The company reined up and dismounted along a creek running the length of the second valley. The riders kneeled on the riverbank and filled their canteens and waterskins with the clear water. Wesley plunged his head in the water and raised it, spraying the water from his mouth. The rest eyed the ridges to the west looking for any movements as they sipped from their canteens. The colonel, Gabriel, and Raif talked openly of the strategy, Raif remarking on the cunning of the Germans. It had been years since Raif had wandered the wastelands, and he doubted the layout of the camp was the same, knowing the foreigners and their capacity for building on the land. Raif's last comment was that their greed for gold could not be sated; it was all they ever talked. It was a heavily armed camp, so the plan was to draw the Germans together and not storm the compound; the company would go to them bearing gold, seeking to buy the magnificent forged field pieces.

Gabriel and the colonel spilled the remaining gold from their saddlebags and the coins tinkled as they bounced on the horse blanket. The administrator and the priest had cost but there was still enough gold left to feed the Germans' lust for it. Gabriel would open first and the order passed among them: if it moved in the camp, it was to die. They went to the second canyon and broke brush until they found a clearing much shaded from the sun; there they penned the horses with sage brush, hobbling the mounts. They planned to sleep for two hours to be fresh for it.

Seth and Toby were sent to the west watch, and they lay flat in the low brush watching the trail the company had ridden out upon from the mission. Seth nudged Toby, and they watched as two young boys dressed in the clothes of the mission were running hard on the trail in their bare feet, the colored sashes flapping and trailing from their waists.

Seth ran back to the company and shook Gabriel awake only to be cussed at and told, "What you shak'n me for—kill 'em; don't let 'em get past; priest warn'n the heathen."

Seth reached Toby, and they reined up and chased the boys, who didn't expect riders from behind them and looked surprised when Toby and Seth rode them down and whipped them with ropes until the boys raised their hands and begged for quarter.

A hundred yards back a third boy, Miguel, lay flat among the gnarled and jagged trees that ran south of the trail. The pygmy trees were blackened by a brush fire that had been triggered by a lightning strike. The sap still oozed from the wounded bark and mixed with the ash creating a cinnamon-red blush along the base of each tree, the rusty crimson broken with flashes of white from the bony thorns that pierced from the crooked branches. Miguel was silent, his breath barely twisting the dust that lay an inch from his lips.

The two captured boys were bound back-to-back with rope and their wrists intertwined. The company rode up and Joe parlayed with the boys, but the two refused to talk, staring at Joe with dark eyes.

Gabriel dismounted and asked Seth, "Why ain't they dead?"

"We reckon'd you'd want to question 'em to see what they up to."

"What for? Priest hedges his bets; sending boys too that sumbitch. I'm gonna burn that shithole of his to the ground; now finish 'em with knives, cut 'em like pigs across the throat, gag'em first so they don't holler."

Before Seth and Toby moved, Abner walked up and stove in the top of the boys' heads with a knotted stick topped with a perfectly round ball of iron. The skulls cracked with a single pop at that crown where the sinewy bone of a baby's skull stays soft the longest. As he turned and walked away, Abner said, "First kill shouldn't be a child. You never forget your first; rest of 'em all run together."

Gabriel glared at Seth. "That's how it's done. Learn from it or you ain't gonna see your sisters again and jest might get your balls burned off. Two of you split up and find their trail, and damn well certify that it's two of 'em and there ain't no other out there the priest sent, I suspect he prefers three."

Seth and Toby rode off, and they saw the main trail split in parts, smaller paths leading off into the thicket of the blackened thorn trees.

Seth said, "I'll ride this small one for a bit and see if there's any sign of another runner."

"All right, I'll ride back a ways on the trail we come up and see if I can find where them two's tracks let off; if'n I find a third I'll ride and fetch you."

Toby galloped down the path but reined up as he neared the

spot beneath the sandstone ridge where the sentinel had watched their passage. He spun his horse back and across the main trail scanning the ground for footprints. He found the game paths for javelinas and the coyotes that tracked the skunk pigs but no other prints. He rode back west slowly and found two sets of tracks a yard off the trail and figured them to be the markings of the dead two. He reined in Ulysses and tracked the prints east along the side of the main trail. He rode beneath the sentinel's perch again and looked, but the aged warrior was not there. He followed for half a mile and was about to gallop off when on a hunch he checked the far side of the trail and found a set of tracks running west, small toes had turned the dusty soil, and he knew they were the tracks of a boy running.

He started Ulysses down the course until the tracks bent hard to the south and disappeared into the thickets of the thorn tree forest. He hobbled Ulysses and pushed his way into the brush. It was thick the way wild forest grows back after a fire, tangled, stumped, and low to the ground. The thorns tore at his face and ripped at his gloves but Toby pressed on know'n that the boy must know of a path or nobody'd try to cut his way through this thicket. He cut east and pushed on until he spilled out onto a small dirt path running north-south through the thickets. He headed south on the trail and felt the soft earth open for the heels of his boots. He stalked slowly until he was almost creeping. The blood was throbbing in his ears, his senses telling him he was closing in on his prey, the hair on his arms tingling.

He removed his boots and crept along the trail bent slightly under the canopy with his pistol drawn. He picked up the track again and followed the path of small feet until they reached a creek that ran hidden under the gnarled vines and overhanging branches. The river twisted lazily under the canopy of trees running to the south. He felt the cool water run over his bare feet as he waded into the stream, searching the rocks for the marks where the lichen had been turned. Rocks glimmered smooth, and he knew the boy had taken the stream south. He followed about a hundred yards until he saw the splash of water upon a flat rock by the side of the crick. He knelt upon the rock and peered through the bushes until his eyes adjusted to the shadows.

As the light diffused, the boy's cotton shirt rose out of the blackness and contrasted with the dark shock of hair that lay thick and long on the back of the boy's head. He was hiding behind a tree, lying still as a snake, searching south for any movement of the white riders. Toby gazed at the boy and appreciated his silence, his stillness, the discipline as he lay in his hide waiting for the riders to move on so he could break for the south. He looked bigger than the other two, and Toby reckoned he was older and had let the other two run ahead like the buck that sends the doe and her little ones out into the meadow, making it their fate to fall with a shot to the heart so he could live to hump another day.

Toby crawled up and put the barrel of his pistol to the back of the boy's head, and he felt the wrack of fear shudder through his barrel. Gabriel had told him never to put his gun to a man's head because a man could whip a hand faster than the pull of a trigger, but he figured the boy was scared and wouldn't try to fight him.

The boy shuddered again and put his hands forward with his palms flat and faced down at the earth. He kept his head down and began to cry and whimpered, *"No me digas el sacerdote, Dios me ayude."*

Toby grabbed him by the hair and flipped him around telling him to shut his mouth, putting the barrel to the boy's lips to signify his meaning. Toby figured the boy to be about ten years old. He had deep bluish-black eyes and wore about his neck a leather strip that had clasped to it a crude odd-shaped wooden cross. Toby felt the handle of his cutting blade slung on his belt. He figured not to fire his pistol so near the Stone Tribe, thinking the passage deal might have been a one-way train ticket, and he didn't want a running fight with spearmen in this thicket. He gripped the hard leather handle of his knife and ran through his mind Raif's teaching on how to finish it quick.

The boy held his hands above his face in a shielding manner, the only sound a thin reedy whimper like a coon-dog puppy yelps the first time you have to snout it to get it to heel. Toby felt his chest and scrotum cinch tight and his breathing grow short. The world started spinning beneath his feet, and the throbbing sound in his ears deafened him to the boy's whimpering. Toby tied the boy's hands and said, *"Andale."* He tied a rope lead to his waist and yanked him along behind him, put his boots back on, and headed north up the stream. He was leading him with no particular destination and for reasons he didn't know and only headed toward Ulysses because he could think of no other purpose. He thought to take him back and have Abner stave in his head, but he knew the company would think him weak.

He passed a thin tree near the riverbank and saw that its thick roots reached out from the earth like a spider's legs. He figured the river flooded in winter and once over its banks it pulled the earth from about the roots of trees downstream. The exposed roots formed a chair of sorts with high elbow rests. Toby knew what needed getting done. Gabriel couldn't have been clearer about that, but he knew he couldn't kill the boy.

He stopped in the water and looked at the roots. He dragged the boy and forced him to sit amidst the thorn tree's roots and bound him thrice around the chest to the trunk and lashed his arms to his ankles like a roped steer. The boy sat like a king bound to his tree throne. Toby reckoned even if he started chewing on the rope it would take him a day to free himself, but he knew he had no real way of knowing. He figured it was just as likely the boy could die a worse death if a critter or ants found him and reasoned again with himself not to send his knife into his neck. He nearly wept but he knew he couldn't kill the boy.

He cursed his weakness and took to cursing the priest for sending a boy on such a charge, saying to himself that the bloodletting would be on the priest. No matter how hard he reasoned the pulsing in his chest would rise and wouldn't let him kill the boy. He returned to Ulysses and headed back to the company.

He caught up with Seth and said, "I only found two tracks, I reckon Abner done ended this one."

Seth looked at Toby and said, "Toby, don't go tell'n anyone, but I reckon I jest couldn't of done them two in like Abner did, they was jest kids."

Toby spit, trying his best to look hard. "We best get go'n 'fore they come look'n for us."

The dark-eyed boy struggled against the hemp cords but couldn't reach the ropes with his teeth. He squirmed and struggled and felt the hemp give only grudgingly to his straining. He knew it would take hours to free himself, and he feared he would suffer the rite if he failed the priest. He looked to the heavens to pray, but as he raised his head he saw the sentinel staring at him. The aged man was squatting, his knees near his ears, his ancient stone-tipped spear held by one hand resting lengthwise across his toes. He was three feet away and the boy had not heard him approach. The sentinel squatted silently, chewing a mild hypnotic nut that grew wild in the thorn tree forest. He let the brown juice slip the corner of his mouth and run freely down his chin.

The priest had forbidden the children of the mission to enter the Stone Tribe lands, and Miguel feared the ancient warrior. The old crones of his village told the children tales of the tribesmen, that they tore the limbs from naughty boys and ate them raw and enjoyed the music of their screams as they were consumed.

The sentinel squatted, still gazing at the boy's eyes as if time and action had no correspondence. He raised up the spear with one hand, and the boy followed the axis of the deep cherry brown wood as it spun, and he heard the slash as the sharpened stone spearhead ripped through the three cords of rope that bound his chest to the tree trunk. The sentinel rose and turned slowly, disappearing into the foliage by the river as soundlessly as he'd approached.

The boy, freed from the tree, rolled onto his knees and brought his hands under his feet with that flexibility only the young know. He began dragging the wrist bindings against the dark, rough bark of the tree, and it began to fray. In minutes the bindings of his hands and ankles lay in bits and pieces in the crotch of the tree throne, and he was afoot again, headed south toward the great stone temple that stood like a sentinel before the lake country.

As the company ranged into the third canyon Raif rode ahead, looking for the stone outcropping above the ridge that held the watch. Raif took off his hat and waved at the rocks, and in return, echoing down from the cliff, he heard, "Raif, hallo, *mein freund.*"

Raif answered, "Is that you, Dieter?"

"*Ja,* Raif, long time; and good to see."

"*Ya, mein freund,*" Raif responded in a weak mimicry of a German accent.

The company kept to the trail, and as they neared the valley it opened to a wagon road with wheeled tracks crossing the dirt and crushed stone. As they crested the rise, the Germans' compound and fields came into view. The fields extended like a lantern's cone shape of light into darkness stretching from the narrow bottom of the valley out into the desert floor. The fields flowed with the vivid colors of verdant land. The conduits of the vast aqueduct system the Germans had engineered had drained the river and spread its gift out into the once-desert land. It was an oasis stretching over the primeval alluvial plain. The Germans had sowed the desert until it bloomed, moving tons of earth from the valley to cover the Ordovician limestone and calcareous shale that had formed an ocean bottom millennia ago. The fields were a patchwork of bounty. The stockade was crude but practical. The homes were raw timbered and lay in tiers rising up the ridgelines.

Entering the main compound, which sat on the floor of the southern valley, you could hear the hammers pounding on the molten steel emerging from the forge. The largest structure was a whitewashed barn, and from its dark interior came a red glow and the hiss and rush of the forge's fire. In neat rows outside the forge doors were three bronze-colored field pieces, the artillery the same type as the one they found spiked near the Old Mission, and which had killed the McCallums.

The Germans welcomed Raif with slaps to the back and great hugs as if he were a long-lost member of their tribe returned home from an odyssey. After he had caught up to Lobo, it was here he had trekked back to with his bleeding wounds, and here the Germans had saved him, searing his wounds before he bled out. Lobo had eaten a few of their members and Raif was a hero to them. The Germans had found a vein of precious metal in the valley since Lobo's time, and had begun mining, selling the precious silver in Tin City. They had bought bronze in exchange and continued to forge field pieces, selling cannon to a rogue Mexican general they had fought for in the Mexican war, who was now planning a coup to take control of the Mexican state that lay to the southwest.

The wealth had paid for the passage of women from their homeland and the compound teemed with husky raw-boned women red from the sun hanging laundry and other chores. They had taken to cradling their infants in hide slings about their chests in the way of the southern tribes and the young ran about in the same white cotton frocks and sashes as the mission children.

Raif and the colonel met with Klaus and the ruling council of elder Germans. The discussion ran to trade, gold, and the price of field pieces and ammunition. Raif explained they were hunting a renegade who'd ventured into North County and stolen a hundred head and left a dozen dead. They were sent by a commission and sanctioned by the army to find the renegade. They told the Germans they didn't know what tribe he hailed from or where he was headed, but they were hoping Klaus could help. Klaus was the honcho, akin to a *burgermeister*, and Raif was cautious because he knew him to be wary and shrewd.

Klaus said that the tribes no longer ventured past the Ash Run, and his people knew of no warlord who would chance passing the Crossing, claiming the days of such ventures was finished for the tribes.

Raif nodded his understanding and asked them to keep an ear out from the locals and see if any were talking about a raid so they could get a fix on the band that done it.

The colonel put his saddlebag forward and took out a thousand in gold, counting the coin out slowly, moving the pieces methodically across the table. The Germans followed the coin with fixed eyes. The company aimed to purchase ammo and a field piece if the Germans had a caisson or wagon that could haul it to sell. The Germans *ja, ja'd* and stared at the coins, nodding to each other. The colonel added that he didn't think they'd need it, but a few rounds would scare the hell out of any renegade, to which the Germans laughed and Klaus said, "*Ja, ja,* we forge it loud for purpose." Klaus and the colonel shook hands.

After the meeting, Klaus took Raif aside and they walked the camp, Klaus pointing out all they'd built and their greater plans for the future. When they were clear of the company, Klaus took Raif by the upper arms and looked him in the eye. "Raif, things are different here now. It's not the same as in the days of Lobo when there was no order of things. It's no more this tribe and that, there is one now—a great chief of many tribes from the south we deal with now. It is not good for your party to be here. He has warned us not to harbor strangers. It's no longer small bands, it is all the same. A small company can't travel through here anymore. It's not the same, Raif, I warn you. You are not enough, they are legion, and the chief is crafty."

"What chief, Klaus?"

"Raif, my *freund,* this is our home now—it's not like it used to be, it's not wild anymore—things are happening here, good things; look around, we can build, the renegades trade now, they can be bargained with; it is different. The trade is good from Tin City to the mission. Much is happening here now, the Mexicans fear the chief and stay away; the Tin City fears the priest—we can do business, we can build."

"You and that padre got it all figured, Klaus."

"Raif, you know the padre knows many things, he knows what's in our hearts before we do. Take your friends back to North County, go now north—I tell you it will be the end of you if you venture south, go back. We owe you this, my friend, but we cannot help you in this quest, go home, Raif, take your brothers and go home."

The colonel paid in gold coin, and the Germans were showing the North County men the best way to fire the field piece.

Toward the end of day, the Germans gathered in a large open barn that had a paddock and stables attached. They set up a number of crude iron steins they had forged and one portly red-faced one began to play the accordion, his meaty hands pumping out the awful sounds.

Gabriel stood with his back to the gathering, his hands splayed out on a long board set like a bridge upon hay bales forming the bar of the makeshift tavern. The Germans dug in the soft earth at the back of the barn and dragged a keg out of the ground. They popped a great stopper from it and put in a tap and placed it on its side and began filling their great steel carafes with a mead they had fermented from wild berries and honey. The laughing and wails rose in the barn as the tart liquor flowed. The portly one yelled out that in a month's time they would have real beer from the hops growing in the fields and a great wail of anticipation rose from the Germans.

Raif walked from group to group talking and joking with a carafe in his hand.

The colonel stood next to Gabriel, next came Abner and Jed; all pretended to drink the thick, viscous liquid in their steins. Joe came over with Wesley and all stood with their backs to the Germans pretending to talk. Seth and Toby were left outside with plates of dinner near where the horses were tied; they were given instructions that once the shooting started they were to break for the main trail and set up in defilade with the long rifles and keep the guard posted on the ridge from firing down upon them. All the North County horsemen faced the rear wall of the bar now, standing like many a man in a saloon with their backs to the Germans, who quaffed the mead in great gulps and sang throaty old tunes from a world lost eons ago. Raif brought out in them much laughter and he appeared without effort to be enjoying their company. He sauntered to the bar and stood between the colonel and Gabriel and raised his iron

251

cup as if to drink.

"I reckon there as 'bout unsuspect'n as it's gonna get," Raif said.

"Good, 'cause I had me jest 'bout enough of that goddamn polka," Gabriel said.

In one turn the eight gunmen wheeled and opened fire on the Germans. In those first few seconds the Germans seemed to be open to their fate, as if they'd expected every day they had rooted themselves in the wastelands that eventually this is how the end would come; that it had to end like this in this world. They had believed it would come from the south and not from the north, by the arrow and not the bullet. The steins dinged and flew from hands, spewing the froth, and the North County killers dispatched life each in his way.

Gabriel drew both pistols and walked toward his targets firing with both hands, wild-eyed, as if killing fed the fire that burned in him, its heat and smoke emitting from his barrels and the sockets of his eyes.

Wesley took a proper shootist's stance, firing his pistol with his arm stretched and propped by the other hand with a precise, slight bend to the elbow. He discharged the weapon with almost no perceptible movement except an easy breath, the fluid mechanics of selecting a target and squeezing gently. He aimed at the bobbing, fleeing heads as if the center mass shot to the torso was beneath his abilities. He fired slowly as if the whole event's meaning in the world was a design to test his marksmanship; he stood oblivious to the chaos of the charnel house and never missed; each rhythmic shot expanding a head and releasing its life in fine mist on the hard, rough-hewn wood of the tables.

The colonel kept his eyes moving and was the only one to issue orders, telling Abner and Jed to concentrate on the barn door as a few Germans tried to break out into the light.

Abner fired his shotgun in a double blast, spraying the lead beads into the legs and splaying out four men.

Jed and Joe walked among the fallen as they desperately crawled toward the thin slant of light, thinking if they could reach the sunlight they would live, but the two took aim and sent the final dispatches into their skulls. It was over in minutes, the Germans lying about in the puppet poses of the dead.

Raif moved about the carnage to the back of the barn and saw three Germans on top of hay bales trying to squeeze out a small window. He shot the top man in the ass, and he fell over backward onto the two still atop the hay bales, and they spilled about the hay-strewn floor. He shot two, and the third, named Günter, looked up at him and said, "Raif, *warum?*"

Raif looked down and said, "Hey, Doc." Günter was a surgeon in the old country and had healed Raif after the killing of Lobo. It was Günter who'd seared his flesh and sewed up his wounds, saving his life.

"*Warum,* Raif?"

"It's North County business. You done sold a cannon to that White Lion, and he done killed a family with it—no hard feelings, Doc, but you all knew this day was com'n whether it be this day or t'other,' Raif said, and paused for a moment before he shot Günter through his hands; the round's trajectory splayed the tips of his fingers, which caused the round to tumble and enter Doc's forehead sideways.

Outside Seth took aim at the watch and saw the man Raif had called Dieter run with his rifle toward the sound of the firing. Seth took a bead on him and dropped him like a deer with a shot to the chest. He rested the rifle in the crook of his arm and looked at Toby, but he did not know what to say.

The German women scrambled about in the melee, dragging their children into the huts.

The North County gunmen emerged into the compound

shooting at any man that still moved, walking past a wailing woman on her knees removing a bloody child from the sling she wore about her chest. They rounded up the horses from the paddock, near fifty of them, and took three caissons and limbered the three field pieces to the caissons. Jed and Abner went from hut to hut and set them ablaze.

The women fled up the valley, scrambling into the thick brush, hoping the predators were sated and had lost their desire to hunt.

The company rode out, dragging the cannons, the Germans laid about in varied effigies of death. The company journeyed to the last canyon, where the White Lion was descending.

CHAPTER SIXTEEN:
THE VALLEY OF DEATH

The company stopped at the south end of the fourth valley's ridgeline to lay out its war plan to destroy the army of the White Lion.

The colonel explained to Seth and Toby that the valleys of the south ran like a right hand flattened on a map; the Stone Tribe held the valley of the thumb they had traversed leading in from the east. The remaining fingers ran directly south, and each was wooded and flowed with a river disappearing under the dry plain to emerge and feed a great lake that lay miles to the south where the southern tribes warred. The high ridges that separated the valleys were thick with trees but rose to rocky crests that were naked of life except for that which slithered or crawled.

It was through one of these valleys that the White Lion would descend and the herds of cattle meant it had to be the fourth valley, because it was wide with water and open grasses the herd could feed upon after the high desert crossing. They needed to set the trap before the White Lion's lead scouts reached down into the valley.

The company moved out again ten miles and turned north up the great wooded fourth valley. The White Lion would pass through here to the great lake of the south where a thousand of his people waited for his victor's march amidst the villages that teemed along the shores of the great lake.

The colonel could sense the army of the White Lion starting

its descent at the northernmost point of the valley. He could feel it in his bones and he drove the company to finish the position.

At the crest of the valley, May was astride the White Lion's mare. She was tied naked, her hands bound at the wrist about his stomach. Clara was stripped and tied to the warrior, Bird, a lean and aged warrior who had followed the White Lion since they had run as children along the banks of the Criss in the White Pine forests of the north. The Lion's warriors had been on the move for twenty hours a day since the northern raid began, moving whenever there was any glow in the sky no matter how leaden or how sparse its light. The renegades were exhausted, and their minds rambled with the expectation of the trilling praise they would receive from the women of the lake.

The young warriors were many, and this had been their first taste of war; as conquering heroes bringing a hundred horses and nearly so many cattle they could expect to be given a bride chosen by the Lion. In their wake, lay not only the shattered land of the white ranchers but twenty dead cavalrymen who had ridden hard to inspect the curious dust cloud on the horizon only to find fifty warrior rising up out of the shimmering plain to slaughter the troop to a man. The Lion had lost five in the siege and fifteen in the fight upon the plain with the cavalry. He was leading only twenty-nine warriors in the final push to the lake and was heading straight into the North County position.

The colonel's plan required the White Lion's stolen cattle and horses to stampede with the first shots of cannon, so the company moved up the valley until it found natural rock outcroppings that lay in the center of the pass. The bulls and stallions would break to either side or try to turn in the valley, creating chaos in the ranks of the renegades. The rocks would protect the company from the charging bulls and horses and keep the Lion from knowing their numbers. The warriors would charge bent on punishing those who would dare to attack the tribe so close to the lake country.

Toby and Seth were ordered to the south to conceal the horses in the thick brush of the riverbank and to watch the creek for a scout; their task was to protect the mounts and not engage in the fight. They bristled at the assignment but held their tongues; they rode off as the rest of the company took positions in the rock outcroppings. The colonel placed the three field pieces aiming straight up the pass and filled them with small rocks and nails taken from the Germans' larder. The company concealed them in brush and sage. The strategy was to let the herd and riders close and fire the cannon, throwing every renegade mount into frenzy and wound as many horses and warriors as possible in the first volley. It would sow the chaos they needed to defeat the superior numbers. The North County gunmen would stay disciplined during the fury and shred the renegades as they charged.

The company waited.

To the south, the boy, Miguel, was running upon the ancient sea bed. The priest had told him to pass the Germans and take the old path through the third valley and to make his way north until he reached the pass in the ridgeline that separated the third and fourth valleys, the break where you could climb across the precipice and down into the big valley. The three were to cross the break and head north up the fourth valley until they found the lead scouts of the White Lion's army and warn them of the North County gunmen waiting in ambush. But the white boy had discovered him and tied him to the tree. He feared that the boy would look for him now and would kill him because of his shame in front of the old warriors of his band. He had seen the others in the sacristy talking with Farinata, and he knew they had the hardness to kill him with no pangs of weakness. He heard the firing from the German camp and saw the smoke billowing from the second valley. The screams of their women bid him to move faster and to change his plan. The white tribe would see him if he tried to run north so he scampered south across the end of the German fields and onto the plain of the desert toward the far hill that marked the entrance to the lake country.

The priest had told them of the ancient temple that guarded the lake country and how they would be sacrificed upon its altar if they ventured to the south. The boy was sure that such a temple would have a sentinel and he hastened south to warn the Lion's warriors, that is, if he could tell them his purpose before they cut out his tongue. He rested briefly from the sun under creosote but only for a moment, and he moved on again trekking toward the southern hills. He stopped again when he found a cactus and sucked on its leaves, but it gave up its moisture grudgingly. He ran again, and the shimmering heat of the plain reduced his steps to a shuffle. He saw the contours of the southern hills growing bolder and it bade him to move faster. The priest had warned them not to venture to the stone temple, but he feared the priest more than the tribesmen and now more than ever because he had failed him.

The boy feared the way the priest looked into his heart with the eye without sight and the way the priest knew his unsaid thoughts. The priest would perform the rite on the stone altar beneath the sacristy of the new church if he did not find another way to warn the Lion. His fear grew, and he moved faster, his heart beating in his chest as he knew he must find a way to save the White Lion to save himself. He headed for the stone temple across the limestone of the ancient sea floor.

The Lion's lookout, Bird, was the first scout to crest the northern boundary of the valley. He rode a mile ahead of the

Lion's war party looking for anything that might surprise the herd. He descended slowly, running amidst the thickets along the edge of the river and out again to the middle of the valley, never revealing too much of his silhouette, using the shade of the trees to mask his advance and forgoing the easy ride of the meadows. He was to the heart of the valley when Toby saw his shadowed form move about the river's edge among the thorn bushes. He crawled from his hide and traversed to the company's position in the outcropping. He told the colonel there's a scout approaching, looks like two riders on a single horse, but he's definitely scouting ahead and you can see some dust rising in the skies to the north; the war party is on the move and close to the valley.

"All right, head back. Raif, we got to take his eyes out," the colonel said.

"I hear you, Colonel, I'll git him," Raif responded.

Raif moved out of the rock cropping on foot and slid into the vegetation that gnarled the riverbank and moved slowly upriver. He reached a spot in a forked pine and slid into its shadows to create his hide, and lay there waiting, hardly breathing, the long blade in his hand, its dark leather sheath concealing it so no errant flash of sunlight would warn the warrior. He waited, his stillness such that a small furry river animal passed a few feet from his face oblivious to the strange animal lying still by the river.

Through the bushes he saw the renegade's dark hair in beads, the tails of his locks running down over his painted chest, the once vivid reds and yellows subdued by a film of sandy dirt he'd collected from the tribe's voyage across the desert plain to the north. The hair lay matted to his chest, mixed with the dust and sweat. He held a rifle in his right hand, the barrel laid across the strip of leather holding his riding blanket in place. He stopped at the river and looked about before untying a leather strap from his waist and dismounting. As the warrior dropped to the ground, Raif saw it was Clara sitting on the back of the scout's painted pinto. She was naked and painted in spots with symbols and a red ocher smeared across her chest. She was tied, and a red bandana was drawn tightly around her mouth, a white cloth wrapped over her eyes to blind her.

It was quiet except for the burbling of the stream. Bird looked about him, turning his entire body around, and then turned and lifted Clara out of the saddle with two hands about her waist and lay her down by the hooves of his horse. The renegade knelt above her and then went still. He listened for full minutes, eyeing the valley floor without a movement. He undid the top of his chaps and placed Clara bent over face down onto the grass and sandy soil near the river and mounted her from behind, pushing her face into the soft earth of the riverbank.

Raif waited until Bird was humping to creep from his hide. He moved up the riverbank. The scout's horse was eating grass, facing north. The wind was from the north so Raif moved straight toward the renegade believing the mount wouldn't spook. He crept to within a foot of the brave, listening to his groaning and Clara's muffled whimpers. He raised the long cavalry blade and drove its tip into the side of Bird's neck splitting the larynx and thrusting it deep and angled until the hilt was the only thing visible sticking out from behind the renegade's right ear. He slumped over dead.

Clara lay motionless, her bound hands out before her and her fingers clasped in a prayer, the red-and-white bandanas still binding her mouth and eyes. Raif could hear her quiet sobs. He didn't reveal to her what had happened but moved her roughly with his hands, trying to mimic the renegade so she wouldn't cry out. He feared if she saw it was him she'd let loose with a wail. He grabbed the renegade by the hair and dragged him across the river into thick brush where he scalped him, stuffing the pelt into his shirt; he then cut off his ears and gouged out his eyes, tossing the parts into the river. He took the reins of the renegade's pony and waited to see if he needed to stab it to keep it from bolting but it stood their docile with no concern for its former owner. He put Clara back in the saddle and led the horse and girl down the river toward the rock outcroppings.

When he reached where the river paralleled the outcroppings he took her down from the saddle, tied the pony to a tree, and moved her into the company's position in the outcropping. The North County men stared in silence as Raif, cradling the naked niece in his arms, approached from the tree line.

Caleb grabbed a blanket and placed it over her shoulders, wrapping her in the fabric like a funeral sheath. Gabriel cupped his hand over her mouth where the red bandana was still taut about her mouth and removed the white cloth from her eyes. She was wild-eyed, scanning the faces about her as if her eyes had no common purpose but each one fell hither and there upon the different men. She began to cry, a low sobbing as if the pain bubbled up from somewhere deep in water.

Jed looked at Gabriel and saw his eyes were a black, lifeless wild. He looked at Raif and his left eye twitched, its gaze wandering off on some unknown path on a tangent of its own design. Jed muttered to Abner, "Well, this is gonna be one interesting fight."

Gabriel warned her not to yell and took the gag from her mouth. He held her briefly and shifted her to a place underneath one of the rocks that had a shelf of stone and then told her, "Keep still. No matter what happens stay beneath this rock until someone comes for you after the shooting stops." Gabriel asked her if May was still alive and she nodded. He said there were no guarantees in the coming dogfight of who'd be there to fetch her and he handed her a pistol. Gabriel pulled her once more tight to his chest and pushed her back under the shade of the rock, saying only, "If it ain't one of us, you need to take that pistol to yourself." She nodded again and said, "Nanna said you'd save us."

Raif, Gabriel, and the colonel split up and took positions separated from each other by thirty feet across the hundred-foot front of stone outcroppings; the massive rocks dropped like pebbles along the valley floor by a glacier thirty millennia before the birth of man. Abner, Jed, Caleb, Wesley, and Joe formed the five-man reserve. Upon the colonel's whistle the reserve would either go to Raif, Gabriel, or the colonel's position, depending on the enemy's action. The colonel would reckon during the fight which position was most vulnerable. Eight men grew exponentially to have the firepower of eighteen using this tactic. The concentration of fire at the vulnerable pressure points would blunt the enemy's tactics of racing in one at a time trying to gain the glory of close combat.

Seth and Toby stewed in the ravine watching the horses. The renegades would shoot and scatter the horses if they spotted them, to strand the company. The renegades would then circle about them on the sides of the valley and kill or starve them out if necessary. If the numbers were too great, the company would need to ride for it. Seth and Toby seethed but recognized the orders were rational and to be followed.

The White Lion's army descended down the pass, and Miguel ran to the stone temple, his steps falling in patters as the heat and fatigue crippled his senses. He stood in a daze as a hunting party of twenty horsemen ran headlong into him and circled him about the desert floor, whooping their terrible cries and staring down at him with their fierce painted faces. A warrior dismounted and raised his blade, but the child cried out that the White Lion was in danger. Miguel told them of the ten whites who had slaughtered the Germans, and that the priest had sent him to warn the Lion. The painted warrior heard it was only ten and rode hard for the fourth valley, sending one horseman to take the child to the temple and then ride to the lake and summon another fifty warriors.

At the top of the valley, the Lion sat high in the saddle with May. She was his prize. He knew the moment he looked into her eyes by the fireplace in the ranch house. His father had been a prince of his nation when they ruled the lands to the north of the Crossing, and, as an old chief, he had taken a dead settler's pilgrim daughter as his third wife. His mother had taught him many things, to speak the tongue of the invader, to read from the black book of old warriors and prophets. She had died of the fever on the Path of Blood to the south when he was seven, but he remembered the gentleness of her touch upon him. She never beat him as the other mothers did their sons. She had taught him her language because she wanted him to recite the useless prayers to the invisible god, but that magic never worked. The priest had shown him the power of the fire gods, the secrets of the flames, the power that burned in this world. When he had returned from the raid with the pelt of a white lion years before, the priest had told him it was an omen and that it was time for the ritual of the flames and his purification as Leon Sagrada.

As he descended down to the valley, he looked over the horse and cattle, and he was pleased with it. He had not seen Bird for two hours, but he considered it impossible for Bird to be taken without a warning shot. He was called Bird because of his sight; he could see in the dark like an owl and in the day like a hawk. The Lion thought of the girl upon Bird's horse and of Bird's weakness, a gnawing anxiety growing in his chest, but his nearness to the lake eased his mind. He looked about him at the youthful faces of his warriors and realized he had lost too many of the tested. The northern raid had been too costly; it would take two winters before those around him would season into warriors, but they had done well, and the raid is what the priest wanted. The herd of stolen cattle and horses meandered with the warriors in its midst in a slow rambling down the valley floor, each warrior nearly asleep on his pony, their horses knowing the way south.

In this dreamy state, the warriors drew nearer the company secreted in the midst of the rock outcroppings.

Wesley, Jed, and Abner crawled in the brush to the cannons and lit the fuses, and a horrid breath of fire, rock, and nail swarmed out upon the renegades. The roar of the cannons engulfed the valley. The cattle reared left and right, and the horses bolted upright, throwing riders into the paths of the steers, the chaos destroying the war party's ability to execute collective action. The few older warriors bade the young forward, knowing that to defeat cannon one had to rush past its maws and into the ranks of those who lit the fuses. Those who survived the initial volley rushed into the cloud of dust and smoke thrown up by the blasts of the cannon only to be met by muzzle flashes in the chaos. The dust and smoke concealed the numbers of the company, and the older warriors feared they had run into an entire cavalry troop. On they pressed, launching their short arrows into the dust cloud, screaming, drawing knives, and rushing into the smoke, only to be cut down by pistol and rifle, the enemy hidden and cagey, firing with rapid succession and en masse. The young warriors fell like corn, dying without knowledge of what was killing them.

The White Lion reeled upon his white mare and spurred her to the far western side, searching for a path past the rock outcroppings, knowing that the strong position was where the unseen enemy was striking. He needed to reach the lake. He galloped past the stone outcroppings and he wended his way down the valley and came upon the twenty warriors riding to the north to join the fight. He told them of the enemy's positions in the stone outcropping and bade them to attack from the south as he fled away across the cracked and bleached seashells of the alluvial plain toward the stone temple.

As the White Lion's army was being annihilated, it braved one last charge at the company. Raif stood to the side of the boulder and watched three warriors bolt from out of the dust clouds before him. Two were to either side of a third warrior who was astride a blue roan. The once wild pony's skin was striated with corn marks, and the color of the old wounds ran black against the gray of its hide. Raif's pistols were empty and he raised from its scabbard the cavalry sword and with his left hand drew from his belt the twisted horn. The wicked rasp of an arrow sliced past his head, and he swore that he felt the feathers of its fletching prickle his ear. Above the din, he could hear the colonel's whistle, but he knew the reserve of gunmen would not reach his position in time. He knew that rider of the blue roan would be upon him and that he was once again alone.

Raif did not move but stayed square and drove his blade into the roan's shoulder joint. The steel raced through the flesh until its tip lodged in the scapula. The horse and rider cascaded into him, and the warrior flew over the roan's head and dove upon Raif with his eyes ablaze with bloodlust. The warrior gripped the shaft of an arrow in his right hand and stabbed, embedding the thousand-year-old flint arrowhead into Raif's shoulder. The two rolled as one back upon the earth. The other two warriors moved to finish him, but Raif's collapse cleared the shot and Wesley and Joe poured fire upon the two, killing them in a hail of bullets. Raif flipped the warrior over and rose up, straddling the rider of the blue roan between his knees, and he drove the length of the twisted horn into the warrior's right eye.

Jed rushed over and grabbed Raif. He pulled him behind the

boulder as Abner sprayed the dead with buckshot. He gripped the arrow and broke off half the shaft. He cursed at Raif and said, "Lord knows it wouldn't hurt to have gotten your sorry ass behind that rock with that pony com'n."

"Well, I was hoping the Lord was done toy'n with me, but I reckon he ain't."

Jed shook his head and said, "Why would the Almighty? Watch'n your silly shit never gets old."

The colonel surveyed his ranks and saw Raif with an arrow sticking out of his shoulder and Abner with a broken shaft sticking out above his knee. Caleb and Joe bled from wounds about the forehead as the two had dragged a warrior to the ground, the warrior slashing furiously with a knife before Caleb put a barrel to his ribs and shattered his innards. The colonel was about to order the reserve to Raif's position when he turned and saw the twenty riders coming hard from the south. He sent Joe to Toby and Seth's position to gather up the last of the ammunition. He didn't think they had enough, and he knew it would be hand-to-hand before the day was out. His last thought was that there were too many and they were depleted now by their wounds. It would be a dogfight among the outcroppings and the Lion was close to home; there would be reserves committed before the day was done. The colonel believed they were finished, and he sent Joe to run to the boys.

Joe reached the boys and grabbed the last bandoliers from the two pack horses and said, "There's a raiding party from the south. They gonna be on us. Colonel says for you two to follow the river and ride north up the valley and head to the fort and don't stop for noth'n. Now, git going." Joe bolted back to the company's position with the bandoliers slung over his shoulders.

Seth and Toby mounted up and reined the horses to ride up the creek north but looked at one another.

Toby said, "That ain't the play and the colonel knows it."

Seth, "Yeah. I reckon he's gett'n us mov'n 'cause he thinks they maybe ain't got enough to stop 'em."

"You know the play, Gabriel run us through it a hundred times. It be hammer and anvil—the horse the hammer; the infantry the anvil. We head south until we at the last of the cover and we lay low, when they ride past we come out behind 'em and drop 'em in the back as they go'n into the charge," Toby drawled.

The boys rode slowly south in the creek bed until the foliage and thick brush gaps grew too much. They held the horses in the stream with the hooves still in the water and moved to a position under the bows of a low brush near the bank and looked out upon the plain. The war party's shields played with the light of the day. The numbers were many and they rode at a steady trot up the valley floor across a meadow of scrub grass. The tribesmen rode past their position, and they counted maybe a score, mounted on painted ponies, adorned in a hundred different colors, flashings of light echoing about the trinkets, stones, and flakes of gold set upon their shields and chest pieces, and braided in their hair. The renegades began to increase the pace; Seth and Toby heard a great cry arise from their ranks, and they began to charge.

Seth turned to Toby and said, "Gabriel didn't tell us one thing."

"The hammer'd be scared shitless."

Seth responded, "I reckon."

The war party's charge pulsed tremors through the ground, and the water in the river rippled, the ground pulsing under their boots with the weight of the war party's hooves upon the earth.

Toby said, "I reckon now's the time—hard out, hard left behind 'em; wait 'til the shoot'n starts and then start plugg'n in the back, I got the right out and in the turn."

"I reckon," Seth responded.

The two boys mounted their stallions and broke from the riverbank out onto the valley floor. They rode straight out hard and then reined a hard left separating by thirty feet and galloped after the war party riding ahead of them. They followed until they heard the company commence firing and heard the colonel's whistle. Toby wished the main party knew they were coming, a wave of fear cutting through the boys that they'd be dropped by an errant shot from the anvil, but on they rode, and he reckoned the colonel knew they was coming.

As they gained on the war party, they began emptying their pistols into the backs of the warriors. The boys rode with the reins in their teeth and emptied the first of two pistols and then grabbed two more that hung from string cords about their riding coats.

To Toby, it was all a slow-moving dream, as if the whole world had stopped spinning and time stretched before him on a path of his choosing so that he was living in this moment and the eternal clock of time was not running against him. He selected each mark with minute detail, a warrior with the shape of a V painted down his back, the axis running from his shoulders down to the point that converged in the center of his lower back above the crack of his ass. He placed his round dead center of the V. The warrior fell to the horse's shoulder and slipped from his pony to be trucked under its legs, animal and man disappearing in a twist of limbs and dust.

The next warrior wore a chain of feathers and beads that adorned his front, but the wind of the ride had sent it awkwardly over his left shoulder. The beads slacked down his back in an emerald chain dazzled in places with long white feathers. Toby selected a single green glinting stone and swore he hit it with his shot. The warrior bolted upright and let loose with a great yell, reining his horse in a short stop, slipping off the horses as its ass reared up. Toby rode past and put the second shot into the warrior's face as he turned to see what had lanced his back, the round chiseling in between the end of the white stripes painted symmetrically on both cheeks. He emptied his third pistol and then his fourth, the last was a boy no more than thirteen, and as Toby came alongside him, the boy looked over at him expecting a fellow warrior only to be dropped from his horse with startled eyes as the round entered his sternum. Toby shot again at a second warrior he came abreast of; this time the round slammed into that hard skin that sits between the tufts of the eyebrows.

He reined up at the rock outcropping staring down at his father, his four pistols spent and smoking, hanging from the cords lashed to his riding jacket. He did not recall missing with a single shot. He looked over and feared Seth was dead but he was only falling with his horse to the ground. Seth's stallion had taken an arrow through its side. piercing its heart, and it collapsed in the dust.

Seth looked up at Toby and yelled, "Weren't that the craziest shit!"

The colonel grabbed Ulysses and spun Toby and horse around and faced him south down the valley, yelling, "Look yonder, Toby! See that sumbitch on the plain? He's got May." Toby looked off in the distance and could see the dust trail of a solitary horse kicking up about a mile off down the valley.

"I see him, sir."

"Ride that sumbitch down and kill him and bring May back. Ride him down, you hear me, boy?"

"You shoot that son-of-bitch and don't let him chant. Cut off his ears and carve out his eyes," Raif said.

Gabriel rushed over. "Toby, that mare is spent, you got to ride him down, his horse'll break 'fore yours, kill him from the saddle, don't scrap with him, kill him with the rifle."

Toby bolted away but the ride was tough, weaving through the valley floor that was dotted with boulders and scrub branches. He looked out and fretted that he wasn't making up time on the Lion. He left the valley and out onto the hard calcareous shale of the plain. He got his toes into the stirrups and raised himself knee-high onto the shoulders of Ulysses. He put his hands together over the pommel and made himself small against the wind and spurred the stallion, yelling, "See 'em, boy? See 'em? We got to catch him! Now go, boy, go."

Ulysses could feel the new position and the grip of his hooves on the hard pack, and it pleased the horse, and he began to run wild and hard.

Toby galloped across the hardpan and could see the White Lion's mare was running awkward; the weight of the Lion and the girl mixed with the horse's exhaustion, manifesting in the animal's humping gait.

As Ulysses caught sight of the white mare, the racing instinct took hold. Ulysses stepped up his speed to catch the lead horse, and Toby felt his true speed for the first time. Toby was up on his toes now, and the horse and boy were one, the horse oblivious that a rider was upon him, the rhythm of their movements now a single vicious animal. The gap closed, and Toby could see the shape of the bowler hat. He was still a good distance from the southern hill. He didn't know if he could close the gap before they reached the hills, so he drew his rifle from the scabbard, and at a full gallop aimed for the bowler hat, its blackness standing out starkly against the shaded brown sand of the stone rise beyond. He aimed high so as not to hit May, and his shot sent the bowler spinning from the White Lion's head.

The impact and whir of the round took a shaft of skin from his scalp, and the Lion reared on the horse and looked back over his shoulder. He saw the speed of Ulysses and knew he couldn't keep his prize. He cut the bind and threw May from the horse, hoping to gain enough speed to reach the southern hills.

It was the mistake and moment Toby needed. He reined up Ulysses, and as the Lion tried to attain speed again Toby took a long aim at the Lion's broad back and fired.

The shot went low and hit the mare square in the ass, the round tumbling through the horse's entrails, collapsing her convulsing body into the sand. She raised a mighty cloud of dust, throwing the Lion in a cartwheel along the ground head over heels three times before he landed in a clump of arms and legs twenty feet from his dying horse. The femur of his right leg had snapped and the bone emitted from the flesh, stretching the fabric of his pants. He drew his pistol from his waistband and raised the pistol to fire, but Toby and Ulysses went flying past him and Toby swung the rifle butt into his shoulder, sending the weapon fluttering away and throwing the Lion onto his back, the force of the blow separating the Lion's shoulder and raising a revolting hump in his shirt beyond his right shoulder. The horse-driven force also sent the bone of his leg ripping through the fabric, and the white shard of bone broke the fabric like a shark's fin breaks the surface of a calm ocean.

Toby reined up and dismounted in one move and stood twenty feet from the Lion.

The Lion crawled on his hand and good knee, dragging his broken body, grunting "Os" and "Um." It was a language Toby had never heard, and as the Lion moved toward him, he hobbled like an injured lizard upon the ground. The Lion was completely bald except for a long gray ponytail that ran down the back of his neck. The top of his skull was traveled with a vicious bleeding wound from the shot, and the blood ran in rivulets about the old jagged scars that crowned his skull. Even on his hands and knees he was massive, his great bulk of chest and shoulders straining against the thin white cotton of his shirt.

271

Toby stared at him, and the Lion rose up on one knee ten feet from him and began to chant. Toby listened to the cadence and his memories went to May and the time they had snuck off to swim by the pool where the Criss bends sharp to the south. The water ran deep in that pool, so deep Toby had never touched its bottom, so deep it stayed cool in deep summer. He dreamed of May there by the pool and how her body would lay close to his as they warmed and dried in the sun. It was as he turned to face her in his dream that he heard May screaming. He climbed from his dream to see the White Lion hopping on one leg toward him. Toby lowered his rifle and squeezed the trigger, but he'd spent the last cartridge, and the weapon's chamber was empty. He looked down at his weapon and then up, and the Lion was upon him, hopping at him like some great kangaroo slashing with a long knife that flashed in the sun. Toby swung the rifle at the broken leg and connected at the knee, causing the Lion to let out a great anguished cry. As the Lion fell, he slashed with the blade, sinking it into Toby's left thigh, the wrenching flash of pain twisting Toby's mind.

The Lion struggled to his feet again, relentless in his desire to kill the boy. Toby drew his pistol in an instant and put it to the Lion's head and pulled the trigger, but all he heard was the sharp click of the hammer going home. He had spent all his rounds into the backs of the charging renegades during the battle and had not stopped to reload as Gabriel had taught him. The Lion reached for him, but Toby fell backward, the Lion's blade sticking out of his thigh. The Lion fell with him, and Toby kicked him with his good leg at the hump sticking from his shoulder, and the Lion let out a moaning groan. Toby pulled the knife from his leg and crawled away backward, the Lion after him, moving clumsily along the ground with his one good leg and one good arm like a sidewinder. Toby kicked with his good leg at the hump of the Lion and slashed at the top of his head with the knife but could not pierce the bone of the skull, and on the Lion came, clawing at him with his left hand.

Toby kept crawling backward, kicking the hump and stabbing the head. He turned and crawled on all fours and leapt to his feet, hoping to reach the bandoliers on Ulysses, hopping on his good leg. He reached the stallion and pulled a single round from the bandolier stitched to the saddle. He could hear the Lion crawling toward him as he opened the chamber, the Lion spewing forth cries and words in that language he had never heard. Toby could sense him, the weight of his approach throbbing through the ground, the weight of his undecipherable oaths piercing the air like a wind. He went to seat the round into the chamber, but it was jammed with a clod of sand. He clawed at the chamber with his pinky nail and blew the dust from it until he cleared it enough to seat the round in the chamber.

The Lion grabbed Toby's leg, sinking his fingers into the knife wound, and dragged Toby to the ground to strangle him with the power of his enormous left hand. Toby looked into the Lion's eyes and put the barrel to his nose and cocked and dropped the hammer in one fluid motion. The White Lion raised his head for a moment toward the sun and rolled over dead upon Toby's legs.

Toby pushed the Lion off him and looked around. He was a hundred yards from the old steps that led into the temple. He limped on his good leg and climbed the steps and entered the cave. He reached the back of the cave and saw a slit of sunlight radiating through the back wall. The shimmer illuminated the stone altars that decorated the cave. He looked out the slit and saw in the distance the great lake. Women were skinning hides along its banks on both sides, the blood swirling in currents of red that spun in the azure water of the lake. The blood flowed like a young woman's parasol, circling and twisting to the heart of the lake. He looked to the far shore, and riding along the lake toward the temple were fifty warriors on horseback in war paint.

He turned to run and saw Miguel hiding in the shadows of the stone altar. He remembered the blue-black eyes of the boy he had tied to the tree. Miguel was holding a feathered wreath, which he held tightly to his chest. Toby walked to him.

The small boy turned his eyes up, and said, *"Dios me ayude."*

Toby gripped his pistol by the end of the barrel and brought the butt of the handle down upon the soft crown of the child's head, knocking the light from his eyes.

He climbed down the stone temple steps and saw May holding Ulysses. She was wearing the Lion's cloth shirt and it lay in awkward folds upon her thin body. He looked at the Lion lying naked in the dust and saw that May had sunk the blade of his knife through the center of his back. He went to the Lion and there was no scalp to take so he removed the knife from his back and sliced off both his ears, putting them in the pocket of his riding jacket and gouged out his eyes with the tip of the blade as Raif had told him. Toby looked at the Lion's pelt on the ground but mounted Ulysses, leaving the pelt in the sand. He swung May up onto the horse and spurred Ulysses.

He reached the company and reported to the colonel that fifty to a hundred riders were making their way from the southern hills, and they had less than an hour on them. The company mounted and headed up the valley. From atop the rise they looked out over the valley floor and could see the mounted war party milling in a great circle about the entrance to the cave where the Lion's naked body lay. The colonel turned and said, "They'll need to parlay to vote a new chief and that'll buy some time," but a moment later the war party was on the move again, headed north to the valley. The company took the cattle and horses and drove them hard to the northern rise of the valley.

At the very top of the pass Jed dismounted and took a position between two rocks, his silhouette hidden in the long shadow of a great boulder. He laid the long rifle upon the rock and took out the last fifteen shells that Drier's shop had casted special for the long rifle, its stock still a glossy cherry wood with its hunters and prey bounding on it.

Raif came over to him and dropped a Winchester with twenty more rounds. The broken shaft of the arrow still stuck out from Raif's shoulder; his arm was tied with a bandana to his chest in an awkward sling. "You need to buy us no more than an hour or two; don't go lett'n 'em get close. We're gonna shit the steers so you hold 'em an hour. Don't go gett'n caught up in it, you heed me?' Raif warned him.

"This ain't my first time at the rodeo, Raphael. You all get going and don't forget to leave me good ponies and don't you go pick'n any, Raif. Toby'll do the pick'n of my mounts. This is perhaps not the best time for this, brother, but you never had no judgment when it come to horseflesh, if'n we're gonna be honest about it," Jed drawled.

Raif looked at Jed. "Buy us an hour or two and then ride hard."

"You're repeat'n yourself, brother, a habit you ain't had for some time. I'll see you at that witch of yours hut," Jed spat out.

When the war party had ridden up into the valley the company had stampeded the steers down the pass and then rode off to put the Ash and the northern mountains between them and the renegades. Jed watched from the top of the valley as the company disappeared on the horizon, and the last time he had ever felt so alone was when they laid his folks in the earth. He returned to the crease in the rocks and watched the war party wind its way up the valley toward his position. He squeezed himself tighter into the rock overhang trying his best to be absorbed by the dark shadow cast by the boulder. He had a good sight down the valley. He put the rounds for the long rifle on a shelf of rock and placed his leather shooting patch under his elbow. He watched the warriors as they wound up the valley and deftly rode their war ponies around the stampeding herd. *What a waste of good cattle,* he thought. The stampede had slowed the war party, but they never stopped moving toward him, winding up the trail in a line of war ponies snaking to the top of the valley.

Jed aimed with the long rifle, and he sent the lead rider tumbling from his pony. He took aim at the next, and he too sprung up like a jack-in-the-box off the back of his horse. He could see in front of him the licks of dust as the warriors fired, but he knew he had the drop on them with the long rifle by a hundred yards, if not more. Jed sighted and fired, and two more fell from their stallions as the round went through the first and out a second warrior.

The rest dismounted, and he could see them making for the sides of the valley on foot. He looked through the long scope atop the rifle and spied the warriors moving in the low brushes to the east, and he fired at the leads. They stayed hidden in the bushes for about two hours, then without warning they started coming on again, running now in bursts of speed and then hunkering down behind anthills, mounds, or rocks, whatever defilade they could find. He aimed and sent another down, but he realized they were not stopping despite taking such losses. He had six rounds left for the long rifle. He prayed they'd hunker down again until nightfall and then move on him but on they came without regard for the long rifle. He fired the remaining six rounds but on they came despite the fallen in the trails. He raised the Winchester and fired but the round sailed past without hitting its mark, and he saw a puff of dirt fifty yards behind the warrior. The elevation was steeper than he reckoned and he feared he didn't have the skill of the sharpshooter to figure angles of such height with the Winchester. He had driven them to move on foot, and he had bought some time, but they were still moving, and he couldn't stop them with the Winchester from this position.

He looked five hundred yards down the valley, and he could see a single warrior leading thirty war ponies with a single tether up the valley. The other warriors were all on foot going around the sides to gain positions about his perch. He checked the Winchester again and lowered the yardage sight. He sighted it down the valley and spotted a warrior less than two hundred yards from him. He fired and the warrior spun in the trail and lumped over to the side. The shot sent twenty hidden in low bushes sprinting toward him, and he knew they were breaking for him between shots. He rattled off three errant shots, but the warriors did not pause. He knew they had figured out the company had left a single man behind to slow them down, and they were willing to take losses from a single gunman. He looked to the east, and saw the warriors gaining on that side, cresting up and out of sight from where he hid. He figured it weren't more than a few minutes before they would be even with his position and come in from the flanks or maybe even behind him. He couldn't see the ones on the far west side, and he knew he needed to get moving.

It wasn't going as he had planned.

He fired into the warriors running the ridge to the east and missed badly, the angle from the side of the valley difficult to judge. The warriors looked to be at his elevation, but the distance and the slant of the sun had tricked his sighting. He fired and missed again. He turned to the warriors moving up the trail below him, and they were now near a hundred yards away. He could see the sweat glistening on their shoulders, the heaving of their chests as they trotted up the valley oblivious to the threat of instant death lurking above. He aimed in on the lead and dropped him in the trail. The warriors following vaulted over the fallen renegade, their bare feet continuing to pound up the steepening trail toward the rocks he hid among without so much as a pause to survey if the fallen still breathed. He aimed in again and saw the dirt spit up at the feet of the next warrior. He had missed, and he looked at his hands and saw they were shaking. He slung the Winchester and long rifle across his back and scrambled from the shadows; his dash sent a dozen rounds pinging about the boulders where he had sniped from. He ran to his horse and rode up the last rise of the valley. He descended down a short path out to the flat plain and raced across the dry plain toward the next mount he knew would be waiting for him at the crossroads south of the Ash Run.

He figured his next stand to be at the Ash; he would cross before they could enter the river's current and he could ding 'em from the far side. He tried to fool himself into believing that maybe they wouldn't even cross, but he spat and cursed himself for his foolishness. He knew the fanciful thinking was rising in tune with the steady flow of fear welling up in his chest. He rode the naggy pony hard knowing he'd have a fresh mount if he made it to the next rally point the company'd set for him. The warriors didn't have a change of pony. Ten miles into the ride, though, his horse started to falter, and he reined up and looked behind him. Jed could see the dust clouds rising from thirty riders in the distance, the dust shimmering in the dying sun to the southeast.

He rode on and came to the old silver mines and descended the switchbacks gouged from the land and found his next mount tied to a rusting mine car. The company had left water in an old tin for the animal, and the pony didn't look to be in such bad shape. He trusted Toby's judgment. Slung across the mount's neck was a bandolier with ten more rounds for the Winchester. He took a moment to study the warrior's long rifle that he'd carried these past ten years before he hid it beneath the rusted flap of an old iron trough, lying to himself that he'd come back for it when they came back with cavalry and more riders and slaughtered the southern tribe. He traded the saddle from his spent pony as it licked feverishly at the small droplets of water at the bottom of the tin and mounted the fresh pony, spurring it up the old cutbacks on the far side. He passed the darkened shanty, which clung to the wall of the cliff like a spider. It rested near a great hole in the side of the rock where Jed'd heard tell a dozen miners were trapped for all time.

At the top of the ridge, he looked back over the mine and on the far side, the war party was descending the switchbacks he'd come down a half hour ago. They were gaining on him. He muttered to himself, "Goddamn sumbitches can ride." He spurred the mount on and pushed for Ant Hill, a pioneer ghost town where every soul had disappeared some fifty years ago, not a trace left; every soul got up and left one day, leaving an empty town. It was there he'd find the next mount. He spurred the pony on and set it on a dead reckoning for Ant Hill. He crossed another dry plain and looked back when he reached the far shore of the ancient sea. The thirty were coming on him like an endless wave. He could see the war ponies bouncing like corks on the incoming tide of the hardpan, a relentless, seething bobbing. The harder he drove the pony the more they gained on him; they came on like wraiths blown upon a dried field by a strong wind. He galloped into Ant Hill and saw what he feared most, the pony lay on its side kicking its rear leg in a last defying gesture at the man in black. He rode up to see the snake with its spine crushed in the middle from a hoof stomp. The horse's leg bloated from the venom of the young viper. Jed looked down at the mount he was riding: its skin glistened with white froth and its breath rattled and labored out the sides of its mouth. He pulled its reins to the right to get a move on and felt that telltale sign, the momentary delay in obeying the reins. Jed knew the beast was spent, that it was asking you to reconsider your decision to ride for your life. The horse wanted to quit; it was ready to lie down and be eaten by the pack. Jed spurred the pony out of Ant Hill and toward the Ash Run, which lay a full score miles north.

Out on the hard pan again, he made decent time, and he and the pony reached a gait that he judged was about right where the pony wouldn't quit, but when he got to the top of a short steep rise, the animal faltered and dropped, dying underneath him without so much as a gasp. The animal's heart exploded in silence within the beast's ribs from the last exertion. He ran to the top of the knoll and looked back and saw the war party still bobbing across the hard pan, riding horses that did not die, that had endless life, their pace always the same. He murmured to himself, "Damn, them sumbitches can ride."

It was a mile to the Ash, and Jed started running. It was now he remembered his squabble with Luther. He had sassed Luther in front of a dozen spring hands, telling him he was a no-good drifter, freeloader, jack-off ass clown. Jed had fired his put-downs so rapid the dozen drifters started guffawing at the old man.

Luther had gazed at him with his dark eyes, and said, "Keep the knife with you, Jed, you know you can't outrun a war party of horse afoot. They're going to string you up by sewing bones through your ankles. Cut your own throat, boy, at the spot where your finger feels the pumper, cut like you seen me do steers in the sacrifice, and cut deep because they'll try to plug it to have their fun for a spell."

Jed muttered, "Luther, you old fart, I was just funning you, you sumbitch."

He felt the knife jangling on the sheath tied to his belt, and he knew the odds were he'd be putting the blade to his own apple. He ran across the hard pan, and he heard their whooping cries bounce past him on the wind. They had seen he was running on foot, and they started whooping. When he saw the last rise before the Ash Run, he turned around with his hands on his knees breathing hard. The war party was five hundred yards back. The weight of day had sunk the glimmer on the horizon, and the war party rode now in the dimness of day that reveals the true shape of things moving upon the plain.

He ran up the rise, and at the top he looked for the copse of white pines where the last pony would be tied up. He turned and saw the war party was at the base of the rise, and he fretted that he couldn't spur a rangy pony quick enough to cross the Ash before they got to him. The war party was riding hard now, not caring anymore that they were going to kill the ponies under them; they were so close now he knew they could smell him. He ran down and his breath was quitting him, and his legs ached from the starvation of air, but on he ran with the knife jangling in its sheath, bouncing against his hip like a church bell tolling. Jed reached the bottom, and he could hear them yelling as they crested the top of the rise, crashing down upon their ponies to the river meadow. He turned to look over his right and left shoulders and he saw the warriors had fanned out to the sides like the horns of a great bull. He heard the tearing of the sheet around him as their bullets and arrows ripped the fabric of the sky. He threw his legs out in front of him to keep up his speed and keep from falling over. He looked to his right and he could see the crush of horses breaking into the vegetation along the river trying to cut him off between the white birch and the river. The hair on his arms prickled out and it tingled as the air crackled with bullets. He fumbled through the underbrush into the copse of white birch.

They'll swarm me at the river, he thought. *The pony'll never get the steam up and they'll swarm me before the river.*

He could hear them now twenty or so yards away whooping and thrashing through the trees, the yelling a horrid clash of whoops, laughter, and cries. He felt the knife banging against his hip. *Jest get it done, Jed, jest git it done. You'll be sorry a week from now when the kids in that village're still poking what's left of you staked to the ground.*

He ran on into the trees and saw flashes of the next mount's coloring through the trunks of the white pine. The hide was a radiating golden amber, and he realized Toby had left him Ulysses. He nearly whooped, but he had no breath and still he knew it would be a close-run thing.

He snatched the tether from the trunk of a white pine and leapt onto Ulysses's back, spurring him to the river. Riding the naggy ponies for so long Jed had forgotten the kick of a stallion and was nearly thrown, but he had a handful of the bridle and the mane, and he held on. Ulysses bolted from the trees straight for the river, as if the animal knew what waited for it if the war party got to him too. They were a few yards from him now on all sides and arrows and bullets flew about in a great tumult as the yelling and whooping mass condensed around him as he galloped for the river.

Ulysses flew into the current without breaking stride, and the crash of water nearly sent Jed floating off again over the stallion's head but he gripped the tuft of mane in one hand and clung for his life, his legs cinched about the neck of the horse. He settled back into the saddle and felt the horse's mighty pull through the river's strong current, pulling nearly straight across despite the force of the water. The bullets and arrows ripped the air past his head, but horse and rider crossed, and he rode hard up the far rise, the stallion scaling the heights in an instant with his powerful thrusts.

He jumped off Ulysses at the top, and swung the Winchester off his back. The war party had entered the water but their tired ponies faltered and did not have the strength to carry the riders. He could see warriors floating with the current and the horses floundering. Two warriors swam the river and in four feet of water on the near side Jed dropped them with shots to the chest and belly as they struggled to run in the low water. Three warriors were midstream still on horseback and the slow pace of the swim gave Jed time to aim, breathe, and squeeze, sending each one into the current. He stood and looked at the war party on the far bank and saw that many had dismounted and were standing in silence. One warrior had dropped to sit on a driftwood log, his head slung between his knees. Jed waited and watched the war party move off singly at first and then in hushed columns back south through the trees. No more entered the water.

As darkness shrouded the river, the far side was quiet and empty. Jed saw a lobo wolf skulk in from the east along the far shore of the river, and sniff at a dying pony that kicked passively at the interest. The lobo sat on its haunches and waited for the animal to die. Jed knew the renegades must be gone. He mounted Ulysses and rode on again to the north at a slow trot. By midmorning he was ten miles east of the fort and an hour's ride to the witch's hacienda.

Chapter Seventeen:
The Healer

The company crossed the Ash Run; Gabriel led them west along its banks without a word, and Seth could only wonder as to the direction that was taking them farther from home. They came upon a hut built into the wall of the riverbank with a single steel pipe spewing gray smoke and a lone window with a pane of melted glass. The hut was surrounded by gardens and fields terraced up the riverbank. The steps of crops bursting with color and a thousand different birds nesting and flying all about the hut. She emerged from the dark of the door in a simple gray frock dress with a thick sea captain's leather belt at her waist. She was aged but lean and hard with ample bosom. She had piercing eyes and a great head of gray hair pulled back, revealing a weathered but beautiful face. She was agile and leapt down from the steps of her hut to the path that led up from the river. She studied them as they rode up. All about her were dark-skinned women in head scarves; one pumped water from a well and eyed them without curiosity.

"Well, well, lookee here, my old friends come to visit. Gabriel, where be my Luther?" She sang it out, her voice rich and dripping.

"He moved on west, no word from him yet," Gabriel said.

"Still searching for his answers, heh? Well, what you bring me, Gabriel? What you bring, Tamara? I see that arrow shaft in Raif. You bring trouble to my doorstep?"

Gabriel dismounted and approached the woman, but kept an

arm's distance. Seth saw she lit a pipe of stone and placed it to her lips, a stream of gray smoke trailing from the bowl. They conferred with one another. The woman shook her head, and Gabriel retrieved a satchel from his saddlebag and doled out gold coins and something shiny Seth could not discern. The woman went to the wagon and touched the young one, but when she felt the belly of the older sister, Tamara shuddered from the feeling of her touch.

"Tamara, see to it?" Gabriel snapped.

"The young one's not ripe, so no lasting harm except to her marrying prospects—takes a mighty handsome dowry for upstanding church folk to overlook a single buck, let alone a dozen. T'other I think is certain; they had at her and you know how they like to rut, heh, heh, heh," Tamara said with a taunting laugh.

"See to it."

"Now, now, Gabe, it ain't like my craft's for free."

"The gold. See to it."

"I want a piece of Luther's wood, a piece can burn for a spell; won't take nothing less to wash the little bitch out." Tamara voiced it soothingly as she caressed the older sister's belly.

"Luther would need to see to that."

"You say Luther gone. They say you can't take it with you. A piece of the wood, else you'll be bouncing kin on your knee, Uncle Gabie, heh, heh, heh?"

"See to it, or give me back the pieces."

"All right, all right, but you bargain'n for a craft takes lifetimes to master and not pay'n what's due. Ain't that the way of it." The woman's eyes fell on Seth and Caleb. "Who be these two? Why, Gabe, you send them out to kill 'fore they even sired a once, what if they didn't come back from the deep? Don't hardly seem fair, bring both on in to the cabin, it warm inside more ways than one and I'll git 'em fixed right, heh, heh, heh."

"Stop your ways, Tamara," the colonel said.

"Now, Colonel, this boy one of yours, ain't he? He has the look of his mother, sometimes nature be generous in its selection. Oh, look at the eyes, he done heard the music; he tasted the deep—heh, heh, heh—what's his name, Colonel?"

"Toby." Toby said it as he looked at her eyes. Tamara moved to his horse and placed her hand upon his thigh and moved it up his leg toward his crotch. Toby felt a rush of blood in his loins as she murmured "Enosh" and then said in an unknown tongue "slain a king," but somehow Toby understood her voice. Tamara turned and whispered to Raif, "my angel, bring this Toby back to me and I'll weave you a dreamcatcher, one that'll let you sleep like a babe in the womb."

Toby had strung the White Lion's ears on a coarse leather thong about his neck. Tamara reached up and fingered the ears of the White Lion. She turned to Gabriel, "It be wood or the ear, or the bitch bears a savage."

Toby wrenched one of the ears free and handed it to Tamara. She looked up at him and pulled his shirt down until his face met hers and whispered to him that she "owed him a debt and that she always pays her debts." Toby tried to pull away but stopped when Tamara's breath flowed over him—it was a blend of flowers, fresh-cut peaches, and the smoke of a cooking fire. He breathed it in and felt the warmth of it upon his face, his heart stammering in his chest.

She released him and turned to the others, "Bring the girls to the kitchen," she said in Spanish to one of the shrouded women. She turned to Gabriel and said, "I'll wash out the young'n, too—you never know." She pointed to a copse of birch and said "Camp yonder, it the only place that don't know wind at night; you can fetch the girls in the late morning; right now I need to see Toby first, then Raif. Toby's wound deep in the thigh, let me see to it before he bleed out in my yard. I'll call out when done with them two, and then take Abner and the rest."

Tamara brought Raif and Toby into the barn and situated them on a flat table. She mixed a potash from stones and herbs and whiskey and crushed it in a clay bowl. She took the paste and smeared it into Raif and Toby's wounds; each writhed upon the table. She drew a hot poker from the fire and seared their wounds. Toby was in agony, and she came to him and again he tasted her warm, sweet breath. The pain subsided and Toby asked her where she was from. She laughed lightly and said, "I am from right here, this spot, Toby, the river is my father, the earth my mother. I was seeded at night, and fed by the rays of the moon. I'm from beneath us, and I am here always waiting for you to return; I'll be waiting for you."

Caleb dismounted and held the bloody bandage tight to his head and asked to the group in general, "What she mean, 'Toby heard the music'?"

"It don't mean noth'n. Can't trust noth'n she says. Renegades think she's a shaman, but she jest uses what medicine she learned back east to fool 'em. Any woman choose to live out here got to learn to play them devils for fools," Abner said.

After the healing, the party unsaddled the horses in the white birch woods. They found a defensible position and lit a fire surrounding it with saddles and bedrolls. Abner was given first watch at a knoll that looked down the river for three miles.

Gabriel, Raif, Jed, the colonel, and Wesley sat on their bedrolls around the fire, eating from flat tins of food brought over by one of the shrouded women. As they ate, Caleb asked Wesley if he'd seen any of them Oklahoma Injuns in the Badlands yet.

Wesley said that he had not gone west but south during his months-long furloughs at the academy. He explained that every summer cadets spent eight weeks with an active troop. His tour had taken him through one dry September to Hawkshaw, Mississippi. Wesley quipped, "The only action I saw was four men lynching a black man because some old spinster said he leered at her."

Caleb asked, "What's the military got cause to be in something like that?"

"Why? Because the law in Hawkshaw wouldn't do anything about it. The major's duty was to maintain the peace under martial law and to also allow the locals to handle local matters with no military interference. Well, this old spinster was apparently the last of a long line of the county's founding families. She claimed a black man leered at her. Four men took upon themselves to lynch the man. The major demanded that the locals arrest the four but one of them was a town trustee, another one a lawyer. The local sheriff was either a coward or corrupt, and refused, saying he didn't have enough evidence to arrest leading citizens. Leading citizens, imagine. The locals did nothing; the local magistrate refused to do anything, saying the investigation and the sheriff needed to bring the charges. The four went about their business as if nothing had happened."

Gabriel asked, "Did he leer at her?"

"Gabriel, you can't hang a man because some old spinster's pretending she's still a southern belle and wants attention. By all accounts he was a good man, worked his own field. Lynching him because of some old spinster's vanity, that's barbarism." Wesley looked around and expected to see nodding heads but found only blank stares. He continued, "Well, if the locals wouldn't act, the major was going to. Reconstruction was to instill the rule of law, so every man would have justice. The four were arrested and placed in the stockade, and we convened a military tribunal. They were given a proper evidentiary hearing, and all the accused rights were observed."

The colonel asked, "You hang them?"

Wesley, "No, not a single witness would come forward to

testify. Hawkshaw was still lost in the old ways—they learned nothing from the war. It was useless, no jury down there would do justice."

Gabriel said, "I know that county, that's how things been done in that county since the first Scots broke ground there. That county always took care of its own business—them folks apply their code to what you're talking to."

"What code? What code is that, Gabriel? To lynch an old hand because some spinster said he looked at her skirt?"

The colonel said, "They weren't defending her honor alone—those folks were protecting the order of things. The four you wanted to hang got the torch passed to them who knew it important to protect a woman's honor, especially in tough country like that—there're mothers and young girls that everyone needs to know if you give offense to there'll be a reckoning—some acts can't stand if the order of things is to keep."

"At what cost, Father? Let's say that hand was innocent; that the old spinster fancied up a tale so people'd pay attention to her. Is the cost of the order of things worth an innocent man going to the rope?"

"Maybe it is, to protect the rest," Gabriel said.

"Well, then, Gabriel, how about two innocent lives, three? How much blood to keep this code you and my father speak of?" Wesley shot back.

"I fear a world of men without that code," the colonel retorted.

"It's the new world. We don't need a code that's based on myth. We have the rule of law; we have a Constitution—laws written so that all can read them, not a few self-chosen men who deem themselves executioners of the invisible code," Wesley snapped.

"Who is the force for those laws, Wesley?" the colonel asked.

"The authority to enforce the law is given by law, and men

deputized to use violence if necessary. Philadelphia has had a police force for a hundred years; Boston and New York for decades. I have seen them in operation. I have walked those streets; it works better than vigilantes making justice on the accusations of old women. They are a society bound by law in the East, a law that all answer to: rich, poor, white, black, immigrant, or citizen. Why should it not apply in some backwater like Hawkshaw?" Wesley replied.

McCallum lit his pipe. "Wesley, in this new world you speak of, what is a man allowed to fight for? What will this law of yours justify a man to fight?"

Wesley replied: "The world is changing. What we did out here a thousand miles from a courthouse is one thing, but there's no excuse for it in Hawkshaw. Law, science, a new frontier, codes, superstitions, myths of honor are relics of the past."

McCallum pulled smoke from his pipe. "I'll tell you what I think, under the code of them four, they decided it was a matter of a woman's honor, right or wrong, that's what they reckoned. That code built up over near two centuries before that major of yours and his army came to that county uninvited. The tooth was not yet cut on this entire country when the first men laid eyes on the Hawkshaw land. Their fathers fought for it and tamed it from wild. Trappers and indentureds look'n for land to farm. Like all new worlds it got tamed by men like them four you wanted to string up. The first men cut that land open and run out the tribes. Once the tribes're gone, that kind tend to need someth'n to fight, and if no one's 'round, they tend to kill each other 'fore long. So families moved out there, well folks begin thinking there's got to be rules different between the hard men and family folks and such. It's hard to tame men that ain't known nothing but the tomahawk; it takes time and so folks build a code to live by—and the first rule is to agree that womenfolk that ain't whores need to leave be; attacking a woman in word or deed is a killing offense."

Wesley responded, "Gabriel, your history may be right, but that code is nonsense. It was the same code that defended the right to chain a child to its mother in the field. It was the same code that allowed four men to go free after they hanged an innocent man on the word of an old spinster."

Gabriel tilted his head and said, "I see where you're going; so answer my first question. What can a man fight over in your world?"

"Self-defense I suppose. Violence is only an answer if there is a threat of violence that you cannot avoid. I would say that, Gabriel. All other things are meaningless; the violent man's justifications for lashing out because of misplaced pride, honor, or base instincts like jealousy, hate are all the fool's passions. The twentieth century is dawning—it's a new world. I've seen it in the east—it's going to be a better world guided by law, medicine, science; people can either choose to board the train or be crushed by its steel wheels."

Gabriel pulled on his pipe and said, "A world with no myths, no creed, no insult or blasphemy that allows for a reprisal? Is that the world you see in the future?"

"That's right, Gabriel, there's no golden idols in the new world. It's not the future, it's in the East now, and it's coming here, it can't be stopped. It will reach the wastelands and even those tribes will be ripped into the new world."

"You say it's going to come to these savages, take their myths and convince 'em the druids is noth'n but rocks?" the colonel asked.

"If you could see what I have seen, the cities back East, you would believe in the future too."

"For a man that talks about such a time, you certainly ain't got no problems pull'n the trigger in the here and now," Gabriel said.

"I never said the future would come without a price. A few chosen will have the burden to be its deliverer."

Toby and Seth relieved Abner at the watch. They lay flat in the darkness on the rise above the birch trees staring south. There was a faint glow from the river where the hacienda rose on the plain; when the wind was right you could hear the moans of the girls.

Seth looked at Toby for a long while before he asked, "What happened to you out there?"

Toby said, "The White Lion chanted to me, it were odd, it took me to dream'n of that spot of grass by the bend in the Criss where it pools deep. It was like I was there, really there, felt more real than it do right now. Me and your sister were all wet from dipp'n, and we were drying in the hot sun, lay'n in the grass together. May's scream brung me out of it. The Lion knew it too, the fear showed in his eyes when he seen me come out of it. He had fooled me with that song, but she broke it with her scream 'fore he got me. Raif said don't let him chant, but I wanted to hear it, I guess. Raif jest told me it's an ancient song born thousands of years ago. Raif's searched for answers to it these past ten years and paid medicine men gold for the secret of it, but the only thing he come to know is the song is called a passage song. Those that know it, sing 'fore they kill— it's like an offering—it's like you give the soul of those you kill to a winged angel on t'other side. Raif said he gave the song but once and even though the man needed kill'n, he still wished he'd never sung it. Said he'd done it for reasons his own, which he didn't want to tell, he fears the price be heavy though when the tax collector comes and he need to pay it back."

"Will you teach it to me, Toby?"

In the hut, Tamara ran the Lion's ear along May's belly, and she knew the babe cradled in the womb was the Lion's cub. She had brewed a sleeping mix from roots that grow wild in the abandoned turtle nesting ground along the river's reedy bank and the potions let the girls sleep. She paced the room—her bare feet gliding along the floorboards.

"What would the priest extract as a price if I sacrificed the Lion's kin?" she murmured to herself. She could fool most shamans, but the priest would find her out. "What would Gabriel do if I let the kin live?"

She placed the ear in an earthenware jar and buried it beneath a stove leg. She riffled through an old case for her mixings and blended a bitter soup that would fortify the child being forged in the womb. She sacrificed a burnt offering. She needed it to foretell that McCallum would send the girls back east to kinfolk to heal up while he rebuilt his ranch. The girl would be too far along before warning could reach McCallum from his east kin. The son would live and find his way back.

In the morning, the company loaded the two girls into the buckboard of a wagon they bought from Tamara. Tamara had fed them more root and they both lay sleeping in the folds of many blankets.

As they finished laying the girls out, Jed trotted up on Ulysses. The company crowded around him patting him on the leg and asking him how it had gone.

He said, "Them got the same ass-kicking anybody stupid enough to chase me gits."

The company broke in a loud guffaw.

The colonel asked, "Is any of 'em coming?"

"No, sir, I left 'em broken bitches back of the Ash."

Tamara looked Jed once over. He was covered in filth and dirt. She said, "I figured your skin to be making a new drum by now."

Jed looked down at her and said with a smile, "Hey, Crazy, good to see you too."

Tamara moved up to Raif and whispered to him. She told him if he brought Toby back to her she would craft him a dream-catcher out of the sinews and talons of a snow owl. It would catch the dreams, and he would sleep like in the days of old before the passage song.

The company rode off and started moving north.

Jed asked Raif, "What was your sweetheart whispering back there to you?"

"She's hankering for Toby. I reckon she either wants to hump him or cut out his heart and eat it," Raif responded.

"I shoulda shot that crazy bitch long ago; never can understand why you were always sweet on her. You gonna bring Toby back here?" Jed snorted.

"Nah, my soul, what's left of it anyhow, is held together with pine tar and spit. I reckon it can't take that," Raif said.

The girls watched from the bed of the wagon as the company voyaged home on their run to the North County. Their route took them back across the flats, up past the Old Mission and retraced the steps they took in the descent into the wastelands. North of the mission the McCallum clan split from the company, dragging their wounded souls in the wagon. The Hansons split off at the Post Road and headed east from there to the Cuchalainn.

Molly and Mother Martin were on the porch when they saw riders approaching; when Molly saw it was three she held her hands tightly over her chest, trying to ease the ache of anticipation. The three came to the gate where she now stood, and she looked at them covered in dust, their faces filthy, blackened with soot. The eyes of all three were pierced and shadowed, still full of hate and an animal's wariness. She looked at Toby, and he had the dried blood of the Lion spread on his riding jacket; it looked like dried clay. He had forgotten to remove the ear of the White Lion, which lay pierced upon a coarse leather rope he wore as a necklace, the ear pendant dangling from the strip of leather.

Molly went to Toby and looked up at him atop Ulysses. He looked down at her in silence, and she saw his eyes reflected no light but sparkled darkly. She lowered her head and cried, "Oh, John, you promised."

EPILOGUE

Walker slept the night and most of the next day, emerging as the sun dipped on the horizon, the fire blazing across the sky. He struggled onto the porch, his legs wobbly beneath him, and the ache going to the marrow of his bones. Toby and Wesley still slept and would for hours longer. He held the jug of whiskey and sat in the rocker looking out at the fire being swallowed by the earth.

Molly came out on the porch and sat on the rocker next to him. "Is there any way to heal him?"

Walker sipped the whiskey and looked off in the distance. He winced, and said "I don't know, some boys come back from it. I seen a few come back after the war."

Molly shuddered.

Walker looked off. "We journeyed to that cave in Miller's bog, the four of us. We found a pool of dark warm water. An old slave, Clarabelle, had told Pierce how to cross the waters to a stone temple on the far side by swimming underneath a rock ledge. Pierce, Addie, Courtney, they were all smiles, the thrill of it, to explore beyond that cave wall, to swim underneath and discover the secrets it held.

"I stood there and the water was black, a deep black so dark it swallowed the torch light. I watched them enter the water, Courtney first, Addie, and Pierce the last. He turned to me, and said, 'This is such good stuff, isn't it, Johnny?'

"When Pierce disappeared into the water, I ran. I ran out the cave and on to the trail into the moonlight, and I kept running. I didn't stop until I reached Sommersville's fence line, and even as I walked in the early light breaking the darkness I could feel something was upon me, searching for me, running my scent. I never really spoke to the three again. I'd see them from time to time and there would be awkward moments. The three were always together after that night, and it was as if they couldn't speak to me, as if their secrets could not be shared with those not anointed that night.

"I had stood on the edge of the world as they had, but I ran away."

ABOUT THE AUTHOR

Thomas Owen O'Connor lives in upstate New York with his family and is a former infantry officer in the Marine Corps (1990–1996; 2002–2004.)

The employees of Five Star Publishing hope you have enjoyed this book.

Our Five Star novels explore little-known chapters from America's history, stories told from unique perspectives that will entertain a broad range of readers.

Other Five Star books are available at your local library, bookstore, all major book distributors, and directly from Five Star/Gale.

Connect with Five Star Publishing

Visit us on Facebook:
   https://www.facebook.com/FiveStarCengage

Email:
   FiveStar@cengage.com

For information about titles and placing orders:
   (800) 223-1244
   gale.orders@cengage.com

To share your comments, write to us:
   Five Star Publishing
   Attn: Publisher
   10 Water St., Suite 310
   Waterville, ME 04901